MISTRESS OF THE RITZ

Center Point
Large Print

Also by Melanie Benjamin and available from
Center Point Large Print:

The Swans of Fifth Avenue
The Girls in the Picture

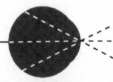

**This Large Print Book carries the
Seal of Approval of N.A.V.H.**

MISTRESS OF THE RITZ

MELANIE BENJAMIN

CENTER POINT LARGE PRINT
THORNDIKE, MAINE

Mistress of the Ritz is a work of historical fiction, using well-known historical and public figures. All incidents and dialogue are products of the author's imagination and are not to be construed as real. Where real-life historical persons appear, the situations, incidents, and dialogues concerning those persons are entirely fictional and are not intended to depict actual events or to change the entirely fictional nature of the work. In all other respects, any resemblance to persons living or dead is entirely coincidental.

The text of this Large Print edition is unabridged.
In other aspects, this book may vary
from the original edition.
Printed in the United States of America
on permanent paper.
Set in 16-point Times New Roman type.

ISBN: 978-1-64358-245-0

Library of Congress Cataloging-in-Publication Data

Names: Benjamin, Melanie, 1962- author.
Title: Mistress of the Ritz / Melanie Benjamin.
Description: Center Point Large Print edition. | Thorndike, Maine : Center Point Large Print, 2019.
Identifiers: LCCN 2019016450 | ISBN 9781643582450 (hardcover : alk. paper)
Subjects: LCSH: Auzello, Blanche, approximately 1897-1969—Fiction. | Auzello, Claude—Fiction. | Ritz Hotel (Paris, France)—Fiction. | France—History—German occupation, 1940-1945—Fiction. | World War, 1939-1945—Underground movements—France—Fiction. | Large type books.
Classification: LCC PS3608.A876 M57 2019b | DDC 813/.6—dc23
LC record available at https://lccn.loc.gov/2019016450

To Ben,
who had to wait for this one

MISTRESS
OF THE
RITZ

LILY

Blanche is dead.

Sometimes death is a mercy, and I believe this is true for her. Because she was once so vibrant and spirited, and that's how I'll remember her. I have so many memories of Blanche: Blanche singing a sailor's sea chantey with a glass of champagne balanced on the back of her hand, Blanche showing a streetwalker how to dance the Charleston, Blanche being gently compassionate to someone who didn't deserve it, Blanche stubbornly turning her back and stomping her foot like a child.

Blanche blazing with courage, defying—foolishly—those she should not.

But the memory of Blanche that remains the most vivid is the memory of seeing her, for the first time, in the setting that suited her best: at the Ritz. Her beloved Ritz.

Blanche wasn't there the day the Nazis first arrived in 1940; she was still making her way back home from the South of France. But she told me how it happened that day.

How at first, the Ritz employees and guests only heard them: the tanks and jeeps roaring into the vast square, positioning themselves around the tall obelisk as Napoleon himself stared down in horror from his lofty perch. Then the metal heels of boots ringing out on the cobblestones and pavement, faint at first but increasing in volume as the Germans came close, closer, closest. They wrung their hands, they looked at one another, and some of them bolted for the service entrance downstairs. But they didn't get far.

Madame Ritz herself, small, gallant, dressed in her best black dress, still in the old Edwardian style, waited inside the entrance to her home that was the grandest hotel in all of Paris. Her bejeweled hands trembled as she clasped them in front of her; more than once she glanced up at the enormous portrait of her late husband, as if his painted likeness could tell her what to do.

Some of these employees had been with her, with him, in the beginning, in 1898. They remembered the first time these same doors flew open; the glittering, gay guests venturing into the richly appointed hall—no lobby for Monsieur Ritz's new hotel; he did not wish for mere citizens to darken its gilded portals—eyes shining with awe. Princes and duchesses and the wealthiest of the wealthy: Marcel Proust, Sarah Bernhardt. Then, as musicians played, as chandeliers gleamed, as the kitchen sent up trays and trays of Auguste Escoffier's finest creations—meringues of vanilla cream decorated with sugared petals of lavender and violet; tournedos Rossini, rich pâtés, even peach melba in honor of Dame Nellie Melba, who had agreed to serenade the guests later—they gave one last touch to their new uniforms and smiled, eager to do their jobs. To fetch, lift, provide, polish, dust, mop, chop, fold, soothe, fix. To pamper; to cosset. They were thrilled to be part of this— the opening of a grand new hotel, the only one in the world with bathrooms en suite, telephones in every room, completely wired with the new electricity instead of gaslight.

The Hôtel Ritz, on the Place Vendôme.

This day, they did not smile. Some wept openly as the Germans stormed through the front doors, their dusty black boots sullying the carpets, their guns slung across their shoulders or holstered. They did not remove their caps, those imperious caps with the eagle insignia. Their uniforms— gray-green, the color of haricots verts—were ugly and offensive against the brilliant gold and marble and crystal of the hallway, the ornate tapestries on the walls, the regal blue of the carpeted grand staircase.

The blood-red band on their arms—the menacing black spider of the swastika—made everyone shiver.

The Germans were here. Just as everyone was told they would be, after the French Army crumbled like one of Monsieur Escoffier's fine flaky pastries, after the Maginot Line proved to be a child's illusion, after the British Allies abandoned France, fleeing across the Channel at Dunkirk. The Germans were here. In France; in Paris.

At the Hôtel Ritz, on the Place Vendôme.

CHAPTER 1

BLANCHE,
June 1940

Her shoes.

It's her shoes that worry her, if that can be believed. Of all the things this woman should be concerned about on this horrific day, it's her shoes.

But in her defense, given who she is and where she is headed, her shoes *are* a problem. They're filthy, caked with dried mud, the heels worn down. And all she can think about, as her husband helps her off the train, is how Coco Chanel, that bitch, will react when she sees her. How they'll all react when she shows up at the Ritz with filthy, worn-down shoes, her ripped stockings practically disintegrating on her shapely calves. While she can't do anything about her stockings—even Blanche Auzello would never dream of changing her stockings in public—she is desperate to find a bench so that she can rummage through her suitcases and find another pair of shoes. But before she can speak this wish, she and her husband are swept up in the wave of bewildered—well, what the hell are they now? French? German? Refugees?—who are flooding out of the Gare du Nord, eager, terrified, to see what has become of Paris in their absence.

Blanche and her husband are part of the great unwashed; dirt and cinders have coagulated in pockets of perspiration beneath their chins, behind their ears, their knees, in the crevasses of their elbows. Greasy faces streaked with soot. They haven't changed clothes in days; Claude packed away his captain's uniform before they left his garrison. "To be worn again," he assured Blanche—or more likely, she suspected, himself. "When we fight back. As we most certainly will."

But no one knows when, or if, that time will come. Now that the Germans have taken France.

Outside, the pair finally push their way out of the crowd so that they can catch their breath, try to corral all the luggage that is slipping out of their hands; when they packed, nine months ago, they had no idea how long they'd be away. Automatically, they look for a taxi in the usual line outside the station entrance, but there are none; there are no cars at all, only one lone cart, hitched to the saddest horse Blanche has ever seen.

Claude glances at the horse, takes in its heavy breathing, the foam dribbling from its mouth, ribs so defined it's as if the flesh has been carved, and shakes his head. "That animal will never see another morning."

"You!" Blanche marches over to the man sitting on the cart, a man with small eyes and a gap-toothed smile.

"Yes, Madame? Ten francs. Ten, and I take you anywhere in Paris! I have the only horse and cart within twenty kilometers!"

"You unharness that horse right now. You bastard, that horse is about to collapse, can't you see? He needs to be stabled, fed."

"Crazy bitch," the man mutters, then sighs and gestures toward the street, teeming with humans on foot. "Don't you understand? The Nazis took every healthy animal when they came. This nag is all I have to make a living."

"I don't care. I'll pay you twenty francs if you just let this animal lie down for a while."

"If he lies down, he won't get up again." The man glances at the poor animal swaying on its crooked legs, then shrugs. "I figure I have three, maybe four jobs left, and then he's done. And so am I."

"I'll do it myself, you—"

But Claude has reached his wife and dragged her away, even as she still lunges toward the hapless horse and his owner.

"Shh, Blanche, shh. Stop. We need to go. You can't save every broken thing in Paris, my love. Especially not now."

"Try and stop me!" But she does allow her husband to steer her away from the station.

15

Because one important fact remains. The Auzellos are still a long way from the Ritz.

"I would have telegrammed to have someone meet us," Claude says, mopping his forehead with his filthy handkerchief; he looks at it and winces. Blanche's husband craves a clean handkerchief as much as she craves clean shoes. "But . . ."

Blanche nods. All the telegraph and telephone poles linking Paris to the outside world had been cut during the invasion.

"Monsieur! Madame!" Two enterprising young boys appear, offering to carry the Auzellos' bags for three francs. Claude agrees, and they start to follow the urchins through the streets of Paris, normally so chaotic. Blanche can't help remembering the first time she tried to navigate the circle around the Arc de Triomphe, so many lanes full of honking vehicles going every which way. But today, she's stunned by the complete absence of traffic.

"The Germans are confiscating every car," one boy, a tall, pale lad with blond hair and a broken front tooth, says with the cockiness of a youth in the unusual position of knowing more than his elders. "For their army."

"I would blow it up first, rather than give my car to the *Boche*," Claude mutters, and it's on the tip of Blanche's tongue to remind him that they don't own a car. But she doesn't; even Blanche knows that now is not the time to make that particular point.

While the ragtag little group straggles along, she becomes aware of something else: silence. Not just from the crowd of stunned citizens stumbling out of the station, spreading out through the city like a muddy puddle of rain, but *everywhere*. If there is one constant in Paris, it is *talk:* Café tables crammed with volatile patrons arguing about the color of the sun. Sidewalks, too, crowded with Parisians stopping to make a point, jabbing a finger in a companion's chest as they debate politics, the cut of one's suit, the best cheese shop—it doesn't matter, it never matters. Parisians, Blanche knows too well, love to gab.

Today, the cafés are empty. The sidewalks, too, are bare. There are no noisy schoolchildren in uniforms playing in the vacant gardens. No vendors singing while they push their carts; no shopkeepers haggling with suppliers.

But she feels eyes upon her, she's sure of it. Despite the warmth of the cruelly sunny day, she shivers and tucks her hand beneath her husband's arm.

"Look," he whispers, nodding his head skyward. Blanche obeys; the windows beneath the mansard roofs are full of people peering out furtively behind lace curtains. Her gaze is pulled toward the sky, caught by something shining, reflecting the light, up on the very rooftops.

17

Nazi soldiers, carrying polished rifles, looking down at them.

She starts to tremble.

They haven't encountered any soldiers until this moment. The Germans had not reached Nîmes, where Claude had been garrisoned at the start of the Phony War. Even on the train to Paris, where everyone was terrified that they would be strafed by bombers as so many people who fled had been; even though every scheduled—and unscheduled—stop caused all conversation to cease as they held their breath, afraid of hearing German words, German boots, German gunshots. Through it all, the Auzellos hadn't encountered a single Nazi.

But now that they are here, home, they do. It's really happened, goddammit. The Nazis have really conquered Paris.

Blanche takes a breath—her ribs ache, her stomach churns, and she can't remember when they last ate—and walks on in her destroyed shoes. Finally, they come to the enormous paved square of the Place Vendôme; it, too, is empty of citizens. But not of soldiers.

Blanche gasps; so does Claude. For there are Nazi tanks in the square, surrounding the statue of Napoleon. An enormous Nazi flag, with its twisted black swastika, hangs above several doorways—including that of the Ritz. Her husband's beloved Ritz. Hers, too. *Their* Ritz.

And at the top of the stairs leading to the front doors stand two Nazi soldiers. With guns.

There's a clatter. The boys have dropped the bags and are sprinting off like hares. Claude looks after them.

"Perhaps we should go to the flat instead," he says, taking out his dirty handkerchief again. For the first time today—for the very first time since Blanche has known him—her husband looks uncertain. And that's the moment when she understands that everything has changed.

"Nonsense," Blanche replies, feeling hot blood surge through her—strange blood, not her own, but the blood of a courageous woman with nothing to hide from the Nazis. To her own surprise, not to mention Claude's, she gathers up the suitcases and marches straight toward those two soldiers. "We are going in the front door, Claude Auzello. Because *you* are the director of the Ritz."

Claude begins to protest but for once does not argue with her. He lapses into silence as they approach the two sentries, who each take two steps toward them but don't, thank Christ, raise their weapons.

"This is Herr Claude Auzello, director of the Ritz," Blanche announces in her best German, a German that surprises her with its smooth confidence, as it obviously surprises her husband. After all, according to him, his American-born wife speaks French with the most atrocious accent he's ever heard, so it's more than a bit stunning to hear this flawless German.

But then, the Auzellos have been surprising each other since the moment they first met.

"I am Frau Auzello. We want to speak to an officer at once. *Mach Schnell*!"

The soldiers look startled; one runs into the hotel. Claude whispers, "*Mon Dieu*, Blanche," and she can see by the way he tightens his grip on his bags, he's doing his earthly best not to cross himself in that infuriatingly French Catholic way.

Blanche—despite trembling limbs—remains upright, even imperiously so, and by the time the officer, a short man with a red face, emerges, she knows exactly what she is going to say.

For she is Blanche Ross Auzello. American. Parisian. Among other things, many other things, past, present, future, that she will have to conceal from now on. But then again, hasn't she been concealing most of them these past twenty years anyway? So she is very good at this, deception. As, she must acknowledge, is her husband.

It is, perhaps, the thing that binds these two even more closely than it tears them apart.

"Herr Auzello! Frau Auzello! It is a pleasure to meet you!" The commanding officer tumbling out the door to greet them has a voice that is both slippery and guttural in the German way, but his French is flawless. He bows to Claude and reaches to kiss Blanche's hand, which she hides behind her back just in time.

For it, too, is suddenly trembling.

"Welcome back to the Ritz. We have heard so much about you. I am here to explain that management has been relocated to the other side." The Nazi bobs his head to indicate the rue Cambon, which runs behind the building. "We—we Germans—have made ourselves at home, thanks to your staff's hospitality, here on the Place Vendôme side. Your other guests are all over on the rue Cambon. And we have taken the liberty of removing your personal items from your office and installing them in another, in the gallery above that side's lobby. You will find much of your staff intact and awaiting your instructions."

"Fine, fine," Blanche hears herself replying—as if she encountered a Nazi officer every day, and she can't help but marvel at her own performance. Damned if it didn't take a German invasion to mold her into the kind of actress she'd always wanted to be. "I expected nothing less. Now, will you have your men take our bags around for us?"

She turns to smile reassuringly at Claude, whose face, she's startled to see, has paled beneath the ruddy tan acquired in the South of France. As the two soldiers begin to gather up the luggage, she can't help but notice that Claude grips his attaché case tightly when they motion for it, the knuckles on his hand white with effort, the ropy muscles in his neck twitching. She shoots him a questioning look, but his face remains smooth and unworried.

They follow the two soldiers through the square, taking a left to the narrow yet impossibly chic rue Cambon. Once again, she's aware of eyes, watching. She reaches out to grasp Claude's other hand; he keeps her tightly within his grip. The two of them, linked this way, won't falter. Of this, she is sure; it's the only thing of which she's sure, at this incredible Wonderland-moment, when nothing is as it should be.

When Nazi soldiers are escorting the Auzellos to the rear entrance of the Ritz.

They follow the soldiers through the smaller entrance, and at once the pocket-sized lobby is filled with familiar faces, stricken and pale but breaking into smiles of relief at seeing the Auzellos return. Blanche, too, smiles and nods to one and all, but they don't stop to chat. Blanche senses that her husband is not up to the emotion of homecoming, of being greeted by the staff he left almost a year ago, his family, his children in the truest sense. Normally her husband would have deserted her while he caught up with them, broke open a bottle of port in his office, listened to all the stories that have waited until his return to be told: The young florist is gone, married to her lover; there is a new provider of butter, because the old one died and his children sold the dairy.

But today, Blanche suspects that he knows the stories he will be told are not pleasant, trivial ones. Stories of staff disappearing in the chaos of the invasion, of young bellhops dying in battle, of that pretty young florist—last name of Chabat—not marrying after all but trying desperately to get a visa to England. Stories of how the Nazis want things to run here in his hotel—yes, her husband thinks of the Ritz as his own despite the fact that the family of César Ritz are the true owners. He is arrogant in that way, her Claude; if Blanche were to be honest—something she allows herself to be at least once a day—it's one of the things she most admires about him.

Claude is in an awful hurry to get to their rooms. Blanche breaks into a jog to keep up with him and the soldiers in their black boots with the steel toes striking hard against the plush carpets. And she finds herself worrying—always the wife of the director of the Ritz!—that the carpets will not stand up to this kind of treatment. Not carpets more accustomed to slinky heels of leather. Again, she remembers her own shoes, grinding dirt into the carpets as well, and for the first time in a very long time, she feels less than her surroundings.

Blanche has grown accustomed, over the years,

to dressing up to the Ritz. There's just something about the place that inspires you to wear your best, to sit up straighter, talk more quietly, drape your best jewels about your neck, check your reflection one last time before venturing out into its marble halls, every surface always shining and polished. Those whose job it is to shine and polish retreat into hidden cupboards and corners the moment they see a guest, so that the overall effect is that of a magic castle lovingly tended to by sprites who only come out at night.

But now she notices the Nazi flag on display in the enormous urns that hold palm trees. The utter silence in the opulent halls and sitting areas; the sense that lurking behind every polished door is an ear, pressed, listening. And she forgets about her shoes again.

The Auzellos are shown to their old suite, conveniently already located on the rue Cambon side of the hotel. The bags are stacked neatly for them but damned if Blanche is going to tip a Nazi; she merely nods as the soldiers leave. Claude and Blanche both turn away from each other, as if the moment of homecoming—nightmarish as it is—after so long away is simply too much to acknowledge. So the two of them, like tourists, begin to walk about the rooms, surveying. Blanche is startled to see that there's a layer of dust on every surface—impossible to imagine, before. There are some small fault lines in the gilded wallpaper—were there bombs dropped nearby, prior to the Occupation? There's a staleness to the air, as if the small suite—by Ritz standards, anyway—has been holding its breath until their return. She opens a window; below her is a cluster of Nazi soldiers talking, laughing, as gleeful as schoolboys on holiday.

"Why were you behaving like a guilty kid out there?" She draws away from the window with a shudder and finally turns to Claude, who is still gripping his case.

"I have . . ." He begins to laugh shakily, his neat little mustache quivers, and his slightly-protruding eyes blink repeatedly. "Oh, Blanchette, you foolish woman. I have papers with me." He thumps the case. "*Illegal* papers. Blank travel passes and demobilization papers. I stole them from the garrison, so I could use them here in Paris for—for whoever might need them. I could have been thrown in prison if the Nazis had discovered them."

"Jesus Christ, Claude!" Now it is Blanche's turn to pale; she collapses into a chair, imagining the scenario playing out. "Oh, Claude. You should have told me when we left Nîmes."

"No." Claude shakes his head, fingers the collar of his shirt. "No, Blanche. There are things you shouldn't know. For your own good." And he's back to normal, Blanche's husband; her infuriatingly *French* husband with his rules and pronouncements and lectures. They've been married seventeen years, and still he's trying to make a docile French wife out of a rebellious American flapper.

"Oh, Claude, we're not back to this old song and dance again, are we? After all we've been through this past year? After *today?*"

"I have no idea what you mean, Blanche," her husband says in his priggish way—and normally, this would be the red cape inciting her to fury. She remembers, with a guilty start, that some of those rips in the wallpaper were there even before they left. Courtesy of flying vases and candlesticks; courtesy of one of their innumerable arguments concerning the very nature of marriage. Specifically, theirs.

But today, Blanche is too exhausted and bewildered to fight. And suddenly, too thirsty. When was the last time she had a drink? Days. She laughs, although it sounds tinny to her ringing ears. A German invasion is a hell of a way to dry out.

"Well, that's that," she says, and finds, to her astonishment, that she has to wipe an unexpected tear from her eye. "It was good while it lasted, I guess."

"What do you mean?" Claude, who is searching

the rooms for a place to hide his contraband papers, frowns.

"I mean that nothing's changed, after all. After that time at Nîmes, when we—when we almost had a marriage. Paris might be under German rule, but you're still lying to me."

"No, no, it's not like that at all," Claude says—sadly, to Blanche's surprise. He drops his case down on a table, as if he no longer has the strength to carry this burden; his face softens, and it looks almost as young and pliant, able to smile and laugh, as it did when they first met. For a moment, he looks repentant, and Blanche leans toward him, her hands clasped over her heart like a young girl. A foolish but hopeful young girl.

But then Claude doesn't bother to explain exactly what it is like and so Blanche shrugs— the one thing, according to her husband, that she does as well as, if not better than, any French woman—and begins to unpack.

"Now." Claude stretches, arching his back, which creaks alarmingly, his usually composed face so weary that, despite her disappointment, she has a momentary longing to draw him a bath and tuck him into bed. "I must go to Madame Ritz and see what is going on over on the other side, where the Germans apparently are residing. Nazis in César Ritz's palace—*mon Dieu*! He will be turning in his grave."

"Go, go. You'll be useless until you've walked

over every inch of your beloved Ritz. I know you, Claude Auzello. But should we go back to the apartment later, though? To check on it?" For the first time Blanche remembers their roomy flat on the avenue Montaigne in the shadow of the Eiffel Tower. The Auzellos' destination, always, from the moment they left Nîmes in the chaos of retreat, had been the Ritz. It is their true north. But they do have another place to stay—a place that is not inhabited by Nazis. And thinking about soldiers lurking around every corner here at the Ritz makes Blanche's skin thrum with the desire to flee, to hide. The fearless imposter who stood outside and ordered Nazis around like peasants is gone; in her place is—a woman.

A frightened woman with no real home—an alien in a country occupied by a terrifying enemy—making her infuriatingly dependent on a husband who disappoints her more often than not.

Almost as much as she disappoints him.

"I think not," Claude says with more than a trace of his usual enraging superiority, and Blanche, in her current state, is relieved to hear it. "If there is rationing or shortages, it's best we're here at the Ritz. I'm sure the Germans will see to it that they have the best of everything, and perhaps we can live on the scraps." Claude, after a moment's hesitation, goes to his wife. He folds her in his arms, and whispers into her ear.

"You were brave today, my Blanchette," he croons, and Blanche can't help but shiver a little, and nestle closer into his chest. "Very brave. But perhaps it is best for you to try a little cowardice, instead? Until we see—? Until we see."

She nods; he makes sense. Oh, he always makes sense, her Claude—except in one area. One very important area. Still, she allows herself to slump a little against him. He is not tall, he is not broad or muscular, her husband. But he manages to make her feel protected anyway, as he has from the very beginning; a man who is as certain as he is, as annoyingly upright and proper, can do that. Even when his hands are small, and his throat as slender and fine as a dancer's. So she clings to him; he is, after all, the only thing she has left. She could have gone back to America when the world started to go to hell. She could have joined an old lover in a different country, one that most likely would remain safely on the sidelines of this grotesque circus. But no, she'd stayed here in France, with this man, this husband.

Someday, she really should get around to asking herself the question of why. But not today; she's already been through too much. And she needs a goddamned drink.

As soon as Claude leaves, with a promise not to be long—a promise they both know he won't keep—Blanche decides to take a good look at herself in the mirror; she hasn't seen her reflection in days. The blond hair—not natural; the ruby ring on her right hand—not authentic. She hocked the jewel years ago and had it replaced with a fake, and never did tell Claude, who would not have approved of her reason. The delicate gold cross at her throat, a wedding gift from her husband—a joke, she had thought at the time, but soon realized it was anything but; the passport in her handbag, creased and soft from carrying it with her, day in and day out—well, they're all a joke, really, when you come right down to it, she thought bitterly.

Everything's a joke now. A farce. A sham.

This new reality, this new nightmare that she finds herself in . . . it's so far removed—light-years, *Biblical* years—from the Paris, the Ritz, the man she met when she first sailed from America. Seventeen years ago, it was. A lifetime ago.

A dream ago. Several of them, actually—dreams. Mostly unfulfilled.

As dreams, Blanche Auzello knows all too well, tend to be.

CHAPTER 2

CLAUDE,

1923

Once upon a time, before the Nazis arrived . . .

"Hey, get a load of this, will you? Hey, mister, hey!"

The young man looked up from his ledger, his brow already furrowed. Unsurprisingly, it was an American calling across the lobby of the Hôtel Claridge. The voice was loud, strident, *insistent.* Americans spoke as if they believed the entire world wished to hear what they were saying; they had no discretion.

But Americans paid his salary, and so, with effort, he unfurrowed his brow.

Paris—*his* Paris—was flooded with these vociferous newcomers. Naturally, it was because of the Great War. Those cocky American soldiers who boasted that they had saved the day— even though they arrived only at the twilight, not the dawn—decided they had to see more of Gay Paree, tantalizingly glimpsed only on their leaves. So they came back in droves, bringing their women, and they took over the cafés, ordering coffee with their meals—absurd!—and drinking absinthe until they went blind. Talking, always talking, even to strangers. "Hello," one of them said to the young man only yesterday, as he took a chair next to him at a café, remarking on its small size. "I'm Bud. What's your name?"

The young man did not tell him, naturally. What business was it of this American? He would never understand this compulsion of Americans to announce their presence everywhere. Why should anyone care?

More than anything, Parisians simply wanted to be left alone. Left to their grief, for *they* were the ones who died and lost. They especially resented the young American men, for in 1923, France had few of them left under the age of sixty.

But the Americans didn't care; they smiled their big, white-teethed smiles and waved their huge paws full of francs and could not stop enthusing about how cheap everything was. What they were really saying was: We're not truly allies; we're better than you.

But the young man—Claude Auzello was his name—swallowed his anger and distaste, for his very livelihood depended on these gleeful foreigners continuing to wash ashore off the boats in Calais and following the Seine into Paris like rubbish.

"May I help you?" He strode over to the loud American woman who was waving at him from across the lobby.

"Yeah, thanks, Mr.—?"

"Auzello. Monsieur Auzello. I am here to take care of all your needs." Bowing slightly, he fingered the brass name tag on his coat, revealing his exalted position at the Hôtel Claridge: *Assistant manager.*

"Well, aren't you the bee's knees?" She batted her eyelashes at him, this brassy woman—in her thirties, Claude guessed with a practiced eye; late thirties, actually. The powder settled in the lines of her face, and the lipstick on her Kewpie-doll lips was far too red for her complexion. She was a blonde—natural, it looked like to Claude. She was tall and broad-shouldered and swathed in furs and jewelry, resembling a mangy Christmas tree.

"Oh, Pearl, you were right. This is the end, the total *end!*"

Another pushy American woman! Stifling a sigh, Claude turned to greet her, a merely professional smile already making its way to the corner of his lips. But this woman froze it there; something gave way in his chest and for the first time in his life he wondered if he, Claude Auzello, was on the receiving end of Cupid's arrow.

For the woman who strode over, hand outstretched in that confident American way, was the most beautiful woman he'd ever beheld. She was blond, too—although Claude suspected from the bottle, but what did it matter when it suited

33

her perfectly? She had big, sparkling brown eyes and this was a combination—blond with brown eyes—that Claude had never been able to resist.

But it was more than her coloring that froze his heart; it was her smile, so dazzling, so unforced. She was younger than her companion by at least ten years; the dew was still fresh on this American Beauty rose. She was also tall—all American women were so tall—so that Claude had to tilt his head, ever so slightly, to meet her dancing gaze.

"Is this your first time visiting us, mademoiselle?"

"It's my first time outside of New York. I can't believe I'm actually here!" How charming! No airs or pretensions of sophistication, as many first-time visitors attempted. This young woman was simply overjoyed and didn't care who knew.

"Then I will make it my personal business to show you Paris," he replied, deciding quickly.

As the assistant manager of the Hôtel Claridge, Claude Auzello was no stranger to showing Paris to beautiful women; he considered it one of the perquisites of his position. In fact, if he were being painfully honest, he would have to admit that there had been a small . . . misunderstanding . . . between a beautiful woman and himself only last month; a misunderstanding that led to the beautiful woman departing the hotel assuring one and all that Claude was responsible for her expenses. A business transaction, most assuredly, that had never been discussed during midnight suppers at Maxim's when this beautiful woman had proven to be charmingly susceptible to champagne and Claude's arsenal of female flattery.

Naturally—and appropriately—he had been chastised by the director of the hotel and warned to be more discreet in the future.

Discretion! Yes, it was handy for a Frenchman, especially for those who had come through the war unscathed. Claude's life had been saved by the luck of an urgent bladder, a small detail he did not like to repeat. He'd left his guard post to relieve himself and while he was in the bushes, the hut took a direct hit from an artillery shell. For that, he had been decorated—such was the randomness of life! And so, unlike many of his childhood friends, he lived to enjoy a Paris that seemed to have five beautiful women to every one able-bodied young man. "Claude," his father had told him after their first weepy embrace upon his demobilization, "Claude, my son. France is yours for the taking, a nation grateful. Do not waste this chance!"

He had not, *cher papa*. He had not.

"May I ask what names your reservations are under?" Claude asked, smoothly.

"Pearl White," the older of the two American women declared.

"My name is Blanche. Er—Ross, Blanche Ross," the younger said with a shy smile and a slight hesitation, as if she were trying out her name for the first time.

They followed him to the front desk, where they handed him their passports. He checked the passports, then, after a slight pause, returned them.

"Ah. All is in order," Claude told the charming Mademoiselle Ross with a smile. He had them sign the ledger—Mademoiselle Ross's signature was quite vivacious, taking up two entire lines—and produced two keys. As he gave one of them to her, he made sure that his fingers touched the vibrant tips of her gloves, allowing them to linger for a moment before—he simply could not help himself!—kissing the top of her hand, and enjoying her surprised gasp.

"This is how we greet beautiful women in France." Claude fingered his neat little mustache, a practical accessory, for his face had not quite matured at the same pace as his personality.

"Well, aren't you fresh?" Mademoiselle Ross smiled at him, her cheeks deliciously tinged with pink. She had on the usual American makeup: lips painted like a ribbon, a fake beauty mark penciled on one cheek. Her golden hair was bobbed and she wore the new flat-chested, long-waisted dress—this was, apparently, known as the "flapper style"—although in Mademoiselle

Ross's case, her ample chest strained against the bodice in a most beguiling way.

"Fresh?" It was Claude's turn to be surprised, for he was proud of his command of the English language. But the word was unfamiliar in this context. "Like a peach?"

"Like a masher."

Claude shook his head, befuddled; his face burned at the young woman's teasing amusement.

"A rake?"

"A garden implement?"

"Like Valentino—you've heard of him?"

Ah—Claude's face cleared. Yes, of course, he had seen Rudolph Valentino in several films. Monsieur Valentino was a funny man with a great many teeth and rolling eyes, yet he was apparently irresistible to beautiful women. So this was a compliment!

"Rudy's no masher," the other woman—Pearl— said dismissively. "He's a queer. Everyone in Hollywood knows that."

Claude stiffened: such language.

"Listen to Pearl," Blanche assured him, placing a warm hand upon his biceps—Claude made sure to flex it beneath his gray pinstriped cutaway jacket. "Pearl's a film star, too. You've seen her, right? *The Perils of Pauline*? This is Pauline! In the flesh!"

He had not heard of Pearl White—Pauline— but naturally, he pretended that he had. But how could this coarse woman—she was actually reaching into her bodice to adjust one of her bosoms, right here in the lobby of the Hôtel Claridge—be a film star? Claude Auzello was dubious.

"Naturally," he addressed the charming Mademoiselle Ross. "I see many American films, they are very popular in France. Mademoiselle Gloria Swanson has stayed here at the Hôtel Claridge many times." And he straightened up with pride; that had been a grand experience, as Mademoiselle Swanson was quite glamorous, and there had been many newspaper photos of her in the Claridge lobby.

"Gloria?" Pearl snorted. "That little shrimp. Nothing but a clotheshorse, if you ask me."

"I'm going to be a film star, too," Blanche confided, lowering her head modestly; her cheeks burned pink, almost as if she were unable to believe it herself. "That's why we're here in Paris. To make films!"

"Ah." Claude could not help it; he tasted dismay. A film star? No, that would never do; while it was a feather in the Claridge's cap to have a film star grace its lobby, film stars—particularly aspiring ones—were, in a purely practical sense, beneath the assistant manager of the Hôtel Claridge, who had higher aspirations. Film stars courted publicity and tended to do all manner of wild things—such as bathe in fountains and remove their clothes in nightclubs—that Claude felt were rather vulgar and common.

But Mademoiselle Ross's breasts heaved most enticingly as her breath quickened; her silky eyelashes grazed her cheeks, they were that long.

"I don't have to start right away. I was supposed to meet someone, but my—my friend—has been delayed a week." Mademoiselle Ross held up a crumpled, tearstained telegram, then shoved it into her coat pocket as if she were ashamed of it.

"A week?" Now that was good news. A week was perfect—finite. No ambiguity, no last-minute sighs and flutters and hesitant wonderings of "Perhaps I could extend my stay. . . ." "Allow me to show you Paris," Claude once again suggested, overcoming his antipathy for the film industry, or at least this particular member of it. "This is your first visit, and there is nothing I would like better to do."

"Well, I'm not sure. . . ."

"Oh, go ahead, Blanche. Enjoy yourself until he comes!"

Ah! There was a "he." Who was away for a week.

Claude smiled again.

"Well, gee, that would be swell, then." Mademoiselle nodded with another radiant smile. "I'm dying to see Paris."

"Let us begin." Snapping his fingers—a bit of theatricality he did not usually employ, but he could not help himself—Claude summoned bellboys to corral the mass of trunks and hand luggage the women had brought with them. He could never understand why Americans brought so much baggage; their clothes were abominable, anyway, and they could purchase much more exquisite creations, very cheaply, here in Paris.

Claude straightened his tie, beckoned for the women to follow, and led them through the lobby of the Hôtel Claridge, proud of the fact that all the chandeliers had been washed just this morning; that the trash cans were emptied every hour; that the brass light switches were polished every two hours. He showed them where the ladies' salon was; he stopped briefly at the American bar, full of noisy patrons listening to a woman singer croon a silly song, something about saying farewell to a person of indeterminate gender named "Tootsie." He pressed the bell for the gilded elevator lift and told the boy to take them to the top floor.

Once there, he ushered the women down the carpeted hall—vacuumed twice daily; he was pleased to see the fresh tracks, still undisturbed—until he reached their suite; opening the door with his gold master key, he stood back and allowed the mademoiselles to enter first.

"Holy moley, Pearl!" Blanche clapped her hands and jumped up and down, so charming and joyful that Claude wanted to take her in his arms right then and there; he desired to hold such exuberance, press it close to his own just as exuberant flesh. Swallowing hard, he switched on the lights in order to show the suite in all its glory. With professional detachment, he opened the door to the bathroom and explained how to use the taps—avoiding the bidet, which, after all, was not proper for a gentleman to point out. Claude also showed the two—Pearl White was more blasé than her friend, who *ooh*ed and *aah*ed most adorably—all the lighted buttons next to each bed that would summon the proper help: chambermaids, shoeshine, laundry, room service.

"And—*voilà*!" With a flourish, he pulled open the ornate draperies to reveal the wide Champs-Élysées below.

It was its usual noisy, chaotic self; cars honking, masses of tourists screaming, laughing, taking photographs with their bulky box cameras. Sidewalk cafés full of people jammed into tiny tables and chairs, souvenir stands with miniature Eiffel Towers and tiny red, white, and blue French flags and cheap berets, dogs barking, restaurateurs waving menus at passing tourists. Claude was not fond of the Champs for all of these reasons and would have apologized for its seedier aspects had Blanche Ross not started squealing in delight.

"Oh! Oh, how grand! It's like Times Square,

isn't it, Pearl? Only so much better! Look—is that the Eiffel Tower?"

"*Oui*, mademoiselle, it is."

"And that over there—what's that?"

"The Arc de Triomphe, built to celebrate Napoleon's victory at Austerlitz."

"And that?" The charming American flapper had opened the window and was leaning dangerously out of it. Claude rushed to grab her, holding her by the waist—out of concern for her safety, he told himself as he encircled that slender torso, felt the firm, ripe flesh straining against his arms, absorbing the heat from her young body, fueled by such innocent enthusiasm that it made his heart do a remarkable thing.

Claude Auzello's heart—that sturdy engine, heretofore reliable and hence unremarkable—made an odd little sound, almost like the *pop* of a champagne cork. It was a sound audible to his ears only, yet he felt the tips of those ears burn with embarrassment. More roughly than he should have, Claude drew Mademoiselle Ross back inside the room and released her without ceremony. Inhaling—rather shakily; he almost removed his handkerchief to mop his suddenly glistening forehead, but reminded himself that he was on duty—he straightened his tie. Unnecessarily, for it was, of course, undisturbed. His tie, it turned out, was much more dependable than his heart.

"That was the Place de la Concorde, Mademoiselle Ross."

"Oh, call me Blanche. If you're going to be spending this week with me, we ought to be on first name terms, don't you think?"

"If you wish." He nodded, knowing that he sounded far more stern and formal than he intended, but at the moment he did not quite trust his voice. "My name is Claude, Madem—Blanche."

"Perfect."

"I'll call for you at seven, if you like? There is a charming restaurant in Montmartre I think you would enjoy. We could walk there, as it's such a warm day."

"Terrific, Claude, just terrific!"

"And what am I supposed to do?" Pearl White pouted—a silly pout for such a weathered-looking woman.

"Oh, Christ, Pearl. I forgot!" Blanche turned to Claude with an appealing gaze in her wide brown eyes.

"Aw, never mind." Pearl began to laugh heartily. "I'm just teasin' ya, Blanche. I have a date already lined up."

Claude did not think he imagined the look of relief on Blanche's face, and so he could not quite suppress a grin as he bid them adieu—kissing Mademoiselle Ross's hand once more—and closed the door, returning to his duties. Despite the charming miss whose supple waist he could still feel in his arms, there were other guests to be welcomed. Then, the night manager to be briefed on the dozens of small problems that had popped up, like clockwork, during the course of the day. The laundry reported that one of the wringers was broken. Some sheets had arrived from the supplier, even though none had been ordered. The chef found out there was no Dover sole for this evening and was threatening to quit—the third time he'd done so this week. Two of the waiters in the dining room had not shown up, so two busboys must be elevated. Mrs. Carter, in the Presidential Suite, had complained of loud footsteps overhead, despite the fact—pointed out to her again and again—that she was on the top floor.

Claude plunged right into these tasks with his usual efficiency, the same efficiency he had brought to his duties in the war. Despite his embarrassment over the circumstances of his survival, he had served admirably. Claude was not one to indulge in false modesty; he knew that he was born to lead, not follow. He had been a captain in charge of a battalion of men and he saw some of those men die around him; he held them while they shuddered out of this life; he had put his hands—he surveyed them now, marveling at the whiteness, the manicure he'd gotten only yesterday. He had put those same unblemished hands in blood and shit and intestines. He had felt the sharp shards of bones protruding from flesh.

And for surviving—such a mindless thing, really, you simply keep breathing while those around you do not—he had been awarded the *Légion d'honneur*.

For merely doing his job, he expected no such honor.

To have his own hotel was his ambition but he was still young—only twenty-five—and patient. So for the present—the assistant manager at the Hôtel Claridge, a decent hotel, yes; many an American movie star stayed here, as well as minor royalty. It was, perhaps, a bit too busy and common for his taste—right on the Champs, so too much foot traffic, and it backed out onto a narrow street lined with jazz clubs, which he abhorred: all that jangling, nervous music. But the Claridge was a fine place for now. Later, however . . . But he must work his way up, learn the job inside and out before he could even think of owning his own place. And to do that, Claude had his sights set on a different hotel.

A hotel in a class all of its own: the Ritz—oh, even to say its name induced in him a little shiver of excitement. Not unlike the excitement that a beautiful blonde named Blanche Ross had also induced.

Glancing at the employee schedule hanging in his office, Claude was very glad indeed that the owner of the Claridge, Monsieur Marquet, was away on business for two weeks. He could easily arrange his schedule to accommodate hers. A whirlwind romance—dinner in Montmartre, the usual stroll along the Seine, lunch in the garden at the Palais-Royal, picnics in the Bois—he'd buy her a small painting from one of the stalls near Notre Dame; that never failed to impress.

Flowers every day in her room, fresh from the flower market on the Île de la Cité where Claude had an account. And a reputation.

And at the end of the week: *Au revoir, Mademoiselle Ross.*

Once again, his heart made that odd little exclamation—what was it? Claude put his fingers to his wrist and breathed slowly, feeling his pulse. Should he take an antacid? Had he eaten something unforgiving at lunch?

Shrugging, he picked up the phone to call the charming little restaurant in Montmartre.

A restaurant known to all in the hospitality industry for its *discretion.*

CHAPTER 3
BLANCHE,
June 1940

Blanche turns away from the mirror, repulsed by the dirt creased into her face, the grit in her hair (as well as the inch-long dark roots at the scalp), the red in her eyes from the cinders of the train, the stains on her clothes, the run in her stocking, the broken heel of her shoe. As thirsty as she is, she draws herself a bath first and while the water is running, she removes a Schiaparelli day dress from her bag, hanging it next to the steaming water so that it might lose some of its wrinkles. She knows she could ring for someone to press it (hell, here at the Ritz, she could ring for someone to go out and buy her a new one) but she's desperate to shed her filthy refugee skin and return to herself, to the Ritz.

She removes all the makeup from her vanity case, lining up the various jars and pots, nearly empty after the months away. She should go down to see if any of her (real) jewels remain locked in the small safe in Claude's office, and then she remembers that it's no longer his office. And so her jewels are probably no longer there.

C'est la vie.

After her bath—not as long as she'd like, but enough to dissolve the first couple of layers of filth—she dresses, sprays the last of her perfume behind her ears, and pulls out a pair of shoes.

A pair of custom satin court shoes from Hellstern & Sons; they are pristine, unworn in all her time at Nîmes. (Christ, what was she thinking, packing like she was going on the Grand Tour instead of accompanying her soldier husband to a small garrison in the middle of nowhere?) They're a lovely shade of apple-green, and she slips her tired, swollen feet inside them and sighs. She remembers the first time Claude took her to have her feet measured at the shop, how excited she was to see her wooden shoe form, when it was finished, with her name on it— *Madame Auzello.*

It was the first thing she'd ever seen with her new, married—French—name. It was the first purchase she made where she said, so proudly, "Put it on Monsieur Auzello's account." She'd felt so *continental;* so sophisticated, emancipated, even. When the reality, as she would discover, was so very different. Still, at the time, the act of having a custom-made shoe charged to her Parisian husband's account seemed the very act of defiance, of rebellion. Back home, as her parents' youngest, unmarried daughter, she'd had to make do with a yearly trip to Lord & Taylor to purchase her chaste wardrobe. Until, anyway, her film career took off—

Which it never really had. But still, the pursuit of it had led her to Paris, and to Claude, and a charge account at Hellstern & Sons, and the first time she'd slipped her foot into a custom shoe, she'd made Claude take her out dancing in Montmartre—something he did only reluctantly—and she'd felt so utterly Parisian, so utterly reborn. So utterly *Madame Auzello*.

Back when being Madame Auzello was a dream come true.

Sometimes Blanche wonders what her life would have been like had she not allowed a certain pompous little Frenchman to walk her feet off all over Paris that week, while he lectured and explained and, at the most unexpected moments, took her hand and kissed her with more passion than his neat little mustache indicated. He bought her armfuls of roses from vendors, romantic paintings of the Seine from starving artists, showed her delights that were not in any tourist brochure—like the little heart, laid by a bricklayer centuries ago in honor of his lover, on the road in front of Les Invalides. Where would she have ended up, had he not revealed, in showing her these private little monuments, his own surprisingly tender heart?

She had not planned for Claude Auzello when she'd packed her trunks, bade a blithe farewell to her stricken parents, and marched up the gangplank of the France-bound ship in New York harbor. No, she had not even *packed* for a Claude Auzello; she had packed for someone else entirely.

She sure as hell hadn't packed for the Ritz.

Now, she surveys her foot, clad in the pristine satin, and thinks—I'm clean, I'm fashionable, I'm *home*. The Ritz and Blanche, they have a deal; they'd made it long ago.

She'd behave herself within its gilded walls; she'd comport herself like a real lady, she'd be a credit to her husband, an asset, even. And in return?

Those gilded walls would protect her—even, perhaps specifically, from herself. Because nothing bad can happen at the Ritz; it was designed to meet every whim, however ridiculous. Would you like a fresh nosegay to sniff while you bathe in an enormous tub with gold swan taps? The Ritz will provide. Would you like your dog walked while you have your tea in the palm-filled court, his meal—prepared by the same chef who prepared yours—waiting for him on a satin cushion at your feet? The Ritz will provide. Did your husband cheat on you yesterday, and would you like to take your revenge upon him, but you don't happen to know any eligible young men?

The Ritz will provide.

And protect. Although it's not only the rich that have secrets, and even the poorest chambermaid might have the most to lose. But it doesn't matter, because once you enter the Ritz, you breathe a little more freely, indulge yourself in ways you wouldn't anywhere else. Because the Ritz will keep you safe—you have no choice but to believe it.

But will it now? Now that its famous front door is manned not by a top-hatted doorman in a black overcoat, but a Nazi soldier?

Blanche shudders, then grabs her handbag and heads out to see a man about a drink.

The Ritz can provide that, as well.

CHAPTER 4

CLAUDE,
1923

*The handsome prince awoke the fair
maiden with a kiss . . .*

"Take me to that Ritz you're always going on
about, Claude," she teased, tickling the back of
his neck before she became quite serious. "Ask
me that question you were about to ask."

Claude had won her, this enchanting American.
Won her after a glorious week that he, for the
very first time, did not want to end. Won her
from her infuriating Egyptian prince, a man who
would never marry this woman, it was obvious; a
man who would only ruin her by making her one
of his harem.

And so Claude asked, and Blanche said yes.
Their lives, joined, forever changed. For the
better, he thought, then. Blanche was a prize—a
fair maiden whom he had rescued from the very
clutches of an Egyptian despot. It was all very
dramatic, the most impetuous, romantic thing
Claude had ever done in his life—completely out
of character. He himself knew this, and so was,

perhaps, a bit too impressed with himself to think beyond the moment of victory. Too intoxicated by his heroics to contemplate how on earth these two—the American flapper and the Paris hotelier—would manage to live happily ever after.

But she did bring him luck, at least in the very beginning. For on the very day, in this very Ritz, that Claude dropped to his knees and proposed—his face still flushed with the triumph of rescuing this damsel in distress—he was also summoned to Marie-Louise Ritz's suite and offered the job of assistant manager.

The very last thing his new fiancée whispered to him before he went was, "Ask to be manager. You're no assistant anything, Claude Auzello."

Indeed, he was not—hadn't the events of the last twenty-four hours proved that? Emboldened by her American confidence, he did just as Blanche told him to. And was rewarded with an impressed, amused smile by the plump Madame Ritz, who agreed. And then asked him to take her dogs for a walk, which, naturally, Claude did without protest.

For doing *that,* he was rewarded with an even more amused smile by his American bride-to-be, who found this extremely hilarious. For what reason, Claude did not know. But, ever the student of human behavior that he prided himself on being, he was determined to find out.

As the weeks and months passed, Claude found out many things about this maiden, this damsel, now miraculously his wife. Things that were not apparent that triumphant day when they marched to the Hôtel de Ville with a marriage license and witnesses—Monsieur Renaudin from the Claridge and Blanche's unfortunate friend, Pearl White—and said their vows in tremulous voices and were declared married by law, and reported back to the Hôtel Claridge for a raucous wedding breakfast. Blanche's and Pearl's friends from the film industry descended upon them; there was much alcohol and laughter and risqué jokes before they accompanied the Auzellos to the train station, where the dazzled couple boarded a train to the coast for a honeymoon and a visit with Claude's parents in Nice. At the station, these theatrical rowdies made quite a scene; there were champagne bottles everywhere. Pearl even insisted on smashing one against the side of the train to christen it, and Claude was relieved when at last Blanche and he could board, and her friends lurched away, so drunk he could only pray none of them fell in front of an approaching train.

Once ensconced in their compartment, Claude learned the first new thing about his Blanchette (the pet name he had determined for her).

"Now that we are married, I will do as Napoleon did to Josephine," he told her serenely, happy to be alone with his bride at last. "I will insist that you drop those friends of yours, as they do not befit one in your position, especially since I'm about to start at the Ritz. You are too good for them, Blanche."

"You—what?" She blinked and squeezed the bouquet of orchids he had given her so tightly, he thought the blossoms might snap off their stems.

"I insist that you drop these friends, Blanche." Claude did not understand why he had to repeat himself; as far as he was aware, she was not at all hard of hearing.

"Hmmm." She reached for her makeup case and began to touch up her face with powder and lip rouge.

"And another thing," Claude continued, pleased to have this opportunity to properly explain things to his new American bride, who might not completely understand her role as his wife, for he did not know how these things were done in America. "I wish you not to use that much paint. I understand that it's necessary for your profession, but not in real life." And not, Claude added silently, necessary for your profession much longer, please God. She had made one film in France since they'd been engaged, a romantic potboiler in which she had to make love to another actor, and Claude had seen the film perhaps twenty times, each time purple with impotence and rage at the sight of his fiancée—now wife—being kissed by another man. But Blanche, Claude had to admit, was not a very convincing actress. Surely it would only be a matter of time before others recognized it?

"You don't need it, Blanche," he continued, relishing his role of new husband, first rescuer, now protector of this enchanting creature. "You are a natural beauty, and furthermore, you are married now."

"And what does that mean, Popsy?"

Claude winced. Blanche had also determined her pet name for *him*. In a moment of pure giddiness, he had shared the—romantic, he had thought—insight that when he first saw her, his heart went "pop." Unfortunately, his new bride had found it quite amusing instead of romantic, and seemed to take great delight in calling him by this undignified nickname.

"It means you are my wife and you will do as I say." Claude smiled anyway. Surely she was joking?

"I'll do as you *say?*"

"It is the way in France, of course. I have no idea how married couples behave in America, but you are in France."

"For the time being," she said, her voice tight.

"I'm sorry?"

"I didn't realize I was marrying a caveman. I thought I was marrying a gentleman who respected me in the way that a certain Egyptian prince did not."

"I do!" Claude didn't understand her meaning—was it the language barrier?

"Then stop behaving like a Neanderthal."

"All I want is that you drop those friends of yours and stop using paint." The train was moving swiftly through the countryside outside of Paris; rolling green hills and small thatched farmhouses and cows everywhere.

"And I say no. I like them. I like the way I look. So do most men."

"It does not matter what other men think about you now." Claude laughed; she was so charmingly innocent. "You are married."

"If you believe I'm going to stop caring about what other men think of me, you're nuttier than J'Ali."

"Do not say that man's name again, Blanche." Claude was no longer amused.

"I'll say whatever the hell I want! *J'Ali, J'Ali, J'Ali, J'Ali!*"

And then he did a remarkable thing. Claude Auzello allowed his temper to overcome his sense of decorum. This young woman, his new bride, had ignited some undetonated bomb—perhaps left over from the war—buried deep inside. She had triggered so many new emotions in these past few weeks, perhaps he should not have been surprised to find she now made him more furious than he'd ever been before. And that he was reduced to growling like the Neanderthal she accused him of imitating, and grabbing her makeup case, opening the window, and throwing the case out of the train.

They both stared at the open window for a long moment, astonished by his actions. Claude started to explain but before he could complete a sentence, she did something even more astonishing.

She ran to the window and tried to push herself out of it.

He grabbed her by the waist and threw her back in the compartment.

They stared at each other, frozen in this absurd tableau, panting heavily, until the train slowed down and began to pull into a station.

Like lightning, Blanche escaped his grasp, dashing out of the compartment and off the train before Claude could even register she was doing so; she was in his arms one moment, vanished the next, and as he tried to understand what had just happened, he grabbed some of their belongings and ran after her. He was barely off the last step before their train began to pull away; darting around startled bystanders, he reached the opposite platform just in time to see his new bride leap onto a train heading the other way; a train bound for Paris. Claude began to run after her, his arms full of things that fell out of his grasp with each step—at one point, he realized that one of her filmy nightgowns was caught on the heel of his shoe—but the train sped away.

Merde.

With clammy palms, perspiration stains on his collar, his arms full of unmentionables, Claude sank down onto a bench and tried to process what had just occurred. The poor man played it over and over again in his mind, as if it was a text he had been forced to memorize but the meaning of which he couldn't quite grasp.

At this very moment, he was supposed to be nuzzling the nape of his new bride's neck, a repast of cold duck and colder champagne in front of them (naturally, Claude had made all the arrangements prior to leaving, and now he winced to think of the puzzled look of the porter wheeling the cart into an empty compartment). He was supposed to be stroking her, kissing her, preparing her for the night ahead. (They had slept together already so there would be no surprises awaiting them, only passion and pleasurable familiarity.)

Instead, he was alone at a train station in some country town, and he had no idea when the next train to Paris would arrive. Or where to find his wife once he got there.

Had Claude perhaps made a mistake marrying this American, no matter how charming, so hastily?

• • •

At last, a train heading north arrived; Claude boarded it, went immediately to the bar car and had a stiff drink, and when the train pulled into the station, the first thing he saw when he disembarked was Blanche sitting on a bench, her crumpled wedding bouquet still in her hands, her eyes red from crying, and when she looked up at Claude and began to sob even harder, his heart did that popping thing once more, and he held her in his arms, forgetting everything that had happened on the train.

Until he made the next discovery.

"Wow, you have an impressive collection, Popsy," Blanche said, soon after they returned from their honeymoon. She was wandering around the kitchen of his bachelor flat, admiring all his copper pots, hanging neatly on the wall. "How do you make them shine so?"

"You polish them," Claude replied, puzzled. "With vinegar and salt."

"Oh." She opened a drawer and gave a little gasp. "And all those knives. So many! Why do you need them all?"

"Because they're different." Claude was, again, puzzled—and growing concerned. "See, this large blocky one is for dicing, this longer one for carving, this jagged one for cutting bread, and so forth."

"Ohhh . . ." Again that little gasp of wonder.

"Blanchette," he said, a queasy feeling in the pit of his stomach, which he should have recognized as a presentiment. "Don't you—don't you know how to cook?"

"Me?" Her brown eyes flew open wide in surprise; she looked as if he'd asked her if she knew how to carve a boat out of wood, or fly an aeroplane, or dance on her toes. Then she laughed; she threw back her head and laughed her throaty, abandoned laugh. "Claude, you're a riot. Whatever gave you the idea I could cook? Of course I can't!"

"What do you mean, 'of course'?" He shut the drawer, irritated. Deceived. "How on earth would I know? Women cook. That's the way it is here in France."

"It's like that in America, too," she admitted, opening up another cupboard and taking out a mandoline, appraising it as if it were an artifact from ancient Greece. "Most girls are brought up learning how to cook and clean, even if they're wealthy enough to have someone else do it. My sisters and I were brought up that way, too— only I always managed to find some excuse to get out of the lesson. I wasn't going to learn that bunk, let me tell you. I had no desire to learn the lessons my mother taught me. I was slippery that way, Claude." She looked up at him, her eyes blazing, her luscious red lips in a teasing pout. "I still am."

61

"Yes, but . . ." Claude was torn between wanting to whisk her away to the bedroom and wanting to march her down to Le Cordon Bleu for some cooking lessons. "But how will you cook for me?"

She shrugged. "I guess you'll do the cooking, Claude. Or we'll go out. I hear there's a kitchen at the Ritz." And she laughed again.

Claude did not know what to say to that; nothing in his life had prepared him for such a moment. So he did, then, whisk her away to the bedroom, because what else could a man do under the circumstances?

After, he made an omelet of chanterelles, shallots, and garlic, which she devoured, and so he had to make another for himself.

What else did he discover in those early days—those heady, passionate, disturbing, delightful early days of his marriage to this charming American who had changed his life so thoroughly that Claude wondered, at times, if she were a witch instead of a damsel? He discovered that she muttered in her sleep. He discovered that she had no qualms about using his toothbrush. That she threw out her silk stockings as soon as they had a run, instead of darning them. He discovered that she liked to wander the streets, with no real purpose; she grew restless as a child if she had to sit for too long. He discovered that she liked cats, tolerated dogs, was enchanted by birds but only if kept out of doors; there was something about a bird in a house that frightened her.

Claude also discovered that she had small feet, of which she was very proud. And that the insteps of these delectable feet were very ticklish. And that she enjoyed having him tickle them, when she was in a certain mood.

Claude discovered that she did, still, want to pursue her film career, which meant that some nights when he returned, exhausted, from the Ritz, his small flat was filled with those inappropriate friends of hers, Pearl White and other actors, smoking and drinking and telling stories about "sets" and "takes" and "goddamned directors." Coarse people, all of them—which surprised Claude, because he refused to see his Blanchette as anything other than a fairy-tale princess, still.

Claude also learned another thing.

He learned that his Blanche loved the Ritz as much as he did.

CHAPTER 5
BLANCHE,
June 1940

"Why do we do it, Pearl?" Blanche remembers asking her friend back in 1923, right after that funny little man, Claude Auzello, bade her adieu with a promise of dinner later that night. She still had J'Ali's telegram in her pocket, informing her that he was going to be delayed a week. "Why do we fall for these men who tell us pretty things just to get us to go to bed with them? Just to get us to cross an ocean without even so much as a contract, let alone a wedding ring?" If she came to Europe with him, he would make her a film star in Egypt, her handsome prince, her lover, had promised. She would be as glamorous as Cleopatra, with her own barge on the Nile. He would marry her.

Except no, he had never promised her that, not in so many words.

"Because we're saps. We're women in a men's world. We're stupid enough to believe that the right man will make us forget that."

"But I love J'Ali. I really do. Crazy me."

"Forget about J'Ali. Go out with that Auzello

guy—his tongue was practically hanging out at the sight of you! Have fun, kid. Real fun."

"But J'Ali wanted to show me Paris." Blanche picked a fleck of tobacco off her tongue and tapped the ash from her cigarette into a black ashtray embossed in gold. *Hôtel Claridge.*

"J'Ali's not here. You think he'd wait for you, if the shoe was on the other foot?"

Blanche had to laugh at that—the thought of J'Ali waiting for her, or any woman. If the world was, indeed, a man's world, then Prince J'Ali Ledene lived in the Garden of Eden; women were put on this earth to give him apples—preferably between their breasts.

But Blanche had followed him to Paris anyway, broken her parents' hearts, left all she knew behind. Simply because she—the defiant flapper, the jazz baby—still didn't know what to do with love. Except to follow where it led her.

But to her surprise, it led her not to Egypt after all.

"Welcome home to the Mistress of the Ritz!"

Poised at the top of the staircase, Blanche grins, bows to the crowd looking up at her. Then she has to laugh.

It's a toy title, something a child would name herself, although Claude is the one who gave it to her. But he did it out of exasperation. He grows weary of her meddling, impatient with her drinking, jealous of her friendships. And when, upon finding her sharing sandwiches and champagne with the staff at the end of a long day which for him is still not over, he purses his lips and calls her Mistress of the Ritz, he does not mean it as a compliment.

But Blanche takes it as one anyway.

Because after seventeen years of marriage, even to a guy whose tongue was practically falling out of his mouth when he first saw you, compliments are rare, while grievances are as common as geraniums in spring. The young man who so ardently wooed her, fought for her, defied even an Egyptian prince for her, has turned into a *husband*. But she can't fault him for that, because Blanche has turned into the most typical of wives.

Only the Ritz can seduce her into forgetting this, on those occasions when her people bow down before her, like now, as she—freshly bathed and wrapped up like an exquisite present and wearing her perfect shoes—descends the staircase to the small lobby on the rue Cambon side of the hotel. She is hugged by chambermaids with tears streaming down their cheeks: "Oh, Madame Blanche, we were terrified for you!" One of them pulls at Blanche's sleeve, turning a pale face with huge brown eyes, smudged from sleeplessness, toward her as the girl whispers, "Madame Blanche, I know you have—we've heard, you see—someone told me you once changed—"

Blanche shakes her head, puts her finger to her lips as her heart begins to pound; she's just glimpsed a German soldier below, standing sentry at the entrance to the long hallway connecting the two sides of the Ritz. She bends to give the girl a kiss on the cheek, murmuring, "Come see me tonight, after ten. Alone." And the girl gasps, almost sobs, before composing herself.

Blanche continues to work her way down the stairs; bellhops grasp her hand in their rough mitts, shaking her arm until it's nearly out of its socket: "Madame Auzello, you're home! Things will start to look up again, God willing!"

"How's it hanging, boys?" she asks, and the bellhops tell her exactly how it's hanging in vivid French detail, until she laughs so hard she bends over, a hand on her aching ribs. She is overreacting, she knows: laughing too much, smiling too broadly. But she has to. Because if she didn't, she'd dissolve into tears. So many beloved faces are missing; the male staff is very depleted. She can only pray that those young men are still making their way back after being discharged, and not in German prison camps.

Then a door opens and there is a hush: no more laughter, no more lewd tales. The bellhops and chambermaids retreat against the railing of the stairs and the walls of the lobby, all eyes trained on the ground. They stand at rigid attention, afraid to move.

For it is her. *Mademoiselle.*

Coco Chanel, that bitch.

She is just coming in the door from the street, and when she perceives the scene before her, she pauses and looks up, narrowing her eyes at Blanche. With an impressive flare of her nostrils, Chanel takes in the vivid Schiaparelli dress—a print, giant pink flamingoes on a bright green background—with undisguised loathing.

"Hello, Blanche. I see the time away has been good for you," she purrs, reaching into her handbag for a cigarette, which she holds out, imperiously, to the nearest bellhop, who lights it with a trembling hand. "You've lost weight, *chère.* Perhaps soon, you won't have to wear rubbish, and can fit in some of *my* clothes."

Chanel, of course, is wearing one of her own creations: a black jersey dress draped so elegantly, Blanche instantly covets it. The woman knows how to make a dress, that's for damn sure.

"Nice to see you, too, Coco, honey." Blanche smiles, knowing that the designer hates it when she calls her Coco instead of "Mademoiselle." "You haven't changed a bit. Still got that stick up your bony ass, I see."

There is silence as each woman assesses the other before bowing, as adversaries do, and Coco commences up the staircase, that alleged stick making her back as straight and unyielding as a narrow brick wall.

But she pauses again when she reaches Blanche; she exhales cigarette smoke only a few inches to the left of Blanche's face and mutters something under her breath. Just one word, one syllable, and she has moved on, disappearing upstairs, but Blanche freezes, unsure. Did Coco say what Blanche thought she did?

Did anyone else hear it?

But no; the bellhops and chambermaids are no longer frozen; now they're all laughing, grinning at Blanche, and one of the bellhops takes her arm and raises it, as if she's just won a boxing match. So she relaxes. For now. And enjoys the moment as best she can, aware—a skin-crawling sensation of being a specimen trapped under glass—that German soldiers are also watching. *Listening.*

But for this moment, it doesn't matter.

The Mistress, by God, has returned.

CHAPTER 6

CLAUDE,
1924

And brought her to his enchanted castle . . .

"Claude," she told him a few months after their marriage. "If you're going to spend all your days with this rival of mine, then I'm going to be there, too."

"What do you mean?" Claude grew nervous; another thing he was learning about his Blanchette was that he would never learn everything about his Blanchette.

"I mean I'm going to spend time at the Ritz, too. It's the best show in town, Claude. All the little dramas, the social climbing, the fashion parade. That place is your life and I want to be part of your life—all of it—and that means I'm going to spend my days there, when I'm not working."

"You are?" Did she mean she was going to sit in his little office all the day long? Trail after him when he made his rounds?

"Yep. I'm going to get to know the Ritz as you do—I'm going to figure out why you love it as much as you love me."

70

Claude gulped, but smiled. Because he was pleased, to tell the truth, that she shared his passion and wanted to be more in his world, even if he suffered a guilty pang over the fact that he didn't share her passion for the movies. But he easily dismissed this pang. After all, he was the husband, the rightful breadwinner; a man had a career, while a woman could only have a hobby.

Claude also knew that there was no better setting for a fairy-tale princess, and it all made sense; why else had he rescued her, if not to ensconce her at the Ritz?

And so they entered into a new phase of their young marriage: a ménage à trois, in a way. The Ritz, Blanchette, and Claude.

He would leave his little apartment—she was already hinting they should rent another, bigger one in a more fashionable area of town "as befits your position"—earlier than she did. He would kiss her sleeping brow, then take the Métro to the Louvre station, where he'd walk the few blocks to the Place Vendôme. But he always ducked around to the rue Cambon side, where the service entrance was. Claude entered through those doors just to see that all the deliveries were being made—the fresh vegetables, the flowers from the market, the linens, the fish and meat.

Once he was certain the deliveries had arrived, Claude would retire to his little office across from the guest elevator, where he would have coffee and a croissant, flaky and buttery and fresh from the kitchen, and go over the schedule for the day. There were always private luncheons and banquets to be arranged, both for guests and for Parisians who recognized that there was nowhere in Paris more elegant. Now that the Great War had destroyed so many fragile empires, displaced minor European royalty roamed the earth like the dinosaurs that they were. And many lumbered into the Ritz.

Every day a newly impoverished duke or duchess or baron or baroness imperiously rang the bell at the desk, insisting on their old suites from their days of glory. It was Claude's job to gently talk them into something more reasonable—something they might actually be able to afford instead of ducking out in the early morning, bills unpaid—while still bowing and flattering and reinforcing their former image of themselves.

Every day, too, pretty American girls, their mamas and papas rich with new money, arrived at the Ritz in pursuit of some of these titles. For there were many bachelor dukes and barons.

And there were the mamas and papas themselves, owners of department stores and gold mines, coming to France for the first time and staying at the Ritz because "Everyone says this is *the* place to stay in Paris. By the way, my name's

George. What's yours?" And Claude would press his lips together before admitting that it *was* the place to stay, and ring for someone to show them to the suites formerly occupied by the now displaced dukes and duchesses. While, naturally, Claude was delighted that these Americans had waterfalls of money, and it flowed everywhere—gushing into the bar, the restaurant, lavish tips that made the bellboys' eyes pop—still, he couldn't suppress a little pang that he had not worked here at the Ritz in its glory days. Back when César Ritz still was alive—every day, Claude said a silent prayer to his enormous portrait hanging in the main hall—back when King Edward VII had stayed here, along with Romanovs and Hapsburgs, and they were all still in power, all still regal, and the Ritz must have looked like an embassy with all the medals and tiaras and gold military braid.

But it is not profitable to long too much for the past, particularly if it is not your own. Claude quite enjoyed the Ritz that he, more and more, ran by himself. He was seldom off-duty. Even at night.

"You do realize, Claude, that most of these midnight summons come from broads?" Blanche asked one evening when their phone rang, and the sultry voice of the Duchesse de Talleyrand-Périgord was on the other end, asking for "Monsieur Claude of the Ritz."

The duchess was staying in a very expensive suite while she searched for a Parisian home. "Claude," she'd confided to him, breathlessly, one day as she returned to the Ritz after walking her poodle in the Place Vendôme, "I have a premonition." She fluttered her eyelashes and breathed heavily, as if she'd been pursued by a ghost; her bosom heaved most attractively.

"What, madame?"

"I've always known it. I've always known that I would be murdered in a hotel!" She shuddered, and so did her breasts.

"Oh, madame, no! Surely you are mistaken?"

"No, Claude—what if I'm not?"

From that moment on, she'd sought his assurance with frequent summons to her room to check for intruders, and now a phone call to his home.

"Claude, you must come at once. You must save me—I'm so afraid!"

Naturally, Claude dressed to go to the Ritz, even though it was after midnight.

"I have to. She is one of our most important guests and it is my job to make sure she remains one," he explained as he tied his shoes, after first washing his face and brushing his teeth and spraying a hint of cologne on his fresh handkerchief.

"Of course," Blanche said, eerily calm—uncomfortably understanding. As Claude hurried through the streets, he worried about that. What did it mean, that Blanche wasn't throwing vases and shoes at him as he left?

The next day, he found out.

"Claude, I've been thinking," Blanche said as they lunched together in the hotel kitchen. The kitchen wasn't a bright or airy place, as it was below ground. But all the stainless steel, the bright white tile, the warm copper pots and bowls, the crisp white chef caps and aprons, the aroma of baking bread and pungently sweet herbs, the perfume of simmering garlic in olive oil competing with the vanilla scent of decadent pastries made it cheerful nonetheless.

"What have you been thinking, Blanche?" Claude waved for another coffee; it had been a late night with the duchess, whose insistent charms he was not sure he could succeed in avoiding without offense for much longer.

"I've been thinking about your late nights. Your many late nights." She gave him a probing look, which Claude returned innocently. "We ought to have rooms here at the Ritz. Don't you think? That way you can still attend to your very important guests, but you won't have to traipse through the streets and then back again. And you won't have to worry about me, all alone in the apartment. So late. At *night*."

Claude was on the verge of assuring Blanche that he did not worry about her being alone at all, for he had learned that she wasn't quite the damsel in distress he had thought she was—in all honesty, he worried more about the hapless would-be burglar because Blanche, as he well knew by now, was in possession of a solid right hook—but decided that would not be in his best interest. Not at all.

"I don't know, Blanche . . ."

"Ask Madame Ritz. Tell her you will be able to perform your—duties—in a timelier manner."

"I'll ask," Claude agreed, for he was already familiar with Blanche's reluctance to let go of certain ideas.

And so Claude did ask, and Madame Ritz—as she fed one of her Brussels griffons a bite of liver, freshly chopped by the head chef of the Ritz, from a silver fork—looked at him piercingly.

"Claude, you are doing very well here, and I'm grateful for all you're doing for Monsieur Rey, assuming so many of his duties while he is ill. I will grant you two rooms on the rue Cambon side. Will that satisfy your wife?"

"Madame, it has nothing to do with satisfying my wife," Claude replied stiffly. "My wife will be satisfied with what I tell her to be."

Madame Ritz smiled, very wisely, and said nothing, and as Claude turned to leave, he felt that women were at times more bothersome than they were pleasurable.

But only at times.

Blanche was thrilled by the two adjoining rooms they fashioned into a suite, appointed with extra furniture and rugs brought down from the attic storage area. The rooms looked out on the narrow rue Cambon and were accessible from the staircase in that small lobby area that was flanked by the bar and the ladies' salon. She moved many of her clothes and a few paintings into the suite, and soon it seemed as if the Auzellos spent more nights here than they did in their apartment. It was quite clever of her, Claude thought with rueful admiration.

Now she would never have to learn to cook.

At the Ritz, Blanche had her favorite haunts: a certain sofa in the grand hallway, which provided her an excellent view of the staircase, a fashion show every hour of every day as royalty, movie actresses, and wives of millionaires descended, each one trying to outdo the other in their dress, in the size and number of jewels draped about their throats and on their fingers. For the point of staying at the Ritz was not only the luxury at hand, but the opportunity to be seen, gossiped about, or photographed by one of the new journalists always clustered outside in the Place Vendôme whose jobs were to write about only the rich and famous.

Blanche also had a special chair in the ladies' salon, where she got up games of bridge with some of the more neglected wives of millionaires, and thus picked up tips that proved useful for some of her poorer friends. She might hear of a matron from Ohio in need of a ladies' maid back home, or a displaced duchess looking for a traveling companion—*et voilà*! Some of her former movie friends now had honest jobs.

Blanche even, once a week, had tea with Madame Ritz herself, who enjoyed Blanche's gossip and humor. And in spite of himself, Claude began to appreciate her efforts on his own behalf; his wife had become an asset to his career. Through her games of bridge, her growing circle of friends both rich and poor, she had brought much new business to the Ritz, convincing people to throw parties here instead of at home, for instance, as they used to do before the war. She even befriended Barbara Hutton, the shy American heiress who might not have made the Imperial Suite her official Paris residence had it not been for Blanche's warm, easygoing companionship.

His wife was becoming so much of an asset, as a matter of fact, that even Claude was able to relax a bit. His marriage might be different from his friends' in many ways; most men left their wives in the morning and only returned in the evening, while Blanche and Claude were together almost constantly. Their pillow talk was always about the Ritz, the employees, the guests—so far, no children had appeared to consume their conversation. But in one way, Claude determined, this marriage would resemble that of his parents, his friends. A very important way. A very *French* way.

It was something of a surprise, however, to learn how differently the French and the Americans viewed the situation.

And Claude's American bride was not shy in letting him know how she felt about those differences.

CHAPTER 7
BLANCHE,
Spring 1941

Where is Lily?

So many people disappeared in the chaos of the invasion: the woman who used to do Blanche's hair, the little old lady with the storefront full of cats who she always bought lace from, an entire family who used to live in the mansion next to the Ritz. Waiters, chambermaids, cooks. A storekeeper here. A perfumer there. When she strolls the streets, Blanche can't help but notice the number of storefronts with broken windows, debris gathering on the sidewalks. Flowers dying in window boxes, unwatered. Neglected—so much of Paris outside the Ritz was starting to look neglected now. She'd always admired how even the tiniest alley or courtyard looked ready for a visit from a king; flowers always blooming, pruned and watered; no litter, no dirt, railings blackened and polished, cobblestones hosed down so that they shined.

Now there is an air of mournful waiting, especially in those tiny alleys and courtyards. And the population appears to be reduced by half, at least, to Blanche's searching eyes.

No, not reduced. For in place of the missing are the *Haricots Verts*, the Hanses and Fritzes and Klauses. They've taken the places of the vanished. And they don't even seem to notice that they are parking their broad German asses in someone else's café chair, someone else's seat on the tour boats, someone else's table at the restaurants, including the Ritz.

Those early weeks of the Occupation passed quickly; it was a hell of a steep learning curve. At first, Parisians fumbled and stumbled about, eyes blinking in disbelief at this strange new world they'd been rudely shoved into, just like any newborn animal. They learned not to initiate eye contact with the Germans, but to respond with a cautious smile when they initiated it with them. They learned not to speak until spoken to. They learned not to stiffen at the sight of German soldiers gleefully buying up goods no longer available (unless you happened to live at the Ritz) when ordinary citizens had to stand in long lines to get a lousy loaf of bread.

Oh, on the surface, if she squints, life here at the Ritz looks a lot like usual: the plush opulence, the polite manners, the idle—and not-so-idle— gossip. But it isn't as usual, nothing is as usual. Yes, Blanche's morning newspaper is still ironed, folded with edges so sharp she could cut herself on them, placed on a silver tray and presented to her with a single rose in a vase. But the paper itself is German propaganda disguised as news with headlines crowing about German victories in North Africa, illustrations of a jovial Hitler, the occasional photo of him in his château in the Alps, posing as if for a fashion spread. His favorite recipe for strudel, helpfully printed for all to see.

There are still flowers everywhere in the Ritz, true—it seems that manure and dirt are the only things not being requisitioned for the German army these days—but those flowers, with their lush petals, dewy stems, can't camouflage the Nazi flags sticking out of them. The soft chamber music always being played, somewhere, in the Ritz cannot mute the harsh German voices.

The bar, though. Ah, the bar. It's the pulsing heart of the Ritz and it always has been. And Frank Meier is its main artery.

Frank was one of the first people Blanche met when Claude introduced her—his blushing fiancée—to his new co-workers, back in 1923. Their surprising engagement coincided with Claude getting his dream job: manager of the Ritz Paris. And when Claude brought her here, proud as punch—although to be frank, she wasn't sure, she's never been completely sure, just what he was proudest of, his bride-to-be or the hotel—Frank was where he always is, where he should be: behind the polished ebony bar, a shaker in his giant paw.

Frank Meier looks like a longshoreman: beefy features, enormous arms, short, thick neck. His hair is always well oiled, parted precisely in the middle. And as much as he seems most at home behind the bar, making up his intoxicating concoctions, he's just as at ease outside it, greeting his favorite guests like lifelong friends, even carrying their bags up to their rooms for them.

But Blanche knows the real reason Frank is so hospitable: The guy runs a gambling ring outside the hotel. Much easier to collect bets away from the gossips and drunks.

"So you're the betrothed," Frank said in his growling voice, giving her a kiss on the cheek when Claude introduced them. "Congratulations! Can I pour you some champagne?"

"You bet your sweet ass you can," Blanche said, and was halfway into the bar before both Claude and Frank were pulling her back outside of it.

"You can't go in there, Blanchette," Claude said with a stern shake of his head.

"Why not?" She smiled; it had to be a joke, right? Because the Ritz had seduced her from her very first step inside.

As it seduces everyone. It whispers your name in a satin caress, it shows you unimaginable treasures—the tapestries on the walls should be in an art museum—it seduces you into thinking, even if you haven't a sou in your pocket, that simply by rubbing elbows with the barons and duchesses and movie stars and heiresses who glide through the halls on the wings of fortune, you, too, are something special. But the spell wore off some for Blanche that day, when she was told that women weren't allowed in the bar.

"What do you mean?" Blanche asked; she, the newly liberated flapper from New York, where she'd rolled her stockings and tucked gin flasks in her garter and knocked on the doors of speakeasies. There wasn't a speakeasy in all of Manhattan that didn't allow women. After all, they'd just gotten the vote!

But women in Paris in 1923, Blanche was about to discover, had not. Married women in Paris in 1923 couldn't open bank accounts and had to turn over all their money to their husbands. Women—married or not—in Paris in 1923 weren't allowed in the bar of the Hôtel Ritz.

"It's simply the way it is," her new fiancé said with the shrug she was beginning to know too well. "It is how it's always been. Ladies wait in the salon, where Frank will be most happy to bring you a glass of champagne, won't you, Frank?"

Frank—his alert eyes scanning her face, piercing through her mask of makeup—nodded.

That day—because, and only because, Blanche

was still anxious to fit in and be a good wife for her Gallic knight in shining armor, and he was about to start work here—she allowed herself to be ushered into the stuffy, compact little wood-paneled ladies' salon, where matrons with yapping dogs sat sipping tea or, at the strongest, one of those glasses of champagne (with a fresh rose in the glass), gossiping about the newest clothes. Vionnet was to die for, but have you seen the new fashions from the young Mademoiselle Chanel down the street? Shocking, simply shocking!

Waiting—impatiently—for her champagne (when what Blanche really craved was a martini), she happened to eavesdrop on two very large women who sat down next to her. They were stuffed into their tight crepe de chine dresses, swathed to their eyebrows in furs, but their feet were clad in very boring, very utilitarian black laceup shoes. They began to talk in German; the language of Blanche's childhood.

"I do enjoy the Ritz," one said as she began to remove her gloves. "It's where I always stay in Paris."

"Yes, I agree," said the other, who evidently preferred to keep her gloves on even as she reached into her handbag and produced a small box of chocolates; she took one and offered her companion a choice.

"They don't take Jews here, of course," said

the one without the gloves. Then she bit into her chocolate, not very daintily.

"I don't think even the staff is allowed to be Jewish," the one with the gloves—Blanche was delighted to see she now had chocolate streaks all over the white kid—agreed as she dug around for another piece. "Or if they are, they aren't obviously Semitic."

"It is a relief. One feels safer, in a way. More at home."

"That is what the Ritz does—it makes one feel at home. Better than at home—I don't have gold taps in my bathroom."

"Who does in Germany? The war has bankrupted us."

And then the two were talking about postwar economics and the new Nationalist party and some guy named Hitler who apparently was in jail, but Blanche didn't care about that.

Suddenly she looked up; Frank Meier was standing next to her, a champagne glass on a silver tray and a grim expression on his broad face. He had heard the women, Blanche suspected. Evidently Frank also spoke German.

They looked at each other for a long moment. Frank handed Blanche the glass and said, so softly concerned, she couldn't believe it from such a gruff-looking man, "If you ever need anything, mademoiselle, just ask me. Anything."

It wasn't long before Blanche did.

And that's how it's been between Frank and Blanche. He was her ally in her fight to open the bar up to women—Christ, it took the Depression to put ol' Madame Ritz over the top about that, but with empty rooms and empty barstools, Madame really had no choice but to let in Blanche and her fellow thirsty sisters. And Frank, along with all of Blanche's new bar buddies—Ernest Hemingway, whom she'd known since he was a poor, starving tagalong to Scott Fitzgerald; Cole Porter, whose little bright eyes shone like polished onyx; Pablo Picasso, whose laughter and speech were as bold and singular as his paintings—celebrated. She was the Mistress of the Ritz Bar—and she's remained on her throne ever since.

Blanche has her own little table facing the door, so she can see, before anyone else, what illustrious personage is entering. Every day Frank places a fresh rose in a bud vase, and there's an ornately framed, handwritten *Reserved for Madame Auzello* sign in exquisite calligraphy (of course, there is a staff calligrapher here at the Ritz whose sole job is to write place cards for private dinners). And it's in the bar that Blanche hears everything there is to hear. This is no different now, even though instead of Hemingway—who disappeared after the invasion—laughing at a table, a row of martinis lined up in front of him, there is Hermann Göring. Instead of Fitzgerald toppling off his seat, because the man cannot hold his liquor but always has to engage in a contest of the liver with Hemingway, there's ol' Spatzy, that German son of a bitch who frequented the Ritz even before the war, charming as ever, but Blanche doesn't laugh quite so hard at his jokes as she used to. She detects the malice hidden inside the humor and shrinks from his hands, always reaching out to caress a shoulder, cup an elbow. Instead of Picasso and Porter whispering about which guest is unable to pay his bill, there are various Hanses and Fritzes in their uniforms, tittering over a Bee's Knees or a Singapore Sling. Instead of Garbo and Dietrich reclining seductively—although Claude forbids them both from wearing their famous trousers here at the Ritz—there's Chanel with her sharp nose and the movie star Arletty with her patrician forehead and etched cheekbones. Drinking with Spatzy and his friends. Doing more than drinking, if you believe the gossip.

Gossip—which, if you ask Blanche, is the main trade of the Ritz—has only increased since the invasion. There's the gossip that Göring dresses up in women's clothing—he's especially fond of marabou feathers, apparently—and dances with the poor waiters he summons to his suite at every hour of the day. He's hopped up on morphine most of the time, too. And he had to have a special bathtub installed just to contain his bulk—this, she heard firsthand from Claude (since she, like everyone else not in uniform, either of the Third Reich or the Ritz, is confined, courtesy of armed guards, to the rue Cambon side), so it must be true. For her Claude, bless his pompous little heart, does not gossip.

There is another kind of gossip, too, now, the air practically snapping with secrets, secrets, secrets. And Frank oversees it all from behind his post. He accepts a napkin, folded just so; he covers it with his giant hand, slides it so fast across the bar, tucks it into a pocket. Minutes later, he goes outside for a smoke. Someone might decide to join him.

So much of what the Ritz—less officially—provides is provided by Frank. Do you need an abortionist? A blackmailer? An illegal gun? Some forged papers?

Frank Meier will provide. And he will keep your secret, too, at only a little extra charge, a small deposit in that bank account he keeps in Switzerland, but he has no idea that Blanche is aware of it.

And so, today, walking past Germans standing sentry, Germans ordering champagne, Germans calling out her name while patting the seat next to them, she knows who to go to about Lily. Blanche has asked Frank for things in the past; things she can't ask from Claude. And Frank has always provided. So what's one more favor, between friends?

What's one more secret between husbands and wives who started out so much more than that to each other?

CHAPTER 8

CLAUDE,
1927

Where they lived together in wedded bliss . . .

She was gone.

Her wardrobe at the Ritz was empty; so, too, was the one at their apartment in Passy—the apartment she had insisted they move into, for she could not stand his bachelor quarters. He had done that for her; he had done so many things for his ungrateful wife! The apartment he couldn't afford; the designer dresses she insisted she needed as befitted his position; the rooms at the Ritz she demanded. Demands, demands—it was all she ever asked of him, it seemed. It turned out that marrying a woman new to a country, with few friends, no family, and a tenuous grasp of the language, required a lot more attention and energy than Claude had planned to give. After all, it was the wife who was supposed to maintain a marriage, who was supposed to provide and soothe and cook and clean.

But what did any of it matter now? Like a child, a spoiled, petulant child, Blanche was gone. And for such a reason as this?

He should have realized; he did have an uneasy feeling about telling her, if he was being honest. Claude had seen how ridiculously Americans behaved about these things—the soldiers on leave during the war who were overcome with guilt. The businessmen who checked in to the Hôtel Claridge under assumed names.

Americans! Why were they so puritanical about sex? Sex was merely a physical act, a necessary act, particularly in these years, and naturally, that was how he attempted to explain it to Blanche.

"My love," Claude began one evening after they had enjoyed an hour of passion; he thought this would be the appropriate time, when she might understand, physically as well as emotionally, the situation from a woman's point of view. For Claude prided himself on being a generous lover, and this was one area in which Blanche seemed to agree with him.

"Yes, Claude?"

"These last years—these last hundred and fifty years, actually—France has been a nation at war. We have committed mass suicide, in a way—look around, how many young Frenchmen do you see in Paris?"

"Not many. Dammit, Claude, you sure have an odd idea of pillow talk." She sat up and put on a thin wrapper and began to brush her tangled blond hair.

Claude watched her for a moment. He did

enjoy seeing women brush their hair; it was one reason why he was not fond of those bobbed hair-styles.

"Blanche, we have just made love—don't you agree, it's a necessary part of life?"

She grinned at him, put the brush down, and plopped back on the bed, arranging her wrapper so that the tops of her breasts heaved most enticingly. "Now you're talkin'!"

"So, we agree—a woman without a man in her bed is half a woman?"

"Hmmm mmmm . . ." She began to nuzzle his chest, her lips making angel kisses against his flesh, and it was with great effort that Claude managed to continue the conversation. But it was imperative that he did.

"So you understand." Claude gently pushed her away; he needed her to hear what he was about to say. There could be no confusion about the matter. "You understand, then, that I will be spending my Thursday nights elsewhere."

"I—what?" She rubbed the middle of her forehead with her thumb—a habit that made her look heartbreakingly childlike and naïve; Claude had to swallow before continuing.

"I will be elsewhere on Thursday nights. That is the night I will be with—*her.*"

"Her?"

"My mistress."

"Your *mistress?*"

"Yes. Only Thursday nights, as is proper. But I did not want you to worry, or to come looking for me. Now, you know. Would you like me to warm up some of the bouillabaisse from last night? I'm quite hungry." He reached for his trousers, for it was chilly.

As he bent down to pull them up, she pushed him from behind, and he fell to the floor in an undignified heap. Claude turned around; Blanche was standing on the bed, her eyes blazing.

"Blanche! Why did you do that?"

"Your *mistress?* You have a mistress? Goddamn you, Claude! You tell me, when we're in bed, after we have just *fucked,* that you have another woman?"

"Shhh! Blanche, lower your voice."

"I will not!"

"Blanche, calm down. I will not discuss this with you until you have controlled yourself."

"Controlled *my*self?" But she did lower her voice.

"Yes. Come, sit." Claude sank back down on the bed and patted the space next to him with a charming smile; she glared at him, jumped off the bed, and took a seat on the small chair next to the window. But she only perched on the edge, looking like a bird—a wild, exotic bird—about to take flight.

"First, I am your husband. I honor, I respect you."

"How can you say that when you have a little chippie on the side?"

"A little—what? I don't understand that word."

"A whore."

"A *mistress,* not a whore. If I wanted a whore, I could have one. But why would I pay for what I can have for free? I couldn't dishonor you in that way."

She opened her mouth, shook her head. "I have no idea what the hell you just said."

"A mistress is not a whore, Blanche. You Americans use the word interchangeably but it is not—"

"Oh, shut the hell up. Don't you dare lecture me, you—you—do you know I can divorce you over this?"

"What?" It was Claude's turn to look perplexed. "First of all, only Americans get divorced. We do not in France—it simply isn't done, it isn't necessary. Husbands and wives have so much more of an understanding of these things here, my love. This is why it's absurd for you to even think about this—I cannot understand it."

"Because you're cheating on me!"

"No, no." Claude almost laughed but caught the violent gleam in her eye just in time. "No, that is not how it is. It is how you Americans *think* it is, but you have it all wrong. How could I cheat on you with a woman I see only once a week, and have told you about? I don't love her, I love you.

I'm not married to her, I'm married to you—you have my name, it is with you that I share my worldly goods, you are my partner in life. She—she is only—only—" Once more, he struggled to find the word in English. But English was not the correct language for this conversation.

"A piece of ass?"

Claude shuddered. "Blanche, that is vulgar." His fairy princess had turned out to possess the vocabulary of a dockworker, to his bitter disappointment.

"*I'm* vulgar? Oh, boy, that's rich. Do I need to remind you what I did, Claude Auzello, when I married you?"

Claude winced; it was the first time she had brought this up, this thing that she had done. Claude had nothing to do with it, had never asked her to do such a thing, although he confessed that there was a part of him—a larger part than he would have expected—that was relieved when she did. But they had agreed to bury it, to forget about it—for the good of all involved.

"This conversation is ridiculous. I did you the courtesy of informing you where I will be on Thursday nights, and you react like a spoiled brat. This is not worthy of you, Blanche, it is not worthy of us—*merde*!" Claude saw stars, felt blood trickling down his forehead.

For Blanche had just thrown a vase at him and was picking up another.

"Stop!"

"You go to hell! You go to hell, Claude Auzello!" The second vase missed and shattered against the wall, and he threw his arms up to protect his face as she began to search for something else to hurl; he ran out of the room and closed the door, holding it shut as she began to pound on it, calling him the most inventive names he'd ever heard, and he had to admire her creativity: "slimy son-of-a-bitch frog," "two-timing no-balls bastard," "cheating, lying, gutless worm of a wanker."

Suddenly the pounding and the invective stopped; all was quiet. Eerily quiet.

"Blanche, I—" Tentatively, Claude opened the door a crack; when the silence continued, he opened it wider. Blanche was standing there, looking perfectly calm with a smile on her face. Then she reared back and punched him in the nose.

He stayed away from the apartment for two days and prayed she would not show up at the Ritz in her current state of mind; it would not help his career to have his wife marching through the hallways shouting that he was a "two-timing no-balls bastard." Marie-Louise Ritz would not stand for that.

Claude rationalized that it was good to give her time to absorb the lesson and cool down.

And he did blame himself, somewhat; he had, once again, discounted the difference between American and French. The French understood that an occasional visit to another land—like a holiday—is good for a marriage. That is all it is; the delight in discovering different flesh, now and again. The restfulness that comes with being satiated physically, without emotional attachment—it is important for a busy man in charge of a household. His own mother knew about his father's mistresses over the years; all she ever asked, like any reasonable French woman, was that he not flaunt them, not introduce them to the children, not allow them to take up more than a modicum of his time and energy and—most important—money. And if she had affairs—impossible to imagine, but perhaps—naturally, no one knew.

Blanche would learn to understand this, Claude believed; she was a quick student. She had proven adept at understanding, even embracing, most other things French. Claude felt a couple of days apart were all that would be needed for her to see the situation more rationally.

However, at the end of the second day, when he returned home to the apartment and discovered that her wardrobe was empty, he grew alarmed, and did the unthinkable—he sent a message via the Ritz messenger boy to Pearl, who replied by telling him to come over to her flat.

Claude had begged Blanche to end her friendship with this woman. Pearl's film career had not been restored here in France. She'd been reduced to lending her name to tawdry nightclubs, where she was trotted out to crudely reenact some of her more famous movie scenes with young men clad only in loincloths. Even that work had dried up, lately.

One night, after too many bottles of champagne elsewhere, she showed up at the Ritz to see Blanche and attempted to breach the bar where, naturally, she was not allowed. Blanche tried to stop her, but Pearl was not to be stopped that night; her old fur stole was stained, her stockings had enormous runs, her makeup was streaked down her face. Blanche wept when she saw her. But Claude saw only a disaster of Pearl's own making. Blanche had told him that she had pawned almost everything she owned and was subsisting on handouts from whatever lover she could dupe at the moment. Blanche saw bravery in this.

Claude saw disgrace.

Even Blanche was appalled that night by Pearl's behavior; the woman had actually struck Frank Meier with an umbrella. Blanche was finally able to coax her out to the street and into a taxi. Claude had not seen her since.

But he made the long trek out to the 20th arrondissement, to a neighborhood of decrepit, narrow mansions all broken up into tiny flats. This was an area devoid of absolutely anything— few cafés, no restaurants, shops widely scattered, some of the streetlights burned out. It was not a place to linger, let alone live.

Pearl had an attic flat, so he climbed six flights of stairs. And he hoped, with each step, that Blanche would be waiting for him at the top.

But she was not; Pearl was, clad in a stained wrapper, formerly trimmed in fur but now the fur was missing in great patches, and what was left was matted flat, shiny with grease. Her blond hair was streaked with gray; she wore no makeup but somehow that made the lines of her face less prominent. Her mouth, devoid of that garish lipstick, was a pale, attractive pink. She was far prettier than she had been the first time Claude met her; some women did grow more beautiful with pain and suffering. He recognized now that Pearl was one of them.

"Hey, Claude," she said, and moved aside to allow him into her flat. He looked around eagerly for Blanche, but she was not there.

"Where is she? Where is my Blanchette?"

"She's gone."

"What do you mean?"

"Gone. Vanished. Vamoosed."

"From our apartment?"

"From France."

"No." Claude's legs felt weak; he had to sit

down, and Pearl hastily removed a torn negligee from the only armchair before he sank into it.

"Yes. What'd you think she'd do, you idiot?"

"I thought—I thought—she is my wife! How can she do this to me?"

"Oh, Claude." Pearl laughed raucously, and it turned into a rib-shattering cough that went on for so long, he grew alarmed and went to the sink (the kitchen, living room, and bedroom were all one space), found a cloudy jam jar, obviously used as a drinking glass, and filled it with water.

"Thanks," she rasped, and she drank it, then started to laugh again. "You men! *How can she do this to me?* What about her, Claude? How could you do this to *her?* Don't you know Blanche by now? She's a little girl, Claude. Not sophisticated like you and me. Blanche, for all her polish, her salty language—that broad can curse like a sailor—is just an innocent little schoolgirl at heart. Everything she does to make it seem otherwise is an act. A damn good one, but an act. She believes in love, she believes in goodness, she probably still believes in Santa Claus for all I know. The thing is—she believes in you, too, you dumb bastard."

"But I love her—surely she understands that. I don't love anyone else but her!"

"You have someone on the side. You told her

about it—Christ, you big dummy, if you hadn't been so damn honest, you probably would have gotten away with it."

That, Claude had not thought of before. To be dishonest about his mistress? A woman—yes, a beautiful woman, a *discreet* woman—but only a woman, still. Not a wife. He was certain he was being honorable in telling Blanche. Yet another way that Americans were so frustrating! Had he not told her—had he deceived her—they would right now be spending a cozy evening together at the Ritz, the picture of contentment. By being honest with her, Claude had lost her.

How was that possible?

"Where did she go?"

He felt, somehow, that Pearl was on his side—and he knew he did not deserve her support, but was grateful for it.

"To London."

"London?"

"J'Ali is there," Pearl added, softly.

"No!" Righteous rage propelled Claude out of his seat; he bumped his head on the sloped ceiling of the flat. "Not back to that man—he does not love her. He does not respect her."

"I know that and you know that, but Blanche—she doesn't. She doesn't see much of a difference between how J'Ali treated her, and how you did."

"But there's a world of difference. I made her my wife!"

102

"Why did you? I've always wanted to know. Do you even *like* her? Because I can't help but think she's not your type. Do you need her?"

"I—well—" Claude had to sit down and take the tumbler of water from Pearl. This was not a question he had ever asked himself; it was not a question any man he knew had ever asked himself. Women were necessary, but that wasn't the same thing as professing a need for them. As for the notion of liking his wife—

He thought of the ways Blanche surprised him, the things about her he'd never thought he'd desired, until he met her—drama, intrigue. Excitement. A keen mind that probed and pushed, instead of simply acquiescing.

"I need her, yes," Claude said slowly. "I need her, for my days would be quite—boring—without her. I cannot imagine now, for myself, any other woman than her. Any other wife."

"Then go get her, Claude. Go get your wife."

"I cannot." Claude picked up his hat, too frustrated to remain—but too proud to cross the Channel. "If she cannot see the difference—if she cannot see that I need her, that she alone is my wife, that there is no other reason that I saved her from that man, other than to honor her in this way—I cannot make her. I will not make her. It is not my place."

"Then you'll lose her." Pearl shook her head and—surprisingly—gave Claude a kiss on the cheek. Again he perceived her sympathy, despite all odds.

"I won't believe that, either." Claude felt surprising tears in his eyes, for her kindness. Perhaps he had been too judgmental in the past. "Try to stay out of trouble, Pearl. Blanche worries about you."

"Blanche worries about everyone—do you know what that crazy girl did? She hocked some of her jewelry so I could pay my rent."

"She did?" Claude's eyes brimmed over again; he was stunned. Claude tended to think of two women as natural enemies, competing with each other for clothing, jewelry, attention. *Men.* That they could be so unselfish and supportive was yet one more revelation in a day full of them, and he suddenly yearned for a good glass of port and a friend to talk it all over with.

But Blanche was that friend—another stunning revelation. In the short time they had been married, Claude realized, he had never once shared a glass of port with a friend or co-worker the way he had before he met her. Now, whenever he had a problem, a bad day, or just a desire to laugh at his fellow man, he went to Blanche.

"Where is she staying in London?" Claude asked Pearl before she could shut the door behind him.

"Where do you think?" She laughed again.

"Ah." Claude chuckled, despite his turmoil.

104

"Of course she is." He bade Pearl good night—after first thrusting whatever money he had in his pockets into her hands. She tucked the notes into her bosom and smiled—a ghost of her old smile, the one he first saw across the lobby of the Hôtel Claridge, when he met the fair maiden he knew he had to rescue.

Claude smiled, too. Because all was not lost, after all. Even if Blanche could run away from *him,* there was one thing she loved that she simply could not turn her back on.

The Ritz.

CHAPTER 9
BLANCHE,
Spring 1941

It startles Blanche to look out of the sparkling windows of the Ritz—where everyone, Nazis and civilians alike, still dresses and drinks and gossips like the old days, retiring safely at night in beds made with fresh linens, maybe starting to be a bit threadbare, but the Ritz seamstresses repair them with such delicate stitches, it's barely noticeable—and witness the displacement of certain families. For now there are new laws, decrees coming down from Vichy, which are really from Berlin: All the Jews in Paris have to register. They're now prohibited from professions like the law, medicine, teaching, or even owning shops. Homes—with their treasures, sculptures and paintings and rugs, all packed up neatly and warehoused in empty stores, archived in great detail by Nazi secretaries and curators—have been requisitioned, leaving entire families out on the street.

Many of these families she recognizes as patrons of the Ritz bar or restaurant, even if the Ritz has always *discreetly,* as Claude puts it, enforced the unspoken quotas against Jews in the past. ("We must always make sure our clientele is comfortable, Blanche. Rothschilds are very much welcome; in fact, they are investors in the Ritz. There are Jews and there are *Jews*," as Claude put it. "And you very well know it, for you Americans are not so very different from us." He's right, of course. It's the same in New York, where Guggenheims are much more acceptable than Goldbergs.)

On her way to have tea with a duchess or simply to get air, because even the rarified atmosphere of the Ritz gets stuffy these days, thick as it is with German accents, Blanche passes more and more of them. Maybe she even goes out of her way to seek them out: Papa in a fine felt hat with an overcoat sitting helpless on the curb while Mama in a fur coat with a brave slash of red lipstick—always a brave slash of red lipstick, and a silk scarf tied perfectly, so French, even now—corrals her children like little chicks and begins to knock on doors or telephone relatives from call boxes. It is Mama, always Mama, who is able to move and think. And plan.

Why does Blanche call them that? Mama and Papa? She always does, in her mind, in her heart, when she encounters these discarded families; when she walks past them, stopping to press money into their hands; when she walks on, walks toward wherever she is headed, free to move, free to return to *her* home, but always she glimpses someone familiar in their faces, someone from a memory. Or is it a nightmare? Someone from an old photograph, perhaps. Or a face conjured up from childhood stories.

She also sees, in their displaced faces—foreign faces mostly, the Jews who had fled to Paris in the last decade from Germany and Austria—Lily.

It's been almost four years since she first met Lily. When Blanche ran away from Claude, yet again.

It had become their pattern, their little game. He insisted on sleeping elsewhere every Thursday, they argued about it, she could not make him see how this humiliated her and he could not understand why she cared. Blanche ran away for a while before returning again—or sometimes he came to her, for the romantic thrill of bringing her back himself. For a few months, they lived and loved in a brittle truce, Thursday night passing without drama. But it began again. It always began again.

And it was on one of these—*excursions*—that Blanche first met Lily.

"Where you say you are going, Blanche?"

"Back home, to Paris."

"Paris." The small woman—she looked like a little girl but talked like a drunken sailor with a tenuous grasp of English—next to Blanche nodded. They both stood at the railing of the steamer, watching as their ship sliced through the Mediterranean, leaving foam in its wake.

"I go, too," she said, with determination. "I go with you. I always wanted to see Paris."

Her name was Lily, she'd said. Lily Kharmanyoff. Blanche asked if she was Russian, but she only shrugged. Blanche asked if she was Romanian, but she only shrugged. Blanche asked if she was from any particular country at all. But she only shrugged.

"You'll fit right in in Paris," Blanche replied, with a sardonic laugh.

"Why you say, Blanche?"

"You've got the shrug down pat." And Blanche shrugged, too, to illustrate. Lily laughed delightedly and clapped her hands. People around them stared, but Blanche was already getting used to that. People had a tendency to stare at Lily.

It wasn't merely that she was tiny, excitable, prone to poking total strangers on the shoulders to ask them the most personal questions. (Which was how she met Blanche.) It wasn't merely that she dressed like an orphan who had gotten into a bag of discarded circus costumes—today she was wearing a red beret atop her short black hair, cut in a Dutch boy style, along with an emerald green sweater studded with rhinestones with patches on the sleeve, a tight black skirt, yellow gloves, and flat purple shoes, the sole flapping at her right heel. Her black stockings were pristine, but too big; they bagged at the knees. She wore no makeup and had a charming smattering of freckles across her cheeks and nose, which gave her an elfin quality.

Yet. There was something about this Lily that made you wonder where she'd been, and where she was going. What she'd seen—and what she'd forgotten. Her eyes were constantly darting to and fro, searching, appraising. Blanche had the uneasy feeling that she knew exactly where all the exits were in a room, where all the windows were, where she might hide if she had to.

"Why you so sad to return, Blanche?" Lily poked her with an elbow. "Don't you want to go home?"

Blanche looked at her sharply. In the forty-eight hours they'd known each other, after Lily sat next to Blanche in the ship's bar and asked her why she was wearing that particular dress, as the color was not at all becoming to Blanche but would suit *her* perfectly, the two of them had: spent a cocktail hour with two smarmy French Foreign Legion soldiers and drunk them both under the table; played shuffleboard using their feet instead of their hands; devised a game wherein whoever went the farthest in a conversation with a total stranger about his or her preferred sexual position won a bottle of champagne (Lily was the victor); won a loving cup in a rhumba contest (Blanche led, Lily followed); and held an impromptu party in one of the lifeboats, inviting only men who wore monocles (of which there were a surprising number).

And during these forty-eight hours, Blanche had laughed more than she had in years. Since the good days, with Pearl. So why did Lily Kharmanyoff ask her why she was sad?

"I'm not sad."

"Sure you are. Every time you look at the sea, your face changes—it slides. Down. Like this." Lily made a sad face. "You'd no be good as spy, Blanche. Or at poker."

"I've been told that before."

"So. Tell me."

And damned if Blanche didn't. As they stood at the boat's railing, sea spray coating their hair and faces, Blanche realized she hadn't had a close friend other than Pearl in a very long time. And Pearl, sad Pearl, was dying, no longer able to think or speak coherently. Pearl was dying despite Blanche's best efforts to save her, perhaps dying because of those efforts, to spare Blanche years of despair. And Blanche had never been close to her sisters who, at any rate, were an ocean away.

Claude, she supposed, was her closest friend and the irony was not lost on her. Because he was the reason she hadn't had women friends in so long. Because every woman she met, now, she couldn't help but wonder: Is it *her?* Is this perfectly nice woman who sat down next to her in the Ritz tearoom, chatting about the high cost of gloves these days, asking Blanche what kind of perfume she is wearing, actually Claude's mistress? Every woman with her own teeth and under the age of fifty was a suspect; Claude had made it impossible for Blanche to trust any female she met.

As far as all her pals at the Ritz—well. Blanche had acquaintances galore, drinking buddies, too. Famous people, idolized people—Hemingway and Fitzgerald and Porter and Picasso and movie stars. But they weren't her friends; she couldn't unload her romantic woes on them the way they did on her, because she didn't expect them to have any sympathy—because they were men. They'd surely side with Claude. And they probably only thought about Blanche when they were inside the fabulously papered walls of the Ritz where she was a fixture, just as constant and decorative, nothing more, as the huge mural of a hunting scene behind the bar. Outside of this enchanted palace, Blanche did not exist for them—and sometimes, she wondered if that was true for her, too.

She missed a woman's friendship, Blanche realized as she turned to this stranger with the big, eager eyes (hungry, almost, Blanche thought); someone to try on clothes with, to lie about your figure, your face, your ability to stave off the ravages of time. Someone you could count on to be on your side regardless, someone who would listen and sympathize, not try to reason. Someone who had experienced the same shitty treatment at the hands of a man.

So Blanche heard herself blurting out to this Lily Kharmanyoff why she was, indeed, so sad.

"It's just that—my husband and I—we, our marriage, it's complicated. For one thing, we're childless." Blanche held her breath, waiting for Lily's response; it was such an enormous confidence. Not something she could talk about, really—especially not with Claude. Oh, it was always *there,* in the air, hovering over every conversation Blanche and Claude had, even if they were merely chatting over breakfast about the most mundane, married-couple things like "Do we have enough milk?" or "I think I'll buy new towels today."

That the absence of someone—or some*ones;* tiny, helpless creatures at that—could add such terrible heft to everything she did or said, puzzled her greatly.

"Ah," Lily said, nodding sagely. As if complete strangers told her this every day.

"Also, the bastard cheats on me, and I drink too much, especially lately. And we seem to—we *disappoint* each other, I guess. Too easily. Too often. We're not who we thought we were, back when—well, you know how it is. We're just not who we thought we were. Do you have kids?" Blanche had asked whether or not Lily was married the night before, but Lily had been vague about her personal life, as if she was used to not revealing too many details when questioned. As if she was quite used to being questioned, as a matter of fact. Blanche had simply assumed she was married, too; currently teaching her husband some vague, misguided "lesson."

Like Blanche was.

"Oh, no, no." Lily shook her head passionately. "No, the kind of life I lead—is not for children."

"What kind of life do you lead?"

"I'll tell you, Blanche, I'll tell you all about. But only after we talk about *you*."

Blanche grinned; it had almost worked, her turning the tables. With any of her other acquaintances—socialites, artists, and drunks, all equally prone to flattery and misdirection—it would have.

"Fine. We can't have children, I guess. I've been to doctors, it's something about my plumbing. Claude doesn't know about that."

"Claude is your man?"

"Yes. My husband—I told you, last night. Maybe something's wrong with his plumbing, too—I have no idea if he's had kids with his other women. I can't bring myself to ask." This fear, above all others, made her unable to discuss this with Claude. But if he had a child by one of his mistresses, Blanche could not have borne it; she could not keep coming back to him, hoping, always, that he would change—Christ, she was so naïve at times. "I don't really know if he wants children. And to tell the truth I'm not sure I do, either, except that it seems as if there is something missing between us. Like—this was what he expected of me, a family to remind him that he's a virile man. While I never, not once, gave him any indication that was what I wanted, because I didn't *know* what I wanted. Oh, we have a grand life—you should come visit us at the Ritz—but it's a different life than most married couples have. But then, we *are* different, we started out believing that we were so, so—"

"Special?"

"Yes, that's exactly it—we had a grand, fiery beginning that just fizzled into—this. Whatever *this* is." Blanche gazed at the horizon, as if the placid, reflective sea could explain to her what "this" was. "I'm lonely and angry, disappointed in him, as he is in me. And I can't, for the life of me, figure out how to fix it. Maybe it's something we can't fix. Yet I feel stuck with the guy, because I don't have anywhere else I can go. I love Paris. I could never go back home."

"Where is home?"

"America. I haven't been to see my family in ages." Blanche had returned a couple of years after her marriage, one of her frequent escapes intended to punish Claude. She'd stayed at the Ritz in Manhattan, naturally, and treated her entire family to fine dinners there, a behind-the-scenes tour, even put them up in a suite for a night, proud to show them what she was used to back in Paris. But Blanche's family—particularly her parents—were uncomfortable and disapproving that Blanche had traveled alone, without her husband. It was not a successful visit; the only thing Blanche had in common with her family, she'd realized with a new, heavy sadness that temporarily made her forget about her marriage, was the past. And the past was the reason she'd left New York in the first place.

"So what do you and your man talk about, if not children?"

"His work, mainly. The Ritz. The people there—they've become our family. Or, they take up the space that children would occupy, I guess. The space between us—something that pushes us apart but when you look at it, there's really nothing there. Does that make sense?" Blanche glanced at her new friend, who was nodding enthusiastically at everything she said—although Blanche had her doubts as to whether Lily comprehended it, given her mangling of the English language.

But it didn't matter; Blanche needed to spill her guts to someone not Claude.

To a woman.

"Yes, yes. I understand. You need a cause, you and your man. Do you have one? Something that you have to fight for, together?"

"What?"

"I don't think it's important to have children, myself. Not now, especially. There is danger, Blanche, everywhere. Bad people. But you and your man, you must have something else to fight for, as you would a child's life, a child's well-being. So, what is your reason to live, Blanche?"

"I—I don't know." Blanche gripped the slick handrail. This creature had taken the wind right out of her sails. No one had ever asked her this before, and she'd certainly never asked herself.

"Pleasure, I think?" Those dark brown eyes were probing hers, searching, seeing—every-thing. "Fun—is that your cause? Drinks and laughter and dance?"

"Well, yes—but don't you enjoy those things?—last night, the way you were arm-wrestling that torch singer—"

"Ah." Lily turned away and spat over the railing, and Blanche had never seen a woman do this; she found the spectacle rather impressive, to tell the truth. "That. That was fun, sure." Again, that mysterious, pan-European shrug. "But it's not a reason for living, Blanche. There has to be more in a life than fun, don't you think?"

"Lily, I was brought up to believe in God

and family and tradition above everything else. Propriety. Modesty. Following all the rules. But none of it ever took with me, and so I ran away, was rescued by a little hotel manager who didn't know what to do with me after he won me—as I had no idea what to do after I was won—and so I've spent the last decade or so having as much goddamn fun as I could. All the fun I was never allowed as a child."

"Maybe is time for you to grow up, Blanche? You think? Maybe is not my place." Lily gazed down at her funny shoes, and her forehead creased; she looked, for the first time in their short acquaintance, as if she was afraid of offending.

Blanche exhaled, gripped the railing tighter. Gazing ahead at the shimmering water, the bleached blue skies of the Mediterranean—no land in sight; no tempting harbors full of casinos, no moneyed yachts anchored, playgrounds waiting to be explored; only the water, the horizon, the clouds, and this odd little creature by her side—she was forced to acknowledge that yes, maybe it was time.

Time for her to grow up. But how? And did growing up mean leaving Claude for good? Standing on her own two feet, for the first time in her life not kept by a man?

Or did growing up mean forcing Claude to reckon with her as a woman, not an idea?

"What are you going to do, Lily, once you're in France? Do you have someone waiting for you?"

Again, that shrug. "Maybe it's a place to hang my bag." She looked at Blanche quizzically, and Blanche laughed.

"Hang my *hat.* That's the expression."

Lily laughed—little peals of delight—and clapped her hands. "That's it—hang my hat. I like it."

"Hang your hat? So it's not permanent—you think you'll be going on to somewhere else?"

"I will wait for Robert. He is my man, like Claude is yours. And then, we'll make plans. I think there's going to be war. The damned Fascists, Blanche. They must be stopped! Spain is very bad right now, very bad."

"So, you're from Spain?"

"Nah."

"Why should you care? And you're a woman, you can't fight. What would you do?"

"Really?" Lily peered up at her, a little cloud of disappointment dulling her eyes. "You think that women can't make a difference in this world?"

"No, but—well, *war,* Lily! What can women do about that?"

"Maybe nothing, in your Ritz world. But in my world, plenty. There is war coming, not just in Spain, and women will be part of it. Children, too."

"I suppose . . . but really, I can't think of what I personally can do about that."

"Your France will be caught up in it, too. This war that is coming."

"Lily, there's already been one world war, and France suffered the most. My Claude fought in it. It won't happen there again, trust me."

"If you say." Lily shrugged, fiddled with the hem of her skirt; Blanche saw that it was coming undone, and she made a mental note to send it to the ship's seamstress. "I wouldn't make a bet on it, though."

"Then why go there to hang your hat?"

"Because I have to get some money before we go to Spain, to fight for the Loyalists, like I told you. We need food, we need arms—maybe you help me, eh, Blanche? Are you rich?"

"Lily!" Blanche had to gasp at her new friend's audacity. "People don't ask other people that!"

Lily wrinkled her nose. "*I* ask. Is the easiest way to find out."

"I suppose so."

"And there are people in France we know who will go with us, to Spain. Hey, why not you, Blanche? You say you don't know what to do—so go with me to Spain! That will teach your man his lesson!"

"Lily!" Blanche laughed at the absurdity of what she was proposing—she, Blanche Auzello, the Mistress of the Ritz, throwing hand grenades and crawling on her belly under fire! Who on earth—*what* on earth—was this strange creature, to propose such a thing? "I believe I'll have to pass on that."

"OK. You can still help me get money. Say, I like you, Blanche. I like you a lot. And not just for the money, although that is nice, too. But for yourself. You OK by me, Blanche. I think you need me." And Lily looked startled by this; she shook her head, rubbed her forehead above her left eye with her thumb, as if she had a headache. Then she did something remarkable.

She laughed, stood up on tiptoe, turned Blanche's face toward hers, and kissed her on the lips.

With a soft, satisfied sigh, Lily pulled away, rocking back on her heels. Cocking her head, she gazed up at Blanche, testing her, Blanche thought, as her hand flew to her cheek in astonishment. Her skin was blazing hot and she knew her face must be scarlet. There was a quivering in her stomach, as if a gusty wind was blowing right through her. She'd never been kissed by a woman before.

"Lily! I—why did you—"

"I felt like it." She shrugged in that way of hers. "You look so pretty, Blanche. So sad. I thought maybe I cheer you up."

"But Lily, I'm—I'm not like that. . . ." Blanche knew there were women who loved women, of

121

course—she had been in the movies, no matter how briefly. Hell, she lived in Paris! There were clubs devoted to them. Chanel was rumored to "be like that" when the mood suited her, and so was Josephine Baker. Not to mention Cole Porter representing the male version of "like that" despite his marriage to Linda. Blanche was no prude, but nothing in her life had prepared her for this moment.

"Like what?"

"Like—well, I'm married, Lily."

"So? I have a man, too, I told you. Robert. I'll show him to you."

"And I, well, I've never—"

"Blanche, Blanche." Lily started laughing, quietly, but Blanche didn't feel as if she were being made fun of—and for that, she was grateful. "Blanche, not to worry. I just felt like it. I like men, too. I like you. I like many things, many people. A kiss—what is it? A normal thing between two people who like each other."

It was Blanche's turn to laugh; Lily sounded a lot like Claude and the way he described his regular Thursday nights.

"OK, then. I like you, too, Lily. A lot." *But not like that.*

Lily nodded, and, after a moment in which she appeared to be deciding something, slipped her little hand into Blanche's, holding her breath as if she were afraid Blanche would pull away.

And with that hesitant, shy little gesture, this ferocious, startlingly sexual creature—whom only a few moments before Blanche was picturing holding a machine gun with flair, entirely capable of mowing down a regiment of Fascists—became a waif. A child, in need of protection.

"You are my friend, Blanche."

Blanche didn't know what to say, she didn't know how to react at all; Lily had provoked so many uncomfortable emotions within the span of thirty seconds, she was utterly speechless. And wouldn't Claude be amused by *that*?

"Thank you," Blanche whispered, and wasn't sure Lily could hear her over the rush of the water, the conversation and laughter surrounding them. "You're my friend, too." But Lily squeezed her hand again, and Blanche knew she had.

"You need me, Blanche," Lily announced in that lilting, vaguely Eastern European accent of hers. "You need me to teach you about the world we live in—the world outside the Ritz. You're like a balloon."

"What?"

"A balloon. Up in the sky, you see? You could float away—like this!" Lily waved her hands wildly, making crazy windmills in the air, and she began to dance, too, her tiny little feet in those absurd shoes stomping around on the slick deck. She wiggled her hips, laughing and capering about.

"I keep you here, on earth," she called over her shoulder. "You keep me from doing too many crazy things. We help each other!"

Blanche laughed, even as she felt skewered to the deck railing by the piercing truth of the girl's mangled speech. Goddamn if she wasn't rather like a balloon lately, blowing this way and that, allowing anger and idleness and gossip and pretty clothes and fancy meals and strong cocktails, infantile petulance—not to mention disappointment that her life had not turned out to be a grand, heroic drama after all, Ritz or no Ritz—to tug at her string daily.

Blanche wasn't selfish enough to blame her current balloon-like state entirely on Claude and his wayward Thursday nights, however. Or even on the lack of a child she didn't precisely know that she desired. But neither was she able to find a way out of it, to recapture a sense of purpose—to act, instead of react.

Until, perhaps, now.

"Come visit me at the Ritz. Day after tomorrow," Blanche called to Lily, who was linking arms with total strangers, drawing them into her dance, and soon there was an impromptu conga line snaking around the deck; Lily grabbed Blanche and absorbed her into it. "Come have tea. I want to introduce you to Claude. I want you to meet all my friends."

"Of course," Lily said, as if it was only what

she'd been expecting, after all. "You have rich friends, I bet! They can help me, too. But forget them now, and dance, Blanche. Dance while you can! It won't last; it never does."

But she said this with merriment, giggling at her own joke—at the inevitability of the last note of the trumpet, the last spin of the waltz. Blanche giggled, too, and allowed herself to be dragged along in a line of strangers, all of them dancing to nothing but the onward rush of the ocean as they pushed through it relentlessly, oblivious to all the other boats in the sea.

CHAPTER 10
CLAUDE,
1938

Until the giant awoke . . .

It was true that the Ritz, throughout its illustrious history, had been home to some unsavory characters. What hotel hadn't? It was Claude's unfortunate experience that people staying at a hotel indulged themselves in ways they never would at home. The matron who kept the tidiest house in the neighborhood had no qualm leaving towels and dirty lingerie all over the hotel floor. Strict dieters threw caution to the wind and ordered every cake available from the kitchen. Early risers found themselves sleeping until noon in the unaccustomed plushness of a cushiony bed outfitted with the softest linens.

So it was unsurprising that indelicate things sometimes happened, even at the Ritz. The baron who died of a heart attack in the bed of his mistress while his wife slept, unawares, in their suite next door. The suicides: There have been more than one, but the most famous was that of Olive Thomas, a silent movie star and the wife of Jack Pickford, whose sister was the more famous

Mary. It was in 1920, before Claude began here, but of course he knew all about it; the demented soul drank mercury bichloride, so the rumor went, because her husband had infected her with syphilis. Monsieur Rey had to quickly remove her so that none of the guests would see; she was taken out through the kitchen wrapped in a duvet, poor girl.

The Ritz, then, had seen its share of shady characters before. But nothing in Claude's experience had prepared him for the startling change in clientele that the Ritz began hosting in the latter half of 1937 and continuing into 1938.

The Spanish Civil War was the reason. The bar was suddenly full of talk of nothing else, and many of the regulars had left to experience it, some in uniform, others as correspondents. Hemingway, in particular, had bellowed long and loud about it being the opportunity of a lifetime; some said he'd enlisted with the Loyalists, but Claude suspected his manner of enlistment was more of a drunken observer on the sidelines— although, according to others, the man could write. Claude did not know; he had more than enough French literature to keep him occupied during his rare moments of leisure.

While the war raged, all sorts of people washed in and out of Paris and France; the country along the border between Spain and France was flooded with refugees, peasants mostly. But certain unsavory characters ended up at the Ritz, too: agents trying to secure more money, more guns, more help—for both sides.

As that war ground on, and as the German Air Force was revealed in all its ferocious power and might, bombing citizens as well as soldiers, others showed up at the Ritz—others with hated German accents, wearing the black armband of the Nazi party, their black boots always shining obscenely, their medals polished to an unearthly glow.

As the Germans arrived, the Americans left. Like rats fleeing a sinking ship, they all disappeared. Overnight, it seemed—gone were Blanche's writer friends, the artists, the musicians. The dabblers in life, Claude could not help but think. But they were replaced by others just as unstable—Europeans treating themselves to a desperate last revelry in Paris, dancing a wild dance, ignoring what was going on about them: The starving refugees from Spain, forced to live exposed to the elements in refugee camps near the border; the dispatches detailing the bombing of civilians. The smiling pictures of Hitler and Mussolini shaking hands, masses of brown-shirted crowds raising their arms in that harrowing salute.

Claude was being run ragged by these dissipated Europeans determined to have the most ridiculous times of their lives. In all his years at the Ritz thus far, he'd organized (expertly, of course) his fair share of wild revelries: The Cubism parties popular in the 1920s, where the guests all dressed in ridiculous costumes of exaggerated angles. The parties that were held here after the triumphant performances of the Ballets Russes, when they hired dancers, dressed as nymphs and satyrs, to work as waitstaff. But nothing had prepared him for the *fin de siècle* flavor of the parties held at the Ritz in the late 1930s.

A dinner party given by a count who insisted on serving his guests elephant feet—somehow, Claude found them by calling every zoo in France, Austria, and Belgium. Elsa Maxwell (technically an American, but she spent most of her time in Europe tagging along after the rich and famous), who wanted to throw a masked ball at the very last minute—she breezed in at two P.M. to say that two hundred of her closest friends would arrive at eight. Claude and his staff had six hours to procure fresh flower arrangements, trinkets for favors, and a trapeze artist willing to perform from a very rickety, hastily constructed gilded trapeze Claude wheedled out of the Moulin Rouge. A revelry for a group of British socialites and minor royalty on their way to fight in Spain; they treated the entire prospect as an impending holiday and bought baskets and baskets of the best pâtés and foie gras, cheese, wines, champagne, and chocolates, to take with them. As if war was a picnic.

Claude knew it was not, but it was not his place to lecture. It was his place to manage, to fulfill every request, no matter how absurd. For that was what he did. He managed.

However. Claude reached his limit one day and did not *manage* to hold his temper when he encountered one more shining, fat German face poking around every corner, every office, and every room at the Ritz.

The most personable of the Nazis who increasingly scurried about the hotel—indeed, the entire city—like a cockroach was a man named Baron Hans Günther von Dincklage, an attaché at the German embassy. He was young, handsome with shining blond hair and cloudless blue eyes; newly divorced and quite flirtatious with all the women, including Claude's Blanchette. This had created problems with Coco Chanel, who regarded von Dincklage—nicknamed Spatzy (German for "sparrow") due to his propensity to table-hop in the restaurant and bar—as her own personal property.

One evening, Chanel met Blanche and Claude as they were ascending the stairs on the Place Vendôme; Chanel's private suite of rooms was on this side of the hotel. Since her fashion house was only a few doors away on the rue Cambon, this arrangement made sense to her, and it was a nice, reliable income for the Ritz.

But not many at the Ritz liked the woman

herself, it must be said. She often sent her meals back down to the kitchen, saying they weren't up to her standards. (Not that the woman ate anything at all, other than liquids.) She'd insisted on redecorating her rooms—not for her the intricately patterned wallpapers, tapestries, gilt, and gold that stamped the Ritz as the most luxurious hotel in all the world; she made her rooms over in the new modern style, which was hideous, if you asked Claude. So much glass, so many straight lines. Horribly uncomfortable, to say the least.

She seemed to really have it out for Blanche, in particular—almost as if she'd chosen the one person universally loved in the Ritz to make a point. A point known only to herself.

"Blanche, do you have any idea what I just heard?" Chanel smiled that night, and Claude was immediately on his guard; she was the type of woman who only smiled when she was about to destroy someone.

"What?" Blanche was more innocent than he was; she stopped on the stairs and folded her arms, as if she were about to be told a funny story. She resisted Claude's attempt to steer her out of Chanel's way, so he had no choice but to listen, too.

"My seamstress asked me the other day if you were a Jewess." Still Chanel smiled, as coolly as a cat. "How unusual of her, don't you think?"

Blanche nodded.

"I told her I'd ask. But you can't prove that you're a Jewess, can you, Blanche? I could ask to see your passport. But how absurd!" Chanel laughed, and her eyes glittered like onyx.

"What a good idea." Blanche sounded amused. "Of course, you'll have to show me yours, too. C'mon, Coco, let's do it—let's show each other our real ages!"

Chanel stopped laughing; she drew herself up and looked down that sharp nose of hers.

"I don't think that's necessary," she huffed, parading with solemn ceremony up the staircase, while Blanche guffawed until she had tears in her eyes.

Claude could not share in her laughter, however. He knew that Chanel was dangerous and not above spreading lies and rumors; she had a habit of conforming her ideals to match whomever she was sleeping with at the time.

And at this time, she was sleeping with von Dincklage.

For now, all Claude could do was bite his tongue, remain vigilant, and warn Blanche—as well as all his staff—to be very careful around these new German guests. And pray that they would remain just that—guests—in the months to come.

CHAPTER 11

BLANCHE,
Autumn 1941

When do occupiers become guests? When does the enemy become a friend?

These are questions Blanche has to ask herself, as the weeks and months go on.

At the Ritz Paris, she knows so well, guests sometimes become more like family than real siblings, spouses, parents. But even those regulars, like Hemingway and the Windsors and the Fitzgeralds and the Porters, leave eventually. But this is different; with the Nazis using the Ritz as their headquarters, Blanche is forced to get to know them, and to her surprise, some of them aren't so bad. And the same uniform that, seen walking down the Champs, instills in her fear and revulsion appears almost harmless in the rosy, flattering light of the Ritz.

There is the young soldier staying in room two-nineteen, an officer but still a boy; his uniform never looks as if it quite fits him, the collar too big for his skinny throat with the prominent Adam's apple. He's homesick, he tells Blanche one day when she comes across him outside in the rue Cambon, leaning against a wall with a pad and pencil, sketching away at the scene on the street. "It's to send back home," he says, showing her his amateurish work; for sure, he's no Picasso, but he seems very proud of the picture he's drawn anyway. "For my mother, who is very worried about me."

Then he tells Blanche about his girl back home, still in school, and he's worried about that, that she'll fall for a student while he's away. And Blanche decides that he's a nice young man, really; a kind person, and she starts to go out of her way to ask him if he's gotten any letters that day, if he's heard from his mother or his girl (Katrin, her name is). She tells herself he didn't decide to invade France, Hitler did. This boy—Friedrich—only followed orders.

Then there's the driver for General von Stülpnagel; the poor man sits out in that car in front of the hotel, day in and day out, no matter the weather. He only comes inside to use the facilities and then he is polite, even deferential, embarrassed to look anyone in the face. So Blanche has taken to bringing him a cup of hot tea when the weather is cold and he is shivering in the seat of the car, all alone. To chatting with him when the sun is shining. It's really terrible, she rages to Claude, the way von Stülpnagel treats him! He's a man, not a goddamn machine. And, she further explains to her husband, who's interested in a distracted sort of way (only humoring her, she suspects), that the driver—Klaus—has a wife back home whom he's eager to talk about. As if, in talking about her, she is real to him; and if he couldn't talk about her, he'd be afraid she would disappear, like a dream. And while Blanche has never sent a loved one to the front, she understands his eagerness to keep her alive in this way, and she listens to him.

And the secretary for Colonel Ebert—a young woman, not so pretty; Blanche sees her looking at the Parisiennes, the chambermaids, even the laundresses, shyly, in awe. The poor girl has to wear the ugly green uniform, the square-cut tunic over the shapeless skirt, her feet in black bricks for shoes. And the uniforms of the Ritz employees are much more flattering and fashionable, not to mention what the guests wear. The girl—Astrid—sits all day taking stenography and typing. She's surrounded by men, none of whom give her a second look; they're too busy ogling the French actresses and socialites who sail in and out of the rue Cambon side. Astrid doesn't have a sweetheart back home or in the army, she confessed to Blanche once, when Blanche saw her at one of the cafés nearby and sat with her as she ate too much pastry.

"Have a cigarette instead," Blanche urged as the girl ordered another Napoleon, but it was no use. Astrid's simply sad and lonely and homesick and finds in food her one comfort.

It's in this way—seeing them every day, knowing them beyond the uniforms and swastikas, observing the things she has in common with them (Blanche has thought of taking her revenge out on Claude in pastry many times)—that they become people, not nouns. Living, breathing, eating, drinking, crying, laughing people. They go to church—there are even Catholics among them; Claude was surprised and disturbed, he told her, the first time he encountered some of them in church, kneeling and lighting a candle before slipping into a pew on Sunday. They buy presents for their friends and family back home. They cry when they don't receive enough letters and wonder if something terrible has happened, and Blanche cries and wonders right along with them.

And then she tries to imagine what Lily would say, if she saw her drying Astrid's tears, or patting Friedrich on the shoulder when he doesn't get a letter. But Lily isn't here, Blanche is; she's the one who has to live with these people, find a way to survive, connect with them, maybe not the worst of them, but with the ones who are only following orders—there has to be something they have in common.

Doesn't there?

Two days after their ship docked in Cherbourg back in 1937, Lily was Blanche's guest at the

Ritz; she remembers, so vividly, Lily's reaction to her first glimpse into Blanche's world.

Gone was the confident miniature revolutionary who strode off the boat and right past all the customs officials into France with no passport, no visa, armed with nothing but cunning and attitude. In her place was a shy child, overwhelmed by her surroundings, clinging to Blanche like a cold sweat. "You *live* here, Blanche?" she kept asking, no matter how many times Blanche answered in the affirmative. She gaped up at the tall ceilings with their plaster ornamentations, she clutched her umbrella tightly, suspiciously, to her chest when the top-hatted doorman rushed to take it from her, she blinked at the rosy light everywhere—the light that César Ritz had decided was most flattering to women, and so had installed throughout his palace. There was no light anywhere in all of Paris like it; only at the Ritz was every woman beautiful, no matter her age, no matter her social position.

No matter her secrets.

"Well, sort of. We do have an apartment, too. Our official address." For the Auzellos had moved again, and now had a lovely four-room apartment, not counting the kitchen, on the prestigious avenue Montaigne, just off the Champs. Blanche had convinced Claude that this address was much more suitable to his position; the wide, tree-lined street was full of fancy dress salons, including Mainbocher, Molyneux, Vionnet, Patou, and Lucien Lelong.

Lily didn't quite understand how Blanche and Claude could have an apartment *and* live at the Ritz, however. And Blanche had to admit, it did seem a little extravagant. So in order not to discuss it further, she steered Lily into the bar and introduced her all around. Frank Meier, Blanche couldn't help but notice, seemed to recognize her; he raised his eyebrows, as did Lily, which was odd, as Lily said she'd never been to Paris before.

"Madame," Cole Porter said with a neat little bow. "It's not only a pleasure but a treasure to meet you."

Lily glared at him skeptically, and Blanche knew she didn't quite pick up on the wordplay; whatever Lily's native tongue was, it surely wasn't English or French. But suddenly Lily beamed at Cole, and Cole beamed back, and it was as if one child had suddenly found another in the midst of a forest of adults; they were almost the same height, their eyes almost identically round and dark, their skin, too, both the same olive tint.

"You must be the famous waif," boomed Hemingway, as he took her delicate hand in his great big paw. "I'll put you in a book."

"Stand in line, Lily," Blanche told her, hitting Hemingway on the shoulder. "He says that to everybody."

"It's the best way to pick up women," he admitted with a boyishly shy grin, and Blanche had to laugh.

"Where's Scott?" She looked around; he wasn't at his usual corner stool pestering Frank Meier, who always had the sense to cut him off when he got too sloppy.

"Back home. To good old America. He and Zelda had to return—some emergency with her family, I'm told."

"I'm sorry, I hope it isn't serious." Blanche didn't really like Zelda—she was too petulant, too predatory, like a hawk, Blanche thought. Her narrow blue eyes always searching for a weakness, ready to pounce. But Blanche did admire her commitment to keeping up with Scott, drink for drink. Even if she didn't always admire the results—she sometimes felt as if there ought to be a crew following the Fitzgeralds around Paris, cleaning up the debris of their drunken sprees, wounding arguments, and shattering explosions.

"Is this where we have tea, Blanche?" Lily had relaxed in the bar, which was easy to imagine anywhere else but in the Ritz, it was so relatively cozy. But Blanche shook her head.

"No, Claude's meeting us in the Garden Terrace." Even though it was October, it was still warm enough to dine outside.

Reluctantly, she bade her chums farewell and

steered Lily toward the Garden Terrace. They walked down the long hallway connecting the two buildings—the Hallway of Dreams, it was called—and Lily's frown deepened with every step as Blanche pointed out the lighted display windows on either side, filled with luxury items such as Mark Cross pens, Louis Vuitton handbags, flasks of Guerlain perfume, diamond necklaces from Cartier—items far beyond the reach of most Parisians, but chump change for those who could afford to stay at the Ritz. The retailers paid a pretty penny to advertise their wares in this way; Claude was very proud of it, as he said there was none like it in any other hotel. But Lily only glared darkly at the goodies that most people drooled over.

She looked the same during tea; her discomfort as item after item was presented—delicate little pâté sandwiches, exquisite fondant-covered cakes, sugared nuts in silver swan dishes—was palpable, but Blanche saw her sneak a few tidbits into her raggedy handbag to take home, as well as some silverware and napkins. She could only hope that Claude hadn't noticed.

Blanche didn't think he had, but he did look as if he needed an antacid. Blanche realized too late that he and Lily would never get along, and she should have known it from the start; after all, Claude had never approved of Pearl, either. How silly of her, how foolishly hopeful she was—like a little girl showing off her new friend. And God forbid that Lily was not, obviously, someone who would be at home at his precious Ritz—Claude the prig, Claude the uptight. He never changed, and it was such a cruel trick that he had so dazzled her in the beginning that she couldn't see who he really was.

But then again, she supposed she'd deceived him, too—no, she *knew* that she had.

Lily's dismay at all the opulence, the whispered, oh-so-polite behavior, the ostentatious orderliness of the Ritz was only too apparent by her refusal to say hardly a word. And Claude's clipped answers, too, spoke volumes. Blanche found herself keeping up an inane chatter the entire time until she was wrung out with exhaustion; the weather, the fashions, salty tales of her travels and her shipboard antics with Lily were all met with stony silence, until she made the mistake of talking about the current political situation in France.

"Socialists!" Claude could barely say the word. "They keep trying to unionize the Ritz—they tried, in the General Strike, but fortunately I was able to stop it."

"Why? What is wrong with unions? People deserve a living wage!" Lily came to life for the first time; she balled up her napkin, her inky eyes blazing.

"Which we pay them, and more. Our salaries are the highest among all the hotels in France, and we are very generous with time off."

"Good for you, then. But is not like that everywhere. Everyone deserves the right to feed their families!"

"Are you a Socialist?" Claude began to pale.

"No, a Communist."

Claude dropped a spoon into his tea glass, splattering the tablecloth.

"How about these croissants?" Blanche offered the silver basket around to her dining partners, who both declined. Claude excused himself shortly thereafter—with a long, significant look at Blanche that told her exactly what he thought of her new friend.

Lily didn't even wait until Claude had left the terrace before she spat out, "Blanche. I know he's your man and I know I shouldn't say, but—how awful he is!"

"No, he's not," Blanche assured her. "He's really not. Claude is so generous, he doesn't like to show it because he thinks it makes him look weak. He's very invested in his staff; he does take good care of them. But you see, he is—very French."

"But the people of France are changing. They're waking up. Just in time."

"Some of them are, I suppose." The new prime minister, Léon Blum, was a Socialist—he was part of the Popular Front party—but the heart of France remained staunchly conservative. Catholic. "Trust me—most of the people in Paris are just like Claude. It's not that they're uncaring. It's just that they're set in their ways."

"But your friends—in the bar—they are not."

"No." Blanche thought of her friends, her drinking buddies, as rudderless as she was. "They're Americans, and they don't give a good goddamn about French politics as long as they can sit and drink their kirs and their absinthe. They love France, but they're not of it. France is a vacation from reality for them."

"Are you part of France, then? Is this where you belong, your home?"

"I—I—I don't know." And Blanche didn't; she didn't see herself as American any longer, but neither did she feel one hundred percent French. Especially in the ways of the heart. "You don't have a home either, do you? You just drift about. You won't even tell me where you're from."

"Ah, is different. I have no home because home is gone—vanished. Destroyed. America is very much still America. I hear it's a great country. I hope to go there someday."

"It is, and it isn't—it's not perfect, if that's what you mean."

"Neither is France."

"Neither is anywhere—or anyone. Not even you, Lily." Blanche felt she had to take her new friend down a peg; she was getting to be a little annoyingly self-righteous.

"You must decide who you are, Blanche— American, French, *something*. You must stand for something."

"Oh, must I?" Blanche arched an eyebrow. "Like you?"

"Yes." Lily threw her wadded-up napkin down on her plate and rose. She nodded in her decisive way. "Yes, like me, like others. Not like here." She gestured to the rest of the court, filled with satisfied, richly clad people. "I thank you, Blanche. But your Ritz—is not for me."

"I guess you'll want to leave those sandwiches and the silver and the napkins behind, then, won't you? If they offend you so, I mean."

Lily flushed and sat back down.

"Listen, Lily." Blanche leaned across the table. "You don't know a damn thing about me or the Ritz. Or Claude, for that matter. Or even Paris. You can't make pronouncements like that—you can't barge into people's lives and tell them how terrible they are."

"You invited me, Blanche." Lily attempted to shrug with her usual insouciance. But she also looked a little intimidated; her freckles seemed to darken on her pale face.

"I wanted to share some of my life with you— that's what friends do. And friends don't walk off with the silverware and napkins in return."

Lily reached into her bag and stealthily put back the items in question, although she kept the food and Blanche didn't call her out on that.

"I'm sorry."

"Well, don't do that again. If you need something, just ask me. I like you, Lily, and I'm not sure why. Except that you make me think about things I generally try to avoid, and maybe I need that."

"I do?"

Blanche nodded, relieved to see Lily—obviously pleased—grin, looking once more like the Artful Dodger.

"I haven't had a close friend in a long while. I'm lonely, sometimes."

"Here? At this Ritz?" Lily's eyes were enormous and Blanche saw herself in their brilliant reflection as Lily must—as an enchanted Alice in Wonderland.

"Yes, I am. I like these people, I think they're interesting in ways they don't even know. But I'm not sure I'm as much like them as I thought I was. I'm not sure I *want* to be like them anymore, to tell the truth."

"I like you, too, Blanche. You are swell. You need me and I am here, thank God." Lily clapped her hands twice and rose, bent down and kissed Blanche's cheek—only her cheek, to Blanche's great relief. She gathered up her gloves and bag and umbrella, ready to leave.

"Maybe you need me, too," Blanche called after her. Lily grinned and waved, unaware of the stares she was gathering, like a lone, gaily decorated little tugboat sailing among proud, great ships.

"Maybe I do!"

The next day, a small nosegay of violets was delivered to Blanche.

Thank you for visit and I'm sorry for being rude because I was your guest. I don't know this soft life but maybe you teach me. But next time, you see me. I show you some of my life like you said friends do. I show you France, real France. A week from Wednesday for lunch. Love, Lily.

What a bizarre message! This odd foreigner who'd only been here a matter of days, when Blanche had lived in Paris for nearly fifteen years—*Lily* wanted to show *her* France?

However, Blanche realized she was looking forward to it; that she *wanted* Lily to—show her, wake her up, tell her something. And that this, perhaps, was the reason she'd invited Lily to the Ritz in the first place. She needed someone to help her to see beyond the gilt and the polish that had blinded her, truly, these last several years, since she'd become Mistress of the Ritz. What was Paris like for Lily, for those who came here from other shores without a franc to their names? Well, like Blanche had, to tell the truth. The only difference between her and Lily, when you came right down to it, was that Blanche had been kept by one man and rescued by another to be ensconced at his castle. At the time, she'd thought herself rather clever, really. But now, she had to wonder at her willingness to be rescued. And ensconced.

But before Blanche could find out the answers to any of the dozens of questions that suddenly were keeping her up late at night, long after Claude had gone to sleep, snoring softly beside her, Lily was gone. And Blanche couldn't help but wonder if she had taken all the answers with her.

So even now, in 1941, Blanche still keeps looking for her, every day when she leaves the Ritz. She ducks into stifling little bookshops tucked into small mews, she checks out dark cafés where everyone stops talking when she enters. Restaurants that serve foods like goulash instead of ratatouille. Blanche searches all the places she'd never normally frequent—places that the Germans, too, seem not to have discovered yet; places where someone like Lily might be. Because she misses her, yes, of course; even though they were together for such a short time, Lily illuminated Blanche's life like a fluttering, persistent firefly. But—

Lily needed her, too; Blanche is certain of that, despite all evidence to the contrary. There was something about Lily that made Blanche want to take care of her, to feed her nourishing soups, to mend her clothing, to take her to get a decent haircut. Perhaps, Blanche muses, Lily is the child she'd never had. But she also remembers that kiss—that remarkable, disturbing kiss. And she realizes that Lily is much more than that. Not just a friend, not just a child, not a lover, either; a complicated engine, that's what Lily is. And engines propel people.

Blanche also searches for Lily because she needs someone to tell her what to do, how to live with these occupier/guests, how to continue to be worried about the Friedrichs, the Astrids, especially now.

Now that, every day, she passes another family huddled together; every day more people disappear into the night. Simply—gone.

And more and more, in her dreams, in her nightmares—

Blanche is one of them.

CHAPTER 12

CLAUDE,
1938

And caused great distress
throughout the kingdom . . .

After the *Anschluss*, Claude urged Blanche, as he urged all his staff, to be more careful around their German guests, particularly around Spatzy. But Blanche—of course!—was fond of the fellow (who was, Claude had to admit, good-natured and as admiring of pretty women as Claude himself was) and enjoyed practicing her rusty German on him, to his great amusement. They would sit for hours in the bar, having dirty conversations in German and laughing like two schoolchildren.

"Spatzy's a regular guy," she told Claude one day in his office. "I like him. Nazi or not."

Claude swallowed, loosening his collar; his wife's timing was most unfortunate.

"Von Dincklage is a member of the *Abwehr*," Claude informed her coldly. "The German military intelligence organization. He reports to Goebbels himself."

"That's crazy." Blanche laughed, perching on the corner of his desk in a bright pink silk dress with the new shoulder pads making her shoulders look sharp and dangerous, nothing like the way a woman's shoulders should. Her hair was shining, swirling up around her head in the front, hanging down her neck in the back. She was so naïve, his sheltered wife. So in need of *protection*—of rescue—and he warmed to his long-forgotten role; it was certainly easier than being her husband. She especially needed protecting in these times. He reminded himself, as he did a hundred times a day, that she was an American. And Americans were so foolish. She might dress like a French woman, she might speak the language fluently—although *mon Dieu*, that accent! She might be able to order a fine wine without Claude's help now.

But she was, deep in her heart, still that trusting American. And it was Claude's privilege—his duty—to protect her. As he had, from the very beginning.

"Your Spatzy all but told me he was a spy, just this minute. I found him downstairs in the wine cellars, snooping around—making a list, actually. Counting the cases, marking the vintages."

"So?"

"So—he is not allowed down there. No one is except staff. But von Dincklage—and other Nazis—have been snooping around the Ritz, Blanche. Asking questions. Taking inventories. Even measuring windows and doorways. And not just the Ritz; I've heard from my friends in the business that they're seeing the same thing. At the George V, the Crillon, the Le Royal Monceau—even the Claridge. The Germans are taking stock, taking inventory. I threw Spatzy out of the cellar—I told him to go to hell." Claude wished that he had a glass of water, for his throat was unaccountably dry. "I should not have done that. He is, after all, a guest. But why, Blanche, do you think he was snooping around?"

She shrugged and wiggled a foot out of a shoe; reaching down, she picked the shoe up and began to massage her instep. How could she be so blissfully unaware?

"Because they are planning to *invade,* Blanche. I'm serious." Claude grabbed her shoulders, looked right into those laughing, taunting—innocent—brown eyes. "The Germans want Paris—they want all of France, all of Europe. What's going on in Spain is only the prelude. There will be war, just as your Lily has said. They're building planes, tanks, roads that lead to the border—that's what I'm hearing. And you, my love, will be in great danger. We all will be, of course—but I never thought that you, my wife . . . and I don't know what to do about it."

For even Claude couldn't protect Blanche from the Nazis, should the day come when they—but no, he would not think of it.

"What do you mean?" Her eyes were no longer

dancing. "What on earth *could* you do, Claude?"

"Send you away, for one thing. Back to America, where you would be safe. America won't be drawn into any European war, at least not for a while."

"Popsy!" She grabbed his waist, pulled him to her, and whispered in his ear. "You can't get rid of me that easily, Claude Auzello, no matter how hard you try. I don't give up. Don't you understand that by now?"

It was what Claude wanted to hear. It was what he was afraid to hear.

"But it is my duty to keep you safe, Blanchette—from the very beginning, when we first met, I knew that—"

"And it is my duty to be by your side. I'm your wife, remember? Will you be called up?"

"It's only a matter of time, I think." Daladier's government had already mobilized two million men, and Claude, at least in his eyes, was still young—only forty.

"Then I will go with you, wherever you are garrisoned."

"No, Blanche." Claude shook his head. "No, you must return to America. I've thought it through. Or even to that—that J'Ali, that man—I would put you on the boat myself, if I thought it would keep you safe." Claude did not quite know what he was saying; he was simply overwhelmed by all that could happen, should the Germans start using those tanks and planes while all of Europe merely shrugged and played on.

"Claude, you're talking nonsense—go back to J'Ali? He's fat and full of syphilis, last I heard. Anyway, I'm staying right here in France, and I'm going where you're going, so I can keep my eye on you. I'm not going to be sent away so you can have your—so that *she* can take my place." Those eyes were now filled with devastation, and Claude flinched.

But he had recently come to a decision; one that was not, after all, that difficult to make.

"Blanche, you must know—there is—I'm through. With my Thursday nights."

"You are?" Instantly she was skeptical, alert. A volcano on the verge of erupting.

"Yes. This is not the time for—that. There is only time for survival. For—for love?" Claude did not approve of the question mark; it made him sound too vulnerable. But he also could not prevent it. In all these years of marriage, he had never asked his wife if she loved him. Claude took it for granted, as any Frenchman would. Or rather—Claude took it for granted that it did not matter much, one way or the other.

But most Frenchmen were not married to Americans.

"Claude!" Her eyes were brimming, and she buried her head in his neck, and he inhaled her scent—Blanche always smelled like ripe fruit,

153

peaches and grapes and luscious pears. "You're getting sentimental in your old age."

"Blanche." Claude shook his head; she was always teasing. When she wasn't throwing things. "I'm serious. I—we have been playing games, you and I, have we not? For too long. I am as much at fault as you are. I've already seen one war and I have no wish to see another—but there is something about war that makes a man assess his life, his accomplishments—or lack of them. I am not—proud—of some things."

"Really?" Blanche's face—she lit up like a young girl, and it pained Claude to observe the fact that he had not inspired such joy in his wife in a very long time. "Do you mean it? I—I don't know what happened between us either. I think we married too hastily, too caught in all the excitement, and before I knew it I had a French passport and a suite at the Ritz and who's going to complain about that? But we never have had a real marriage, have we? Two people who are everything to each other—who don't need the glitz and the glamour the way we seem to. But perhaps we can start over? Whither thou goest, and all that jazz?"

Claude could not help but laugh, as Blanche was forever mangling Biblical passages on purpose; she did not take religion seriously, as he did. No weekly confession, no fasting during Lent. She complained every time she had to kneel, on the rare occasions she accompanied him to Mass. But then again, he must give her some leeway, considering her background.

"I would like that, Blanchette. I would like a chance to—to get to know you better." Claude winced, because it dented his pride to admit that he did not fully understand his own wife— no, it dented his pride to admit that he *wanted* to.

But these days, pride seemed a luxury few could afford.

"So it's settled. I'm staying by your side—I'm not leaving you. And besides, who will look after Lily when she comes back? She needs me, too."

Claude sighed. What was the strange attachment that drew Blanche to this dangerous woman? Take the incident of the rug, which Blanche was not aware that he knew about.

One day, soon after she invited that person to tea at the Ritz, Blanche came to him, all innocent giggles. She had "accidentally, because I'm such a butterfingers!" dropped one of the heavy oriental rugs belonging to the Ritz out the window of their suite, in a misguided attempt to shake the dust out of it. While it was in the street, before Blanche could rush downstairs, some terrible woman had stolen it! How awful! Blanche—charmingly—shook her head at her own clumsiness, sat on his knee and played with his tie as she told him this tale.

Of course Claude hadn't believed her (although he had quite enjoyed the interlude upon his knee, which led to an interlude upon the bed). For the sake of peace, he pretended that he did, however. And not two days later, on her way to take a train to Spain, Lily had come to him to explain. She had asked Blanche for money for her journey. Blanche and she had arranged this farce; Lily was the crazy woman in the street who had taken the rug to be sold.

"She is a good woman, Blanche," Lily told Claude, and though she looked absurd, like an orphan in a baggy gray cardigan sweater over a tight black skirt, she also was as earnest a person as he'd ever encountered—with the exception of Pearl White, when she had told him the same thing, years before.

And despite his distaste for this person and her ideals—and her presumption in telling Claude anything about his own wife—he did have to ponder the coincidence of these two similarly exasperating women reminding him how lucky he was to be married to Blanche. He was accustomed, of course, to valuing a woman through another man's eyes—if he looked at her retreating backside when she left their table in order to powder her nose. If he winked at Claude with admiration as they passed by, his hand possessively on the small of her back. If, after a few drinks, his pals thumped him on his shoulder and made enviously lewd remarks about what must go on in the boudoir.

But to have his wife's worth reflected back to him by other *women*—it was a novel experience. And not an unpleasant one, Claude was surprised to discover. Even if one of these women was this bedraggled little *Communist* on her way to fight in a country not her own, and good riddance.

"Lily can take care of herself," Claude told Blanche now, and truer words were never spoken. "She will most likely end up the new president of the Republic, should her side win."

"Popsy." Blanche bent down to put her shoe back on; she straightened her silk stockings and smoothed the front of her dress. "You are a real stick-in-the-mud, you know?"

"That is an unfamiliar expression. But I sense it is not a flattering one."

Blanche laughed that hearty laugh that he so loved to hear. It was a sound he hadn't heard much of late, until Lily came into her life, and for that he was grateful. That, he could admit.

Claude kissed his wife, more passionately than the director of the Ritz should have done. But then, what good was being the director of the Ritz if one couldn't kiss a beautiful woman in one's office?

And kissing—touching, exciting, upending— that had always been good between them. The one thing they could count on never to disappoint.

Claude cleared his throat, about to say something more—precisely what, he didn't quite know—when his wife pushed him away, laughing, even as she made an odd motion toward her face, as if she were brushing a cobweb away from it. For a moment, they couldn't look at each other; their mutual vulnerability was too unfamiliar, too much.

Blanche waved and drifted off so that he could return to his duties.

Claude hoped she would not drift off to the bar. He did not approve of how much time she spent there; he did not approve of how much Blanche drank with these people—not her friends, but the people who called her name in delight, bought her rounds of martinis, told her secrets and lies and enchanting stories. He did not approve of the fact that she sometimes got so drunk she misplaced her handbag, or lost a shoe, or had to be discreetly placed in a chair behind the bar where Frank Meier could keep an eye on her while she snored softly, before waking up in a haze and talking nonsense. Or sometimes, the truth.

For the truth was especially dangerous now, when spies were everywhere. Even in the plush environs of the Ritz.

CHAPTER 13

BLANCHE,
Autumn 1941

Parisians have grown used to sitting next to Nazis in cafés, theaters, on the Métro—it is no longer the sharp, wounding blow that it was in the very beginning. The Germans now merely are suffocating with their presence; the soldiers try to be courteous, in their own way. Deferential, helping old ladies cross the street, carrying heavy parcels for pregnant women—that kind of thing, that Boy Scout show.

But always with guns holstered or rifles slung across their backs.

Blanche thinks that if Lily was back in Paris, she would have shown up at the Ritz by now. Frank Meier—who knows everything about everybody—isn't any help; all he can say is that Lily crossed the border into Spain sometime around the beginning of 1938 and no one's seen her since. Which is a damn shame, because Blanche needs a friend right now, more than ever.

Because her husband is cheating on her again.

"There is time now only for love," Claude had said that day in his office, before the wispy puffs of conflict had turned into thunderclouds of war. She'd believed him. Like a fool, like a wife. And those nine months in Nîmes had been a revelation; no Ritz, only a small apartment and the two of them (well, the two of them and an entire regiment of French soldiers who, Blanche discovered, loved nothing more than sitting around drinking coffee and arguing politics past, present, and future, when they weren't drilling and preparing for an invasion that kept being postponed, until it was over almost before it began). But in those months, Blanche and Claude had to rely upon each other in ways they'd never had to before—at the Ritz. Not merely for creature comforts, the everyday busywork of a marriage that can be the subject of more conversation and concern than Blanche had ever suspected: the cooking and polishing and laundering. But the Auzellos had also had to rely on each other, solely, for company, for support, for earnest conversation about topics much more important than who was sleeping with whom, and where, and when; who had not paid a bill; who was going to throw a party.

They talked about a future that loomed dark and unknowable; they reminisced in the way of lovers who have only met—eager to quickly build a shared history. In the Auzellos' case, a history that was not full of deception and recrimination, reflected back, dazzlingly, by polished mirrors and chandeliers until it blinded.

In Nîmes, in a country town within a stone's throw of the blue Mediterranean, where the most excitement was who would win the weekly bocce tournament held in the town square, this future, uncomplicated, even boring, seemed possible.

Now, however—

Now that they're back in Paris, now that war has come and moved on, leaving this crazy reality; now that the world has splintered into shards of unrecognizable images, puzzle pieces that will never fit together, and the only real thing, the only thing that makes sense, is love—

Now that once again Claude nags, scolds, lectures her to carry her passport, to behave herself, don't antagonize the Germans, he's worried sick about her, what was he thinking, not putting her on a boat to America himself, back when he could, *mon Dieu*, what would he ever do without her, his Blanchette—

This imagined uncomplicated future doesn't seem possible, after all.

Blanche had thought that the one good thing that had come from this nightmare was that, at least, she and Claude were finally over all the—*Frenchness* of their marriage. The stupid arrogance—and inability to keep his pecker in his pants—of the French male, as embodied by her husband. He'd sworn, he'd promised, that day in his office, when he first voiced his fear about the Germans, that he was through with *her*. That

Blanche was the only thing that mattered to him, from now on.

Ha!

A month ago, when they had just turned off the lights for the night, the phone in their suite rang once, just once, and Blanche wondered if it was a signal of some kind. Then she chided herself for imagining that everything these days is a sign or a code or a portent of impending doom, and not simply an accident or a coincidence.

However, Claude leapt up out of bed at the ring, but didn't attempt to answer it; instead, he threw on some fresh clothes and splashed cologne on his face. "Your mistress?" Blanche teased, for she didn't really believe it. And so it was like a slap across her drowsy, stupidly contented face when Claude, after only a moment's hesitation, said, "Yes."

And left.

Just like that.

And it happens again and again, and it isn't always a Thursday, like it was before the war; the phone will ring its one ring of betrayal any day of the week now and Claude runs off, eager as a teenage boy, no longer the beaten-down man, barely recognizable to her, who'd first returned to the Ritz. No, Blanche's husband is newly energized, filled with purpose—a man's purpose: sex, vitality, vanity—and she knows the reason why.

And is it even the same "her"? Or is this a new one, maybe a fräulein instead of a mademoiselle, for the city is lousy with sleek blond German secretaries, all of whom make themselves up to look like Marlene Dietrich?

Blanche has no idea, and when she taunts Claude, baits him, tries to get him to reveal more; when she throws a bottle of precious perfume across the room, runs to the door to prevent him from leaving, calls him a bastard, a son of a bitch, and every other name she can think of—all he does is press his lips tightly together, gaze at her sadly, and push her aside on his way out. To *her*.

And Blanche—the American who married a French man and finds herself, in a time of world-upending chaos, unable to leave, is, for the first time in this marriage, unable to punish him. And worse, reliant on him, the man who cheats on her, for her very survival.

But Blanche has to torment her husband somehow; it's the price she must extract from him, the bounty that keeps her own morals in check and so, one day, she leaves the hotel. She hurries down the narrow rue Cambon, around toward the wide open Place Vendôme. It used to be filled with a long line of the most luxurious cars you could imagine, Rolls-Royces, Bentleys, all accompanied by chauffeurs in livery, standing idly by or polishing the chrome while they waited for their owners inside the Ritz. Now, the only cars in view are the hated black Mercedes with the taunting swastikas on the doors. And an absurd number of tanks, as if, should the Allies invade, the Nazis plan to make a last stand at the Ritz.

Blanche makes her way through the Tuileries, damp and cold today, some late-blooming flowers—mums, roses—still valiantly giving their all. No longer does she stroll the Champs; it's too full of Germans playing tourist—snapping photos with their cameras, posing with civilians who try to smile, forced as they are to pose with their captors—so she ducks across it, walking narrower streets, passing café after café with the words written, accusingly, menacingly, on blackboards perched on the sidewalk: *Les Juifs ne sont pas admis ici.*

Jews are not allowed here.

These signs are everywhere now; the Nazis "encouraged" all store owners and café owners to put them up. Chalkboard by chalkboard, letter by letter, Paris is turning into Berlin. The street signs are being replaced: German names for the streets are on top, with the French names in smaller print on the bottom. German films primarily play in the cinemas. Radio Paris, as well as live music—the string quartets of the Ritz or the brassier bands in the Luxembourg Gardens—is now an odd combination of works by Strauss followed by works by Debussy. German music to educate the French as to the superiority of the Aryan race, but French music—dutifully performed by artists such as Maurice Chevalier and Mistinguett—to pacify them and keep them in their places. Although, according to Claude, the Nazi officers who walk around singing snippets from Wagner in public, privately, in their suites, play records by American artists like Glenn Miller and Tommy Dorsey.

No jazz, however. All the black musicians who were so popular in clubs such as Chez Bricktop before the war, like Louis Armstrong and Cab Calloway, packed up their horns and left right before the Nazis came; their "black music" has been outlawed altogether. Even Josephine Baker, so beloved here, skipped town in a hurry, once the invasion started.

Every Sunday, as if they think it's a special treat for the citizens, the Germans march up the Champs. Regiments of soldiers, their black boots striking the pavement, rifles against their shoulders, heads held high. Every Sunday, this damned parade. Just to remind Paris—as if it could ever forget—who, exactly, is in charge.

Synagogues and temples are empty. Curtains in the Marais—the poor Jewish quarter—are always drawn tightly. Lest the light from the Shabbat candlesticks escape. Lest a chant be heard.

Blanche doesn't walk in the Marais very often these days. She used to; it reminded her of parts of New York, the vendors and the men in their long black coats and tall black hats, the women with their heads covered. There was a time when she sought the Marais out, more often than she probably should have, for reasons she couldn't always explain.

But no more. Blanche can't bear to see the Nazis pounding on doors. The first time she witnessed a family—they spoke German, so they probably had fled to Paris only a couple of years before—herded into a truck, the children crying for a misplaced pet, the parents with terror and resignation both etched into their faces, she flattened herself against a wall, her heart beating so confusingly that she heard her pulse in her ears. She had seen images of this in newspapers and newsreels, before the Germans came.

Blanche couldn't believe, however, that it was happening on the streets of Paris. She couldn't comprehend that she was one of a group of Parisians watching this, horrified, but also untouched. As if this was a play, happening to actors. Not people. Not people who breathed the same air as she did, who ate the same bread, who drank the same water. Because if this was happening to people, not actors—

It could happen to her, too. To any of them.

That day, she rushed back to the Ritz; even though the same uniforms she'd just seen on the street doing despicable things were present

166

there, too—standing sentry at the front entrance; strolling the Hallway of Dreams, deep in discussion; off duty, their hats removed, their jackets folded over their arms, walking up the stairs of the Cambon side with certain French guests or signaling for a drink in the bar—still, she felt safer.

Was it because Claude was there? Or because it wasn't quite so hard to pretend to be who she had to be, in the rosy, flattering light of the Ritz?

Blanche shudders as she passes a Nazi soldier now, patrolling the sidewalk of the avenue Montaigne; he nods at her, and she nods back, and it is such a normal exchange, yet it still feels strange. Menacing. But he's just a foot soldier, nobody important; she tries to forget him as soon as they pass.

This is rather a posh neighborhood, and she still can't believe she convinced frugal Claude to lease an apartment here. The luxury fashion houses—Patou, Vuitton—are all dark and boarded up; their owners have fled somewhere, wherever the wealthy of France with an ounce of sense *have* fled; sometimes Blanche imagines them all on an island in the Mediterranean, running out of champagne and turning on one another, burying one another in the sand.

She inserts her key in the front door of their building, and nods to the concierge, a nasty old woman who has never liked Blanche, who looks startled to see her. Then she climbs the stairs up to the fifth floor, and lets herself into their apartment, calling out, "Elise? Elise, it's Madame Auzello."

Claude has forbidden her to come here, explaining that despite the ever-present Germans, it was still safer for them at the Ritz, where they could not be taken in the middle of the night without anyone knowing, and where they would always be assured of food and electricity.

But now, Blanche knows better; she knows exactly why Claude has tried to keep her away. It's not as if she thinks she's going to catch him in flagrante delicto; Claude is too Catholic to have an affair during the day, when it would interfere with work. But even if she knows she's not going to see anything she shouldn't, she still had to come. The need to punish, to defy something, someone—because good God, Blanche is damn sick and tired of not doing anything, simply watching and accepting and crying into her pillow at night about Nazis, Jews, Claude, all the people gone, Lily, Pearl—is too strong to ignore. She *has* to do this, this insignificant gesture, but still it is an act of rebellion. Because if she doesn't, she knows that one of these days she will do something more foolish—perhaps even kick a Nazi right in the balls—and then Claude will really have something to worry about.

So will she.

Elise dashes out from the kitchen, pale, clad in a plain black dress. She looks as startled as the concierge did; she gapes at Blanche. And she does not, Blanche notes sourly, appear as relieved as she should, to see Blanche alive and well after all this time.

"Madame Auzello," she finally manages, her voice hoarse.

"I thought I'd—I thought I'd see if everything was intact. And I wanted to thank you for taking care of the place, of course." Blanche stiffens and tries to sound imperious, because at the moment she feels like an unwelcome guest in her own damn house.

"Oh, madame, it is nothing. It is my pleasure!" Elise curtseys, nervously; she's never curtseyed before.

Blanche smiles, puzzled—what does Elise want her to do, give her a knighthood?—and looks around; the furniture in the sitting room is draped in the same dust covers she draped them in before they left for Nîmes, the chandelier is encased in a sheet, too. The fireplace mantel is bare, as they'd packed away the trinkets, the candlesticks and mantel clock, objects from Claude's childhood home that he'd inherited after his father passed away before the war. Their few paintings—a small Picasso that he gave them a deal on, one of those odd Cubist paintings from Gerald Murphy, the usual watercolors of flowers that are in every single Paris home—are stored away in the attic, so the walls are bare. But negatives of the paintings remain; the paint is slightly darker where they used to hang.

Behind her, Blanche is aware that Elise has scurried away and she hears heavy footsteps, a thud or two, coming from the bedroom. Elise is probably removing any evidence of a "she" that is not Blanche, and Blanche allows her; it's not Elise's fault that Claude is a pig, so there's no reason to involve her in this little escapade. And that's all it really is; it's not as if Blanche is searching for physical evidence, a tube of lipstick that isn't her shade, a negligee in a size either too small or too large for her. She doesn't need to see, to touch; objects won't make her any angrier than she already is.

Besides, if she knows anything about Claude, it's that he's meticulous to a fault.

Still, to allow Elise her little adventure, Blanche takes her time inspecting the dining room—the china is still in the buffet; they hadn't had time to pack it all away—and the compact, tidy kitchen that remains the lone cheerful place in the house, as it's warm from the oven and smells of garlic and rosemary.

Finally Blanche makes her way back to the bedroom; everything appears undisturbed. The bedspread is smooth, the night tables empty except for a few personal photographs, including one of Claude and her on their wedding day, and she can only hope Claude has the decency to turn the photo away when he makes love to—*her*.

Blanche picks up the photograph and stares at it; she wore a smart dress in the twenties fashion— oh, Lord, that dropped waist looks so old-fashioned now! Claude wore a pinstriped double-breasted suit. They looked happy. Gobsmacked, actually—as if they couldn't believe their good fortune in finding each other, as if the world was too much for them in that moment, and all they could do was grin like idiots, so stunned were they.

With the photograph still in her hand, Blanche rummages through her wardrobe, retrieving a couple of dresses, placing them and the photograph in a small hatbox she finds on the bottom, and prepares to leave. She has no idea what else to do; at least, tonight at the Ritz, Claude will see the photo and know that she defied him and went to the apartment, and that will have to be enough. For now.

"*Au revoir*, Elise. I can't say when I'll return, so until happier times." Blanche embraces the tense woman, and to her surprise, Elise returns the gesture fiercely, kissing her on both cheeks.

"*Au revoir*, madame. I will remain here until— until I no longer have to." She has tears in her eyes, and her gray hair, scraped back into its usual severe knot, has come undone a bit.

After one last wave, Blanche descends the stairs, emerging onto the avenue once more. Strolling slowly, she dangles the hatbox from her finger; while she wasn't eager to remain in the apartment, she's in no hurry to get back to the Ritz, either. And Blanche has lost any delight in simply wandering the streets as she used to—as Claude taught her to do when he was wooing her. Back in 1923.

Back when she was the only woman he could even see, in a city full of them.

"Paris is not to be hurried through," he'd said, holding Blanche's hand when she let him. "Paris is like a beautiful woman—like you, Blanchette. She must be savored. Like you." And then he'd nibbled her neck, and her stomach dropped, and suddenly she was dizzy—the man and the city, in that moment, became so mixed up in Blanche's mind, so entwined, that she wasn't sure which one she was falling for.

Sometimes she's still not sure, if she's telling the truth.

But J'Ali—he knew. Oh, boy, did he know.

"That man!" J'Ali paced up and down his room in the Hôtel Claridge, his face ugly with rage. Blanche had an arm full of clothing; they were leaving the next day for Egypt, and he'd told her to start packing.

J'Ali—impossibly handsome Prince J'Ali

172

Ledene, who had picked her up off the floor of a film studio in Fort Lee, New Jersey, and promised her a star-studded, Arabian-Nights-filled future—had arrived the week before, and Blanche had immediately forgotten all about the dapper, lecturing little Frenchman. Or so she'd thought, while J'Ali and she had a fabulous time driving all over the city in his Stutz Bearcat, going to the races at Longchamp, dancing until four A.M. in clubs in Montmartre, screaming in delight at the Moulin Rouge. Quivering with delight in bed.

But the week was over, and Blanche was packing to go to Egypt. To be a film star. To be a—

Well.

"What man?" Blanche dropped the clothing on a chair.

"That Frenchman. That *desk clerk*." This last, dripping with disdain.

"Claude—my—Claude?"

"Yes, Claude. *Your* Claude. What did you do before I arrived, Blanche?" J'Ali gripped her arm, hard; she cried out but he didn't release it. "What happened between the two of you?"

"Nothing! I mean, he simply showed me Paris, that's all. You were gone, remember? You left me here alone."

"That's all—he was only a tour guide? Why did he come up here a moment ago? Why did he threaten me, as if he had a right?"

173

"What do you mean Claude came up here?" Now Blanche was panicking; after all, she barely knew this Claude Auzello. Was he one of those Frenchmen you read about in novels, going about threatening duels? She couldn't imagine Claude—priggish little Claude—doing so, but what did Blanche know? He *was* rather passionate, at surprising times; she blushed, remembering his touches, his kisses, his whispers.

J'Ali, glowering at her—noticing her blush—was more obvious. He *definitely* was the kind of man capable of a duel.

"That little man. He came here and said he would not allow me to take you to Egypt."

"He—what? How did he even know our plans?"

"I told him, when I was arranging our transportation. So he came up here and threatened me—*me!* Prince J'Ali Ledene! That little frog!"

J'Ali had dropped her arm, but she didn't care to placate him. She was too angry; angry at J'Ali, angry at Claude. Furious at these ridiculous men, each claiming to own her in some way. Didn't she have a say in anything?

"Excuse me." Blanche spun around and marched out of the room, J'Ali shouting after her, "Where on earth do you think you're going, woman?"

"Wherever the hell I want!" She jabbed at the button for the elevator, rode it down to the lobby and strode right into Claude Auzello's office.

He was seated behind his desk, pouring himself a glass of wine. He looked brooding, angry— until he saw her. Then he bolted up, knocking over the glass of wine, which spilled all over the papers on his desk, and Blanche saw that he was desperate to mop it up and save what he could, but instead, he chose to rush to her.

"Blanche . . ."

"No." She held out her hand. "No. What right did you have to talk to J'Ali? What right did you have to tell him I couldn't go with him?"

"The right of a man of honor. A man in love."

"Honor? Love?" Blanche laughed. "You pompous little ass! What do you know of J'Ali? What do you know of me? Nothing. Maybe J'Ali's a saint. Maybe I'm not deserving of any man's honor—or his love."

"You don't believe that," Claude said, his dark blue eyes piercing through her armor.

"No," Blanche admitted. "But I'm still angry with you."

"You will never be honored as long as you're with that man. You will be dragged all over Europe just as you've been dragged all over Paris to those clubs he likes, those absurd jazz joints—"

"How did you know where we went this week?"

"I—" Claude adjusted his collar, as if it had suddenly become too tight. "I—"

"You were following us, weren't you? I knew it!" Blanche would have laughed had she not been so furious—it was ridiculous, like one of those Keystone Kops movies. Dignified Claude, skulking behind trees.

"I did, yes. Because you needed me to—you needed someone to look out for you."

"You have no idea what I need. I'm not some innocent little lamb being seduced by the big bad wolf. I know exactly what I'm doing. You men! You think you own us!"

"I don't think that, Blanche, but I hope—I hope you will see that you belong here, with me. I hope you will see that I will treat you like a goddess, a wife—not like a whore, which is the only kind of woman that man understands. Which is what you'll be, if you stay with him. The whore of Europe."

Crack!

The sound shot through the room like gunfire; she heard it before she knew what she was doing, before she saw her hand drop back to her side, before she felt the sting.

"Oh, Claude, I'm sorry, I'm sorry!"

For Blanche had slapped him across the cheek, and his eyes had tears in them. Tears, and disappointment. Disillusion.

"Oh, Claude!" Blanche started sobbing, torn in

two—how could she have hurt him so? It killed her to think that she had—and this realization stunned her, caused her to look at Claude as if he'd only now come into sharp focus; as if the entire week they'd spent together, he'd merely been an idea, not a person. Because she knew she would not feel sorry if she'd slapped J'Ali; in fact, she had, more than once. But she'd only felt that the bastard had deserved it.

But Claude—he did not. Claude was noble, dignified—*honorable.*

And he saw her as the same.

Blanche's shoulders shook with sobs and shame, and somehow Claude's arms were around her and she was resting her head on his chest, surprisingly broad and stronger than it looked beneath the stiffly proper attire. Her eyes were closed and he was cooing soothing words in French that she didn't understand, but yet—she did.

Of course she understood. That this man, in this moment, loved her. That he wanted to rescue her from something she hadn't understood she needed rescuing *from.* That he saw something in her of much more value, worth, than did the prince upstairs—

"Blanche!"

They sprang apart; J'Ali was in the doorway of Claude's office, and someone was behind him—the director of the Hôtel Claridge. Claude's superior, Monsieur Renaudin.

"J'Ali! What are you doing here?" Blanche felt her face; it was blazing. She was a boiling pot of unexpected emotions.

She was also more than a little thrilled by it all.

"I'm making sure this little frog is sacked. For fraternizing with the guests."

"I did not fraternize. I am in love. I am honorable." Claude addressed Renaudin instead of J'Ali. "I love this woman, and I want her to marry me. This man has no honor. He treats her like a concubine."

"Claude—" Renaudin began to speak, but Blanche had had enough.

"For God's sake!"

The men stopped their glowering and their grunts, and all three looked at her.

"I'm nobody's woman, I'm my own self, and I will not be discussed this way. Claude, I'm sorry I got you involved in this but you're at fault, too. Monsieur Renaudin, please don't sack Claude, though."

"Blanche—" Claude began to speak, but she shook her head and marched over to J'Ali.

"Blanche, I swear, if you slept with this man, I'll—"

"You'll what?"

"I'll murder you, then him."

Renaudin gasped, but Claude only paled. Slightly.

"Oh, J'Ali." Blanche had to laugh; he looked like an actor in a bad drawing room comedy, glowering, pacing, turning to look at her with such theatrical gestures. *He* should be the film star, she thought. His entire life was like a melodramatic costume picture, what with his talk of camels in the desert, moonlight filtered through palm trees.

And harems.

"Swear it, Blanche, as if I had the Koran with me. Swear you'll never see this man again."

"I won't do it."

J'Ali looked at her in astonishment; so did Claude. And even gripped in this undertow of swirling emotions, Blanche couldn't help but register the differences between the two. J'Ali was so handsome—the strong eyebrows, mesmerizing brown eyes, chiseled chin. Claude was not so handsome—he didn't really have much of a chin at all, to tell the truth—yet he was very attractive, radiating such quiet authority.

Such—honor. Integrity.

"What? You refuse me—me, J'Ali Ledene?"

"Yes. Furthermore, I have something to ask of you. Forget about the contract, forget about making me a film star. Tell me the truth. Will you ever marry me? I need to know. I need to understand what you have planned for us. For the future."

"Blanche." J'Ali's voice—that rich, plummy

179

voice, Arabian Nights with an Oxford education—dropped low. Oh, Blanche knew that voice; she fell asleep dreaming of that voice when he wasn't with her. She also knew its intent—seduction. Lies. Pretty, pretty lies. "Blanche, my angel of angels. Let's not worry about the future. We have each other now. And tomorrow, you will be on your way to Egypt, and you will have your own barge on the Nile just like Cleopatra, as befits the most popular movie actress in the world."

"Oh, J'Ali." Blanche let out a deep, tired sigh. She was weary; weary of the fantasies, the "pretties," as her mother used to call elaborate fabrication, intended to soothe. Blanche had fallen in love with someone who told her beautiful bedtime stories. But it was time to wake up. "No, J'Ali. Tell me the truth. Now. Will you ever marry me?"

"Blanche, it's not that simple. My father, my religion, yours—it's impossible. You know that, Blanche—don't pretend that you don't, that you haven't all along. I've never made a false promise about that."

"No, you haven't." Blanche admitted it to herself, finally. "So what will I be to you in Egypt? What will I be in the eyes of—well, everyone?"

"My lover. My angel of angels."

"Your mistress. Your whore."

"Those are your words, not mine."

"But you don't dispute them."

J'Ali looked pained; he shook his head.

"Then I'm not going with you. I should have decided this long ago." Blanche stood on her tiptoes, kissed his cheek. "Goodbye, my love."

Slowly, she turned to Claude.

Who looked—stunned. Stunned by joy or terror, Blanche wasn't exactly sure and for a moment, she was frozen with the fear that she had chosen very, very badly. Until Claude Auzello held out his arms, and she walked right into his embrace, put her arms around his neck, pulling him close, kissing him passionately, feeling him melt into her as she did into him.

When at last she came up for air, J'Ali was gone. But the hot little office was suddenly filled with bellhops and chambermaids who were all clapping and cheering and toasting to true love, while Renaudin stood beaming like a proud father.

Claude pulled her to him, his arm strong, possessive about her waist as she buried her head in his chest, embarrassed but content—and oh-so-dazzled by the sheer romantic theatricality of what had just transpired. So dazzled, her vision wasn't quite to be trusted—she realized that, later.

But at the time, she saw only where her future lay.

In Paris, this magical city she never wanted to leave, this city that had cast a spell upon her. In Paris, with Claude, *her* Claude, she'd called him that without knowing exactly why. Her knight in shining armor, her Don Quixote, tilting at windmills—and princes—for her.

Whatever happened next didn't matter; she believed that just as sincerely as she believed in the gallantry of Frenchmen.

She was wrong about both these things, as it turned out.

CHAPTER 14

CLAUDE,
Autumn 1941

For the first time in their marriage, Claude sometimes hesitates when he leaves his wife at night. Especially after the nine months away at Nîmes, just the two of them actually living like other husbands and wives, no room service, no gay, glittering gossip, no late-night calls from sexy duchesses.

The first time the phone had rung, just once, Claude did pause; his wife's innocent gaze when he turned on the light did give him a troubling moment of doubt. But finally, he answered the summons; he had instigated the assignation in the first place. Although in his defense, he had no way of knowing precisely the outcome of that initial, fateful meeting; he had no idea of the depth of the entanglement, the longevity of it.

He only knew he was grateful, because finally, for the first time since the invasion and the disgrace of laying down arms, defeated, he feels like a man. A French man.

The day after the Auzellos returned to the Ritz after their journey from Nîmes, they were paid a visit—"A courtesy only," he said, smiling smugly—by Colonel Erich Ebert, a typical Nazi type. He sported close-cropped white-blond hair, a mustache, and was stocky but solidly muscular.

"I have heard much about you, Monsieur Auzello," he said, taking a chair in their suite even though they hadn't offered one. Claude shoved his hands into his trouser pockets; at that moment, he made a vow. He would never shake a German's hand. He would treat them courteously as befit the director of the Ritz, do their bidding as far as morally possible. He would not visibly make waves; he would not endanger any employee, Madame Ritz herself, or most vitally, his Blanche.

But he would not shake their hands.

Fortunately, Colonel Ebert did not appear to notice this slight. Blanche hastily shoved some lingerie—she had been unpacking—into a drawer, and she sat down, too. She was pale but composed; she took a Gauloise out of its pack and just as the German reached into his pocket to take out a lighter, she quickly lit a match herself. The German put the lighter away, with a short laugh.

"I am grateful you speak German, Herr Auzello," the man continued. "I wish that I spoke French. You are most gifted in languages, I understand."

184

"You do?"

"Yes." Colonel Ebert reached into his attaché case and produced a sheaf of papers. "This is your dossier. We know all about your—commendable—service in the Great War, and your command of the garrison at Nîmes. We admire how you handled the General Strike here in Paris. We could not find a more excellent director for the Ritz, so we are pleased to have you continue."

"Thank you." Claude barely got it out; being forced to thank a German for allowing him to continue at his job!

"For now, at any rate," Ebert continued, grabbing one of Blanche's cigarettes for himself; she opened her mouth, but caught Claude's look and closed it. "General von Stülpnagel will be arriving here shortly, and he may make changes. Who's to know?" The man shrugged, as if Claude's entire livelihood was merely a minor annoyance. "One more thing." Ebert held up a page with the word *Enjuivé* stamped across it, in menacing black ink. "The Ritz is famed for its hospitality, but we will not allow Jews to strain that hospitality any longer. Let them stay in their hovels. They are no longer welcome here, although we are pleased that your hotel has never been completely welcoming of them. You were born in America, were you not, Frau Auzello?"

Claude, struggling to keep up with the man's abrupt change of subject, glanced at his wife; she took a few quick draws on her cigarette.

"Yes."

"How is it you speak German so well?" Ebert picked up another sheaf of papers—her dossier, Claude assumed—and shook it at her. "Our soldiers were most impressed with you yesterday."

"I speak German and French, as well as some Italian. What can I say? I have an ear."

"Where were you born in America?"

"Cleveland, Ohio."

"I have been to America myself, once."

"Oh? How nice."

"Yes. I took the train from Chicago to New York once on your Fourth of July. Alas, I did not see any of your famous fireworks."

"That's a pity, but I'm not surprised."

"Oh, you know that part of the country?"

"Yes, as I said, I was born in Ohio." Blanche dangled her arm—holding the cigarette—over the back of her chair. She puffed again and looked at Ebert with unconcealed amusement. As if she were a cat, and he a mouse. "In fact, you could have looked out the window of that train and seen my house. I often used to listen to the trains at night. At least, until my family moved away, to New York. I suppose that's when I developed my ear for languages. Our neighbors, now that I think of it, spoke German. They were originally from Munich, I believe."

"What a pleasant coincidence. I hope you learned some of our beloved customs."

"I have a fondness for schnitzel, if that's what you mean."

Ebert laughed at that (to tell the truth, Claude almost did, as well); he gathered up his papers and shoved them back in his case and left with a sharp salute and an assurance that they would be seeing much of him in the future.

As soon as the door closed, Claude grabbed Blanche by the shoulders; he wanted to shake her, he was so furious at her insouciance—but also, more than a little admiring of it. Instead, he pulled her fiercely to his chest, as if he could keep her there always and protect her from the evil around them. After all, he rescued her once.

But even Claude doubted that he could do so again, under the circumstances.

"You idiot," Claude whispered. "You beautiful idiot! You were actually teasing that man."

"He didn't know that." She giggled into his chest. "God, Claude, you were white as a ghost when he started questioning me. It's a good thing he wasn't looking at *you!*" But she stopped giggling and released an enormous, shaky breath. She was not as strong as she sometimes appeared; Claude always had to remember this about his wife.

"Blanche, be careful—it is more important than ever, now. Think of—"

"The Ritz?" she asked, wryly. But there was a darkness in her gaze: Accusation. Resentment. "It's always about the Ritz with you, isn't it Claude?"

"I didn't say that! You didn't give me a chance—but yes, of course, the Ritz. Remember my position. It's particularly precarious now."

"As if you'd ever let me forget it." She pushed him away, tidied up her hair.

Claude hesitated, but then he consulted his watch; he had a hotel to run, and he had no idea how to do it under these circumstances. Rationing, Germans, a skeletal staff, secrets, secrets, secrets; the enormity of the task ahead suddenly settled across his shoulders, and he knew that even he, Monsieur Auzello, director of the Hôtel Ritz, would stumble a little before he figured out how to distribute its weight. "Blanche, I'm sorry, I don't have time right now—"

"Well, I see one thing hasn't changed." She picked up her still-lit cigarette from the ashtray and inhaled quickly. "The Ritz calls, you run."

"Blanche, it is my job—a job that I hope, God willing, will keep us safe and feed us during this time. But please, one more thing—I believe that man was lying about not speaking French. They will be listening, all the time. Even in the bar. We were lucky today, but we must be cautious in the future."

"Oh, Popsy!" She resumed her unpacking. "You worry too much."

"Because you don't worry enough," Claude retorted before he left to try to figure out how to run a hotel when the majority of its guests were the hated conquerors of the staff.

Soon after the Auzellos' return, postal and telephone service resumed. Ration cards were distributed to all citizens—including the German military—and a curfew enforced. General von Stülpnagel, a man with a sharp nose and face and a permanently suspicious air about him, arrived amid the pomp and circumstances the Nazis insisted on displaying to the conquered citizens at every opportunity—a lineup of officers along the front steps leading to the Place Vendôme, a military flourish, clicking heels, drawn swords. Accompanying him was Hans Speidel, his chief of staff. Speidel, Claude liked, despite himself; he had a round face made rounder with rimless spectacles, and a warm, easy manner. But Claude guarded against this feeling, naturally. For the man was still a Nazi.

Göring, he of the marabou feathers and morphine, commanded the Imperial Suite when he was in the city but also took over an enormous mansion on the outskirts of town. So many wealthy Parisians were displaced by the Germans commandeering their lavish mansions that some decided to live permanently at the Ritz for the duration, like Coco Chanel (whose garishly decorated suite was relocated to the rue Cambon building), the film star Arletty, assorted citizens who had answered the door in the days after the invasion and found themselves agreeing, after an extremely persuasive conversation, to trade their homes and paintings and silver and antiques and family heirlooms for an indefinite stay at the Ritz. It was surely a better bargain than many in Paris were getting these days.

Despite the orders from the high command that Paris carry on as usual—the theaters reopened, Maurice Chevalier and Mistinguett were back performing in the cabarets, and Edith Piaf sang her sad songs—most Parisians in those first days and weeks were too appalled, too shell-shocked, to think of laughing again. Claude could not understand why these performers would take the stage for the Nazis—who were eager to be entertained in the fashion Paris was best known for—until Blanche pointed out that he was doing the same thing, in a way.

"But it's my job," Claude said curtly. "And what would happen to me—and more important, to you—if I refused to do it?"

"If they refuse, what do you think the Germans will do to them?"

Claude had not thought of that. Although it

still seemed wrong to him. And he began to comprehend, then, how murky it all was going to be; how many choices Parisians were going to have to make on a daily basis, questions they would have to ask themselves that had no correct answers. Yet if you blundered, if you made the wrong choice, you would likely be thrown in prison for a few days. Or worse. And if you made what appeared to be the right decision for now, how would you be held accountable for it in the future?

Claude had no answers. The only thing that mitigated his misery was that he knew no one else did, either.

At the Ritz, von Stülpnagel ordered a sumptuous banquet his first night there.

"I will do my best," Claude assured him, detailing the fresh flowers that the Ritz could provide, the musicians they would arrange— for heaven knew there were fresh flowers in abundance, and musicians with too much time on their hands. In many ways, Claude reminded himself sternly, this was simply another banquet held at the Ritz. Another revelry for him to plan.

But there was one small catch.

"I will need your ration books, naturally."

Von Stülpnagel looked down his sharp nose at Claude.

"I hardly think that is necessary. These are all

the highest-ranking officers. You will provide us with the type of banquet the Ritz is famous for, Herr Auzello. This is why we decided to keep you on."

Claude did not reply; he simply bowed and left to arrange it all.

But when the doors to the banquet room were opened the next evening, revealing perfectly set tables groaning with flowers, crystal shining, silver gleaming, a string trio playing Strauss in the background, the Germans sat down and waited for their food.

They waited, and they waited.

"Again, Herr von Stülpnagel, I must have your ration stamps before I can serve you the food. It is in the very orders you have given." Claude tried not to betray his nervousness—more like terror—as he whispered into von Stülpnagel's ear. But he felt this was an important thing to do; to show them that the Ritz was still a hotel, not their command headquarters. All guests at hotels and restaurants were now required to present ration books with stamps to be collected. Claude felt that if the Ritz was going to survive, they would treat the Germans as guests, not occupiers. Their most valued, exalted guests, true—guests who carried weapons with them and had the power to throw any one of them in jail, or worse—but naturally, that is how the Ritz had always treated its guests, from kings to film stars to couples who had saved everything to spend their honeymoon night in the very smallest room.

And the Germans—please, God—would respect them (and him) for that, and not, in the end, loot all the silver and the wine and the paintings and the linens; they would not destroy or even desecrate Monsieur Ritz's palace. And that was important to Claude, God help him, even in these times—particularly in these times. It was vital that this beacon of Paris, this iconic jewel, this world-renowned symbol of French taste and hospitality, remain as it was before—unsullied by German hands.

So Claude held his ground and tried to conceal the tremor in his fingers as he straightened his tie and waited.

"Fine, Herr Auzello." Von Stülpnagel—after a quick consultation with Speidel—laughed. "You are right to ask. My aide will retrieve them and present them to you. However, from now on, here at the Ritz we will provide our own food from our own warehouses so we won't have to bother with this ration book business."

"Perfect," Claude replied, thinking rapidly. "And I am happy to assist in procuring the finest vegetables and the freshest meats for those warehouses. After all, I have my connections with the local suppliers, and you do not. Shall I arrange to do this for you?"

"Of course." Von Stülpnagel waved him away. Claude fairly danced out of the room, quickly told the staff to bring the damned Nazis their food and ran to his office. There, he picked up the phone and arranged to have the largest lorry he could find out back in the morning. He would fill it up with food for the Germans—

And for all the rest of them on the Cambon side, and all his staff, and if there was any food left over, he would arrange for it to be distributed to those most in need. And in that way, everyone at the Ritz would survive.

There is one other thing Claude needs to do, however. One other burning desire he needs to fulfill, in order to survive however long this occupation will last; it cannot last forever, please, God. It will end sometime; the Germans always conquer but they never manage to hold on to their spoils for long.

Soon after the banquet, Claude had discovered that all the other fine hotels had been commandeered by the Germans, too. He decided to meet first with his compatriot at the George V, François Dupré, to see how his fellow hotel directors were handling things.

"Claude!" Dupré embraced him with tears in his eyes, bestowing upon him two wet kisses, one upon each cheek, which Claude returned. Despite the fact that the two had not been close friends before, Claude now regarded him as his brother. That is what war can do to men.

They were in the lobby of the Hôtel George V; armed soldiers like the ones posted at the entrance of the Ritz patted him down when he entered and asked why he was there but paid him no further heed. Unlike the Ritz, which did still operate like a hotel, at least half of it, the other hotels were strictly German headquarters; no paying guests allowed.

That day, for the first time since his return to Paris after the bitter defeat, Claude felt himself growing agitated, excited; moved by the new rumors rustling through the narrow streets like the winds of the mistral. There were whispers of group meetings in basements. In back alleys. Outside of town. Calls for resistance. A general named de Gaulle—one of Pétain's former aides—had escaped to Great Britain during the invasion and was making secret radio addresses urging for France to keep fighting, although few heard the broadcasts themselves, only the rumors of them. It was thrilling, it was frightening, it was the backbone the French needed.

"How are you doing, François?" Claude accepted a glass of brandy from a rattled young waiter; Claude studied him, then shook his head. This young man would not be working here long. Far too nervous a disposition.

"Ah, Claude, it is terrible, is it not? What

has happened? *Mon Dieu*, I still cannot believe it even though I saw it with my own eyes, that day. Germans, marching beneath the Arc de Triomphe!" Dupré, to Claude's dismay, was obviously one of those who had already given up. While some citizens were finally stirring after the stunning shock of the invasion, others remained broken. There had been many suicides since the tenth of May. Dupré was gray, his hands shook as if he were eighty and not fifty. His eyes were red-rimmed, as if he wept day and night.

But he was still the director of the George V, a man Claude had long admired.

"We who run the hotels, François, are in a unique position, are we not? We have ringside seats to everything that goes on in the German high command. We will most likely know who is meeting whom, when someone is posted elsewhere, when troops are moved around."

"So?" Dupré only shrugged and picked at a thread on his cuff—in fact, his cuffs were most obviously frayed—and Claude was astonished, for he'd never seen his colleague look anything but pristine.

"I don't have a definite idea, but don't you think—" Claude glanced around, and lowered his voice. "Don't you think this is something we might be able to take advantage of? This knowledge?"

"Claude, Claude." Dupré trembled all over; his

head, his hands, his knees. He raised his watery eyes to him. "Claude, you are young, still. You are a man. I understand your passion. But I cannot share it."

"I am only ten years younger than you," Claude snapped. "We are French, still. We must do *something* to remind ourselves of that." Claude's voice had risen, and German faces turned his way; he sipped his brandy and forced himself to calm down. "We cannot simply display our famous French hospitality to the *Boche.* We must not roll over like the Army did, the Navy—our so-called leaders living like moles underground in Vichy. Moles, blind to the light—that is not for us, we men, we leaders."

"I admire you, young man." Dupré sounded sad, however, not admiring. "But I cannot agree with you. France is lost—*mon Dieu*, I never thought I would say that in my lifetime. The Germans are the victors. Now let us find a way to live as the defeated."

"I am sorry to hear this." Claude had not truly known what he was seeking—was he looking for advice? Words of rebellion? Simply a confirmation that Frenchmen were still men? One thing was certain: He had not come looking for this. "*Au revoir*, François."

"*Au revoir*, Claude."

Claude left him to his sorrow—good God, the man's very clothes reeked of despair and cowardice, and Claude almost held his nose as he proceeded to the other hotels, where he encountered the same despicable, vile-smelling odor of defeat, to a man. And he was finally reduced to walking along the Seine, sputtering to himself like an idiot, calling them all names he'd never imagined calling his fellow Frenchmen, most of whom had served, as had he, in the previous war. *Idiots. Toads. Pigeons. Fools. Children.*

Cowards.

He collapsed on a bench and caught his ragged breath; he was on the Left Bank, across from the Île Saint-Louis. Notre Dame took up its usual bulk of the evening sky. The bells had been silenced since the invasion, and many of the newly restored stained-glass windows had been removed and hidden somewhere, lest the Germans decide to treat them as souvenirs. It was shadowy in the twilight; the lights were out, as they were out all over Paris. The gargoyles were mere smudges, hard to discern. But shadowy or not, it was there; reassuring in its ancient history, dating back to the twelfth century when Paris was just a muddle of wooden huts and rickety buildings, when cows walked in the streets and people believed in saints and sorcerers, both.

What did the saints think of them now? Looking down on Paris from their high perch; watching as first its citizens fled when the gray-green uniforms goose-stepped in, then came crawling back, heads cowed, spirits broken?

And where were the sorcerers? Besides de Gaulle, Claude could think of no one who could break this spell of defeat and cowardice. And de Gaulle was on the other side of the Channel. He did not have to walk, as Claude must from now on, upon soil that was spongy with defeat.

"*Pardon.*"

Standing in front of Claude was a young man. He was wearing a leather motorcycle jacket, pegged trousers, a silk scarf around his throat.

"*Oui?*"

"You are Monsieur Auzello of the Ritz." This did not appear to be a question; indeed, the stranger seemed delighted with his perspicacity. He snorted a small laugh, took a last draw on a cigarette, threw it to the ground and crushed it beneath the heel of his boot.

"Who are you?" Glancing around, Claude perceived that no one else was near, save a young couple nuzzling each other's necks on the bridge nearby. Ah, some things did remain the same—Claude was unaccountably aroused, and he shifted his legs, embarrassed; there was one way, at least, in which he could feel like a Frenchman. He was surprised by the thought, but he did not dismiss it.

"My name is Martin." The man turned his back to Claude, appearing to study Notre Dame, watching a few shadows scurrying about its foundations. A boat *putt-putt*ed in the river on the other side; behind them, cafés and nightclubs emitted their usual music and laughter, muted because curfew was at nine o'clock and it was almost eight.

"I do not wish to know your name," Claude replied curtly, hoping the stranger would find him rude and leave. It was not the time to make new friends, not when they might be taken away in the middle of the night. For already there were rumors of people simply disappearing; stories of hearing cries behind closed doors, cries silenced by German voices.

"That's a pity." Martin still didn't turn to him. "Because I believe I have something to say that you would like to hear. Man to man—*Frenchman* to *Frenchman*."

Claude had been half-rising, but now he froze.

"I also understand," Martin continued, still so casually, "that you have a wife. An American."

Claude sat back down again.

"I am very good with wives." Martin chuckled. "Personally, unlike your friends, I am not interested in playing dead until this is all over. I see in you myself—a man, looking for adventure, for romance, women, eh? Perhaps even opportunity in treacherous times. Would you care for me to elaborate?"

How did this stranger expect Claude to answer?

Even if he hadn't mentioned Blanche, Claude would have stayed. For here, at last, was a Frenchman.

But since he did mention his wife—his American wife—Claude had no choice but to remain. And listen.

Claude Auzello had listened well. He took notes. He made plans.

And now, he is a man again.

A Frenchman.

CHAPTER 15

BLANCHE,
Autumn 1941

"Madame!"

Blanche looks up, surprised to find herself back in the dim nightmare of the present instead of the rosy romance of her past—surprised, even, to find herself still holding the hatbox she'd taken from the apartment. She's also disoriented; she's no longer on the avenue Montaigne, but instead has turned down a side street. Slowly she recognizes it; it's full of familiar little shops—a cheese shop, a wine shop, a patisserie. She used to spend time here, back—before.

"Madame!"

Someone is beckoning to her, head swiveling back and forth in a doorway, looking out for something. Or someone. It is an old man, standing in the doorway to a chocolate shop. In his hand, he holds a box of chocolates, wrapped in a pretty ribbon.

"Madame, for you. Please. Come—a gift."

"What?"

"Come—I give you a gift!"

"What on earth do you mean?"

"A gift! Of reunion!"

She shouldn't; she knows she shouldn't. Hasn't Claude told her that often enough? Hasn't she heard the stories of people—ordinary citizens—snooping around where they didn't belong, and then disappearing? But she can't help herself; she decides to investigate. Glancing around to see if anyone else is watching, she follows the old man into his shop, where he thrusts the box of chocolates at her and says, excitedly, "You are American, I remember! We haven't seen you in so long."

"Yes, well . . ." Blanche has no idea why he's so damn happy to see her; it isn't as if she'd been his most frequent patron. To tell the truth, she rarely bought chocolates here; there are better places nearer the Ritz.

"Come, come." He grabs her hatbox and hops—one leg seems stiffer than the other—toward the back of the shop, which appears to be empty. She follows—she has no idea why, except she's curious. What an odd little fellow.

"Here!" He opens a door—a storeroom, windowless—and shoves her inside. "Look," he says, accusingly.

There, seated at a table, is a young man in clothing far too big for him: a thick fisherman's sweater, tweed pants, gaping boots. He's pale, gaunt, reddish-blond hair sticking up all over his head. He blinks at Blanche, as surprised to see her as she is to see him.

"Speak to him," the old guy urges Blanche, and a younger man—introduced to her as the proprietor's cousin—nods eagerly. "Talk to him in English. He doesn't understand French."

"He showed up at my door," the cousin says, rubbing his hand all over his face. "I cannot be responsible!"

"Hello?" Blanche says in English to the boy, and he immediately bursts into tears. The other three look at one another in alarm.

"Oh, Christ, I'm sorry!" The soldier wipes his eyes, shuddering. "It's just been so bloody long since I've heard my native tongue."

"You're British? What happened? Why are you here?" Sitting down, Blanche accepts a tumbler of red wine from the old man and wishes it was something stronger.

"Got shot down months and months ago, and I've been hiding from the Krauts ever since. Passed along from place to place like a parcel, trying to get back home. Last night I missed my contact, or he missed me, and I knocked on this bloke's door." He points to the cousin, who shakes his head morosely at his bad luck. "I don't think he's happy about that."

"No." Blanche glances at the other two, twitchy, agitated as oil in a hot skillet.

"You will help? Take him?" the cousin asks her in French.

"Now?" the old man adds, desperately.

"What can I do?" She asks it twice, in both English and French, and no one has an answer in either language. So she stands, paces a bit, pausing to study the airman. He's so boyish; even though he hasn't shaved in days, there's very little stubble on his thin cheeks that still have a babyish softness to them. He's so young—

He could have been her son.

"OK," Blanche says, taking charge; and once she makes the decision she realizes she's excited, energized, despite the danger that surely lies ahead.

Because finally, she's contributing; finally, she's *acting*. Not passing by the walking wounded, merely pressing money into their palms. Not plastered against a wall, a silent witness to a family being destroyed before her very eyes. This time, she's doing something—something—

And then she realizes. She really has no idea *what* to do. But she suspects she knows someone who does. "May I make a phone call?"

"If you think it's wise." The old man shows her an old-fashioned stick phone on a wobbly end table. Dialing the Ritz, she identifies herself to the new switchboard operator—a German girl, naturally—and asks to be patched through to the bar. She'll have to be very careful; Claude has warned her that the Germans listen to every conversation.

"Frank? Frank, is that you?"

"Blanche?" There's a noisy din in the background, but it's Frank Meier's voice on the other end. Frank, who can provide.

Anything.

"Frank, I—I have an unexpected guest. You know how terrible the mail has been, he sent a letter, but it never arrived. The thing is, I don't have—I don't have room for him, and I thought you might know someone who does."

There is a pause; she hears the clink of glasses, the shaking of ice, the language of Nazis. Spatzy bellowing his hearty laugh in the background.

"And where might this guest be?"

"We're buying some chocolates for him to take back home. Seven rue Clément-Marot?" Blanche looks at the old man, who nods, a broad smile of relief on his weathered face.

"Sit tight," Frank replies, hanging up.

Plopping back down on her chair—nervous perspiration causing her blouse to stick to her chest so she airs it out and asks for another glass of wine—Blanche stares at the clock. For agonizingly long minutes, no one speaks; the young airman actually puts his head down on his arms and is soon snoring. The two Frenchmen gape at each other in astonishment, then a bell dings; the old guy leaps up, Blanche's heart pounds, but as soon as he hops back up to the front of the store, she relaxes; it's only a customer, a woman buying some candied orange peels with black market Reichsmarks. Blanche hears him wait on her and, finally, his uneven footsteps leading back to the storeroom.

She jumps up, knocking her chair over in her relief. For it is Greep who is with him, Greep who looks at Blanche, then at the young man who has raised his head, sleep in his eyes, and nods.

"*Allons.* We get to work."

"What do you mean?"

"There is a place. A barge, on the Seine. It is a contact point. If he gets there he'll get home, God willing. I can take him there."

"You?" Blanche studies him; Greep looks like, well—Greep. She's known him for close to twenty years, this small, gnarly magician; he's one of Frank Meier's "friends," a specialist in the lost art—or so he says, with a sad shake of his head—of forgery, the last of his kind. Do you need a death certificate for an inconvenient body, but don't wish to contact the authorities? Greep will provide. Do you need a marriage certificate in order to collect a widow's pension that you haven't legally earned? Greep will provide. Do you need a new passport, perhaps, one with a different name, a different country of origin, a different religion?

Greep will provide. For a price.

Greep smiles, jumpy as ever; he's a caffeine addict, originally from Turkey, she thinks. Maybe? Like Lily, Greep is not one to talk

207

much about the past and it occurs to Blanche, for the first time, that this is something she has in common with the mysterious, scrappy refugees she seems to be drawn to lately. Blanche notices the permanent ink stains on Greep's right forefinger and thumb and can't help but smile. But an expertise in forgery isn't what's required here, is it?

"You've done this before?" Blanche asks, dubiously. "You've—helped in this way?"

"I've done it once. With a friend."

"Where is that friend now?"

"Ask the *Boche*. I haven't seen him since they captured him." Greep laughs, as if this is a colossal joke. He wipes his eyes—they are streaming tears of mirth—and says, only a trifle more seriously, "There are German sentries along the route, so we should go soon, while it's light. They don't stop as many people in the day."

"But what would you do if they did stop you?"

Again an amused shrug. "Run!"

The young airman, even though he speaks no French, looks alarmed at this; his eyes are big, bright, and terrified.

"No." Blanche decides in that moment. "No, I'll do it."

"You?" It seems to her that all four men say it at the same time, in the same language.

"Yes, me. I speak German. Does anybody else?"

No one answers.

"Right. That's what I thought." Surveying her clothing—plain, nothing special, just a skirt and a blouse and sensible shoes—she decides it will do. The boy—well, there's no hope of getting a German soldier's uniform for him, even as Blanche is fairly certain that Frank Meier could provide this, too. But in his current attire, which is hanging off his bony frame, the young Brit can pass for an invalid. He's certainly pale enough; Blanche wonders when he last saw the sun.

"He's a convalescing German soldier, that's what he is," she explains to Greep and the other two. "And I'm taking him out for his daily walk. If the *Boche* ask any questions, I can answer; they'll think I'm his German nurse. And he's fair, too." She appraises the young man, who looks at her with absolute trust in his eyes. Trust Blanche hasn't yet earned and might not, of course—so many obstacles lie ahead she can't bring herself to count them all—but she represents his only hope. He has no choice but to convince himself that she will succeed.

She has no other choice, either.

"Tell me where I'm taking him again?"

"A barge. It's a place for crippled pigeons— you'll see. Beneath the Pont d'Austerlitz."

"All that way?" How long can Blanche keep this young man from crumbling beneath the strain? He's already been through hell, and he doesn't look as if he'll be able to bluff his way out of any situation.

Greep shrugs. "It is what it is."

"All right." She beckons to the boy, explaining it all in English. "I'm your German nurse. You are a German soldier, sick, being taken out for his daily walk. If anyone talks to you, just say *Jawohl*, do you hear me? Nothing else. Not a single word. You can nod, you can shake your head, you can sneeze or cough, you can say *Jawohl*. But I don't care if anyone points a gun at you, I don't care if you see me stand on my head or start speaking gibberish—you don't run, do you hear me? And you don't say a word of English."

"I don't think I can do this," he says softly. His eyes begin to fill with tears. Christ, he can only be about nineteen or twenty. What this fucking world is asking of boys like him fills Blanche with enough rage for the two of them.

"You can. You were in an airplane shooting down at these bastards. You can walk right through them now. I'll do all the talking." She places a hand on his shoulder; he's trembling. "Trust me."

And when she says it, she's filled with an otherworldly calm—almost spiritual. Not based on anything she's ever experienced before; if she were a different person she'd say it was the spirit of her ancestors, guiding her. Or maybe the spirit of Lily, somewhere.

"OK." It's time to move; Greep's right. They don't want to be out when the sun starts to set. Blanche gathers up her young ward, nods to Greep and reminds him, "If I'm not back at the Ritz by midnight, tell Claude," and waves farewell to the two Frenchmen, who are clutching each other and weeping with relief at seeing their burden taken from them so quickly.

She's almost out the door before she remembers something.

"I'll take those." Sprinting back to the store-room, Blanche retrieves the chocolates the old man had waved at her, ages ago now, but in reality, only forty-five minutes have passed since she left the apartment. "You gave them to me, after all. I'll be back for the hatbox."

Tucking the chocolates in her handbag, she steers the young man out the door, and then they are walking. Walking out in the sunlight, he squints at it, his eyes tearing up at its radiance; he must have only known night, all these months. Yankee Blanche is walking through German-occupied Paris with a British pilot and they could both be shot, no questions asked, if they're found out. But the sun is shining—it wasn't, before; the trees are so beautiful with their reds and golds, leaves crunch beneath their feet, warm chestnuts are being sold on corners, children are playing in gardens. It's such a pretty day, she almost remarks upon it—in English, and thank Christ she bites her tongue just in time. And Blanche tastes blood, and it reminds her that flesh is permeable, bones can be broken, veins slashed. Ashes to ashes. Dust to dust.

Still they walk. Her legs are much steadier than her nerves; they appear to know exactly where to take her. The pair trots down to the Métro station at the Champs; Blanche chooses a car with only a few German soldiers in it and she prods the young man into a seat, while she stands, makes a decision, and clears her throat before she speaks.

"*Es ist immer so überfüllt, nicht wahr? Nicht wie zu hause.*" Blanche turns, with a shaky but charming smile (she hopes!), to a German soldier, his gun in his holster, holding on to the pole next to her. He grins, even as she spies, out of the corner of her eye, her young soldier tense.

"*Ja, immer. Und auch schmutzig,*" the soldier agrees with her.

Blanche offers him a chocolate; he takes one with a smile before turning back to his companion and they begin to discuss how terrible the postal service is between here and home, and her young man relaxes. Blanche doesn't venture anything further with the Germans; suddenly she's shaking, too. But she thinks—she desperately hopes—it was enough.

Blanche and her "ward" get off at the Bastille stop; keeping a firm grasp on the young man, Blanche forces him to walk slowly, not bolt as she senses he's gearing up to do; she reads it in his face, the panic, the desire to flee. She feels it in his muscles, so tense and hard, she could strike a match off them.

She feels it in herself—she could outrun a panther, the way the adrenaline is pumping through her. She's soaking wet; her blouse is once again sticking to her chest. But she holds on to him and keeps them both going, slowly but steadily. Occasionally she instructs him, loudly in German, to rest, and he understands because each time, she nods at a bench. So in fits and starts they make their way through the quieter streets toward the Pont d'Austerlitz, one of the more ugly *ponts* in Paris. Even Claude has never been able to muster much enthusiasm for it. Instead of the charming, flower-bedecked little houseboats that are tied up closer to the heart of the city, here are industrial commercial barges. Blanche searches them, looking for a clue, and finally she spies a smaller one, with a birdcage hanging from a pole on the front. And in that birdcage are two birds with broken wings; the wings are bandaged, and they hang loosely by the sides of the birds' bodies.

"The crippled birds," Blanche whispers in English.

The airman's pupils dilate, and he looks where she's looking.

"There. You see?"

He nods.

"You have to go there on your own. It wouldn't make sense for a woman to accompany a simple barge worker onto his boat. And that's exactly what you look like. You shouldn't be questioned, now. You're home free."

"I don't know—I don't know what to say," he begins to stammer, and dammit if she doesn't have a tear in her eye, a warmth in her heart that's never been there before. She shakes her head; she won't allow him to see her this way. She's not his mother. He's not her son.

But as she pushes him away, and watches him walk slowly, hands in pockets, head down, across the *pont* to the other side, and then shuffle down the steps leading to the river's edge, and finally step onto the barge and disappear from sight, she realizes she doesn't know his name; never once has she asked. So desperately does she now need to know this that she almost dashes across the *pont* herself. She desires a connection—something that will outlast her memories of this extraordinary adventure. Something that will link her to another human being, whom she helped; truly helped, not passed by or stood watching from afar or merely showered with money. If she has his name, she can write it down and one day—dear God, surely one day this will all be over?—look him up, or maybe he'll come back to find her, but no, he doesn't know her name, either.

But she understands that it's better this way. Better for both of them, should—should the thing she can't bring herself to contemplate happen. So Blanche turns, blinking away her tears, and walks briskly back toward the Ritz. It's a long walk, but she can use it.

She needs to be above ground. Among the living, among the hunted, among the *doers*. For she finally feels, after these long months—after these long years, all the years of her marriage, even—as if she's taken her rightful place among them.

"Claude, I—" She bursts through the door of their suite once she's back at the Ritz, after she's smiled broadly at Frank Meier behind the bar, who grins back in relief. "Claude! Popsy—you won't believe what I just did—"

"Where have you been?" Her husband glares at her, then consults his pocket watch, old-fashioned, just as he is. "It's late, you've been gone for hours. Where have you been, you selfish child? Did you not think of me, how I might be worried about you? But no, you think only of yourself, don't you?"

Her husband. Once her savior. His face is tight with anger. He doesn't see her: Blanche—Blanche the Bold, Blanche the Brave. Blanche in Need of a Good Strong Drink. No, he can only see his wife who is so much trouble, so much of a burden these days. After all, he has a hotel to run, a hotel full of Nazis he has to bow and scrape to, run and fetch for. He has no time for her antics, Blanche the Disappointment, Blanche the Nag—hasn't he told her this, time and again?

Her words—of accomplishment, of pride, of bravery—flutter to the ground, unspoken. Claude can't see them there, these broken, ruined things, stillborn.

But Blanche can. She steps over them on her way to the bathroom where she shuts the door and heaves into the sink. Outside, in the bedroom, the phone rings once.

The room to their suite opens, closes.

When finally she emerges from the bathroom into the empty suite, she can still see them there on the floor, her words, her story. The story she will never share with her husband now.

For it's far too good for that cheating bastard.

CHAPTER 16
CLAUDE,
Autumn 1942

The phone rings, that one telling ring. Claude glances at his wife, who is dressing to go out, for reasons she hasn't made clear. It's late afternoon, too early for dinner, although he had intended to take her out somewhere, even if it means using up all his ration stamps to do so. Normally, they dine here at the Ritz, of course; that's the whole point of remaining here, there is always leftover food from the Nazi banquets for staff and their families; food that doesn't require a ration stamp.

But there's something new to Blanche these days, both a recklessness and a brooding quality, and it worries Claude almost as much as it angers him. As if he has time for one more worry! She sometimes starts a conversation, one Claude senses she has wanted to start for a long time, then abruptly stops herself. She speaks more boldly—sometimes rudely, sometimes playfully—to the Germans, especially her old friend Spatzy; she flirts with him so brazenly, Claude fears that Chanel will one day push his wife down the stairs. He himself is of two minds about this new development: On the one hand, if she plays nicely with the Germans, there's a greater chance she won't bring ruin down upon them all. On the other hand, Claude detests seeing her cozy up to them as if they weren't evil to the core.

Of course, he imagines she detests seeing him do the same.

The other day, while they were in the restaurant (the only room on the Place Vendôme side where civilians other than hotel staff are allowed; it is insulting, to have to be patted down by armed guards every time he crosses that long hallway that links the two buildings), von Stülpnagel sat down, unasked, at the Auzellos' table.

Naturally, they could not tell him they wished to be alone; there is no such thing as being "off duty" to the Germans these days. The Ritz employees, all of them, are now the Nazis' adjunct staff. Claude, of course, is used to being treated casually by the rich and famous. But before, he was well paid for the honor and, for the most part, they were decent people. There is no honor now. And little pay.

As for decency, that word has no place in the world in which they find themselves.

"Claude, my friend," von Stülpnagel said, waving his arms expansively; the German seemed genuinely happy to see him.

"And his lovely wife," the man added, still smiling; was he drunk? "The *American*. Now our enemy, too. So many enemies of the Reich." He nodded at Blanche, his eyes half-closed, and he almost sounded sad.

"Thanks to the Japs," Blanche said coolly, fingering the long stem of her glass of wine; Claude stiffened, afraid she might be tempted to throw it in the man's ruddy face. "They're responsible for finally getting America into the war."

"So you wanted your country to fight us before?" He leaned forward, made an effort to open his eyes wider, as if he were merely curious. Claude couldn't figure him out—was he laying a trap for his wife? Claude clutched his knife tightly, watching von Stülpnagel, searching his face. But the man didn't seem menacing at all, only slightly tipsy and in a surprisingly expansive mood.

"As astonishing as it might be, Franklin Roosevelt doesn't actually consult me on these issues," Blanche replied with a shrug Claude could only admire.

Von Stülpnagel laughed; he actually slapped the table in delight. "A witty woman! You are a lucky man, Herr Auzello. I know a lucky man when I see one because I am lucky, too. My wife, you should meet her. She is almost as charming as your wife." The German inclined his head at Blanche, with a courteous bow.

Blanche gave Claude a look of surprise, which he returned. Neither knew what to do with their dinner guest, who was now beckoning to a waiter and asking for some brandy.

But one of the other officers, seated at the next table, had heard their conversation for he rose, raised a glass and exclaimed, "To Washington! Our next conquest—*Heil Hitler*!"

Blanche was trembling; her hand clutched the stemware of the glass so tightly, Claude was afraid it might break. He could not reach across the table to grab her; von Stülpnagel was between them, glaring at the officer who had risen. Almost with reluctance, it seemed to Claude, von Stülpnagel rose, too, lifted his glass and mumbled, "Heil Hitler." And the entire restaurant filled with Nazi officers did the same.

"Excuse me," Claude said, getting up from his chair, quickly pulling his wife out of hers and propelling her toward the door, even though they'd only had their soup. "I realized I've not yet ordered tomorrow's fish." And with a bow—he detested himself for it, he saw himself as if from above doing this despicable thing, bowing to the Nazis, but decades of being in this industry betrayed him; Nazis or not they were, still, guests of César Ritz—Claude propelled his wife out of the dining room.

As they reached the armed guard standing at the beginning of the long hallway back to the rue Cambon side, the young man grinned at them, tipped his hat. "Good evening, Frau Auzello."

"Good evening, Friedrich," Blanche replied tightly, but then she sighed and paused. "Did you get a letter today?"

"Yes!" The boy beamed and reached inside his pocket. "Would you like me to read it to you?"

"Some other time." Blanche allowed Claude to continue dragging her back down the endless marble passageway. "What's your hurry, Claude?"

"I—I was afraid you might say something foolish."

"You mean tell the damned Nazis what I think about their chances of taking Washington?"

"Well, yes."

"Oh, boy, wouldn't I like to do just that!" She threw him off and marched away, and he had to run to keep up with her. "I just may do that, now that you mention it." She pivoted and started marching back toward the hallway, but Claude grabbed her just in time.

"Get your damned hands off me!"

"No, Blanche, no. Not here."

"Why the hell not? I don't give a damn about your precious Ritz, Claude Auzello! How can you keep bowing to them like a servant? I don't care how charming they are—I don't even care about Friedrich anymore, he's just like them, isn't he, even if he is just a boy, a boy like—" And then, to Claude's astonishment, his wife began to weep, bitterly. "Oh, it's just so damn sad, Claude. So damn wasteful. What can I do?"

Finally, he got his weeping wife up to their rooms—she wanted to stop in the bar but as it was full of officers off duty, he wouldn't let her— where she was free to rage and fume at him, at the Nazis, at all men in general. "You all act like big brave beasts, pounding your chests and grunting at each other but it's only because you're all weak, you're all pretend; and meanwhile here I sit and it's not enough, it's never enough"—until she finally fell asleep, her makeup streaked, her lipstick faded so that her mouth looked like an Impressionist brushstroke.

Claude sat down, wiped his brow, eased his breathing. She was right, of course, in the abstract—it was a shame, it was a waste, a horror, men were, indeed, just as she said and more. Men were awful, himself included.

But in the reality in which they were trying to live, trying to survive, his wife could not have been more wrong. She must remain aloof, she must sit and watch, for her own good as well as his—and the Ritz's.

Would he be able to avert a crisis like this next time—avoid a raging Blanche shouting like a lunatic, perhaps revealing things she shouldn't? The fact was that he did not trust his wife, particularly when she drank. He had never been able to trust her in the ways a man should be able to trust a spouse: to be discreet, to soothe instead of ruffle, to put his needs before hers, to understand and comfort. There would surely be more moments like this in the future; the combustive combination of an alcoholic American wife plonked into a nest of viperous Nazis made it inevitable. Claude could see them all, an endless parade of little bombs that only he could defuse. And he did, for the very first time, wonder if he—the unflappable Monsieur Auzello—was up to the task.

He wondered if his own wife might, in the end, be the downfall of the Ritz, his Ritz, his wartime assignment—that was how he looked at it now. He might not have a battlefield assignment in the truest sense, but he viewed his responsibility to see the Ritz through this safely, keep it and its staff intact, alive, in exactly that way.

His assignment. His responsibility. His duty. As a Frenchman.

The phone stops ringing, and Claude must answer its call. He is a man, after all; a man in whom war has stirred up familiar longings.

Blanche—in the act of putting on her earrings—stiffens. He flinches before she can even say a word or pick up the closest item to hurl at him—he throws his arms up, to protect his face in anticipation of the battle to come. A battle that is ancient, moth-ridden; an old play, the two of them actors wearily saying their lines, going through their paces for an audience that has fallen asleep.

Tonight, however, it appears that Blanche has gone up on her lines. She is silent.

Claude lowers his arms.

Blanche starts humming a little tune, something from a theatrical production, maybe American—it's faintly familiar to him, but not enough so that he would know the words. She continues to make herself up, putting on her lipstick, blotting it with a tissue, doing that odd thing she does—she puts her index finger into her mouth and pulls it out, and wipes the lipstick off her finger, too. She claims that by doing this, her lipstick won't get on her teeth.

She then steps into a pair of shoes and reaches for her purse.

"Have fun tonight, Claude, darling. Tell her hello, give her a good time—oh, and don't wait up for me!"

"Where—where are you going, Blanche? You know I don't like it when you wander the streets. You never know what might happen—"

"Too bad, Claude" is all she replies as she sails out the door with a bright smile.

Claude, for once, is at a loss for words. He does not know the dialogue for this particular play. He sits on the bed, befuddled.

And then, immediately, suspicious. What did she mean, "Don't wait up"?

As violently as he desires to run after her and ask—or to trail her like a spy, like he once did back when J'Ali was squiring her about Paris—he cannot. Someone is waiting for him.

He splashes on some cologne, straightens his tie, combs his mustache, opens a closet, retrieves a notebook from a coat pocket. Claude locks the door of the suite and descends the curving stairs, glancing inside Frank Meier's busy domain, hoping, for the very first time in their marriage, to see his wife seated at her table, bending her elbow.

She is not there.

Frank Meier might know where she is, and Claude is halfway to the mahogany bar before he stops himself; it would never do to share his marital concerns with Frank, who, after all, is technically Claude's employee. No, that would never do; it's bad enough when his and Blanche's quarrels attain decibel levels that cannot be contained by the walls of their suite.

So Claude spins on his heel and pushes his way out the door, out of the hotel. He really has no other choice.

Because someone is waiting for him.

CHAPTER 17
BLANCHE,
Autumn 1942

Lily is back.

The note—delivered to Blanche with a bouquet of violets—says to meet her on a bench at the flower market, although it doesn't say which one. But the only market Blanche knows well is the one on the Île de la Cité, near Notre Dame, and that is where she goes this late afternoon, after first deciding—oh, good God, the look on his face!—to bedevil her husband and ruin his evening. What came over her, what imp whispered into her ear, she has no idea; she's just tickled she did, and wishes she'd done it years ago. Why not torture him as he tortures her?

Why not let the bastard believe that she has a lover, too? It will do him good to think that. It will do her good to let him. And it isn't as if she's not thought of taking a lover before.

It's just that she's never been able to bring herself to. Because there are things about her husband, she is forced to admit, that she loves. And unlike the French, Blanche was raised to believe that love and sex very much were synonymous. It's a habit she's never been able to break—the Puritan in her (in all Americans, according to Claude) is too strong.

But she loves the way he presents himself—to her, to everyone. Even if Claude has a day off and plans only to sit with her in their apartment, reading, he shaves, he splashes his face with cologne, he grooms his hair, he dresses impeccably. Blanche can't help but be touched by his arraying himself like this, just for her.

She loves the way Claude reads through the mail first, in case there's something in it that might upset her. She loves the way he settles her into bed before they make love; he must fluff the pillow, arrange the sheets perfectly, arrange *her* into them with the delicacy of an artist deciding upon the perfect frame for a finished painting. She loves how he takes care of her needs, before his.

She loves how he reads a book, even—slowly, licking his finger to turn the pages with great care, always using one of his beautiful leather bookmarks with his name embossed upon them, making notes in a special leather-bound notebook, the pages gilded. Watching him read sometimes reminds Blanche of how he makes love, to tell the truth. And she's never in her life met a man who could turn her on simply by turning the pages in a book.

She loves her husband, goddammit. But that

doesn't mean she isn't savoring the triumph of making him wonder about her.

By the time Blanche crosses the Seine, however, her husband is no longer on her mind. She takes long, sure—masculine—strides, impatient to walk through the pretty little market full of blossoms and birds in cages, songbirds mostly, vivid with blue feathers, yellow. Blanche, despite her fear of birds, finds them charming, for she'd never seen anything like them back in the States. Although they don't always sing, and they don't always look happy, still the collective impression of these cages, filling tables, hanging from poles, is one of delight. It is so very *Paris*.

She selects a bench near the water and faces the market. And then Blanche sees her. Darting through the crowd, laughing before she even gets to Blanche, wearing her usual costume of mismatched clothing: a plaid scarf wrapped sloppily around her throat, black lace gloves, a baggy green woolen skirt, an aviator's leather jacket, far too big on her.

Blanche stops herself from jumping up and waving; after all, Lily might be under surveillance; Frank Meier had hinted at this, when he delivered the note and the violets. And of course, the market is patrolled by the usual German soldiers, pausing now and again to flirt with the country girls minding the stalls under the watchful eyes of their papas. So Blanche remains where she is, looking straight ahead, until Lily sits down beside her.

Lily's hand reaches for Blanche's. Their fingers entwine, and Blanche's heart skips a few beats before racing to catch up.

She had resigned herself to never seeing Lily again. Lily was dead, vanished; eulogized and buried in Blanche's mind, her presence rationalized, filed away—she was just a woman Blanche had met on a voyage. A funny, strange little thing who made her laugh, that's all. They knew each other for such a short time. People do that, of course—they come into your life, illuminate some dark corner you'd not even known was there, then they disappear. True connection is rare, but that's just the way it is.

And yet, now that Lily is back, Blanche can't contain her happiness. That rare, precious connection between two people who understand each other without having to explain it—she hadn't imagined it, after all. Because after only one glimpse at Lily, Blanche knows that now, something good—or at least, something exciting—will happen. And Blanche needs that. Since her escapade with the British airman— that's how she thinks of it, as an escapade, a lark, trying to downplay in her heart and mind how recklessly dangerous it was—she's been restless.

But it wasn't merely a lark. What she'd done *was* dangerous. It was important. She had been courageous, resourceful. She had saved a life.

And she's aching to do it again.

Ever since that incredible afternoon, she's wondered how she can truly get involved in what people are starting to call, whenever the Germans aren't within earshot, the Resistance. She even sought out Frank Meier about it, in a café near the Palais-Royal on a rare day off from the bar, but he'd raised his hand to silence her even before she could complete a sentence.

"Nothing doing, Blanche," the big man said. "I was glad I could help you—that time. But Claude would murder me in my sleep if he found out I got you involved further. And you know the reason why."

"Yes, but—"

"Blanche, I don't envy you. I know it looks like you have everything but you and I both know that you don't."

Her cheeks felt hot; she was overwhelmed by his confession and so she studied her coffee, to hide her face. To disguise how touched she was that someone saw her, truly. Someone recognized her loneliness, her restlessness—and knew the reason at the root of it.

"But Claude—your husband is my employer. I hide a lot from him and I don't mind that I do. But you, well, you're different. You're his wife, and he cares deeply for you and worries."

"He has a strange way of showing it." But she

didn't elaborate. Frank—who knew everything that happened at the Ritz—surely was aware of Claude's nocturnal activities.

"I'm in no position to judge anybody" was all Frank would say about that, and the subject was closed.

That didn't mean she was content to resume her shadowy seat on the sidelines, relegated to watching the horror unfolding all around her, hidden by the brocade curtains in the Ritz. But she had no idea who else to turn to, who else to ask how she could do more.

Until Lily sits beside her again.

At first, Blanche thinks she's simply going to gossip about where she traveled, how she got her new cropped haircut, what the wine was like in Spain. The kind of conversation that Blanche is accustomed to, at the Ritz.

So it takes a few moments for her mind to catch up; it takes a few moments for her to register that Lily is telling her fantastic stories not of sightseeing and hotel rooms but of battle, of gore, of nights spent in caves with peasants, of bombs falling from the sky. She mentions someone named Heifer, someone named Muscat.

Lily tells her of making love in the open air with Robert at night, after fighting, their guns on the ground beside them.

And Blanche imagines that love must be sweeter, when death is so close you can touch it.

Now Lily is telling her about Paris, it seems—Blanche has to concentrate, so overwhelmed by the pictures in her head that she hasn't been keeping up with the torrent of words flowing from her friend's mouth, as if she cannot stop them, as if they've been locked deep within her until this moment when Blanche hands her a key. Blanche studies Lily, suddenly concerned, and sees, finally, how thin her friend is, how pale, how her eyes burn with fury.

Lily is talking about a man now. A man who made a noose out of the tricolor flag and hung himself off the Pont de l'Alma the day after the Germans marched into Paris. And nobody stopped him, not even her.

Apparently, Lily and Robert joined forces with students in the early days. They fought back when ordinary French citizens, too stunned by the tidal wave that had swept over them, could not.

"How is Robert?" Blanche finally has to stem Lily's words; they are too terrible. "I hope I can meet him this time. You were in such a hurry to leave for Spain—"

"Robert," Lily interrupts, "is dead."

"Oh, Lily." Blanche's eyes sting with tears—absurd, she thinks, to mourn someone she's never met. She's shaken by her emotion, when Lily's eyes are as dry and unblinking as a doll's. So Blanche studies a bird in its cage, in an end stall of the market. It's a mustard-colored bird with iridescent blue on its wings, and it hops up and down, from its perch to the cage floor, over and over as if it's having a fit.

"Early days," Lily continues, as if Blanche had asked. "Right after the filthy Germans invaded us. Maybe I tell you someday. I pray they fry in hell."

"I know that some of them are terrible, yes, but there are boys among them, boys who didn't want to be here, who aren't as bad as the others—"

"They're monsters, Blanche. Things aren't like in your Ritz now. What's going on in Poland, in Austria—it's happening here, too."

Blanche's stomach churns with revulsion and guilt—right this moment, in all probability, Claude is serving tea to the very monsters who murdered Lily's Robert. And she—why, she had made it a point to tell Astrid how pretty her hair was this morning. She'd sat with Friedrich yesterday while he read a letter from his girl back home—she'd even hugged the boy when he revealed, with big tears in his blue eyes, that the girl had another beau, a soldier in the SS stationed in Berlin.

And Blanche understands that she has to get out of the Ritz. She has to see what is happening in Paris beyond those walls. If she doesn't, how can she live with herself?

How can she atone for her lies?

"Seeing you is good for me," Lily says, and Blanche is touched, deeply, although she knows she doesn't deserve Lily's friendship. "And I have other lover now. He hates the Nazis, too, and he has bigger plans, fine plans." She wipes her nose with her sleeve, refusing Blanche's offer of a handkerchief, and grins. But her freckles are like black ink spots against her pale skin.

"But he's not like Robert, is he?"

"No, Lorenzo is not my man. He is just *a* man. There is difference."

"And don't I know it." Blanche sighs, knowing that for her, Claude has never been "just a man." He is infuriating, pompous, possessive, immoral. All the things J'Ali had been—all the things "a man" is. But in the beginning, at least, Claude had been so much more.

"Come meet my friends, Blanche. Well, not my friends, not like you—these people, I don't care about like you. But we have fought together. And that does something, you know?"

"Battle brings people together. Claude's told me so many times."

"But I also—I also have to ignore them—how you say? Deny them? If I have to. I have to leave them behind, for bigger good. I couldn't do that to you, Blanche."

Blanche looks at her, sharply, not sure if Lily's telling the truth or buttering her up for something, because nothing Lily has said or done in the past has indicated that she has any attachment to anyone other than Robert. And even he, Blanche suspects, could have been sacrificed to what Lily felt was the greater good.

But before she can ask, Lily declares, "Is time, now."

Blanche has a choice, she understands; the moment is upon her, the one she's been seeking. She could use a swig of gin to steady her racing heart, dry her sweaty palms.

Blanche looks around; the market is crowded with German soldiers patrolling, even as some of the vendors are starting to put sheets over the birdcages, preparing to pack up and leave as it's getting very close to evening.

And she watches Lily disappear into the maze of stalls.

CHAPTER 18

CLAUDE,
Autumn 1942

As calmly as possible, Claude strolls out the door, walking the streets—it is getting to be early evening, but he still has plenty of time. So he stops at a café for a glass of wine and to pretend to read the paper that is nothing but Nazi propaganda and lies, all the while wondering about his wife. Where did she go? Why was she so calm, insouciant? Could she possibly have a lover, too? How was that even possible when she's been, by and large, right under his nose at the Ritz all these months?

But no, of course she couldn't. She is his wife. Unthinkable—

So why is Claude thinking it?

He can scarcely sip the wine, his stomach is roiling so, but he realizes that appearances matter. So he drinks it, pays the bill, nodding at a couple of guests of the Ritz who are out and about, too—"It is a fine evening for a walk, is it not, Monsieur Auzello?" "*Oui*, the finest so far this autumn."—and he resumes his stroll, hoping to be able to calm down, shrug away his suspicions. For he has to be able to perform his duties; it is vital that he does.

Passing soldiers who tip their hats to him, Claude remains rather stunned by the politeness their occupiers continue to display, their obvious efforts not to offend the citizenry. Claude has witnessed German soldiers get up and give their seats on the Métro to French women. But it is all for show; he keeps waiting—everyone does— for the shoe to drop, for the Nazis to show their true colors. Especially after that abominable exhibition they held about the Jews—*Le Juif et la France.*

Claude continues his perambulation, all the way over the Seine, to the Left Bank, which is not as teeming with German soldiers as the Right. He makes his way toward the Panthéon, crossing the Luxembourg Gardens, which are crowded with lovers, mothers and their children, the carousel still in operation, a band playing in the bandstand. However, it is a German military band playing beer hall music, loud *oom-pah-pah*s that assault his sensibilities, not to mention eardrums.

Still, Claude marvels at how peaceful, unmenacing, the world can appear while the sun still shines, even if faintly. Nights, of course, are different.

"*Bonsoir, mon ami!*" The young man beckons to Claude from an outdoor café table, shoved against a window. It isn't too far from the coal brazier, so he keeps his gloves in his coat pocket. The younger man rises when Claude joins him and kisses him on both cheeks before they take their seats.

The two women already seated, one blond, one brunette, smile; they wear a little too much paint for Claude's tastes, but they are appealing—noticeable—in their gaiety, their easy laughter, their easier blushes; he kisses them both on the cheek and takes the empty chair next to the blonde.

Claude studies him. There is something so rakish about this fellow, Martin, and Claude's curiosity, as always, is aroused. Devilishly handsome with black curly hair and green eyes, he dresses with panache—always the silk scarf about his neck, like an aviator—and every female within a mile is irresistibly drawn to him. Claude himself has never commanded such attention from the fairer sex, not even in his younger days, and he is man enough to admit that he is jealous of this fellow, especially since he must be at least fifteen years younger. Claude is very glad that Blanche has no cause to meet him.

As Claude orders his coffee, he finds himself wondering, again, what Martin did before the war. (He has no such curiosity about the women, even as the blonde nestles against his shoulder and plays with his lapel.)

As far as Claude is aware, Martin does not have a permanent home, although naturally Claude has no cause to know for sure. They keep those kinds of details from each other, even though Martin is quite aware of Claude's position at the Ritz. And of course, he understands all about Blanche, somehow; it is his bargaining chip.

"I am curious, Martin." Claude decides to ask him, for they have grown to truly like each other these past few months, or so Claude tells himself. It isn't simply that they are business associates in an unusual time. No, even if Claude had met him before (like all Parisians, Claude has divided his entire life, his entire way of looking at people and situations, into before the invasion and after), Claude likes to think that he would have been Martin's friend. Claude admires his associate's mind, constantly churning, seeing three moves ahead of any chess game. His *savoir faire*, his ability to imbue even the smallest movement— like signaling for more coffee, as he does now— with flair.

"Curious about what, my friend?" Leaning back in his chair until it's balancing on the two back legs, Martin smiles, devastatingly, at two women seated next to them, even as the blonde and brunette—Simone and Michele are their names—scowl. The other women immediately giggle and simper.

"What did you do before?"

"Claude, Claude, you understand the rules." Indeed, he does. No personal questions. No one at this table, save for Claude, has a past.

"Claude," Simone purrs into his ear. "You are a naughty boy!" She squeezes his thigh, not unpleasantly.

"Yes." Claude smiles at her, as one does at an irritating child. "But you must allow me. I am a student of human nature. One must be, to run a hotel. And you seem to know plenty about me."

Martin sighs. He rights his chair and leans over the small café table. The lamps from inside the restaurant backlight him so that his curly hair resembles a halo. All about the foursome, people are chatting; there is French music— an old recording of Mistinguett singing "Mon Homme"—it's scratchy, the music thin to the ears, but it is still French. If you try, you can almost convince yourself it is a typical Paris autumn evening; the air carries only waning hints of warmth and the geraniums are starting to fade in their pots, their brave reds and pinks no longer standing out so colorfully against the black wrought-iron railings.

That is, until it dawns on you that dotted among the tables are those gray-green uniforms of the ordinary German soldier, speaking his ugly native tongue. Until you register the absolute absence of motor traffic on the streets. Until you take a good look at the bicycles propped against railings and streetlights and see that the rubber tires have been patched and patched and patched again. That on every table is a ration book. On every French face, every so often, flashes a startled look, as if one has just awakened from a dream. A wonderful, elusive dream.

"Claude, that is fair. OK, my friend. You really want to know?"

"I do."

"He does," Martin repeats to Simone and Michele with a broad grin. The girls giggle and shake their heads.

"Martin is a naughty boy, too," Michele says with a knowing wink. A German officer, two tables away, stares so intently, obviously, at her that she winks at him as well, and the officer—young, glassy-eyed from too much wine—blushes and looks away.

"Yes, I was," Martin acknowledges. Then he leans back in his chair and lights a cigarette. After he inhales and blows two smoke rings, he laughs. "I was a gigolo."

"A—pardon?" Claude nearly upsets the coffee that the waiter has just now set before him; the waiter grins as he walks away.

Simone and Michele laugh their bright, magpie laughs; all around, heads are turned toward them but Claude knows that no one sees anything but the two glittering, gay women and their devastatingly handsome male companion; Claude is invisible. Which, of course, is the point, however it might wound his pride.

"A gigolo," Martin repeats with a shrug. "I could be bought. I *was* bought—heavens, my friend, I am bought still, eh, ladies?" He winks at the two at the table next to them; they blush again and look away. "By wealthy women, mostly. I have been to your Ritz many times, but you never noticed me. I was always on the arm of some matron, some stout *madame* dripping with jewels. It was the matrons you noticed and bowed to. Not the handsome fellow on their arms. That is how I know you, my friend. I am very aware of your reputation, and your business."

"My God." Why does this surprise Claude? Martin is so strikingly good-looking, so confident. Without fear, which would be an asset, Claude recognizes, when dealing with bejeweled matrons in possession of husbands.

"You do not think less of me, do you, Claude?" Martin's eyes betray a flicker of anxiety, which touches Claude. He realizes this man puts a lot of store in Claude's good opinion, and that is flattering, naturally.

"No, no, I do not. What does it matter what we did before? War, occupation—it creates new opportunities for those smart enough to take advantage of them."

"I am glad you see it that way, my friend. Now." Martin takes out an order form from his pocket. The girls, bored, begin to talk about films they've seen lately, as the two men get down to business. "How many apples did you go through this week? And how many do you expect you will need next?"

"Not so many, I'm afraid—only about two hundred. But there was quite a demand for artichokes, surprisingly. I'd say we need three dozen of those."

The two men continue their haggling over vegetables and fruit; produce required for the Ritz kitchen, Martin making notes on the order form, occasionally pausing to consider, flicking the ashes from his cigarette. Claude sometimes reconsidering his needs, changing his mind when Martin, after angrily muttering, lowers a price. It is past curfew before they are done, but they are not in any hurry to leave, now that the haggling is done; the tables remain crowded around them.

Finally Simone, who has gone to the toilet, returns; she does not sit, but instead, she takes Claude's arm and drags him out of his seat.

"Come, it's time, I'm tired. But not too tired," she purrs, and others around them—including a table of German soldiers—laugh, and nod knowingly as the other two rise, as well.

Michele clings to Martin's arm with a cooing sigh, but she ostentatiously cups his crotch and proclaims, "This one is never too tired. *Mon Dieu*, I get no sleep!"

And there is even more laughter; the Germans, Claude has noticed before, are very appreciative when the French act the way Nazis think that the French *should* act. Overly amorous, prone to theatrics.

"Oh, Claude, one thing." Martin, tightening his scarf, lowers his voice under cover of the lingering good cheer from their neighbors. "I hear there are some mass deportations. Just starting, but I have it on good authority. Jews, mostly. Being taken from their homes in the night, entire neighborhoods of them."

Claude shoves his hands into his gloves to keep them steady. He dares not look at Martin, he dares not look at anyone; he struggles to keep his face neutral. "*Merci*, I appreciate this."

"I just thought you should know." Abruptly turning, Martin bends down and kisses one of the two giggling women still at the table next to them while Michele howls her displeasure; the woman turns scarlet, her eyes sparkling, as she gasps.

He winks at her, then at Claude, and with an insouciant wave he and Michele disappear, arm in arm, into the night, so darkly ominous. There is no blackout at the moment, but streetlights are no longer turned on, regardless. Only the light from the cafés illuminate the streets.

Claude, Simone clinging to him, resting her blond head upon his shoulder, which is not at all distasteful, picks his way through the tables, and the couple begins to stroll through the dark streets. Still entwined, they cross the Pont de l'Alma and head up the avenue Montaigne. The avenue is quiet, empty.

Despite all that he is thinking, measuring, calculating, Claude is not immune to the blonde's charms; Simone smells like lilacs, her hair is soft and shining. Like most Parisiennes these days, her clothes are worn, mended several times, but clean and flattering, embellished with little touches—silk flowers, rhinestone pins, bits of lace removed from other clothing. The girl does not wear nylons—few women do anymore—but has drawn seams down the backs of her bare legs with an eyebrow pencil. She is, finally, a woman. A soft, pliant, *convenient* woman.

They reach the Auzellos' apartment building; Claude gazes up, and sees the lamp shining in the window. Just as Claude turns, with a smile, to Simone—she has blue eyes, and a penciled-on beauty mark of which Claude does not approve—a German soldier walks by, rifle slung across his chest.

"Get it over with, or get inside," the soldier barks in German. "It's past curfew, you Frogs."

The two of them stiffen; then Simone turns to the German with one of her brilliant smiles; she tosses her shining hair and wiggles her hips.

"Perhaps you'd like to join us, eh?"

The soldier stops, sputters, almost drops his

rifle. Simone laughs, grabs Claude's arm and they are inside the building before the German can stop his stammering.

"That will give him something to talk about," Simone says as they climb the steps up to the apartment. "He won't forget me anytime soon."

Claude is still a bit stunned, to be honest; he was quite terrified the German was going to take Simone up on her offer. So all he can do is nod as the girl—nonchalant, breezy, brave—begins to chatter about what she plans to do tomorrow: mending a torn handkerchief; meeting a girlfriend for what passes for lunch now, watery soup and maybe a crust of bread; standing in line for some meat—what she wouldn't give for a nice filet of steak, but of course, no one can expect that these days, all she can hope for is that it's not dog or cat. . . .

He follows her up the stairs, and into the apartment.

All the while wondering where his wife will be sleeping tonight.

CHAPTER 19

BLANCHE,
Autumn 1942

Grasping her hand, Lily pulls Blanche through row after row of stalls overflowing with flowers—autumn flowers, lanky sunflowers, giant mums, and purple coneflowers—and then, with one quick glance around, so furtive Blanche almost misses it, Lily tugs her down a narrow aisle toward the back of a stall; she lifts the canvas flap, and Blanche finds herself in a cramped, dark little tent filled with overturned crates, buckets of blossoms in water, straw scattered on the floor. A couple of lanterns emit a yellowish glow; at first, she can scarcely make out the faces watching her with guarded interest.

Perching on the crates are Lily's "friends." One woman, a lumpy, dull-looking girl with her dirty blond hair in braids. The others are all men. All bearded, all wearing hats, fisherman's caps, pulled low over their faces. Their clothes are inconspicuous: workers' clothes. One reaches out to pull Lily to his lap in a proprietary, hungry motion; this must be her lover.

But while Lily introduces her—"This is

Blanche, my friend I told you all"—and fires off their names in return, Blanche understands, by the way they barely acknowledge them, that these are not their real names. She also understands she should not ask why.

The man Lily says is Lorenzo—her lover—continues to stare at Blanche long after the others resume their conversation, and she feels, absurdly, flattered. Perching gingerly on an offered crate—surely not good for the woven silk skirt she is wearing—Blanche listens while the others talk, in hushed tones, in French, in many varying accents. She detects a couple of hard-consonant Russian affectations, a rough Polish accent. None of them appears to be native-born French.

And it dawns on her, slowly, that what Lily and her friends are discussing—"Tomorrow, we will shop for silk scarves at the Galeries Lafayette," "Next week's dinner party will have only four place settings"—isn't what it seems.

It dawns on Blanche—it illuminates her, like a warm shaft of daylight has suddenly penetrated the gloom—that what they are talking about are acts of sabotage.

Acts of *resistance*.

"She might be of help," Lorenzo says once, indicating Blanche. "Look at her, very rich."

"Yes, but—" Lily flashes her smile at Blanche. "Money only."

"Maybe more."

"No!" Lily says decisively. "Not Blanche. I do not want Blanche involved too much, like us. She is my friend, yes, she can help maybe get money because of the Ritz, maybe food or ration books. But nothing more. This is not why I brought her here. She is my *friend*." Lily glares at them.

Blanche blushes; every eye is turned on her, and she feels their skeptical gazes taking in her nice clothing, her silk stockings (darned, but still presentable), her impeccable coif, fresh from the beauty shop at the Ritz. She feels shame at having her privilege exposed like this, the comparative ease of her life; nobody here looks as if they've bathed or had a hot meal in days.

But they do look as if they've struck blows against the Nazis, while Blanche has spent her time playing bridge with them. Despite her clothes and stockings, she is the inferior one here.

Then she remembers her "escapade." She thinks of Claude, a native Frenchman, so damn smug about his country, so pompous—what has *he* been doing since the invasion? Nothing. Nothing except getting his conquerors—his guests—everything they desire. Presenting it to them with a smile and a bow that turns Blanche's stomach.

And she is suddenly itching with anger, with

purpose. *One* of the Auzellos has to defend the honor of the Ritz.

"I want to be part of your group," says Blanche.

It isn't as difficult as she'd thought it would be, after all.

CHAPTER 20
CLAUDE,
Winter 1943

Every day, someone from the Ritz disappears. An absence will be noted at the morning staff meeting. Faces will pale; eyes shift, afraid to linger too long on any one person. Feet will shuffle; a chambermaid might whisper a strangled prayer to the Blessed Virgin. Claude has learned not to ask if anyone might know the reason for the absence.

No one knows anything, while seeing, hearing, everything. This is how it is in Paris these days.

Sometimes the missing staff member will show up in a day or so, amid cries of joy. "A bottle of champagne," Claude will call out, and one will appear from the store they keep hidden, at another location, from the Germans. Sometimes this person will have fresh bruises, raw cuts that will soon harden into thick scars. Sometimes an arm in a sling. Sometimes a hand bandaged, digits missing.

Claude watches this person very carefully, in the days following. He keeps everything that could be used to poison locked up in his desk; he sleeps with the key beneath his pillow. There will be no accidental dose of lye in the soup delivered on the other side of the long hallway. There will be no hemlock tucked in the leaves of a salad. Claude fears this kind of retaliation for the foolishness that it is—one Nazi down, but how many of his employees would they take in return? It is his job to keep these people—*his* people, for it's *his* Ritz—safe, as best he can. What they do on their own time, he doesn't want to know. He doesn't want to care.

Sometimes, however, the missing employee doesn't return. They've learned to give it time—a week, maybe two. After that, Claude fills the vacancy.

But he writes down the names of the missing, keeping that list in the same drawer in which he keeps all poisonous items and the revolver Frank Meier procured for him. Why does he do it? Perhaps he has some vague idea of trying to find them, when—when this is all over, if it will ever be over. Perhaps he simply needs to mark their existence by noting their absence.

The list increased in the days after the tragedy at the Vél d'Hiv. And that was a particularly black day in Claude's mind, because it was the French that did it, not the Germans. They rounded up their own people, for the very first time, and no one could convince Claude that it was in order to protect all citizens. The French rounded up Jews who had come to France, some recently, some decades before, seeking refuge, a better life. They rounded up Jews—immigrants from other countries—who had become French citizens. They dragged infants out of their cots, mothers nursing their babes in arms, toddlers clutching their ragdolls. Women and children, predominantly; the men had already been taken, less visibly, and sent to the labor camps that the Germans said were for the making of ammunition and war materiel.

So what threat did they pose, these women and children? They were sorry enough as it was, waiting for their men, existing in shadows, the only bright thing about them, ironically, the yellow Star of David on their clothes. Why tear them from their garrets, their closets, their one-room flats and shove them inside the glass-domed velodrome, deny them food, the sanity of even a one-holed lavatory? It was the French police that did it; their gendarmes, their prefects; they drove the trucks, they knocked on the doors, they pointed the rifles. They shoved the poor souls in the hothouse that became a hell house and only after five days—five days with little water, less air, and no hope—were the survivors taken on to the camps at Drancy, Beaune-la-Rolande, and Pithiviers. Or places unknown.

Who had ordered it? That was the burning question in the streets of Paris among those who were fortunate enough only to have to witness.

It was the gossip in the bar at the Ritz. Frank Meier insisted it was the Vichy government; others said no, it had to have been the Nazis, forcing Vichy to do their bidding. Claude agreed with Frank; he knew the anti-Semitism inherent in French culture. He—like everyone else of his generation—had been weaned on *L'affaire Dreyfus*.

The Ritz lost ten staff members that day, reliable, hard-working employees, mostly women. They never came back.

The Germans celebrated; they toasted, they chortled, Adolf Eichmann came to the Ritz to gloat with von Stülpnagel. Eichmann, whose name already invoked terror. Sitting in the terrace—it was July, such a beautiful day, Claude would always remember how the lilies were in bloom, the air perfumed with roses abuzz with bees—they laughed, they sang songs, they exulted in the fact that "To think, today there are ten thousand fewer Jews in Paris than there were yesterday," as Eichmann said.

"Already the air seems purer," von Stülpnagel agreed.

Claude, watching, rushed to them when beckoned. He bowed, he signaled for waiters to bring them caviar and more champagne.

There are, despite Eichmann's glee, still Jews in Paris. Those born here remain, although sometimes they leave, too. Less obviously. The knock on the door in the middle of the night instead of the summons in the harsh light of day. But every Jew in Paris now has a star, has a card on file in Gestapo headquarters. And no one is safe; it is foolish to think they will stop with the Jews. What about the effete young men in Claude's employ, the ones who are the favorites of the matrons, the ones who wear green carnations in their lapels when they are off duty? What about the maimed—like little Greep, whom Frank Meier does not think that Claude knows but of course, he does. Greep is lame in one leg. What about the few Americans who remain, like Blanche?

The first time Blanche and Claude saw the yellow stars, they stopped in their tracks. Yes, they were aware of the decree, but it was only a concept, unimaginable. They even joked about it—would Chanel come up with a brilliant design of her own, a yellow star with flair, and charge a fortune for it? Until the day they were walking home from a pleasant lunch at a café.

It was part of Claude's plan to keep Blanche away from Lily since she—unfortunately—has come back. If Claude spends more time with Blanche, he reasons—time he does not have to spare—perhaps she won't seek this woman's company. For being with Lily brings out the worst in his wife; the two of them seem to do nothing but drink all day, all night. They stagger into the Ritz holding on to each other, trying to stay upright, laughing hilariously at a private joke. Lily often has to sleep it off in their rooms, curled up in an armchair while Blanche snores on the bed and Claude spends an uncomfortable night on the small sofa in his office.

"Claude, you A-OK," Lily murmured to him one night as she kicked off her shoes—a pair of men's combat boots, for heaven's sake—and settled down in the chair, her eyes half-closed, tucking herself into a little ball just like a cat.

"Claude's a peach, aren't you, Popsy?" Blanche agreed with a hiccup.

Claude wrinkled his nose and left them to their hangovers. Wondering, the whole time, what mischief they might have gotten themselves in, for Blanche had a tendency to blurt things out when she was drunk.

Wondering if Lily was only a cover, if Blanche was perhaps seeing a man—oh, wondering about everything in this topsy-turvy world!

The day that the Auzellos first saw the yellow stars on the street, Blanche grabbed his arm, just as he grabbed hers. While in fact there weren't a lot of them, simply because the latest decree forbade Jews from gathering in public places or walking in the major thoroughfares, still, it seemed as if everywhere they looked, they suddenly saw these hateful badges. There, sewn to the lapel of a schoolgirl's blazer—a blazer too small for the girl, who hadn't been able to attend school since the Nazis decreed that Jewish children could no longer do so. But still, the girl wore the uniform, and Claude had to wonder why. Was it hope, pure and simple? Nostalgia? Or simply a child's whim?

And here, attached to the breast of a man in a blue tweed jacket, a man who looked no different than Claude; a man with a very French nose, long and suspicious. A small mustache. Manicured nails. Hair trimmed weekly and scented with pomade. Shoes polished so that they reflected the yellow star every time he took a step.

Over there, an elderly couple, both wearing their stars, his on a ragged sweater, hers on a prehistoric fur coat, possibly from the Victorian era. They sat side by side on a bench, shadowed by a tree—Claude had noticed, lately, that Jews tended to keep to the perimeters of things, even in the few streets and parks and sidewalks where they were allowed. Always trying to hide, although there was nowhere in Paris where they could escape notice. The couple sat on the bench and he had his hand on her knee, very proprietarily. She clutched her handbag on her lap with both hands, and they both sat looking forward, and they never did stop blinking at the world passing them by, this world they no longer recognized. Her handbag was enormous, and Claude wondered if, inside of it, she kept everything dear to her—old photographs, birth certificates, jewelry. A change of clothing. Just in case.

Blanche and he did not comment on the stars. They did not linger too long. Without saying a word they both began to walk, more rapidly than usual, back to the Ritz, back to their rooms, and still without speaking, they both crawled into bed, fully clothed, atop the sheets and blankets. They lay side by side, his arms about her, and she trembled, or perhaps it was him, or perhaps it was both of them, and she finally spoke, for the first time, of the thing they had never been able to speak of.

"Thank God we never had any children, Claude," said his wife of nineteen years.

He could only nod, while he clutched her to him, his wife. The princess he had rescued who had turned into a confounding woman with a warm, vibrant body, her more vibrant mind, her generous heart. Her goodness, her boldness, her courage, her fears. Her recklessness, her stubbornness. That temper, barely concealed beneath her designer clothing. Sometimes, he could admit, he neglected to remember that his wife was a *person* and not an abstract feeling (irritant, usually); a beautiful, infuriating mass of cells, a contradiction of soft and hard, logic and emotion, just like all women.

But in the eyes of the *Boche*, some collections

of cells, combinations of bones and flesh, pulsing blood, beating hearts, weren't people at all.

"Blanche, please, stop seeing Lily," he breathed into her ear. Immediately, she stiffened. "Please, I have a bad feeling about her. I don't know what she might make you do. But you must be careful, and when you drink . . ."

"When I drink, what?" Her voice was sharp. Suspicious.

"You get careless. You can't afford to do that. No one can these days."

"Let me make you a deal, Claude." She rolled away from him, sat up, and smoothed her hair. But kept her back turned to him. "You stop going out every time the damn phone rings at night, and I'll stop seeing Lily."

"Blanche—" For the first time, Claude was tempted. Tempted to halt his nocturnal activities, which were growing more frequent, more exhilarating as the *Boche* tightened the noose about Paris in the wake of the Vél d'Hiv roundup.

Curfew is now strictly enforced—which makes furtive meetings in the shadows more feverishly exciting. No gatherings of more than four people are tolerated, not even in cafés or nightclubs. There have been some shootings of Nazi soldiers, which have resulted in roundups and shootings of citizens—mostly Jews, but not always—in retaliation.

But no. It is more important than ever to find

relief for his stress, of the juggling he has to do, daily, to please everyone—his wife, his employees, his guests who aren't really guests. The memory of César Ritz. The memory of Claude himself, who he used to be. Only outside the Ritz can Claude find himself again, and he won't stop his meetings with Simone—and Michele, and Martin. Meetings that have expanded beyond vegetables; now Martin is in the business of selling other things. Things Claude needs and things he wishes he had no use for, but still he takes them off his friend's hands, sometimes keeping them—the cupboards in the Ritz are large and mainly hidden from view—and sometimes passing them on to someone else.

However discreet Claude believes himself to be, he is always assessing his behavior, on the watch for any dereliction of his duties. He has, it pains him to admit, sometimes slipped up. The other night, he visited the basement kitchen right around ten-thirty. There was an air raid going on; British bombers dropping their payload on the docks outside of town, docks integral to the German war effort. The Ritz, Claude happened to know, was on the precise latitude to aid those bombers flying over a city blacked out at night. Should someone happen to leave the kitchen lights on . . .

And sure enough—strangely enough—Claude found the lights burning brightly, despite the blackout. And if the Nazis found out, if they discovered who had left them on . . . Claude shuddered, imagining. He felt a lightbulb; it was barely warm. So whoever had done this had only just left; he thought he smelled a whiff of something familiar—perfume, perhaps, or hair oil—but dismissed it. And made a note to be more observant of his staff—he would find out who had done this, and put him or her on notice.

He turned around and took the stairs back up to his rooms, where Blanche was just now taking off her shoes and stockings, her breathing heavy, irregular—"The damned blackout, I couldn't find my way back here for the life of me!" And Claude forgot all about the light in his anger at her for being out so late during an air raid; soon the two of them were arguing so vociferously, they drowned out the heavy vibration of the bombers overhead.

The next morning, he was summoned to von Stülpnagel's office and not-so-gently interrogated before being dismissed with a warning that the incident was not yet over. For those kitchen lights had shone a beacon along the straightest path to the docks, easily visible from above. The Allies had done quite a job of it, apparently.

So Claude must be careful; he must not allow his passion to interfere with his work, and bring hell down upon the Ritz.

He is, in his way, proud of his activities. Until he sees the sadness in his wife's eyes, the resignation that he has lived down to her expectations of him. His wife is disappointed in him, in his lack of faithfulness to her, in his work, as well; he cannot ignore the disgust in her voice when she mocks him for bowing to the Nazis, running to do their bidding. In the days after that air raid, Claude doubled down on his efforts to please his Nazi guests, even going so far as to personally polish von Stülpnagel's boots himself, since the man had expressed displeasure at the regular boot boy's efforts in the past.

"Claude, you would make a very good German," von Stülpnagel said, admiring the gleam of the polished black leather. "Maybe you can come to Berlin with me and run one of the hotels there."

Claude smiled and said, *"Merci."* He said, "I would like nothing better."

Tonight, then, when the phone rings again, Claude is even more eager than usual to answer its call. Blanche smiles that unfathomable smile she has of late and gives him a slap—mild, desultory, almost as if it's a fond reminder of better times—and leaves first. She always, lately, leaves first. And comes home last, incoherent and glassy-eyed, her clothes reeking of gin and vermouth. While Claude does what a Frenchman has to do, even in the Paris of 1943.

He shuts his eyes, but still he can see stars—the stars she has given him with her slap. The yellow stars on the streets of Paris.

For a moment—he looks at his watch, counting the seconds, allowing himself only sixty of them—Claude despises this world, this war, this occupation, this stain, this plague, this nightmare. He doesn't know what to call it anymore.

The minute is up, and he shuts off his hate, locks it tightly in a little compartment in his heart and tucks away the key where he can find it again without too much effort. It's time. He has to go. Claude splashes some water on his face, straightens his tie.

And ventures out into the night to meet a beautiful woman.

CHAPTER 21

BLANCHE,
Winter 1943

A few months after Lily returns, more violets show up at the Ritz for Blanche. Another meeting on the same bench in the flower market—although this time with Lorenzo, not Lily.

"Where is Lily?" Blanche asks, snuggling into her fur coat for warmth; she always forgets how unforgiving Paris winters can be.

She is answered by a glare, and then she remembers the first thing she was told about the Resistance—*no questions.*

"I have something for you," Lorenzo says. Blanche twists the nosegay of violets and listens. It's dangerous, he continues; he won't lie to her. They—a nonspecific "they" that Blanche knows better than to inquire about—have come into some microfilm of planned troop movements along the coast. The Germans are looking everywhere for it. It has to be given to a contact at the Gare du Nord, who will get it out of the country to the Allies. And Blanche is to take it to him. She speaks French, so she can pose as the contact's wife.

She can walk away, she knows. The old Blanche

would have. The Blanche who once thought that having lunch with the Duke and Duchess of Windsor was something to be proud of (she even wrote her parents about it and included a photo); the Blanche who used to spend hours curled up on a velvet sofa, watching the rich, famous, and delusional strut through the doors of the Ritz, their jewels ostentatiously displayed for all to see.

This new Blanche follows Lorenzo to the back of a different flower stall without a word. He hands her a tin lunch pail and a French identity card proclaiming her as one Berthe Valéry. Listening intently, she understands that she is simply taking her husband, Moule Valéry, who works on track five, his lunch. Blanche is shown a snapshot of the man—he looks as if someone has just shot his favorite dog, his expression is so morose—before Lorenzo tosses it in a coffee can and sets it on fire. He hands her a plain dress and a housewife's kerchief—then he seems to take in her chinchilla coat for the first time.

"You look too goddamned Ritz," he snarls, bending over a pile of old clothing, pulling out a cloth coat with a pocket flapping, torn. "Leave that ridiculous fur here—I can sell it, get some money."

"But—it's—" Claude gave her this coat on their first anniversary; she remembers his face, so shyly proud that he could afford this on his new salary at the Ritz. She doesn't want to part with it; it's like parting with one more memory—and there are too few of them anyway—of a fading, more tender, more hopeful, past.

"Do you want to help or not? We can buy passports, petrol, train tickets, things that will help. Guns, too. I thought you were willing to fight, Mistress Ritz?" Lorenzo looks at her with such unveiled disgust and arrogance; she longs to wipe that look from his face.

"Of course, take it. Get as much for it as you can."

He doesn't even thank her. Instead, he says, "As soon as you give him the pail, leave. Right away, just walk out. Are you sure you can do this?" He leans toward her, fixing Blanche with his doubting gaze; challenging her. And she realizes that to him, she is expendable, as useful for the moment as her fur coat, nothing more.

"I could do with some excitement," Blanche replies.

"Are you sure?" Lorenzo scowls; he takes off his cap, scratches his head, and looks about, almost as if he's hoping someone else will pop out from behind a flower bucket and take her place. "You understand what's at stake here? You know you cannot talk about this to anyone, and if you're caught, you're on your own. You can't reveal names, you can't talk. Or else."

"Or else what?"

"If the Nazis don't murder you, we will."

She represses a shudder, but says nothing.

"When you are done, don't come back here."

"Where do I go? My clothes—" Blanche pats her dress, the printed silk that she slipped on so thoughtfully this morning. "What do I do with them?"

"I'll sell those, too." He laughs at her foolish, feminine concern and stands there, arms folded across his chest, waiting for her to strip.

Blanche shrugs, does so, and changes into the costume; the housedress is a little too tight, while the coat is a little too big. Emerging from the tent with the pail, she stops to arrange the kerchief low on her forehead. Lorenzo doesn't follow; she doesn't recognize anyone as she makes her way through the market, pausing now and again to look at flowers—mainly bittersweet branches, a few hothouse flowers under glass—simply another French housewife spending a few coins on flowers to brighten her table. But every Nazi soldier she brushes against is like an electric shock to her system; she recoils, her heart hammering as she grips the pail tighter, but none give her a second look. So she begins to walk toward the Seine. Toward the Gare du Nord.

This isn't like the other time, with the young airman. Then, she was entirely swept up in the moment, a giddy, reckless adventure, as if she were an understudy suddenly called upon to step into a role she hadn't rehearsed. She didn't have time to contemplate the consequences.

What if she never sees Claude again? The question catches her off guard and makes her think, once more, of the coat she has just given away, and all the memories attached to it. Until today, she realizes, she hasn't thought of her husband as a person in so long; he is the source of her distress, the excuse for her drinking, the reason she runs away. Will she grieve, if she can never see him again?

Will he grieve for her?

This conundrum drives away all the other, more immediately terrifying thoughts until she realizes she's almost at the station, and that she is actually swinging the precious bucket, like it is a handbag or a picnic basket and not the hiding place of stolen microfilm that every Nazi officer in France is searching for. For a terrible moment, Blanche fears she's lost the fake identity card— did she leave it back at the flower market, with her real clothes? But then she remembers it's in the pail, on top of the checkered cloth that covers the sandwich that protects the precious microfilm. She pats her cheek to hide her fear, then she shows the card to the Germans at the entrance. She makes herself look them in the eye; she can't appear nervous or suspicious. The soldier who takes it barely gives it a glance before thrusting it back to her and continuing a conversation with his friend.

As soon as she steps inside the great, cavernous, noisy station, Moule—looking just as sad as his photo—runs up to her (How? He's never seen her before, as far as she knows); he grabs her by her shoulders, scolding her in a torrent of French.

"What took you so long, woman? I am starving! It's not enough that I slave all day for you, but you can't be bothered to bring me my lunch on time?"

For a moment, Blanche is too stunned to react; has the man lost his reason? Then her former acting instincts kick in.

"You vile excuse for a husband! How dare you? I was trying to make myself pretty for you!"

"Ha! You did not succeed."

A fascinated audience has suddenly assembled to witness their volatile domestic drama.

Blanche slaps Moule. He growls, then she grabs his collar and kisses him, passionately, on the lips. The man is so stunned he drops the pail.

She stifles a panicked cry; Moule's pupils dilate with a terror that matches her own.

They both, at the same time, look down.

The pail is intact; nothing has fallen out of it, not even the soggy sandwich. Giddy with relief, Blanche grabs Moule and plants another, more passionate kiss on his lips. This one, he returns.

The German soldiers watching burst into applause and one shouts, *"Vive la France!"* Blanche—finally releasing the stunned Moule—is so exhilarated that she almost bows. But she catches herself, just in time, and spins on her heel and marches away, cursing all Frenchmen and their follies at the top of her voice.

By the time she gets back to the Ritz, her arms are still swinging, and she's grinning, madly—only dimly, in the back of her mind, lies the thought that she could still be arrested; she's convinced herself that would only have happened during the drop. *The drop*—she's already thinking like a militant, a spy.

But now she's back at the Ritz, where nothing bad can happen to her, and so she can revel in the rush, the thrill. She's done it, done it brilliantly—she replays the entire scene in her head, and she grins, remembering how she kissed that poor bastard, his gasp of surprise. Oh, she wished that Claude could have seen her! She wished *someone* had seen her, someone like—

Lily. Who is sitting on a chair outside the Ritz bar when Blanche pushes through the doors of the rue Cambon side, still exultant but in dire need of a stiff drink, a reward for a job well done. Lily, who bursts into tears as soon as she sees Blanche. Blanche grabs her, pulls her into the bar, ignoring the stares—of course, she's still in these ragged clothes, although she does tear off the kerchief and tries to rearrange her hair. Frank Meier, without a word, only a probing look, pours them both martinis.

"I told him no, Lorenzo—I told him not to have you do this. He sent me off on wild goose egg chase, to get me away. Oh, Blanche—you shouldn't have, you fool. It was great danger. I will kill him, that Lorenzo!"

"Hush . . ." Frank hisses, inclining his head, ever so slightly, toward the German officers at the end of the bar whose conversation has grown less animated as theirs has grown louder, and Lily finally calms down.

"But you did OK, Blanche?"

"More than OK. Lily, I was grand!"

"I should have done this. But I have to lay low. . . . I shouldn't be here." She glances at the Germans at the end of the bar. "But I had to see you with my eyes. I don't trust that Lorenzo. He doesn't care about people. Not at all, not like Robert. Blanche, I'm afraid for you."

"Lily, I can take care of myself. I want to do this. I want to help. I want to save, too. You won't deny me that, will you?" Blanche puts her arm about her friend. Lily shakes her head, but hiccups a little as she tries to stop her tears; suddenly Blanche is crying, too, although she has no idea why—probably the adrenaline draining away, replaced by jangly nerves. And so the two of them are head-down on the bar, weeping softly, as Frank slides another round of martinis toward them.

"Blanche!"

Blanche, startled, raises her head and gapes at her husband, who is glaring, with unconcealed disgust, first at Lily, then at her.

"Blanche, what on earth—where are your clothes?" She looks down at the too-tight house-dress with the faded flower print, the raggedy cloth coat in a heap at her feet. She remembers, with a guilty little start, how she gave away her fur coat. *His* fur coat.

"I, well—"

"Blanche, she spilled things on herself so I gave her some clothes to wear. She was a mess— we were having fun, like this!" Lily leans over her, lifting her martini glass in a drunken toast. "Cheers, Claude! Have fun with us!"

Claude ignores Lily. Instead, he takes Blanche by the arm, preparing to haul her away. "Come lie down. I can't have you looking like this. Not here."

The Germans, Blanche notices—the martinis have not yet kicked in, although she can feel them buzzing a little at the base of her skull, the edges of her vision starting to blur—are enjoying the little drama, their gazes knowing. How typical, how *French*—the two drunken ladies, one of them the director's wife, at the end of the bar. That's all they see—what Claude sees.

Lily and Blanche—two drunken friends out on a spree.

She kisses her husband on the cheek—it's a very moist kiss and she leaves a lipstick smear which she tries unsuccessfully to wipe up with the sleeve of her borrowed dress—and says, "I'm sorry, Claude, but it's been a hell of a day."

She tries to smile at the look on her husband's face. But it's far too real—smug, resigned—and so, dizzy, she shuts her eyes against it, knowing she's going to have to shut her eyes against his disgust, she's going to have to disappoint him on a daily basis for a long time to come.

By letting Claude believe what he wants to believe—what he's so eager to believe about her—she can hide her activities from him. If he thinks she's just a sloppy drunk, a nuisance, he can't be questioned, can't be accused of anything if she's caught. And it's how she can hide Lily, too.

"Popsy wopsy was a bear, Popsy wopsy has no hair," she murmurs, eyes half-closed, watching her husband's face as it settles even further into the familiar disgusted grooves. Satisfied, she closes her eyes all the way and giggles. "Ol' Popsy wopsy. Another round on him!"

She hears her husband sigh, then leave, as she reaches for another martini.

CHAPTER 22
CLAUDE,
Winter 1944

It is that woman, of course it is. That Lily.

This woman! This slender, minuscule person! She is the one who corrupts his Blanche, who awakens and encourages the most irresponsible aspects of his wife's personality. Oh, yes, Claude knows Blanche enjoys drinking; he's known it from the moment they met. Her incessant campaign to allow women inside the bar— what was that about, other than her own thirst wanting to be sated? Her pleasure in idling her days swapping drinks and stories with the Hemingways and Fitzgeralds. Drink allows her to forget, Claude believes; forget her family, so far away; forget the life she left behind, the things she gave up to be his wife. But—the defensiveness creeps in, for Claude is only a man, after all—he never asked her to give them up.

And she did so quite readily.

But with Lily, his wife's carousing takes on a more careless aspect, as if she is actively courting danger. As if danger isn't already lurking everywhere. Even at the Ritz.

Hans Emliger, his manager, says to him one day, so casually, "Claude, I understand that you—that you are working, late at night, sometimes. If you would like for me to help in any way, I would be glad to. I can keep your secret."

Claude assures Hans (not German, Dutch, thank heavens!) that he must be mistaken; how is Claude to know if he is friend or foe? How is Claude to know to which secret of his Hans is referring? One cannot take the chance of trusting these days; everyone is an enemy. Until that miraculous liberation they all pray for, when all might be revealed. Although it does not seem possible, not at the present.

Frank Meier is also troubling Claude. Oh, Frank is as always—large, wary, keeping his own counsel, the way he's been since Claude first met him, as his service at the Ritz predates Claude's own. Watching, always watching, behind that mahogany bar; it seems as if he never leaves it, and at times Claude suspects he might be sleeping behind it, this large man from Austria who apparently has no family, no life beyond these walls. In his white jacket, he is inscrutable, both in his manners and his demeanor.

However.

Claude knows more about Frank—indeed, about everyone at the Ritz—than he is given credit for. For example, Frank has various ventures on the side—his gambling ring, for one. Claude also knows about that little Turk, his friend Greep, who is famed for his forgery; many passports, death certificates, and other official documents have been altered or created by his hand. What Claude can't discern is if either Frank or Greep is engaged in the Resistance.

And what, exactly, *is* the Resistance? It isn't a defined group of people, not as some would believe; there is no official insignia, no membership dues. It is more amorphous, popping up now here, now there. Some people who never held a gun are part of it. It is at once cerebral, engaged in false diplomacy, and bloodily violent, intent on blowing up bridges and entire regiments of Nazis. It is more of a mood than an action, Claude sometimes believes; if you do something, however small, to make their "guests" squirm, feel unwelcome, or in danger of their lives, you are resisting.

Frank is passing on messages, Claude is certain. From whom—agents, double agents, the Resistance, the Allies, the select Germans who, sickened at the squandering of millions of German lives in Russia, are starting to plot against Hitler—*that,* he doesn't know. But Frank is also funneling money, money that should rightly be paid to the Ritz, and this is the troubling part. In normal times, Claude would have no choice but to accuse him of embezzlement and sack him.

However.

Where is the money going? Is Frank procuring passage to America for those who cannot afford it? Procuring fine clothes for himself from the black market? Who can tell? Who dares to ask? And so Claude must allow him to continue to do this thing, this siphoning off of money that belongs to Madame Ritz, because at the moment the only jury is one comprised of Germans, and Claude will not throw him, nor anyone else in his employ, on their mercy.

After the incident of the kitchen lights—Claude still doesn't know who turned them on—Claude himself came under scrutiny; in fact, he spent two days in jail. Two days being treated very pleasantly—the interrogating officer had been von Stülpnagel's guest at luncheon more than once and so he knew Claude very well, and fondly, because Claude always ensured that the man had his favorite wine, a Burgundy, and an entrée of quenelles, to which the officer was most devoted. While Claude was questioned, naturally, it was done with the good humor and easy camaraderie of dinner companions. He supposes even the Germans find it difficult to torture those who provide them their favorite meals. Claude was asked, gently, about whom he might suspect of having turned on those lights; he was also accused—again, tentatively—of being a Communist; a list had appeared—a list of mysterious origin—and upon that list, in the category of "suspected Communist," was the name *Auzello*. The officer said that, naturally, he might very well be mistaken about that, but one must ask.

That last accusation, mild as it was, Claude could not stand. He told the officer—after reminding him how very much he loved those quenelles—in no uncertain terms exactly what he thought of *Communists,* those who would infiltrate society, do away with its structures, all in the name of mischief. He reminded this officer that he himself had swept the Ritz from attic to cellar, getting rid of any employees who were known to sympathize with such rabble.

Between his gentle interrogations, Claude was held in a cell no bigger than a broom closet at the Ritz, but it was separate from the others, at whom he dared not look lest he recognize any of them; and while the food was swill—*mon Dieu*, what they called soup!—the cot was comfortable. And it had a window; a window through which he saw *her.*

Both days around two o'clock, Claude's wife took a seat at the café directly across the street, smoking Gauloise after Gauloise, pale, nervous. But there. Keeping watch just across from the prison where he was held. Understanding, somehow, that Claude would see her. That he might find strength in her presence, which he did. Much to his surprise. For it had been a very long time since he'd seen his wife as anything other than a headache.

When he was released—with a clap on the back, a laugh, and a thinly veiled threat that should more unfortunate activity occur at the Ritz, quenelles or no quenelles, he would personally be held accountable—Claude teased his wife about her vigil. Because he couldn't bring himself to confess how much it had meant to see her there. He couldn't begin to reveal how frightened he'd really been that these would be the last glimpses of her he would ever have.

Claude also couldn't tell her how much her anguish touched him; that he was surprised by it, even. That he was astonished that he could still be deeply affected by her presence, and she by his absence.

"See?" He kissed her, breezily, on the cheek when he arrived back at the Ritz, and she flung her arms around him with a strangled sob. "Poor Blanchette—you can't bear to be away from me even for one day!"

"Don't flatter yourself, Popsy," she'd said, pushing herself away and reapplying her lipstick. "I was simply dying to see if your mistress would show up, too." But her hand shook as she held the lipstick.

Claude pressed his lips together and returned to his duties.

When he closed the door, however, he heard her

burst into tears, and he, too, felt sadness, like a ponderous, musty overcoat, drape itself over him. What on earth had this war done to them? It had not been perfect before, no; Claude could admit that, and admit his fault. But shouldn't war draw people together instead of tearing them apart? Didn't that Hemingway write of these things, of love and passion while bullets rained down, in that book of his about the Spanish Civil War?

Once, Claude had thought that his and Blanche's story was the most romantic he'd ever known. Now, he only knew the bitterness of a punctured dream.

A moment later, Blanche passed him in the hall, on her way out. To drink with Lily.

Lily.

Who Claude knew—it was simply only a matter of time—would endanger them all.

CHAPTER 23

BLANCHE,
Winter 1944

"Jeepers creepers, do I stink. How much gin do you think I poured on myself?"

"All of it."

"You were slurring your words so much, I think you invented a new language."

Lily giggles. "I was good, huh, Blanche?"

"Good. As usual."

"So were you." And Lily immediately turns serious as Blanche changes clothes. As fond as she is of gin, this is too much; she smells like an entire juniper forest.

"How did it go, Blanche? Tell me. I still don't like this, although you are proving to be very good at it."

"You think so?" Blanche pokes her head around the corner of the door of the suite, pleased beyond reason. She *is* good at "it"—but that doesn't mean she doesn't appreciate hearing it from others. She would love to be able to share this with Claude, to let him see her this way, as she truly is, and not as he thinks she is.

But she can't, so she has to make do with Lily's admiration, instead. As far as Claude is aware,

Blanche spends her days—when she's not here at the Ritz playing dull games of cards with dull women who still are mourning the loss of fashion and not lives—out with Lily. Carousing. Drinking. Making a damned stupid fool of herself, as usual.

And Blanche lets him think the worst of her. Because this way she won't enmesh Claude and his damn precious Ritz in her actions; he can remain above the dirty, dangerous work of resistance and keep serving, providing, fetching for these monsters. Sometimes Blanche can't even bear to look at him, her former brave knight who is now a simpering servant of the most dangerous dragon of all.

"You can never tell Claude," Lily cautions. "We can't trust him. He's too close to them. Thinking only of his own survival."

Blanche nods, but her disappointment isn't in hearing him discussed this way. Her disenchantment is more intimate: the tragedy of seeing a man she once thought truer to himself than anyone she'd ever known reduced to a puppet.

So Claude doesn't know. He *can't* know that the night he thought Blanche was too soused to come home at all and had to crash at Lily's was the night she was actually on a train to Le Mans, another forged passport in her handbag, chatting fatuously with two German soldiers who would not leave her alone while she pretended to be, once more, a German nursemaid, accompanying another downed flyer disguised as a convalescing soldier. (They were dropping from the skies like flies these days, as the Allies stepped up their bombing of Germany.) These two soldiers took a shine to her—they flirted, they tried to get her to agree to an assignation once they got to the town. She couldn't shake them, no matter what she said, and all the while the American airman sat with his head between his knees, vomiting steadily into a knapsack, and still the Germans wouldn't walk away. She finally managed to evade them at the station, when she shoved the young Yank, now too weak to walk, into a convenient wheelbarrow, and *pushed* him through the crowd—attracting fascinated stares but no questions, perhaps because they were so brazen; by the time she got him to his contact, a farmer peddling vegetables in the market, she was wrung out with the exertion of pushing a six-foot-tall American.

This was the first time she'd been allowed to carry a firearm; she had a small pistol, given to her by Lorenzo, in a handbag. It was not that different from Claude's gun—the gun that he thought she didn't know about.

But she did; she'd found it in his desk drawer one evening when she was rummaging through it (of course, she had a key; again, something he wasn't aware of), looking for the passkey to the wine cellar, where she'd hidden some stolen German uniforms behind a lot of thirty-year-old Burgundy. She'd been startled; Claude was not the kind of man to walk around with a pistol in his pocket, especially at the Ritz where anyone, no matter their title, was at the risk of being stopped and frisked. She'd picked up the pistol, admired how clean it was, how polished, cool in her hand.

And she tried—and failed—to imagine a scenario in which her husband would use it.

Claude will never suspect that the time he berated both Lily and Blanche for being thrown out of the Brasserie Lipp for being too rowdy, they were actually creating a diversion that allowed Lorenzo and Heifer—the big girl with braids—to steal a German military ID from an officer. The officer was extremely interested in the spectacle of two beautiful women (Blanche had pinned one of her evening dresses to fit Lily's more delicate frame) engaged in a spirited catfight over an astonished young Nazi lieutenant, who had no idea who either of them were but enjoyed the attention.

Claude, Blanche is sure, also never dreams that Frank Meier is passing coded messages to double agents in the bar. He never realizes that Blanche turned the lights on in the kitchen one night, to aid the Allied bombers trying to find a particular dock on the outskirts of Paris during a night raid.

Claude doesn't know—anything. Of that, Blanche is certain. He doesn't see anything, know anything, think of anything—other than his goddamned beloved Ritz.

The deceptions work, too well, and she's exhilarated—who doesn't enjoy the pleasure of a lie well told?—and determined not to plumb her disappointment in Claude. Blanche is thrilled to be of use; thrilled to do something against these Nazis more devastating than kicking them in the balls. Her activities allow her to resume her old insouciance at the Ritz; once again, she can play cards with Spatzy and Chanel and never once want to throw a glass at him or call her a skinny collaborating bitch. She even jokes with von Stülpnagel—as much as one could joke with such a humorless pig; they have an ongoing bet as to which of his officers will get the clap first because, according to him, all French prostitutes naturally are diseased.

Blanche still has her favorites among the men who are posted as sentries, although she misses Friedrich who, like most of the German boys, has been assigned to the Russian front. Most of the soldiers now posted to the Ritz are older, surlier. Easier to see as merely Nazis instead of people.

Blanche can sit next to these *Haricots Verts* in cafés, and instead of wanting to kick them in the balls, she demurely sips her coffee and laughs at their stupid jokes.

And every time she receives a delivery of violets, she has another opportunity to strike a blow.

Does it pierce her heart that Claude is so easily deceived; that he so readily believes the worst of her? Will they ever be able to recover from this, once the war is over?

Because it is growing more and more evident that there is no room, in wartime, for tending to a marriage.

CHAPTER 24

CLAUDE,
Spring 1944

"Monsieur Auzello! Monsieur Auzello!" No courtesy knock; he bursts in, this young bellhop who joined the staff only a couple of weeks before. Claude has his suspicions about the youth—he has no references, seems to have no family or background—but took him on anyway. The boy is young and able-bodied and not too stupid, and they are no longer favored with many of that kind in Paris. Most young men are conscripted and sent to labor camps to make arms for the Germans (they wouldn't trust a native Frenchman with a gun, which is the only reason they're not sent to the front).

"What?"

"General von Stülpnagel demands to see you at once!"

"Why?"

"He wouldn't say."

Sighing, Claude puts down his papers and crosses over to the Vendôme side, nodding at the guards standing alert in all the doorways, pistols in holsters, who are not alarmed by his presence here. After all, he is Herr Auzello—practically one of them.

Von Stülpnagel has been even more unpredictable than usual, lately—one moment snarling orders to round up civilians to be shot in retaliation against acts of the Resistance, one hundred or so per attack.

One hundred civilians for a lousy German or two. How odd, that this has seeped into Parisians' consciousness, their conversation, even. It is simply the way it is. They are in danger of becoming immune to the horrors surrounding them. This is what an occupation does—it wears you down until you accept evil. Until you can no longer fully define it, even. Let alone recognize it.

Then von Stülpnagel will grow expansive, friendly; inviting Claude into his office to share a glass of brandy as if they are truly friends. In those moments, the man seems almost human.

Until the next roundup of civilians.

Claude tries to avoid him as much as possible, as of late, because of his unpredictability. But a summons is a summons—

Unless it is not. For when Claude attains the Nazi's office and is ushered in by the sentry, von Stülpnagel looks at him in confusion.

"No, I did not request you, Herr Auzello," the German says and Claude notices that today, it is "Herr Auzello" and not "Claude, my friend." A useful distinction, and so Claude immediately is on his toes, alert.

There are papers all over the German's desk, and it requires of Claude every ounce of constraint not to look at them, not to see if there are names of those he knows—perhaps has loved—on them.

"My apologies." With a bow, Claude turns to go.

"But wait—while you're here, Auzello, my tea is cold."

Ah. Now it is merely "Auzello."

"I'll have someone bring you a new pot momentarily." Claude turns back around with a smooth, professional smile.

"Since you're here, you can do it yourself."

Claude stiffens; it is not his job and this man knows it well. He is smiling too smugly; he is watching Claude too intently, almost as if he's hoping that Claude will argue. But Claude tells himself this: Do not make him angry. Do not make any of them angry. If they are happy here, within these majestic walls where I am in charge, then perhaps they won't round up as many citizens today.

There have been times lately—like now—when Claude marvels at how he is able to fill out his clothes, resemble a body with structure, bones, and muscles, when he feels liquefied by rage and helplessness. Cells and molecules—how can they retain their structure, when such evil fills the world, fills the Ritz, tainting it with its putridness?

When the Germans leave, Claude vows, he will scrub the place from top to bottom with bleach with his own hands, if necessary; he will convince Marie-Louise to re-wallpaper it, tear out the old carpets and rugs, buy new. *Everything* new—crystal and china and linen, even the chandeliers, such a matter of pride to her. Anything to be rid of the merest whiff, faintest memories, of these vile men.

And the memories of himself bowing to them, doing his job, just as he always had done. He knows that he will continue to bow to them in the days, the weeks, the months, the years ahead.

"Of course, Herr Stülpnagel." Claude takes the cold silver pot as if it is an honor, and leaves.

As he walks back toward his office, he searches for the young man who summoned him, but the boy has vanished. However, Claude does recognize his wife seated in the lobby of the rue Cambon side, nonchalantly reading a newspaper—something she does not usually do—and an unfamiliar melody begins to play in his brain, a tune of foreboding, suspicion. Especially when she drops the newspaper as soon as Claude appears, and nods at someone across the lobby.

That same young bellhop, who colors bright

red when he sees Claude, and sprints away like a startled hare.

Claude hands the empty teapot to another bellhop, returns to his office, takes two antacids, and waits.

He doesn't have to wait very long.

By nightfall, the rue Cambon side of the Ritz is crawling with German officers, the alert having gone out that members of the Resistance are hiding somewhere in the Ritz Paris. On the Place Vendôme.

It doesn't take long for Claude to uncover the truth. The young bellhop is easily persuaded to spill all, over a glass of wine and a promise of more responsibility. The lad is part of the Resistance, he says too eagerly—Claude shakes his head, afraid for this young man's fate if he is so willing to reveal the truth when barely pressed—and there is a wounded man who needs medical help. Claude's wife—his lovely wife, the youth says admiringly; his *wonderful* wife—has offered a room at the Ritz while the man recovers from his gunshot wound, accompanied by his friend, a woman.

And what is the name of this friend, Claude asks, although he already knows the answer.

Lily, of course. Lily Kharmanyoff.

It transpired that when Claude was over on the other side of the hotel, bowing to von Stülpnagel, the two had checked into four-fourteen as a honeymooning couple, thanks to Blanche's intervention. Claude dismisses the young man, grabs his house keys, and takes the stairs two at a time up to room four-fourteen. In his anger, he doesn't bother to knock; he unlocks the door and bursts into the room. He was fortunate, he realized later, that he wasn't shot on the spot.

Lily, wearing some of Blanche's clothes—Claude recognizes them at once—is seated on the edge of the bed, which is occupied by a swarthy-looking man, shirtless, so that Claude can see the bloodied bandage around his abdomen. He automatically winces; blood is the only thing that the launderers cannot remove from sheets. And new linen is very difficult to attain these days.

As soon as Claude enters the room, Lily springs up, and makes for a pistol on the nightstand. When she sees it is him, she puts it down with a laugh.

A laugh!

"Claude, you give us scare," she says merrily. "My God! This is Lorenzo."

The man—his eyes half-closed in pain—grunts.

"What in the hell are you doing here?" Claude snaps, trying to keep his voice down. He has no idea if the room is being watched or someone has an ear pressed against the door; he tries his best to keep on the lookout for that kind of thing but the truth is, he can never be certain. Claude suspects that there are some German spies among the staff. Not many, but probably one or two. There have to be. The *Boche* wouldn't be stupid enough not to plant spies on this side of the hotel, even though they maintain it is Claude's alone to run.

Lily lowers her voice, too; she is no longer laughing. Her eyes never stray from his as she tells Claude the tale. "Lorenzo, he was shot. So was the Nazi. Only one of them is still alive. We didn't know what to do with Lorenzo, so I got Blanche. We had him in the back of a café around the corner. Blanche say that we could come to the Ritz, and he could rest here. She knew a doctor, too. He gave Lorenzo morphine and we checked in like new marrieds. Blanche, she—she made sure you weren't around when we did. She sent you off on wild goose egg chase."

"Yes, I know." Claude is shaking with anger—and terror. This is the first time, to his knowledge, that the Ritz has harbored an actively sought member of the Resistance. The Germans must be knocking on doors all over Paris looking for this man. And he is here. In Claude's hotel.

And Lily has involved Blanche in it.

"How dare you ask Blanche to help you?" Claude is too angry to be as guarded as he usually is.

Lily only shrugs.

"She's not to be trusted, Lily. I hate to say it about my own wife but the way she drinks—

and I know why she does and I don't blame her—but Blanche, she's like a child, refusing to grow up! And the way you two carouse and play around—how on earth did you get involved in all this?"

Lily sits down on the bed again, careful not to disturb Lorenzo, who has drifted off to sleep.

"Do not be angry with Blanche. Is all me. I promise she—she has never done anything like this, anything dangerous at all. I was desperate, you see?" Lily's eyes fill with tears, and she starts to wipe her nose with her sleeve, but Claude can't allow that. Reluctantly, he offers her his own handkerchief.

"Desperate," she continues, her narrow shoulders shaking with sobs, her big eyes swimming up at him, repentant. "Blanche is my friend, my very good friend, and I love her, I want her to be safe. Like you. But one thing is different between you and me, Claude." Suddenly those eyes are dry, suspicious; the change startles him.

"What?"

"I see Blanche. I see her truly. Not like you. But like you I don't want any harm to come to her. I promise, I won't do this again."

"Good. How is he?" Claude can't help but be concerned; Lorenzo, even in his sleep, is moaning.

"He'll be fine. He can't be moved, though."

"For how long?"

She shrugs. "Two days? Three?"

Claude paces while Lily watches him, that gun still within reach, but Claude pays her no mind. He is thinking. Another delivery for Martin—he can call him up, say he has two more packages than he needs, and can Martin take them off his hands?

That was the code they had devised months ago: "packages" were those who needed to be hidden, "parcels" were those who needed to be exposed. Bushels of apples denoted troop movements. Vegetables were substitutes for the German high command—they'd gleefully decided on the code word for Göring: "potato."

This was the game Claude was playing. This was what allowed him to walk proudly again like a Frenchman; this was what he left to do when the phone rang at night. He did not, as Blanche thought, run off to meet his mistress. No, he ran off—as eagerly, as ardently, as a lover—to meet Martin, who had been able to organize some of the other hotel directors. Through Martin's "business" of supplying produce to the hotels via outside contacts in Switzerland, they were able to relay what was going on in the hotels to the Allies. It had only started out as information being shared.

But now, they had moved on to people, as well. Fortunately, the Ritz had very large cupboards—

as did most of the hotels that the Germans had commandeered and that remained open.

The women—Michele and Simone—were mere window dressing (although Claude suspected that the two were involved in other, more dangerous games when they weren't hanging on to Martin's and Claude's arms, but that was one of the rules Martin had set down: *no questions*). The Nazis were generally so dazzled by these two brilliantly beautiful women, they didn't pay attention to what Claude and Martin were discussing at the table right next to them, or in the club where they were all listening to jazz, or on the bench along the Seine. And Frenchmen walking off, arm in arm with Frenchwomen—again, the Nazis didn't think this unusual enough to pursue.

No one need know that, once upstairs in the Auzellos' apartment, Claude and Simone slept in separate beds, and she always left before dawn. It wasn't as if Claude couldn't have made love to this beautiful woman—she'd let him know that she was willing; and he was certainly, most nights, aroused enough, exhilarated by the game they were playing, the blow they were striking against the *Boche*.

But Claude had promised Blanche, that day in his office, before they left for Nîmes. He had never made such a promise earlier in their marriage and so his affairs, before, were guiltless. But he had promised her, and she was a vulnerable, unstable woman. While it disturbed him that she *thought* he was sleeping with another woman, he felt a perverse sense of honor in not doing so. Even in a time of war.

Especially in a time of war.

Watching Lily—so fierce, so tired, so dirty—Claude makes a decision.

"If you don't leave this room, if you do not, under any circumstances, pick up that phone and ask for anything, or answer the door, or open the drapes, you may stay—and I can get him out of the country to recover, if that's what you think he needs to do. I have—some contacts."

Lily's dark eyes flicker—in surprise, Claude realizes. Then he winces, as the astonishment blossoms on her face.

"*You?* You—Claude—you? I can't—how—I never would have guessed!"

Claude holds himself as if he were a much taller man; he looks down his nose at this girl. "I am a Frenchman, Lily, after all. But one thing—you must not tell Blanche. Not a word. She can't know—she can't suspect, because she can't be endangered. There are things—there are things you don't know about my wife, trust me. I think you ought to leave the country, too; and frankly I'd be relieved if you did, because I can't have Blanche put in danger again."

"I think you are wrong about some things, Claude Auzello. About your wife. But is not my place. I thank you, but we will stay in Paris, Lorenzo and me, as long as the damn Nazis are here. We have work to do."

"Three days, then. That's all, you understand? I can't keep him here longer than that. I can't endanger the staff. But I can send you somewhere else, nearby."

She nods and reaches over to brush Lorenzo's hair out of his eyes and in that moment, Claude sees Lily as a woman, a tender-hearted woman, and he doesn't despise her.

"I'll send up some food."

"Blanche already did."

"Of course. Well, don't involve Blanche further. Lily, do you understand me? I can't have that."

"*You* can't have that?" Again, she looks amused, narrowing her eyes at him. "Really?"

"Yes. Now, do as I say."

She nods and begins to unroll a fresh bandage. Claude turns to leave.

"You a good man, Claude Auzello," she says.

He opens his mouth to reply but does not. He simply leaves them there; what should it matter to him, what this woman thinks of him? But there is an unfamiliar warmth in his heart that causes him to admit that it does matter because he longs to have a woman admire him again—

No, not merely *a* woman. He longs to have his *wife* admire him and look at him the way she did, once.

He cannot afford that vanity, for too many reasons, one of which is the unfortunate fact that he cannot trust her, so he cannot tell Blanche that he knows of her involvement in this. Let his wife think that she has deceived him, for once. Let her have her fun, her little child's adventure; she deserves it, he supposes. After all, she truly must be bored by now, simply waiting, idling, even at the Ritz.

However.

As luck would have it, even as Claude was talking to Lily and Lorenzo, more chaos invaded the Ritz, this time aimed at Coco Chanel herself. For Mademoiselle managed to get herself kidnapped by two *other* members of the Resistance. It was as if they were multiplying even in the short time it took for Claude to talk to Lily, and he had to wonder what was stirring them, all of a sudden.

Well, perhaps "kidnap" was too strong a word. The two were waiting for Chanel in her suite— no one will admit how they got in, but Claude has his suspicions—and they threw a bag over her head and took her to a deserted warehouse, where they told her they knew of her relationship with von Dincklage, and that when the war was over, she would pay.

Two hours later, they returned her. Chanel was fine, and not too rattled. Naturally, Claude called on her as soon as she was back, to offer his sympathies and his regrets and a promise to get to the bottom of this, as much as was in his power—that this could happen to Mademoiselle Chanel! In the Ritz! How unspeakable! How terrible!

(How appropriate, Claude thought, even as he stormed and vowed and placated. The woman was an embarrassment to her country, a traitor.)

Chanel may have been appeased by Claude's little show, but von Dincklage is furious. So furious that he informs Claude he believes the two members of the Resistance are still in the hotel, and that the Germans are going to search every room on the rue Cambon side. And if Claude does not cooperate they will break the doors down themselves; and naturally the Ritz will be responsible for the price of replacing them, and Claude's name will be written down on a list that he would rather it not be written down on.

Spatzy, Claude sees immediately, will not be distracted by quenelles.

Nodding thoughtfully, he stalls for time searching for his house keys. Even though the Nazis are not at the moment searching for Lily and her lover, the fact remains that they are here and Lorenzo might be recognized. Lily, of course, is known as Blanche's drunk friend so she will probably be fine—and for the first time, Claude wonders about that, the convenience of it—but then he pushes it out of his mind because there are more pressing matters at hand.

Finally, Claude "finds" his keys and follows the four German soldiers, weapons drawn, out of his office, his pulse pounding in his ears, his hands shaking so that the keys make a jaunty musical accompaniment.

He cannot believe it, Claude simply cannot believe it. Weapons are drawn—in the Hôtel Ritz, on the Place Vendôme. For the first time danger, real danger, the kind of thing that takes place elsewhere in Paris—in alleys, abandoned lots, dark streets at night—has permeated the hallowed walls of César Ritz's palace.

Finally, the war has truly come to the Ritz. And there is a part of Claude—the part that is not currently pulverized by fear—that is relieved. Perhaps—jubilant? For they are all in the fight, now.

Then the horror takes over. Never before has Claude had to pound on the doors of their guests and summon them unceremoniously, with no regard as to what they are doing.

Starting on the second floor—there are no rooms on the first—they begin, methodically. Claude knocks, doors are either opened or not; and if they aren't, he inserts his house key and the Germans sweep inside, looking beneath beds, behind draperies, in wardrobes, bathtubs, even outside of windows even though there are no real

301

balconies. They roughly paw through trunks and drawers, tossing silk blouses, satin negligees, houndstooth jackets on the floor like rubbish. They knock over lamps. They grab towels with their dirty hands and throw them into the sink.

Claude can't help himself; he automatically starts to calculate the man hours it will require to restore order but gives up, for it is too much.

If the doors are opened, he is shoved aside by the soldiers who grunt out their questions to startled guests facing the barrel of a Nazi rifle. Guests of the Ritz, questioned at gunpoint; Claude closes his eyes, grateful that César Ritz is no longer alive to see this.

And as they progress from room to room, German voices that have never been raised inside these walls now barking out threats and warnings, Claude is aware of activity ahead of and behind them. He doesn't think the Germans notice; they are too intent on the task at hand. But he catches, out of the corner of his eye, the young bellhop, the member of the Resistance (he shall have to be sacked after all this, of course—or perhaps given a raise; at the moment, Claude really can't decide), darting to and fro. Claude hears frenzied whispers every time he and his Nazi dogs turn a corner. It's as if this side of the hotel is suddenly an anthill that has been stepped upon, and all the ants are scurrying about, not sure what to do.

They reach the Auzellos' suite, and Claude hesitates.

"Your rooms?" one of the soldiers asks. Claude nods, but the man points his rifle at the door anyway.

"We still have to search them."

Claude knocks and Blanche answers, paling when she sees the soldiers with their weapons drawn. And they allow these vile creatures to ransack their rooms without a word. Claude informs his tense wife, in normal, conversational tones, what happened to Chanel, and why the search is necessary. She nods. She sidles close to him. She opens her mouth, about to whisper something—to tell him about Lily and Lorenzo, Claude realizes, but he shakes his head just in time.

"I won't be long," he says—his voice higher, more artificially unworried, than he's ever heard it. "Why don't you just stay here, my dear, and I'll come back as soon as these fellows are finished?"

Blanche nods but her fists are clenched by her side. So that the Nazis do not see her this way, Claude takes her in his arms. "Do not worry about your friends," he whispers.

Blanche gasps; she looks up at him with eyes that are wide, incredulous—and suddenly shimmering with tears.

"Claude—"

He shakes his head, kisses her on the forehead, and follows the Germans out the door with one last glimpse of his wife, who is finally looking at him like he is a man deserving of her. Just to keep that look in her eyes—he hasn't seen it in so long, this tangible evidence that knocks the breath out of him as if it is a weapon, a blunt instrument of love—he knows, in this moment, that he will do anything to keep it there. Even if it means hurtling himself in front of the Nazis' guns in order to protect Lily and Lorenzo.

Although of course he does hope that it won't come to that—if only because he wants another chance to bask in his wife's love and admiration, for it washes over him, but gently, soothingly, quenching a thirst he'd grown so used to, he'd never even noticed how his very skin was shriveling, parched. Dying.

Finally, they reach room four-fourteen.

"Ah," Claude says slowly, loudly, consulting his guest list. "A honeymooning couple. Let's leave them to it, eh, fellows?" Claude winks at them, praying that they—being men, that much they all have in common—will respect lust, and move on.

But the soldiers shake their heads.

So he knocks, and when there is no answer, he inserts the key in the lock with a hand that is shaking so violently, he isn't sure how he manages it, and it takes him a couple of tries to get it right. Holding his breath and shutting his eyes, he throws open the door, steeling himself for shouts, gunshots, he has no idea; they could turn their guns on him before he can get back down to Blanche—

Claude hears, to his astonishment, laughter. Hearty German laughter.

Opening his eyes, Claude beholds a gloriously naked Lily astride a wheezing but game, equally naked, Lorenzo. Lily twists her torso toward the door, her small breasts exposed, compelling. So compelling, Claude realizes in a flash of admiration, that the Germans will never even look at her face—or poor Lorenzo, who is now gasping as he tries to complete the task at hand.

"What? You bastards! What you do? Have you no shame? Want a closer look, you guys? Here— look here!" And she cups her breasts, jiggling them, and finally the Germans shut the door and collapse in guffaws.

Somehow, they do not notice when Claude draws out a handkerchief to mop his sweating brow.

"Ah, love," one of the soldiers chortles.

"Lucky bastard," another says with a wink. And they talk about their girlfriends back home as they continue down the hall.

After everything settles down—the Nazis do not, after all, find the two who kidnapped Chanel—Lily and Lorenzo sneak out after midnight in one of the Ritz laundry trucks, driven by the young bellhop.

Claude is astonished to find that he doesn't want Lily to go. Instead, he wishes the two of them could sit down somewhere and have a drink and talk about what they're doing. The desire to share his activities, his accomplishments, with someone is fierce, something buried deep within him, hiding all this time. Until now when it lunges up, almost too forceful for him to contain. And he would like to hear what Lily has been doing, too. He suspects, given the last couple of days, that it's much more dangerous than what he has done, but Claude, ever the military man, the manager, recognizes that not all soldiers can be in combat; paperwork is also necessary in order to win a war.

But Lily has gone, gone with her man, who looks as if he will recover. For the first time, Claude hopes she'll be back. Even if it means more trouble for Blanche. Blanche, who must have known, then, about her friend's activities? Why else did Lily seek her out when she was in trouble? Blanche must have— Has she *done* something, in the past, to earn Lily's trust?

But no, no, of course not. Claude warned Lily about his wife, how she can't be trusted. It must merely have been a matter of Blanche happening to reside in a hotel with many rooms, and Lily taking advantage of that.

Claude returns to their suite, with a bottle of brandy and two glasses, and assures Blanche that Lily and Lorenzo are safe for now. He resists the natural masculine urge to expand his role in the drama, and keeps it at that. She is relieved and grateful—and surprisingly dry-eyed; Claude had expected her to burst into tears, at the very least. She embraces him, and Claude falls into his wife's arms, welcoming her warmth, her calm assurance.

Claude realizes this is really the first crisis they've weathered together since returning from Nîmes. He has not shared his daily life with her in so long, for fear of upsetting her, of igniting her temper, of endangering her.

This night, however, Claude and Blanche are allowed an interlude of reconciliation; they retire to bed, they don't risk words—words can be wounding and they know, too well, how easily each can choose the precise ones to ruin a moment like this. They love each other, they look into each other's eyes during the loving, they kiss passionately after they're done. It is as perfect a night as they've experienced since returning to the Ritz.

But neither Claude nor Blanche Auzello is a fool. They both understand that this moment won't last, not as long as the Germans are still inside the Ritz, patrolling the streets of Paris. Rounding up, mowing down, assaulting. Plotting. Planning.

What none of them can know, however—neither von Stülpnagel currently tossing and turning in his big bed, his brain churning with code words and checklists, trying to convince himself that he is doing the right thing for his family, for Germany, that he and his fellow conspirators have no other choice, not if they want to preserve the fatherland and its current annexations, because the Führer simply is insane: he wants too much, he is too ruthless, too egomaniacal; nor the blade-like, wrathful Chanel as she paces in her suite, smoking, planning, plotting her future, a future she has just now glimpsed, should the Germans be defeated, unthinkable, but still; nor the bouncing Lily and Lorenzo, trundling down the cobblestone streets in a laundry truck, him groaning but occasionally turning to look at her with a smug grin for having risen to the occasion, so to speak, never suspecting that she is thinking not of him but of Robert, the man she should be risking her life for, the one she would have taken a bullet for happily, not resentfully; nor Martin, sitting in a chair in a room in a building on the outskirts of town, drinking absinthe alone, having sent Michele away for the night, pondering the loneliness of a man whom so many people want to love, but daren't even try, and so he risks his life daily in order to feel something, anything; nor Blanche and Claude, slumbering deeply in their shared bed, naked beneath the sheets, for the first time since the invasion not feeling compelled to sleep fully clothed in case of horror visiting during the night—

What none of them can know is that the beginning of the end—no, to quote someone on the other side of the Channel, "the end of the beginning"—is gathering on a distant shore.

Boarding transport ships, climbing into bombers.

Getting ready to step foot on French soil, for the first time since 1940.

CHAPTER 25

BLANCHE,
June 1944

The Allies have arrived! The Americans are on their way—*the Yanks are coming, the Yanks are coming,* she sings it in her heart, over and over, that catchy little ditty from the previous war. Soon, they will be here—everyone in Paris knows it, prays it, breathes it.

The Germans know it, too, and are even more paranoid than before, just like the cornered animals they are. More executions of citizens to retaliate against the increasingly brazen acts against them; more trucks screeching in front of buildings, removing people—Jews or not—from their very beds, throwing them into the backs of those trucks, and then disappearing into the night. For there is a spark in the people of Paris and it is only now, now that it has been rekindled—they walk more sprightly, smile frequently, dare to hum bits of "La Marseillaise," dare to cluster in the streets to whisper rumors, good rumors, not rumors of death but rumors of liberation—that they realize how it has been missing these long, cowed years since 1940. June 1940, to be exact.

It was precisely four years ago that the horror began.

And the Yanks are coming. They *have* to be! The Allies landed at Normandy, up the coast, on the sixth of June. Today is the tenth. And Blanche feels like celebrating.

Claude, naturally, is more cautious. But again, he always is. "Blanchette, we mustn't assume. The Allies are on our soil, yes. But if I were them, I would bypass Paris and go straight to Germany. Paris is out of the way, you see—they would waste precious petroleum, not to mention men and munitions, to liberate Paris when the true objective is Berlin."

"You're nuts, Popsy!" It seems like ages since she's called him this. For some reason, when the world turned dark and dangerous, pet names rarely seemed appropriate. "The Americans are coming! Of course they'll liberate Paris. It's a symbol, you know. It would definitely give the world the message: The damned Nazis are over. Defeated!"

"Yes, it's a symbol." Claude looks worried; he rubs his nose with his forefinger. His hair is thinner now, Blanche notices as if for the first time; graying at the temples. There are lines bracketing his mouth. Well, hell. He *is* older. Four years older. A lifetime older.

She must be, too—but she refuses to gaze too closely at the mirror today. Now is not a time to take stock, to sum up, to account for—that will come later. Now is a time to celebrate, not mourn.

"A symbol," Claude continues, thoughtfully. "A symbol the Nazis might want to destroy, actually. If the Allies don't get here first. Think what a statement that would be, Blanche. For the Nazis to blow up the Eiffel Tower, the Arc de Triomphe, the Louvre. Leave the city in ashes, for no one to liberate. I wouldn't put that past Hitler."

"Oh, Popsy." Blanche refuses to allow him to dampen her spirits. She hasn't felt this gay in years. "You're not going to ruin this day for me. I'm going to Maxim's to celebrate. Will you come with me?"

"Maxim's?" He frowns. "Blanche, are you serious? You know the Nazis have made it a headquarters. It's too dangerous there."

"How is it more dangerous than here? After all, the Ritz is their headquarters, too."

"I . . . It—it just is, Blanche!"

"Oh, Claude, you pompous old darling! You still can't let anyone say a word against your precious Ritz, can you?" But she kisses him on the cheek so he won't be angry. "Champagne and caviar at Maxim's! I haven't had caviar in forever, and I'm going to have some today, even if it takes every last ration card and my feminine wiles. I'm going to have some fun, goddammit! I deserve it—we all deserve it. Are you in or are you out?"

"Out." He shakes his head in that prim little way of his. "I have work to do. For despite your enthusiasm, the Germans are indeed still here, and more demanding than before. Be careful, Blanche, please? Promise me?"

"You old fussbudget." She kisses his cheek. "But then again, you were a *young* fussbudget. I'll call—I'll find someone."

"Not Lily," Claude warns. Even though Blanche admits he was so, well, *gallant* about Lily and Lorenzo, weeks have passed since. And Claude is back to his old dislike of her friend, and how she so easily corrupts Blanche. And how easily Blanche is corrupted.

Although there have been several moments—unexpected tender moments between her and her husband—when she has been tempted to reveal to him just what she and Lily have been up to. But tempering that desire is a new, surprisingly fierce resolution that *she*—in an unexpected turnabout of their previous roles—must protect *him.*

Once, she wanted to punish her husband. Now—perhaps it is because the phone calls are much fewer and far between—she knows she has to protect him. She has to keep him safe, so that when this is all over, their marriage might finally have a chance. There is a promise—she glimpsed it that day when he saved Lily and Lorenzo—that she must follow up on.

So Blanche smiles, very sweetly and properly,

like a good little French wife. "Of course not, Claude. I told you I wouldn't."

"Good. Find someone else suitable. Or stay here?" Claude gazes at her, hope softening his stern eyes.

And she knows—in a giddy rush of discovery—that he recognized it, too, that promise. That must be why, all of a sudden, they are *nice* to each other, so carefully attentive. He looks shy around her at times; she's making more of an effort to look pretty for him, to comb her hair a certain way, to not spend so much time in the bar. While there is still wariness between them, it's a wariness that is flexible; not the brittle suspicion and disillusionment that existed before.

"I'll find someone suitable." Blanche begins to dress, pulling out a silk blouse she hasn't worn in months; searching for a pair of stockings without ladders in them, but that's impossible, so she does what every woman in Paris has been doing for the last couple of years: She draws a line down the back of her legs with an eyebrow pencil. Taking her least worn shoes out of the bottom of the wardrobe, she examines them; despite a tear in the leather that the Ritz cobbler attempted to repair with glue, they're her most presentable shoes—the only pair she has left that doesn't have wooden soles. She's destroyed all her shoes in the last couple of years, wearing them out in her wanderings, her work. Now she's just like everyone else in Paris—all the leather has gone to the Germans, so citizens have had to make do with wooden soles, and that hollow clomping over the streets mingles with the steel boots of the Nazis until sometimes Blanche's ears ring from the din. Despite the shocked acquiescence of these last years, Paris is still quite a noisy city. Just in different ways than it used to be; it's changed, too.

They all have.

Deciding to dress defiantly—the colors of the tricolor flag; the colors of the Star-Spangled Banner—Blanche pairs a red scarf with a white silk blouse and chooses a blue skirt. Then she leaves the Ritz—after a surprisingly *healthy* kiss from Claude that makes her toes curl up in those patched shoes—to try to find Lily at one of the various rooms she uses to "hang her hat."

But Blanche knows she'll turn up somehow. That girl has a pure genius for sniffing out a free meal.

"Ah, Blanche, is nice," Lily whispers, her eyes enormous as she takes in the resplendence that is Maxim's. Blanche is pleased to be the one to introduce her friend to it, for before the war it had been one of her favorite spots.

"It sure is." Blanche relaxes into the plush banquette, luxuriating in the Belle Époque splendor—heavy Art Nouveau lamps with

Tiffany glass lampshades, mirrors everywhere, dark wood paneling. It's a little faded, a little patched—the carpet is worn, the tablecloths still pristine white but mended—just like everyone who has survived thus far.

After a glass of champagne—Blanche orders in confident German to get better service—Lily loses her awe of her surroundings and begins to relax. Blanche insisted on dressing her for the occasion; she couldn't take her here looking as she usually did. So Lily is wearing a decent skirt, pinned up so she won't trip on the hem, and a short-sleeved cashmere sweater that had shrunk too small for Blanche, but fits Lily just right. She found a pair of flat shoes that are actually made for women, not men, in a size small enough for her childish feet. Her hair is growing out; it's shiny, straight, about chin length.

Lily sighs happily, gazing about at the gilded mirrors, the red wallpaper, the chandeliers. Maxim's still looks like it must have during the Belle Époque, when French men proudly paraded their mistresses about, walking from table to table. Only the tables are filled with German soldiers parading their mistresses, now.

But not for long, Blanche tells herself. Not for long.

"I like." Lily hiccups, then giggles. "I like it here. You know, the war has changed me."

"How?"

"I think I learn to enjoy things more. The fighting—always the fighting. I'm tired of it. There will always be more fighting. More Fascists, more dictators. More bad men—and women." Lily glances, significantly, at the French women dining with German soldiers. "But maybe my time is over now. I miss Robert," she says, very softly, and her eyes threaten tears. Blanche is shocked, because she hasn't seen Lily cry in a long time, not even when she got her hand slammed in the door of a lorry full of vegetables (hiding guns and ammunition) that they were in a hurry to drive to the countryside near Orléans one moonless night. Lily had broken three fingers on her left hand and never once uttered a sound.

But now, when the end is so near, Lily, of all people, is weeping. She glances up at Blanche, smiles ruefully, asks for a handkerchief.

"You never have handkerchiefs on you," Blanche scolds, handing her one of her own.

"Maybe now I do, Blanche. Maybe now I cry more."

"Why now, Lily? It's a time for joy, not sadness. We've done wonderful things, you and I! The last thing *I* want to do is cry. That's all over; it's done."

"For you, yes." Lily grins at her, admiringly. "You know what, Blanche? I never told you, but when I lost Robert, I didn't want to be tied to this world anymore. He was, what you say—my anchor. But now *you,* Blanche. You make me see things different like Robert did. Like nice things, and pretty things. Like talking, not fighting. You make me care again—I don't want anything bad to happen to you. Is nice, to feel that again. Not so alone in this."

"I do?" Blanche is stunned—and touched beyond measure.

"Did I ever tell you how Robert died?" Lily whispers.

Blanche shakes her head.

"He was rounded up with some students. They were tortured, their privates cut. Then they were lined up against a wall and shot. Like dogs. I couldn't go to his body, after. They wouldn't let anyone near. I don't know where they took him."

"Lily, I—"

"No—let me finish. I did things then. I brought Nazi soldiers to my room, I plunged the knife in, I fed their bodies to pigs. I forgot to eat—Heifer tried to give me soup sometimes. But I couldn't see her, I couldn't see anything. But once I saw *you.* They were putting a family in a truck, in the Marais, and you were there, watching. There was something in your face new to me. You were upset, but also—how you say? Vulnerable? Seeing you like that made me want to be good again so I could go to you. I didn't think you'd like me the way I was, so bad. So I tried again. To live, live good, so you would be my friend

318

again. Thank you for that, Blanche. Thank you."

Blanche finds she can't look at Lily right then, so she fiddles with her napkin, toys with her champagne glass. It's true that she's often wondered what Lily has seen in her, why she came back into her life—and why she stayed there. Was it only for what Blanche could give her, materially—money, clothes, food, coupons? Only to recruit her in her everlasting fight against fascism? To hear that it was something more, something bigger—vital, even—renders her speechless.

She only hopes it's not too late.

Lately, Blanche has been aware that she looks at people solely as arithmetic problems—three go out, two come back, we need one more to take the place. Five Nazis are better than ten Nazis but zero would be better still. Ten thousand Jews are now eight thousand Jews are now five thousand Jews and the Nazis keep trying to whittle it down to none. And she's horrified by this change in her; she fears falling into something—well, like what Lily described. Something dark, consuming. Unlike Lily, Blanche doesn't need to keep fighting.

But she does need to keep *saving*. She needs to find something, someone, worth saving in this world again.

Blanche takes another sip of champagne,

savoring it—savoring a new vision of the future, a future without Nazis, but with Lily. Her friend, that she's brought back to life—Goddamn, but isn't Blanche wonderful? Isn't Lily remarkable? Aren't they both the bee's knees—she remembers Pearl, so long gone, who used to say that a lot: *Isn't he the bee's knees?* Blanche raises a toast to Pearl.

And one to Claude.

It's funny, she often thinks. She's helped so many people these last few years, people who were strangers to her, really; she had no idea if they were good people or bad, if they cheated on their wives or if they kicked their dogs. She helped them, no questions asked, because they didn't wear a Nazi uniform. She can at least try to do the same for the man who once loved her so. She can at least remain by his side, no more running away, and help him become the man he used to be.

She is very good at this, Blanche understands. Saving—fallen airmen, wounded Resistance fighters, lonely German soldiers, Lily. Now Claude. This damn war—it's shown her that, at least.

"So maybe now you will see me at the Ritz. I'll live there—with you!" Lily grins. "And Claude—won't he be surprise? I'll have a room, we'll do nice things together—you'll show me how to be a lady! And you have friends, important friends.

Maybe they write my story in a book, eh? I would like that. I would like to be famous."

"I'm sure as hell that Hemingway would love to put you in a book—he can write one featuring both of us. *For Whom the Cocktail Shaker Tolls*." Blanche raises her glass in a toast, Lily clinks hers against it, and they order two more. "I wonder where he is right now? Arm-wrestling a German somewhere?"

They are giddy, the two of them, these two warriors hiding in pretty clothes. All the times they pretended to be drunk, to fall off the Ritz barstools, to sing in the elevator—they'd never had as much fun, they'd never laughed, as they are laughing now. The world looks different—the colors brighter; there's music in the air even when the violinists in the restaurant pause their playing. There's music *everywhere;* Blanche's ears thrum with a beat, a vibration. Everyone is laughing, too—they are, the Germans are, along with their girls.

And that's what starts to get to Lily—the girls.

"Look at them," she whispers. "Those girls. Those no-goodniks. What shame do they have?"

"Oh, forget about it." Blanche spears a bite of melon, savoring its refreshing flavor. "They'll get theirs, when the Americans come."

She says this loudly—more loudly than she'd intended. Because the Germans at the table next to them freeze. So does Lily.

321

But—another gulp of champagne, the promising future so bright and close she could touch it—Blanche decides she doesn't give a good goddamn. Because it's true—nothing matters! The Americans are coming and *they* will soon be gone, these vile, filthy Nazis in their uniforms the color of pine trees, their fat well-fed faces, their obnoxious, guttural voices, explosive laughter, evil, evil thoughts and deeds. People are gone from Paris—vanished, forever. Because of *them*.

"To the Americans," Blanche sings it out loud for the world is so bright, almost too bright; she's not felt this vivacious in so long, she needs to shout, to dance—she struggles out of her chair, giggling, and after a moment, so does Lily, and they clink their glasses together and Blanche shouts out—

"To the Americans! Coming to rid us of these German swine!"

Dimly, she's aware of a collective hush, of shocked faces, frozen smiles, but who the hell cares? She is *gorgeous,* this Blanche, and so is Lily—they are gorgeous women who have done heroic things and it will soon be all over, the sun will always shine from now on.

Next to them, the German soldiers abruptly stand. They raise their own glasses in a toast—reaching out to clink glasses to Lily and Blanche.

"*Heil Hitler!*"

Her arm shoots out; Blanche flings her champagne in the face of one of the soldiers.

"God damn Hitler and all of you to hell," she sings, laughing triumphantly—until, abruptly, she stops.

As Blanche realizes what she's done, she can't breathe, can barely think. Staring into the enraged face of the soldier, she knows she ought to beg his forgiveness but the words won't come, not in German, not in French, not in English. He wipes the dripping liquid from his face with a napkin, but otherwise betrays no emotion. His companions do, however; one of them lurches toward the two women, but is stopped by the man whom Blanche has so recklessly baptized. The liquid has darkened the front of his shirt but the buttons are glittering, dripping champagne.

"*Nein*," he says to his companions.

"Lily, I—" But Lily shoots her a look, and Blanche instantly understands. In the stunned silence, everyone heard her name—the companion of the woman who just threw a glass of champagne in a Nazi officer's face. And *her* name is in their books. Maybe Blanche's is, too, by now. Certainly, her face is better known, at least to some of the patrons here, for she recognizes many of them from the Ritz.

"Let's get out of here," Blanche whispers as the maître d' makes an elaborate fuss out of handing out napkins and mopping up the mess. Blanche is certain that they'll be arrested before they step a foot out the door, but they have to at least try to get away.

They make it out of the restaurant, shuddering with every step; Blanche believes that each breath she takes will be her last, and is astonished by every new one. She leads Lily down the street, away from the river toward the Ritz, toward wherever Lily hangs her hat these days. They don't speak.

Finally, they stop running; they face each other for a moment. Blanche opens her mouth to say something—that she's sorry, that she's not—but before any words can form themselves, Lily darts away.

But then she spins around, runs back, and hugs Blanche, fiercely, before vanishing into the dark.

Blanche makes it back to the Ritz, looking over her shoulder the entire way. Stumbling up the stairs, she hurries into the suite, locks the door and sits there, waiting for Claude, as the light of this formerly brilliant day—a day of hope, a day of jubilation—fades to the familiar sinister darkness. Every step in the hallway is meant for her, it has to be. She waits and waits for a knock on the door, a summons that must inevitably come, and by the time Claude finally turns his key in the lock and opens the door, she's so tightly wound that she runs to him, falling into his surprised arms with a hysterical laugh.

"Oh, Claude, Claude—you'll never believe what I've done now!"

CHAPTER 26

CLAUDE,
June 1944

"**W**hat? See here, Blanche, what is it?" She's so distraught; her eyes are wild, her makeup smeared into a grotesque mask. Taking her by the shoulders, Claude sits her down, glancing at his watch. It's late; he's hungry.

What *has* she done now?

She begins to explain, at first haltingly, then finally it all pours out of her as if she is at confession. She tells him what she's done at Maxim's, with Lily. She tells Claude everything, finishing with the part where she threw her champagne into the German's face.

Blanche threw champagne. Into a German's face.

"My God." That is all Claude can say at first. He darts to the window, peering out onto the rue Cambon, glimpses nothing out of the ordinary, but pulls the drapes shut. As if that will prevent them from storming the Ritz, from tearing the place apart. From taking her away.

She looks so vulnerable, so bruised, sitting on the bed. Like she did on their honeymoon, when she'd done something almost as foolish—tried to throw herself from the train—and ran away, and he found her, eyes red from weeping, at the train station. Too fragile-looking, too slight, to have done the thing she says she did. Claude at first wants to take her in his arms, soothe her, put her back together again.

But then the rage, surging through his veins, lassoes him when he's halfway across the room, arms already reaching out to embrace his wife. All he's done! All the care he's taken to keep her safe, to keep them *all* safe under his watch; to preserve the Ritz for it means something to him, yes; something important, the one part of France that is his to keep from being tainted, from being stomped under Aryan boots. All the effort he's made—to the point of ulcers, he's certain of it— to control *his* temper when each day, serving and scraping and bowing, his every muscle strains to reach out, to slap, scratch, pummel. How many times has *Claude* longed to throw champagne into a fat German's face? To tell him—and his Hitler—to go to hell? To get out of his Ritz, his France?

But Claude does not. Because he is a sensible person, an adult. Unlike his foolish wife. The anger overpowers everything else, and he allows it to do so.

"Blanche, Blanche, I told you. I told you not to see that dangerous woman. I forbade it! And look at you, you idiot, you *fool*. You did it anyway, you disobeyed me and isn't that what you always do? You're not a woman, you're a child. A spoiled child, for too long I've protected you. Do you have any idea what they'll do to you for this? They're killing anyone who even looks at them crossly, let alone throws a drink in their faces. They know the Americans are coming, they're doomed, and they're lashing out."

"Maybe they won't," she falters, as if she doesn't believe what she's saying, either. "After all, you—the Ritz—"

"The Ritz can't protect you now, Blanche."

"But I've done so many other—"

"You've done what? Tell me, Blanche. I'm your husband. If you've done anything else, you must tell me. I demand that you tell me. It is my duty to try to protect—"

"Protect me? From what? You just said the Ritz can't protect me now. And maybe I don't want it to anymore—maybe I'm sick of you treating me like a child."

"Because you act like one!"

"No, I don't." She says this quietly, firmly—in a voice he's not accustomed to hearing from his operatic wife. It is this voice that punctures Claude's rage. Blanche is composed, serious. A steel glint in those usually soft brown eyes, a look that says *I must be reckoned with*. Claude has never seen this look before.

"Blanche, of course you do—the hysterics,

the drinking, the playing around with Lily while I'm trying to keep this place running, keep you safe—"

"Keep kowtowing to the Nazis?"

Claude winces. But he will not be judged by his wife, the woman who just threw a drink in a Nazi's face. "It is my *job,* Blanche. You seem to forget that the reason you've been able to live out this occupation with enough food to eat, a soft bed in which to sleep, is because of my job. You have no idea, truly, what I deal with every day."

"Why don't you try telling me?"

"Because you—you aren't to be—"

"You don't trust me, do you, Claude?" Blanche—instead of looking devastated—appears amused; is there *laughter* in her eyes?

"Well, Blanche—given your—habits—"

"Do you want to know something rich? I don't trust you, either."

Claude cannot believe this. All his life, he has been the most trustworthy person he's known. Others have said it. It has been the most memorable part of his personality and he's learned to embrace it, stop wishing that he was memorable for other things, like that fellow Martin. How can his own wife say she can't trust him? It is the most wounding thing she has ever said to him in a marriage full of words that are missiles, aimed at the heart.

"I haven't trusted you since you first took a mistress," she continues, so coolly that the words seem to slice into him—not missiles, but knives. "But I especially don't trust you now, the way you behave to your *guests*. Maybe you'll turn me in yourself."

"Blanche! How can you say such a thing? I have done nothing dishonorable. You have no idea *what* I've done, these past years—"

"And you have no idea, truly, what I'm capable of—"

"Throwing drinks into Nazis' faces? *Very* brave, Blanche. *Very* stupid. Not to mention extremely selfish."

"Selfish?" She laughs, a disturbing, bitter cackle. "Oh, that's priceless. You, accusing me of being selfish. What about your mistresses? So many I can't count? What about you sneaking away even now, even during this horrible war?"

"That's different, that's—" Claude has to sit down; how has this escalated so quickly? One minute Blanche is crying, confessing to him her folly; the next, they're chasing around the same old, tired argument, as if nothing has happened at all these last four years.

When, in fact, *everything* has happened.

Blanche continues—but still in this eerily calm manner. And so, he has to wonder if she's right; if, perhaps, he hasn't any idea of what she's capable of. "You say you worry about me, that you want to keep me safe, that I'm to sit here and do nothing while the whole world is upside down. While people are *dying*. You don't think about what that does to me—to sit idly by, to *watch*. But you leave me anyway, you run off every time the phone rings, and what am I to think about that? I think that I'm not enough. But then I've never been enough for you, have I?"

"Blanche, why must we go through this again? I chose you—you're my wife. I respected you enough to rescue you from that man. I *loved* you enough to marry you, when that scoundrel wouldn't."

"But then you didn't know what to do with me, did you?" she said with a sneer.

"If you were a French woman—if only we—"

"If only we what?" Blanche looks down at her hands in her lap, suddenly apprehensive.

"If only we had a child," Claude says bitterly, giving this loss a voice for the first time. "Why didn't we, Blanche?" He steels himself to hear the truth. "What was wrong?"

"I went to the doctor, once." She shudders. As if she is remembering a cold, sterile room, white enamel basins. Being poked and prodded by a strange man—Claude shudders, as well. "There was something about my uterus. I forget—it was long ago."

"But why didn't you tell me, Blanche? Why?" Claude sits down beside her but forces himself

331

not to touch her; if he does, he is certain he will crumble. He must cling to his anger, his righteousness, for it is the only thing that will give him strength. Love certainly won't; it never really has, has it?

Anger—carefully tended, stoked when necessary. It is what has allowed him to do the things he's done these years. Anger at the Germans, at the French who caved and let them in. Anger at his wife.

Anger at her secret.

"I don't know, Claude. It didn't seem to be anything we could talk about, did it? We could talk about Paris. We could talk about how much I drank, how much you ignored me. We could talk for days about those subjects! And the Ritz, always the Ritz—we could talk about *that,* your true mistress. But we could never really talk about us, could we? The important things?"

"I don't know." Claude slumps, his head in his hands; it really has been a long day. Von Stülpnagel has been unusually demanding as of late. "Blanche, you have no idea what I sacrifice, every day—"

"Is it as much as *I* sacrificed?"

Finally. It is here, it's walked right into the room without knocking. The secret they've kept hidden for decades. They had agreed, back in the beginning, not to talk about it. They each had their different reasons, but on that they agreed.

What was done was done; there was no use discussing it.

Until now.

"I never asked you to, Blanche," Claude says, immediately on the defense. "Never once did I say—"

"Say what? That you wouldn't marry a *Jew?*"

Jew.

Juif.

Juden.

The word is incendiary, no matter the language. Claude winces to hear her say it out loud. Only the Nazis speak that word; everyone in Paris pretends it doesn't exist. Just as everyone in Paris pretends that *they* don't exist. Except as problems to be solved, and it's always been that way.

Even back in 1923.

"My name is Blanche Ross," she said, as if trying out the words for the first time. And when Claude Auzello, manager of the Hôtel Claridge, asked this charming young American woman for her passport so that he could check her in, she hesitated before handing it to him, unable to meet his gaze.

And he could not meet hers, either, as astonishment and disappointment flashed over his face too quickly to hide. For the name on that passport was Blanche *Rubenstein,* not Ross. And her religion: *Jewish.*

She'd searched his face, so anxious, yet

defensive. He ironed out his dismay by reminding himself that she was only a charming woman he intended to take out once or twice, so what did it matter? He was not a prejudiced man, himself—of that, Claude Auzello was most certain. Yes, he enforced the unwritten quotas at the Claridge—not *too* many Jews, one mustn't make the other guests uncomfortable. But it was that way in every fine hotel in Paris. And Claude—had he not fought next to Jews in the war? Did he not know several now? The man, Bloch was his name, whom he often encountered at the Louvre—it seemed they always chose the same paintings to study at the same time, they'd even laughed about it and had a glass of wine once while they discussed Raphael's use of shadows. And that old farmer near his parents' house, Jacoby, who had that pretty daughter. Claude always made a point of stopping at their stand when he visited the south. No, Claude was not a prejudiced man.

Anyway, what did this young woman's religion matter to him? It wasn't as if he was going to marry her, this charming American actress.

This charming American Jew.

And when they did marry, she was the one who offered to have a new passport made (Claude did not approve of the word "forged"). "I've been thinking of changing my name anyway, Popsy. You know how the movie business is. Everybody does it." And he'd believed her; he'd been overjoyed, actually. When she proudly showed him her new passport, the handiwork of that little Turk, Greep, he'd given her a small gold cross on a chain that used to be his grandmother's, and promised he would help her get instruction in the Catholic faith.

Claude was as thorough a Catholic as any Frenchman raised by a devout mother and indifferent father. He went to Mass once a week, he celebrated the feast days, he made confession before taking Communion. So when Blanche never got around to converting, it had disappointed him more than he had anticipated.

The passport had been officially renewed, many times over. The gold cross, she only wore after 1940. It was a costume, nothing more. Claude looks at it now, hanging delicately off his wife's slender throat. Visible, always visible, to their German guests.

"But it was a good thing you did it, after all," Claude says. "Even if it was for your vanity."

"Vanity?" Blanche recoils from him. "You *fool*. If you don't know by now, Claude Auzello—I did it for *you*. For you, for your career here at your precious Ritz! The first time you took me here, I knew what I had to do. I knew a Jewish wife would be a liability for you. So I did it: I changed my religion, erased my past, not for me—I knew I had no chance in the movies—but for *you*."

"No—" Claude's vision is blurry, as if he's had

335

a blow to the head. "That's not what you said, back then—you said you'd thought of doing it before you even came to France."

"Thinking about it and doing it are two different things. Had I not met you—had I not fallen in love with you like a damn fool—I'd still be Blanche Rubenstein." She says it bitterly, and her face is twisted—with guilt, Claude recognizes. Guilt, for hiding in plain sight, for *surviving,* while so many Jews no longer existed.

Guilt. For marrying him.

"Every day I see them rounded up, I hate myself a little bit more." Her words are jagged stones, shattering the protective bubble he had thought he'd encased her in here at the Ritz. Not to mention the nobility he sometimes felt—yes, he could admit it—in marrying her in the first place. "I hate you, too."

"Yes, I—I understand," Claude says, wearily.

"If we understand so much about each other, Claude, then why have we lived all these years so—so—apart?"

Claude can't answer. They are facing each other, and there is despair in her eyes, despair he is feeling, too. Despair—and wariness. *All* their lies, they cling to them with fierce loyalty, they will not give them up. Not even now. Perhaps these lies are the fuel that drives the Auzellos, each of them, to do—what it is they have done.

But are these the last moments they will have

336

together? Because of what she just confessed—he's almost forgotten, so tangled up are they now in their shared disappointment with each other. But yes, of course—Blanche did a terrible thing. A brave—but foolish—thing.

Isn't it time to tell his wife the truth? To have one moment of candor, of love, before she's wrenched from him?

He takes a breath; he wonders if this is actually the bravest thing he has done: deciding to speak honestly with his wife of twenty-one years.

"Blanche, I have not done what you thought I have, those nights when the phone rang."

Her eyebrows raise questioningly; he notices, for the first time, that her bottom lip has a small red mark on it, she must have bitten it at some point; it looks tender, sore, and he wonders if she's in pain.

"I have not been seeing a mistress. I have been—working, in my own way, to get rid of them. The Nazis. To disrupt them. I have been passing on information to someone else. I have, occasionally, helped transport, sometimes hide, people. Jews—even here." Again—why does he have such trouble with the word? They never say that this is who they are hiding, Martin and himself. They know, of course. But they never say it; they never give these unnamed people any kind of heritage or past. And isn't it, really, what the Nazis are intending to do, but in such a more terrible way? *Erasing* a people? Eradicating an entire race? He and Martin, in truth, have reduced the Jews to a problem that needs to be solved. Nothing more.

"Claude, you have been—part of the Resistance, too?" Blanche sits next to him and—to his astonishment—takes his hand.

"Yes—what? What do you mean, 'too'?" Now it's Claude's turn to gaze at his spouse in disbelief.

"Claude, all those times you thought I was drunk, out with Lily—'carousing,' as you like to say—I was working. With Lily and her friends, Communists and students, mostly from other countries. I've—I've gotten people out of France. I've passed on information. In a different way, I think, than you—I have pretended to be other people. I've been to the coast. To farms out in the country. I haven't stayed here at the Ritz, or even in Paris."

Claude can only stare at her, this small woman. Her smile, her voice, her attitude have always been bigger than her physical body. His wife. His princess, in need of rescue. His problem, in need of solving.

His Blanche—a soldier of the Resistance?

"But when Lily and that Lorenzo, when they came here—?"

"It was more than merely a little adventure for me," Blanche confesses, but with a touching, proud lift of her chin. "We'd been working together for a long time by then. I've given them things from the Ritz—clothing, stolen ration cards, food. But I didn't want them to come here. I tried to keep my activities elsewhere. The only time I really did anything here was one night, during an air raid—I turned the lights on in the kitchen, for the Allies."

"That was you? I thought—I went down to do the same, but they were already on."

"Oh, Claude." Blanche laughs, but it's a rueful, sad sound to his still-unbelieving ears.

"So all this time, we've been doing the same thing? We've had the same goal? And all this time, we've been at each other's throats."

"It's a damn shame, isn't it? And now—"

"And now it's too late." Claude pulls her hand to his chest, just above his heart.

He does not know what else to do with this woman. Not a princess, no, not at all. Not in need of rescuing anymore—if she ever was. She is flesh and blood. Jewish. And far, far braver than he has ever imagined.

"Now what, Claude?"

"We wait—I could try to get you away, but we haven't succeeded much lately, Martin and I. The Nazis are everywhere now that the end is near, and it has not ended well for those we've tried to save. It's better for you to stay here, I think. We can only hope that my influence, the Ritz, will make a difference. So tonight, like everyone else in Paris, we wait."

She nods, and they stay like this, her head on his shoulder, his hand in hers, for a long time, until finally they stretch out on the bed. They remain fully clothed; tonight, they need to be ready.

At one point, Claude realizes he has drifted off because he awakens with a jolt. He was so certain he could not sleep a wink. But the revelations, the unfamiliar emotions—they have taken their toll. He holds himself very still, and hears his wife's steady breathing. So she must be asleep now, too.

This is the moment when Claude remembers—remembers that he has a gun.

He eases himself out of the bed, creeps down to his office—the German soldiers on patrol don't give him a second glance—and unlocks a certain drawer in his desk. He checks the chamber of the pistol for bullets; it is full. He has oiled it and cleaned it every month, despite the fact that he's never had an occasion to fire it. But there is no sense in owning a gun unless one maintains it.

Tucking it into the pocket of his jacket, he nods at the soldiers on his way back to his suite. He crawls into bed, so carefully, and gazes at his wife.

Blanche is lying on her back, her eyes closed, her lips parted. She is breathing regularly, shallow breaths, so she must not be deeply asleep. Claude still cannot quite fathom this woman doing the brave deeds she says she did. But he believes her. Because he needs to believe her, he needs his marriage to mean something, *be* something more than he thought it was. Because in war, a man needs someone to fight for. He's had the Ritz, true. And a wife.

But he didn't know how heroic, how remarkable—how precious—she was, until now, his wife.

His *Jewish* wife.

Still gazing at her, Claude curls his finger around the trigger of the gun. Can he do it? Can he truly put the gun to her head and pull the trigger?

He turns away from her, shuddering with horror, with revulsion; he buries his head in the pillow, unable to blot out the picture of Nazis tearing up the Ritz, looking for her. Blanche being tortured or raped; lined up against a wall and mowed down by those Germans. His *guests*. The people he's bowed and scraped to these last four years.

How can he let that happen to her? Even if it means doing the impossible?

Tucking the gun beneath his pillow, Claude shuts his eyes against the sadistic images that continue to assault him no matter which way he turns his head.

They make it through the night, the gun still

cool beneath Claude's pillow. He showers, dresses, and conceals the gun in some laundry that he tells Blanche needs to be done. She doesn't reply; she only prepares to shower herself. She has inky crescents beneath her eyes; her face, devoid of makeup, is pale and her bottom lip now has a purplish bruise.

She is beautiful.

"See, I told you." Claude knots his tie with shaky fingers. "It will be fine, I'm sure. But stay here today, just in case, please, Blanche? Don't go out."

"All right, Claude." She meets his gaze, steadily—bravely. For now, there is nothing more to say other than "I love you."

They embrace, these Auzellos. A tender, forgiving, acknowledging embrace neither wants to end.

But Claude is the one who gently pushes her away; he picks up the laundry pile and leaves his wife. All alone. Unprotected. But no. She is at the Ritz. Nothing bad can happen to anyone at the Ritz—Claude told her that, long ago.

Two hours later, Frank Meier comes running to Claude in his office, out of breath.

"They've taken her, Claude. The Gestapo. They've taken Blanche."

And all Claude can think of is the chance he had, the night before—the one chance to save her from this. But he couldn't do it; he was too much of a coward. Too much of a husband—the kind of husband she's deserved, all these years. The kind who can't bear to hurt his wife.

Claude dashes up to their rooms, but it is just as Frank said.

Blanche is gone.

CHAPTER 27
BLANCHE,
June 1944

Which one of these bastards turned her in? Who at the Ritz said, Yes, of course, she's in room three-twenty-five? Was it the one who handed her a fresh rose just the other day? One of the chambermaids—Blanche had caught one, she said she was Hungarian to cover up her odd accent—searching through her wardrobe last week? Was it Astrid—who has turned into an even more pathetic version of herself, her hair hanging loose and uncurled, her lipstick smeared as if she's always just applied it before eating something, her smile nonexistent?

Was it someone even closer?

As she is marched out through the Place Vendôme doors, Blanche cranes her neck and torso, despite the fact that her hands are tied behind her, searching for him. But Claude isn't here—why isn't he here? Who will tell him she's gone? What will he say? What will he do, that husband of hers who said he had to protect her, no matter the cost?

The man who also said he had to protect the Ritz?

Even as she's shoved into the back of a canvas-covered truck with other women, all in handcuffs, still Blanche twists her body around to look back at the Ritz as the truck pulls away; she longs to see him running after her—the need is so deep it's a physical craving. The gallant little man who rescued her so long ago—where is he now?

But then she thinks, if the final glimpse she has of him is that last one, when he paused in the doorway and gave her a look of such lingering, wistful love, it will be enough. At least, they had last night. When they finally told each other the truth. And allowed the secret they shared to come out of hiding. To seek the light.

When she finally said it out loud, after all these years—

She, Blanche Auzello, is a Jew.

Le Juif et la France.

It was autumn of 1941. The propaganda arm of the German military had decided to put on a show—let's put on a show, kids! But this was no family musical starring Judy Garland and Mickey Rooney. Not by a long shot. Claude and Blanche went to see it, for all the Nazis at the Ritz kept asking if they had. And the Auzellos knew they really didn't have a choice; it was something on the scale of a command performance, a litmus test for everyone working at the Ritz.

So the Auzellos dutifully went. There were

no yellow stars on the street—not yet; that came later. On the surface, Blanche looked as she'd looked these twenty or so years. A blond American Catholic from Cleveland, Ohio, married to a French Catholic from Paris, France.

Before they left, as Blanche pinned her hat in her hair with trembling fingers, she remembered being told, back when she was younger, more careless, that she didn't look "too Jewy." A film producer told her that. He meant it as a compliment.

And Blanche took it that way.

But now, it made her sick to remember how easily, eagerly, she agreed with him. How delighted she was that she did not look "too Jewy."

This day, however, she knew it wasn't going to be as easy as it usually was—or as easy as she'd *convinced* herself, over the years, that it usually was. Blanche understood it from the moment they were greeted, upon approach to the Palais Berlitz where the exhibition was held, by an enormous mural, four stories tall, of an ugly cartoon of a Semite, complete with hooked nose, beady eyes, and gnarled fingers, clutching a globe. The symbol of the Jew out to destroy the world—the message was not subtle, Claude whispered.

Blanche felt her nose—she couldn't help it, her hand flew up to touch her damn nose, to see if it had suddenly grown three sizes, developed a hook where there had been none before.

Claude took her hand and held it tight within his. He kept his wife this way—so close against him that she couldn't fall down—the entire afternoon.

The Auzellos shuffled like conjoined twins, as if his non-Semitic blood could seep through his skin to change hers, to make her, inside and out, "less Jewy," through room after room of exhibits. Exhibits explaining—in German with French subtitles—through photographs, through artwork, through damned dirty lies, how the Jews wanted to take over the world, wanted to squeeze every sense of decency and morality out of it, wanted to kill Christians in their sleep. Jews were ugly, were venomous, were sick. They were responsible for Communism and Marxism. They had poisoned French culture with their art, their movies, their music.

They were unworthy of kindness, dignity. Unworthy of life itself.

And all that Blanche had convinced herself that she'd left behind in New York when she first sailed to France came flooding back, threatening to smother even the shaky breaths she was taking. She was overwhelmed with memories; old photographs, the starched white dress with the red embroidered collar she wore one Passover, the equally ironed and stiffened black dress with huge leg-of-mutton sleeves she wore to her grandmother's funeral, as well as the enormous black taffeta bow her mother used to tie back her hair so tight, she had a headache the entire time; tradition, family, oft-told stories, dreams, Mama and Papa and her sisters and her brothers and glimpses of her grandparents and distant aunts and relatives, all her worst fears, everything she spent a lifetime leaving behind and why had she? Blanche couldn't remember anymore, not when confronted by such slander about them. About her.

Lies about people like her grandparents, who had come over from Germany; they never learned English, so the family always spoke German in their presence. They were kind people. Gentle people who only wanted the best for their children and grandchildren. These were the same monsters that were supposed to be plotting to murder all Christians in their sleep? Blanche's grandfather Rubenstein couldn't harm a fly—a memory flashed through her mind. A memory of how, once, a mouse had gone on a spree in the kitchen of his small apartment, the first home he and her grandmother had rented in America, the apartment he'd never been able to give up despite her parents' urging. But Grandfather couldn't kill the mouse, despite her grandmother's haranguing; he grabbed his old-fashioned top hat (like Abe Lincoln's) that he insisted on wearing even though it was long out of fashion, and scooped the mouse up in it. He carefully released it out in the small patch of yard behind the building, where a cat promptly killed it, and Grandfather wept like a child.

That top hat was the nicest thing he brought with him from the Old World, when he arrived in America. In the Rubenstein family album, there was a photograph of him as a young boy wearing it, his face too young and small for such a towering hat. But he had such a proud expression on his face.

That young, hopeful face—that was what Blanche saw as she read the hateful propaganda proclaiming the Jews the evil of the world, the scourge of humanity.

Her own face, too—suddenly she saw it as if looking in a mirror. Saw it as it had been, before she'd so eagerly decided to seek a different life, a better life, although wasn't the laugh on her? Here she was, a Jew in Occupied Paris, surrounded by Germans every single damn day.

But her own face—brown eyes, cute little nose, dark hair that she'd started dying blond so long ago, she wouldn't recognize the real color now—she saw her own face in the images of the photos, the cartoons, the artwork.

How Can You Recognize a Semite? one of the displays asked.

How, indeed? Blanche sure as hell didn't know

anymore, even though the display helpfully provided an answer: By greasy hair, beady eyes, hooked nose, grasping hands.

But they left out a few other traits. How can you recognize a Semite?

By the terrified pounding of her heart. The liquid in her bowels. The tangible relief—really, she could touch it every time she caressed her passport—that she had erased her identity decades before. For reasons that seemed so ridiculous now: to help her husband's career; to further escape a past that, in retrospect, didn't seem all that terrible; because it was a day ending in a "y"; because the sun was shining.

Because, because, because—it didn't matter, it had been so easy; Blanche talked to Frank Meier who introduced her to Greep who, with a few expert scribbles, a photograph, and fifty francs, erased her past and gave her a new identity. So easy, she wondered why everyone didn't do the same. Change names, change nationalities, change religion—delete a few years, too, might as well—as easily as a flapper could change the color of her hair or the brand of her cigarette (Lucky Strikes for Gauloises).

Confronted with so much hatred in this exhibit—it was like running into a wall made of barbed wire, rusty nails, flayed flesh exposing organs still pulsing with life—Blanche knew it wasn't as easy as that, after all.

Not in this packed exhibition that reminded her, with every step she took, that there were people who were so anxious to be told that their worst fears and prejudices were understandable, if not admirable, that they believed every single lie they were told. She saw two men laugh at a horrible cartoon of the former prime minister—twice he was elected to that office!—Léon Blum, depicting him with a nose the size of a banana; they laughed until they had tears in their eyes.

Blanche overheard a mother earnestly telling her daughter, who couldn't have been more than nine or ten, that it was true, yes it was: Jews sometimes ate little girls like her, and so it was a good thing the Nazis were here, to save her.

"They are animals," Claude hissed beneath his breath, as he gripped his wife's arm so hard she knew there would be marks. "These Nazis have no conscience. This would never happen in a free France."

Blanche nodded toward the mother and daughter. "Do you really believe that, Claude?" After all, he was the one who first told her about the quotas that certain hotels and restaurants unofficially enforced. He was the one who had told her all about the decades-long *L'affaire Dreyfus*, and how his own parents had been pleased when the innocent man had been found guilty and imprisoned.

He was the one who did not try very hard to talk her out of changing her passport, right when he started at the Ritz.

Blanche's husband—eavesdropping while the mother went on to explain to her daughter that it was a good thing the Germans had put on this exhibition, because some of their neighbors didn't share their beliefs, but now, thank heavens, they would know the truth because one thing was certain: Nazis didn't lie—did not answer.

But he did grip his wife even more tightly and hissed into her ear, "Thank God you had the foresight to do what you did, back then."

He'd never thanked her for doing it. He'd never really acknowledged it at all; it seemed natural to him: the American Jew converting to Catholicism in order to marry a Frenchman. It was a building block of the Auzellos' marriage, one of the foundations—as essential, if unspoken, a truth to the story they told about themselves as the circumstances of their meeting, what she was wearing, how he almost forgot the ring for the ceremony.

Once this was all over, she would leave, she told herself as they left the exhibit. Leave Claude, leave their convenient marriage—for that was what it was, by this time; a convenient excuse for her not to go home—and return to New York. To her family that she'd too easily left behind.

To the religion she'd too easily abandoned.

As the truck pulls out of the Place Vendôme and onto the rue de la Paix, Blanche stops thinking about the past and begins to register, fully, what is happening now. She is no onlooker; she is no actress; she is no fake sophisticate, no *Parisienne.* She's no longer Blanche Ross Auzello.

She is, finally, once again—Blanche Rubenstein.

How can you recognize a Semite?

Throw her in the back of a Nazi truck with her hands tied too tightly behind her back, and point a German gun at her head.

CHAPTER 28
CLAUDE,
June 1944

He races down the stairs, her passport in his hand. She's forgotten it, and all he can register is that she needs it now; she needs to prove she's Blanche Ross Auzello, Catholic. So he runs through the lobby, waving the passport like a madman, shouting, "She forgot it! She forgot her passport! Blanche—she forgot it!"

And then he realizes that all the Germans in the Place Vendôme side are staring at him in amusement. Where his wife is going, no passport is necessary.

Still, he whirls around until he can glimpse a kind face—and there is von Stülpnagel, trundling down the wide staircase, tucking his shirt in his pants.

"What is going on?" There's a sharp *click* and Claude realizes that a soldier has pointed a rifle at him, but he can't be bothered by that right now. He actually puts his hand out and lowers it, as if it is merely a fly to be swatted away.

Blanche is gone. Blanche is gone—it's a hammer repeatedly striking a gong in his brain, the only words that matter, the only sound that he hears.

"My wife—Herr von Stülpnagel!" Claude Auzello, all dignity forgotten, throws himself on this man, this Nazi. He has no shame, no pride. All the months he's fetched and carried for these swine—surely it means something? Surely they will remember, and help him? "My wife, Blanche—she was just taken! She forgot her passport!" Claude waves the precious leather book right in the man's face.

"Herr Auzello, please." Von Stülpnagel pushes Claude away, but gestures for the others to return to their duties. The soldier with the rifle holsters it and walks away.

"Herr von Stülpnagel, I beg of you. I know she did a reckless thing—she told me all about it. But she is my wife! She is the wife of the director of the Ritz! She's foolish, yes. Impulsive. But she's done nothing terrible, nothing that warrants being arrested."

"It is not my decision, Herr Auzello." Von Stülpnagel sits down, wearily, on a small gilt chair—it is too delicate, too fine, for this German in his gray-green uniform. "I am not the Gestapo. I only told them where to find her when they came here looking."

"You? You told them?"

"I had no choice. I answer to a higher command, you know that—you're a soldier, too. I tried to—I tried to talk them out of it." The man's shoulders slump, and Claude has a moment of hope. Perhaps this Nazi has a soul, after all. "But she committed a grave crime against the Reich. She desecrated a lieutenant's uniform; she disrespected him in public. We cannot have that. It will give the citizens the wrong idea if we tolerate it, especially now. Even Frau Auzello of the Ritz can't get away with that."

Claude sinks to his knees; he has never done such a thing. But for Blanche, he does.

"I beg of you, please. Talk to the Gestapo, ask them to let her go. I'll take her away, I promise. I'll take her out to the country, where she'll be no threat, where she'll live quietly until—"

"Until what?" Von Stülpnagel removes his glasses, rubs the bridge of his nose, puts them back on, all the while glaring at Claude. Daring him to complete his thought.

"Never mind—I didn't mean—just let me take her away, I promise. She will do nothing further, nothing that disrespects the Reich."

"I told you it's out of my hands, Herr Auzello. Even if I wanted to—and I'm not saying I do—the Gestapo will not listen to me. They answer directly to the Führer, not the military."

"At least tell me where she will be taken?"

"I don't know. Drancy, maybe. Fresnes? She could be in one of the smaller jails in the city, I suppose, but that's not likely. I'm sorry, Herr

Auzello. I, too, have a wife. I haven't seen her in months, and it's likely I won't see her anytime soon. All leaves are canceled until further notice. So I understand, but I cannot do anything about it."

And to Claude's astonishment, the man does look sorry; he looks miserable, actually, still slumped in the chair, bowed down by so much responsibility, so much collective hate passed down from his superiors.

Finally von Stülpnagel rises, wearily. "I would like my usual lunch brought up to my office now, Herr Auzello. Please take pains to see that it is warm this time. Yesterday, it was cold." He peers at Claude, hesitates; he places his hands on Claude's shoulders. "We have to keep at our jobs, don't we? There's nothing else we can do but keep working. It would be foolish, dangerous, to think we can do more than that, Herr Auzello. You understand?"

Claude nods, but he balls his hands into fists, his vision swims so that all he sees are red dots; his head is throbbing with anger—anger, also the color red.

Red—the color of the background of the flags with the swastikas, hanging from the ceilings, covering the antique tapestries.

But Claude Auzello is nothing if not disciplined; he remembers, just in time—everything, all. His training, his duty. His responsibilities.

His wife, in these creatures' hands.

"Of course, it will be my pleasure to arrange your lunch, Herr von Stülpnagel. And—thank you." But for what, Claude doesn't quite know—other than showing him a glimmer of humanity, when he most needed it. "But please, if you will—can you make sure whoever has Blanche gets this?" Claude hands the man the passport.

Von Stülpnagel takes it, then he trudges back up the stairs, to his office. Claude understands that he should not take too much to heart the man's unexpected kindness, but he can't help himself; his eyes fill with tears, and he feels, for a moment, not quite so isolated in a terror that is his alone to bear.

Then he has to walk past German soldiers—the same Germans he's soothed and catered to for four years now—toward the long hallway. Back to his office, to at least attempt to resume his duties, as von Stülpnagel advised.

But the Ritz, for the first time, seems false, like a pasteboard cake covered in icing that is used to decorate the window of a pastry shop. Beautiful to look at. But hollow inside.

Inside his office, Claude can't bring himself to focus; he picks up the phone, desperate to talk to Martin, who might have an idea, he's such a clever fellow—but he remembers all phones are tapped here at the Ritz. Tapped by their guests. And for the life of him, Claude does not know what the code words are for a situation like this.

Claude remembers, finally, the gun. In the locked drawer, with the hemlock, the ant poison, the lye. He opens the drawer and surveys the bounty, so tempting. A drop of lye in von Stülpnagel's tea. Hemlock in Speidel's soup. Why stop there? Hemlock for all! A banquet of poison, he could surely find some allies in the kitchen who would be more than happy to cook up such a treat for their German guests.

Or maybe something quieter? Something more personal, an intimate dance between himself and some random German soldier, the grand finish simply a little matter of a bullet in his brain? Then he would get himself arrested, he would be with Blanche wherever she is being taken, they would be jailed together—

And he would never be able to help her, now, would he? *Of course not, Claude, you fool. Do not think like a passionate lover. You had your time for that. Now is a time for more rational, clearheaded thinking.*

His hands are shaking—not a mere tremble but a body-rattling earthquake. Claude shuts the door, sits down, puts his head in those unstable hands. Tries to think, comes up with nothing.

He remains this way for the rest of the day, anything to delay returning to his rooms.

Where Blanche will not be, to greet him.

CHAPTER 29

BLANCHE,
June 1944

She is only one of many women, also shackled, bouncing around in the truck as it rumbles through the cobblestone streets. One of them asks the soldier pointing the gun where they're going. He doesn't answer but another woman does.

"You'll see. Fresnes. The last stop before hell."

"Go ahead and talk," the soldier finally says, good-naturedly; he takes a cigarette out of his pocket, lights it, throws the lit match at a woman three feet away from him. "It'll be the last time you do, so why not?"

This shuts them up.

It's a warm day. Is it a warm day? It's still June, still summer; only yesterday Blanche was walking in a short-sleeved blouse with Lily. Through the streets gaily bordered with flower boxes, ivy bursting into greenery, birds chirping. So it must be still warm, Blanche thinks, yet she's turning inside out with cold, her body shaking so violently she thinks she's going to be sick.

"Stop it," the woman next to her says once. Then she says no more.

Trundling along in the back of the truck like potatoes, the women are silent, except for some sobs, as they're driven out of the city. Soon they're in the suburbs, dull and charmless, and eventually the truck stops in front of a guarded gate, is waved through, and pulls up in front of a gray fortress, and they're shoved out of the back of the truck as roughly as they'd been shoved into it. More soldiers with rifles march them into the building, where they are corralled into a windowless, spare room packed with even more women in various states of shock and terror. There are more soldiers. Some officers, too. Watching them, rifles at the ready.

Blanche searches the crowd, stands on tiptoe, weaves through it, looking for—

"Lily!" She can't stop herself, she rushes to Lily's side, pushing her way through the other women with her shoulders, as her hands are still cuffed.

"Lily!" Blanche is so relieved to see her alive that she forgets everything she's been taught. Do not recognize a fellow member of the Resistance, if jailed. Never—*ever*—betray knowledge of one another.

Blanche blows it. Just as she'd blown it yesterday, and she gasps, tries to stumble away, praying no one heard her. But then she hears her *own* name, uttered softly.

"Blanche." Lily's face—it's so pale, and Blanche expects to see hatred in her eyes, disappointment, disgust at her stupidity.

Instead, she sees only a strange, startled softness, almost happiness. Almost as if Lily is glad to have been recognized. But no, it can't be—but before Blanche can ask, a German voice booms out: "The Communist Lily Kharmanyoff!"

Blanche watches as Lily is marched off, defiant, chin tilted up, hands behind her in cuffs—and a last, lingering look at Blanche. Who finally recognizes it, this look—of gratitude.

Of love.

And Blanche is left achingly alone, despite the fact that she's surrounded by wailing women, surrounded by her own terror and guilt for what she's done. To herself. To Lily. To Claude, who must surely be out of his mind by now.

"Blanche Auzello!" And now it's her turn to be marched off and thrown into another room, given a change of clothes—rough wool gown too big for her, enormous wooden clogs for shoes. All her other clothes, her jewelry—the gold cross, the chain snapped off her neck, it's such a wisp of a thing, after all—are taken from her. But not her passport—she closes her eyes, remembering. It's back at the Ritz.

Will she need it here? Will it matter? There is no way of knowing. She can only wait and see.

"Why am I here?" Although she knows very well why she's there, she feels compelled to ask it into a void; there are no humans present, only impassive, soulless German faces.

There is no answer.

She's thrown into a cell, all alone. There's a pot. A cot. Three mice to keep her company.

Night descends, she must have fallen asleep, for the next thing she knows a priest is being shown into her cell, and she is stunned. Stunned to realize that they still haven't figured it out, these stupid Germans.

They still have no idea she's a Jew.

So they must have her passport now—maybe Claude brought it? The realization fills her with hope for the first time since they knocked on her door at the Ritz.

The Catholic priest—an old man, one of those priests who's well fed and well pleased with himself—looks smugly superior as he calls her by her name and blesses her. But he looks with disgust at the mice and the pot, and he remains standing, obviously afraid to sit on her louse-ridden cot. Then he proceeds to ask questions.

"Where are you from in America, my child?"

"Cleveland."

"What church did you worship at there, if I may ask?"

"Our Lady of Who-the-Hell knows. It's been a long time, Father."

"I see. Do you want Communion? I'll have to hear your confession first."

She shakes her head. "Sorry, Father, maybe you're an OK guy. But maybe you'll run to the Nazis and tell them everything you hear. I'll take a raincheck."

He sighs, blesses her anyway, and leaves.

For two more days she remains in the cell. Blanche almost convinces herself they've forgotten all about her, that they made a mistake, that they'll change their minds and set her free to go back home—to Claude. She's given brown mealy bread with worms in it; she spits it out. Gruel with worms in it; she spits it out. Soup with worms in it; she's so hungry by then that she gobbles it but it's no use. It comes right back up again and she has to sleep that night with a puddle of sick on the floor.

At least it keeps the mice away.

And then they come for her, the first time. The steel boots—she's heard them walking up and down the hall day and night, but this time they stop at her cell, insert the key in the lock, prod her with rifles, and she walks, willingly, on her own two feet where they tell her to. Because now, they'll set her free; they'll tell her it was all a mistake; they'll send for Claude, who will come for her.

For she is Madame Auzello of the Ritz.

Blanche is shoved into an office, where an

364

officer sits at a desk, a file folder spread before him. A folder with a picture of Lily—looking startled, her hair whipping about her face, she's younger in the photo, her hair longer—paper-clipped to the front of it.

"So tell us, Madame Auzello. How is it that you, from the Ritz—we know your husband, he has been most civil to our officers staying there, quite helpful—got mixed up with this filthy Jew Communist whore Lily Kharmanyoff?"

"What? I—I thought I was here because—"

"Yes, yes, you did an impetuous thing at Maxim's. We know all about that. But we are more interested in your relationship to this Jew whore, whom we've been looking for. How did you meet?"

"We met on a boat. Long ago." A lifetime ago. She'd been running away from Claude like a child, a willful child. Lily picked her out of a crowded bar, saw her sadness, saw her need—maybe saw something brave and true, as well—and came to her. They drank, Blanche remembers. They laughed. They even danced.

"Why were you on the boat? Where was it coming from?"

"From Morocco. To France. I'd taken a vacation. I was returning to the Ritz."

"Why was she on the boat?"

"I don't know."

"We have kept track of her activities, from

Spain until the present. She is a Communist, a traitor, a murderer of Germans. Do you know how many she has killed?"

Blanche shakes her head. *No questions.*

"Thirteen. She has murdered thirteen of our soldiers."

Blanche wants to say, "Hooray." She wants to say, "Only thirteen?" Blanche wants to say, "Good for her!" But she doesn't dare.

"So it is simple. Just say that Lily is a Jew and a member of the Resistance—yes, we know of your activities, but we will be generous toward you, and we will let you go. After all, you are the famous Madame Auzello. Your home has been our home these last few years. We don't want to harm you—it would not be good publicity."

"I don't know," she replies, telling the truth for once. "She never told me. We've never discussed it." And Blanche is grateful—so grateful—for that. Because here, in this prison, she understands that she is not quite the actress she once thought she was. What will she say, when the Nazis ask her if *she's* a Jew?

Blanche Rubenstein Auzello has no earthly idea. And so it's fortunate that they don't. This time.

She's returned to her cell, thinking that at least she got through it, it wasn't that bad—not the horrors that Lily had described, that Robert had to endure—and so the worst is over, only to find

366

that it's just the beginning. The beginning of days alone. Days that turn seamlessly into nights when she is sick—a fever one day, dysentery the next, mysterious rashes that chafe against the rough wool of her garment. Cries echoing in the halls of this prison, all women; there are no men in this section, they are separated here at Fresnes. Occasional defiance, always cut short in mid-cry.

How many days has she been here? She loses count. She tries to keep track by her menstrual cycle, which she can do nothing about but let the blood trickle down her legs. But it happens only once.

Soon after the blood stops flowing, a soldier comes into her cell, matter-of-factly; she assumes he's there to bring her back in for interrogation. Instead, he shuts the door behind him and starts unbuttoning his trousers, a smug grin on his face. She cowers against the wall, she tries to scream but nothing comes out, she's so weak she's like a dry leaf in his hands, crumpling at his rough touch. It's over quickly—she's so brittle, the pain sears her vision, but thank God, he's done almost as soon as he enters her.

The whole time, she shuts her eyes so she can't see his blue ones as he grimaces and grunts and sweats and pushes, as he does this ugly, invasive thing—as he *rapes* her. Goddammit, Blanche, don't let them steal your words as well as your soul. If she doesn't look, if she doesn't retain a visual memory, then if she ever gets out of here maybe she'll forget it ever happened. And if she forgets, she won't have to tell Claude.

Who, she knows, could not handle this. He's not as strong as she is.

Always, almost every day, the questioning. She's hauled out, taken to some officer who looks over the same file with the same picture of Lily. Some days she's accused of harboring fugitives—"Known Semites"—at the Ritz, shown photos of people she's never seen before in her life. People like her. Other days, she's falsely accused of murdering an officer, blowing up a bridge—it's all right here, in her file.

But it always comes back to Lily.

"Tell us. Tell us Lily Kharmanyoff is a Jew. So you can go home."

There are times when they turn charming, her captors; when they offer Blanche a seat, tea, a pastry—not full of worms—that she devours like an animal, ashamed but too ravenous to stop herself. They laugh and ask her, genuinely interested, about her famous friends at the Ritz—they are particularly fascinated by "the writer Hemingway"—and she understands that they're trying to break her by reminding her of all she's missing, all she might never see again. They're reminding her that a goddamned pastry is all it takes to humiliate herself in front of them. Those interviews are actually the cruelest for they bring back to her the memories of before, when she'd been charmed by von Dincklage, been concerned about Friedrich, tried to cheer Astrid up with a new hat. When she'd thought these specimens were human beings, deserving of laughter, deserving of her good cheer.

In all this time, Blanche is never accused of any of the crimes against them that she actually committed, never confronted with the truth of any of the lies she's told and she knows, then, that they aren't very bright, these Germans. But intelligence isn't required when you have evil on your side.

"I can sentence you to death any time I want," Blanche is reminded frequently, always by a German whose words try to lure her into betrayal. "All I need is the suspicion of truth. Tell me, this Lily. She is a Jew, right? A Russian Jew spy? A Jew whore?"

"I don't know, I don't know," Blanche repeats. Sometimes a spark will ignite, a spark she thought was extinguished forever, and she'll throw her head back and spit out words from another person, another Blanche. She'll tell them the food is rotten, that the hospitality is certainly nothing like the Ritz. She'll relish her defiance, but it never lasts long, it can't. Not here.

Sometimes she'll torment herself, lying alone at night, trying to shut out the sounds—she's not the only woman the soldiers rape. The door to a cell opening, closing, grunts, moans, silence, the door opening again. And really, what else are she and her fellow prisoners there for, if not for their pleasure? Pleasure in torturing, in punishing, in breaking, in raping. But how they can do it when the prisoners look like skeletons, when their hair falls out in clumps that the mice take away to use for nests, when their bowels are water and lice crawl all over them—Blanche has no idea.

Lying on her cot amid this terrible nightmare, Blanche further punishes herself with thoughts of the Ritz.

She'll recall the bathroom in their suite, larger than this cell, ten times as large as this cell. The tubs of the Ritz are big enough to hold an army; she remembers how Claude told her the story about King Edward VII getting stuck in the bathtub, and so his good friend Cèsar Ritz ripped out all the tubs and installed more accommodating ones, fit for a king.

She'll remember the ease of picking up a phone and having anything brought to her, no matter the time of day. She'll recall when those things would delight, fulfill—a time when a new dress would make her dance around for days. Or a new bracelet. Or a particularly elaborate bouquet of flowers. When *things* mattered—when her life was filled only with *things* that she hoarded, saved.

Before she started saving *people*.

"So maybe now you will see me at the Ritz. I'll live there—with you," Lily said that last day, and Blanche had thought she'd saved *her,* too. But Claude, he wouldn't have liked that—no matter where they begin, her thoughts always end with Claude.

This man. *Her* man. Who had roared like a lion in the face of J'Ali. Who had made her believe she was a prize worth fighting for. Who'd made it so easy for her—a life at the Ritz!—to forget where she came from.

Who had hurt her, but Blanche can't remember, anymore, why she'd ever been so angry with him. What is sex, after all? Nothing, compared to love. And he does love Blanche. After that last night together, she is sure of it.

Sometimes Claude gets a startled expression on his face when he looks at her, then he becomes stern, as if he's embarrassed by his feelings, as if nothing in his prim and proper little life could ever have prepared him for her.

As nothing could have prepared her for him. She sees him clearly now, in a way she could not until war first wedged them even further apart, then patched them back together. She sees his intellect, his surprising passion, always revealed when she least expects it. His sense of duty. His love of his country. His bravery, these past years, in keeping the Nazis happy while undermining them right beneath their noses.

It's not his fault that it was so easy for Blanche to live down to his expectations for her, when her life lacked meaning and purpose. And it's not her fault that it was so easy for Claude to live down to her expectations for him—a typically chauvinistic Frenchman—as well. Because truly, they had no idea what to do with each other after such a startling beginning, except to paint each other with the broadest of strokes, to revert to a type—and to allow the Ritz to seduce and distract them both. So that it was easy, at times, to forget that they might actually need to rely on, to trust in—to love—each other.

Lying in her cell, alone, terrified, there is only one thing that is clear to Blanche now.

If she is allowed to live, she will never leave Claude again.

CHAPTER 30
CLAUDE,
July 1944

Marie-Louise Ritz, in the touching belief that she can ease Claude's mind, has taken to inviting him up to her suite every evening. She worries about him returning to his rooms, where he will be alone. So she invites him to hers; Claude accepts, polite to a fault even now, and they have tea. Although she thoughtfully provides something stronger for him.

And she tells him stories.

Stories about the old days. The present is too terrible to contemplate, so she takes refuge, more and more, in her past. She recounts stories about Marcel Proust and the cork-lined bedroom in his flat; how he asked to be taken to the Ritz before he died and, since he couldn't, how he asked for one last beer from the bar and it was on its way to him—of course, the Ritz takes care of its own—when he expired.

Stories about her husband, César Ritz himself, and her belief that overwork killed him. She sometimes tells anecdotes about her younger son, the one she lost; but only stories about him as a child, and not as the troubled young man who took his own life, according to Frank Meier.

Stories about herself as a young bride, not accustomed to anything so grand as the Ritz, but even then, in her husband's fevered eyes, she could see it taking shape. Stories about how they got the financing together—she still cannot say the word "Rothschild" without wrinkling her nose in distaste—and her delight in traipsing all over the world procuring the fabulous antiques, paintings, tapestries, furniture with which she furnished it.

And Claude sees it through her eyes; this grand hotel, this shrine, this Taj Mahal—it is, at its simplest, a woman's home. And Claude wonders that they never really have had a real home to themselves, Blanche and he; that they've been so content living like itinerants—spoiled, yes, but itinerants nonetheless.

If they'd had a house of their own, the same bed every night, one address instead of two—if she'd had the work of running a home herself, cooking, cleaning, arranging, to keep her occupied—would she be here with him still, his Blanche? Would he have been able to keep her safe somewhere else—anywhere else—but the Ritz? Once, it had seemed the most sheltering place in the world; once, it had received more of his time, his energy—yes, even his love—than did his wife.

But after that last night, when Blanche told

him what she'd done for him, and for Paris—for France itself; when he had seen her, finally, as others—Lily, Pearl—had seen her, brave, not selfish; giving, not merely taking—Claude cannot look at the Ritz in the same way. It has become yet another casualty of the war; the scene of his last tender words with a wife he was only just discovering, before the Germans took her. As they are taking everyone.

If they don't leave first.

"Claude, I'd like a word," Frank Meier says to him one day—all the days have begun to blur, since Blanche is gone; Claude, who was the master of any calendar—the master of time itself, corralling it, organizing it, parceling it out in appropriate increments—suddenly has trouble remembering what day of the week it is.

He doesn't sleep much at night. He stares and stares at the empty pillow beside him, and tortures himself with visions of what she must be going through. If she is still alive.

In all Claude's years at the Ritz, Frank and he have had very few actual conversations. He is such the king of his domain, Claude has left him to it. Beyond ordering alcohol, seeing to it that stemware is regularly replaced, linens repaired or bought, fresh lemons and limes in abundance (these last only a memory now; Claude hasn't been able to procure any citrus in months, to the Germans' displeasure). Claude rarely spends time in the bar, himself. Blanche spends enough time there for them both. And he does not think it wise to be seen drinking with the guests; they—and his staff—would think less of correct, responsible Monsieur Auzello.

So Claude is mildly surprised—surprise, like all his emotions other than fear and terror, is muted these days—as Frank steps outside of the bar. This is after the plot to kill Hitler had been foiled. That much, Claude can keep track of, a plot that had ensnared many of "their" German officers, including von Stülpnagel. Who disappeared himself, before Claude could glimpse, again, his humanity. But von Stülpnagel had, astonishingly, been one of many German officers who gathered daily in the bar pretending to drink to the Reich, but in reality, planning to assassinate Hitler. Proving that not all Nazis were alike, despite their uniforms.

Claude, even as he pretended not to notice—sometimes he believes that pretending not to notice is his only job, these days—was not unaware that the plot was hatched in the Ritz bar, under Frank Meier's nose, and probably with his full participation regarding his role as "mailbox," as Claude believes those in the espionage profession call it—a person who receives and passes on information without full knowledge of what he is receiving or passing on.

"Look at her," Frank says from the doorway

of the bar. He is indicating, with a nod, a sleek blond French baroness seated with one of the new German officers—so many have rushed up to Paris in these weeks since the Allied invasion and the plot was foiled that Claude cannot keep track of them. The baroness, attired in a black silk dress with fur cuffs, enormous diamond rings and bracelets ornamenting her black satin gloves, is toying with a glass of champagne, looking up at the German with what some call "bedroom eyes."

"What of her?" Claude is disgusted; disgusted by some of these French women. Not all who have kept company with the Germans did so for personal gain, of course; he knows of a woman with three sick children whose husband never came back after the beginning of the war. She's had no word from him, so has no idea if he's in a camp or dead. And when the Germans came knocking on her door, threatening to take whatever meager possessions she still had, she seized upon the situation in order to provide food and medicine for her fatherless children.

Claude cannot—will not—pass judgment on a woman like that and, besides, she has the decency to be ashamed, to try to keep this business secret. But this baroness is different; she is an opportunist who thinks only of herself, who has dined out with these Germans every night here at the Ritz, or at Maxim's, or the Brasserie Lipp—parading about with them in public.

"The baroness is desperate, but trying not to show it," Frank says, amused. "She placed all her bets on the Germans winning the war, and now that the Allies are on the march, she wants this Kraut to take her back to Germany with him when he leaves. Good thinking—the Germans will go far easier on her than will the French, mark my words—but this guy isn't about to take her home to meet his frau. No matter how many diamonds she offers to give him."

"I wish they would hurry up and leave."

"They will. But Paris is the biggest prize they've won, and they're not going to give it up so easily. Come with me, Claude." Frank starts up the stairs and he follows him, to Chanel's suite. Frank takes out a key and inserts it in the door.

"Wait—how is it that you have a key?"

"She gave it to me." Frank smiles—not something he does frequently and so the effect is rather disturbing; he has a very coy smile for a man that large and blocky. "Coco and I—we have a history."

"*Mon Dieu*!" For Claude doesn't know what else to say to this startling bit of information, and immediately the image of the two of them in bed—Chanel so sharply slender and imperious, Frank so meaty and gruff—comes to mind. Despite his best efforts to prevent it.

The two men enter Chanel's suite, in its monochromatic—mostly browns and creams—

Art Deco glory. She has some good paintings, but overall the place has no personality; although Claude acknowledges that the woman herself has enough to compensate for this. Frank shuts the door.

"Frank, is it you?" Chanel emerges from the bathroom with towels in her arms; she places them in a trunk, one of many open. Her maid is scurrying about, filling them, but stops, curtseys, and leaves after Chanel gives her one of her dismissive nods.

Claude stands, dumbly; he has no idea why he is here, he feels an intruder.

"Are you leaving us, Mademoiselle?"

"Yes, for a while. The atmosphere is getting a little close here in Paris, I think."

"She's running away to the Alps with Spatzy," Frank interrupts, and is rewarded with a sharp, piercing look from Chanel. "Running away from the Allies, from the citizens, who might not look too kindly on her actions, like those two who kidnapped her. Right, Coco?"

"That's one way of putting it" is all the woman will allow, before she goes to one of her closets, opens it, and produces a key, which she inserts into a safe. She removes some jewelry cases from the safe and puts them in one of the trunks.

"But before she goes—"

The staccato of gunfire just outside interrupts him; all three rush to the window—foolishly,

Claude thinks later, for they have no idea where the gunshots are coming from. There, in the rue Cambon, are three Nazi soldiers lined up facing a wall, about a block away; a crumpled body lies before them. A crowd has gathered but slowly they begin to walk away. The body remains, but Claude cannot see, from his vantage point, if it is young or old, male or female. All he knows is that it is one less French citizen.

The three turn away at the same time, and they don't even discuss it. It's not the first time any of them has seen this, although it is the first time Claude's seen it while looking out a window of the Ritz. This place—it cannot protect them anymore, not from the horrors of war or the horrors of retribution once the Germans leave. And who among them will be spared? Not even Chanel can count on that.

Claude has helped his country to the best of his abilities, he sincerely believes. He would have fought to the death for it, had he not been instructed, that black day in 1940, to lay down his arms and give up. So he found other ways to fight, while protecting one of the shining examples of French culture and taste—and protecting those citizens who work for him, too.

But will it be enough to satisfy the bloodlust—one can already sense it rising—of the citizens, once they are free to think and act once more?

"I'm leaving too, Claude," Frank says, lighting

a Gauloise. He inhales. "I have to. Things are heating up—well, you know better than anyone."

"Yes." Everyone in the hotel knows about Blanche, but they don't speak of it; they avert their eyes when they see Claude. And every time he does his job, every time he replies to one of the Nazis—"Yes, of course, Herr Enreich, I will see to it that your private dinner with the actress will be served precisely at nine o'clock." "Herr Steinmetz, your new uniform has just arrived from the tailor. Shall I have it brought up to your room?" "How can I help you, Herr this, Herr that?"—Claude knows that *they* are keeping his Blanche, that they ordered her arrest, and he cannot do a thing about it. Except keep serving them, keep them satisfied, pray that this will not go unnoticed.

Get down on his knees and beseech the Blessed Virgin that all this will result in Blanche's return.

"So I'm going to leave," Frank continues. "For good."

"Why are you telling me? Why don't you simply go?"

"Well, Claude, you've been decent to me and I think you deserve an explanation."

"About the money?"

"What?" Frank, for the first time in their acquaintance, is caught off guard; he actually drops the cigarette but picks it up before it can leave a burn mark in the cream carpet. Chanel, still rummaging through drawers and closets, makes a hissing sound, but does not pause in her packing.

"The money you have been skimming. Money that rightly belongs to Madame Ritz."

"Who told you? Blanche?"

"No—what? Blanche?" But of course, Claude realizes. Blanche has always known more about the inner workings, the secrets, the whispers—the truth—of the Ritz than he has.

"Yes."

"She did not tell me, but she didn't need to. I count every sou that comes in and goes out of this hotel. What I don't know is how you've been using the money."

"And I won't tell you, for your own good."

"So you can't repay it?"

Frank shakes his head, sighs, leans back against the cushions.

"Very well then. Of course, in a different time, I would have to fire you for this."

"Which is one reason why I'm leaving—to spare you, to spare us both that."

"Fine. Go. And don't tell me where."

"I won't. But I thought you might want to hear about Blanche."

Claude gasps, burned by the suddenly leaping flame of hope that these words ignite. He'd asked Frank about her before—of course he had. He'd knocked on every door of both sides of the hotel, cornered maids, collared bellhops. But nobody knew anything. Or so they said.

"How do you know? Have you seen her?"

Frank glances at Chanel, who frowns, her hands full of filmy lingerie, which Claude tries very hard not to notice. Then, after abruptly flinging the lingerie into a trunk, she sits down, very noticeably perturbed. Claude almost apologizes for inconveniencing her.

She crosses her arms, her sharp elbows jutting out. There is nothing soft about her at all, Claude recognizes. Her nose, her chin, her pointy heels, her talon-like fingers. The slits of her eyes, allowing a sliver of a dark gleam.

"Blanche was taken to Fresnes," she finally says, her words, too, sharply biting. "Spatzy told me."

Swallowing—difficult to do with a throat so very dry—Claude nods. He'd assumed she was in Fresnes. He did not think she was being held in any of the smaller jails in the city; he would have found her by now.

But then it fully sinks in.

Fresnes.

Fresnes—on the outskirts of town, about fifteen kilometers to the south—is the last stop before the work camps; once you are there, your fate is sealed. During the entire Occupation, Claude has never once heard of anyone going to Fresnes and returning. Alive.

"Is she still there?"

"Yes." Chanel inhales her cigarette, blows the smoke out, staring at him as if he is a specimen at a zoo, an animal whose behavior puzzles her. He thinks she doesn't know what love looks like, this woman. That she has never known it, cannot understand it.

"Thank God for that, anyway," he whispers, voice shaking. "Is she—how is she—?"

"I have no idea; it is not my concern." She stabs her cigarette out in an ashtray and rises.

Frank, who has been watching Chanel—almost daring her not to disappoint him—grunts. "Once people are inside that place, there's no way to know anything more. She and Lily both were taken there. I suppose you know by now what they were up to? So Blanche, she has a file with the Gestapo. Von Stülpnagel didn't tell you that."

"No." Nor had any of the new officers who have replaced him, for naturally, Claude asks each and every one. He's gotten only a shrug, a disavowal of any knowledge. Claude wonders if anyone knows anything in the Third Reich; it is crumbling before his eyes, officers running around, eyeing one another distrustfully, telegrams flying back and forth between Berlin and Paris. But what does that matter, when Blanche is still gone?

"I have to admit, I am surprised," Coco calls over her shoulder as she's bending down to lock a suitcase. "I didn't think Blanche had it in her."

"Courage? Decency? Honor?" Claude rushes over to her, and almost shakes her. "More of a Frenchwoman, a patriot, than you?"

"Calm down, Claude." Chanel narrows her already-narrow eyes at him, bemused. "I admire her, if you must know. It can't have been easy for her these years, being a Jew. I suppose, in a way, I understand why she's done the things she's done. Even if I think they're pitifully rash and stupid."

"You knew about Blanche?" Claude stares at Frank, disbelieving. "You told her, Frank?"

"No, Frank did not," Chanel declares. "I'm simply very astute. Unlike our German friends."

"Have you—was it you who turned her in? I swear upon the flag, if you did, I will—I will—"

"Nonsense." Chanel's entire bony body stiffly registers outrage. "No one turned her in, Claude. She was recognized by almost everyone at Maxim's, that day. Everyone saw what she did. And they knew where she lived."

"You've used the Vichy laws to your advantage, though, haven't you? In trying to get control of your perfume company back from your Jewish partners? You have no love for the Jews, mademoiselle. It's well known."

Chanel shrugs. "I'm a businesswoman, what can I say? But I have no business with your wife, Claude. I quite enjoy her, as a matter of fact—our little sparring. It's amusing."

"Claude," Frank breaks in, glancing at a clock. "You must know—the Nazis, they came for Greep yesterday."

Claude stares at him, not comprehending—until he does.

"Oh." Claude has run out of words today, it would appear. Or—perhaps there are simply no words to describe the horrors. The words they've used—*occupation, occupiers, taken, rounded up, disappeared*—do not, cannot, begin to describe the reality.

"They came for Greep," he repeats, understanding what Frank is saying. So they must know, by now, like Chanel, that Blanche is a Jew—Greep very likely could have confessed his role in all that. Claude truly didn't realize how much he'd been hoping that somehow she'd be able to continue to hide her secret, until this moment when some small spark, infinitesimal but essential, seems to escape his body; he sees it fly away, dimming with each heartbeat.

"But the man killed himself. That damn little Turk—he jumped off a building before they could get him." Frank chuckles, admiringly, and Claude reaches for that last little firefly of hope that was fluttering away, snatches it, cups it in his hand again. It is weak, it is sputtering. But it's all he has.

"So I have to leave, before the Nazis come for *me,* because I don't have the balls that little Turk had." Frank rises, removes his white jacket—not a spot on it, there never is; how he spends all his time behind the bar with liquors—chartreuse, ruby red grenadine, even yellow absinthe—without spilling a drop upon his person, Claude will never understand. And while Frank and he have never been close, Claude doesn't want him to leave. He doesn't even want Chanel to leave—he is not her friend, no, and she is dangerous and despicable.

It's simply that too many people have left Claude lately.

Even Martin; he, too, is gone, since the invasion. Their dealings have dried up, there is too much chaos and many of their contacts are no longer at their posts, but still. Claude would have liked to say goodbye before he—left? Was taken? He will probably never find out, and perhaps that's for the best.

So Claude says it now, to Frank; the two men embrace, even though Frank generally, as an Austrian, is not fond of the French greeting and farewell. But war—occupation—terror—tragedy; again, the words cannot express, describe. Whatever it is, it will do this—cause men to behave in ways they once would have believed utterly impossible.

Frank then turns to Chanel, who is standing, her arms by her side, so brittle, so wary and dangerous, watching him. "Farewell, Coco. It sure was fun once in a while, wasn't it?"

"Take care of yourself, Frank," she says in a voice that, to Claude's surprise, is capable of sounding soft, wistful. "Wherever you may go."

"You, too. If you want my advice, get rid of that Nazi as fast as you can."

"Good advice, I'm sure. But the heart doesn't always want good advice."

Frank chuckles, kisses Chanel's cheek, then leaves. Claude turns to her, bowing stiffly, remembering his duties as the director of the Ritz.

"We will keep your suite intact for your return, mademoiselle."

"Thank you. I'll be back, of course—my business, I can never leave that. But for now, I think it's best that I take a little holiday. Don't worry. I'll still pay my bills."

"I never thought for a moment that you wouldn't. And—thank you. For telling me about my wife. Can you do something for her—can von Dincklage? I would, of course, forever be in your debt."

Chanel shakes her head. "Spatzy doesn't have that kind of influence, Claude. I already asked."

Claude can't trust himself to say another word, so he can only bow once more as she resumes her packing. Before he leaves, however, he takes one more look out the window. The body in the street is gone, removed by someone—a grieving loved one? A Nazi? Who can know? He cannot even see the bloodstain on the wall or pavement, although it must be there.

War is nothing but attrition, it seems to him in this moment. There is nothing gained, only lost. Except—

Perhaps this war has given Claude Auzello a few things. Compassion, for one. He doesn't think he's ever been a cold man, but he can accept that he was, at one time, more attuned to his head than his heart. Except for when he met Blanche; that is the only time Claude can recall when he allowed passion to rule his actions, until now—now that war has amplified the connection between his emotions and his reaction to the world about him. Which is why, he presumes, he is so touched by Chanel's words, he wants to frame them.

This war has also bestowed upon Claude clarity, for he realizes something, now that Blanche is gone: Marriage is not defined by what we hope to gain, but by what we are willing to sacrifice. And Blanche sacrificed her whole self for him—her entire past. What did Claude sacrifice for her?

Not a thing. And that will change, God willing, when she is returned to him.

With a brisk *"Au revoir,"* followed by a whispered, "and God bless," Claude takes his leave of Coco Chanel, and returns to his office.

CHAPTER 31

BLANCHE,
August 24, 1944

Blanche doesn't know the names of the Germans who haul her out of her tiny cell day after day, drag her past all the others in their shadowy cells, all the others who won't meet her gaze in case she doesn't return. That's a trick you learn real fast here: Don't get too attached.

All she cares about is the pain; her left shoulder, dislocated, she thinks, during an interrogation. She can recall only that she passed out when the Nazi slammed her against the cement wall, and when she awoke she found it no longer moves properly—she tries, sometimes, to raise her arm past her waist but the pain is so violent—icy hot javelins piercing her muscles—that she cries out.

All she cares about is the hunger that is so constant it's a part of her, just like the lice setting up camp on her head, the filth under her ragged fingernails. Sometimes, she pulls her thin woolen dress tight against her body, feels the ribs poking through the fabric and thinks, "Finally, I'm thin enough even for Chanel, that bitch." And she longs to laugh, she tries to laugh, just as she used to. But she's forgotten how.

All she cares about is survival. Sometimes, when she can't sleep, she tortures herself—as if the Nazis needed any help—remembering some of the things she's said to Claude in the past, the petulant arguments, the whining. The times she threatened to leave. The times she did leave.

Always, she came back, or he found her.

It's been months since she's seen him. Is he even looking for her? She doesn't know anything outside this terrible prison that echoes with the cries of those who are already lost but don't realize it. Those who do don't cry, for they know tears won't save them.

And the boots—those steel boots clomping up and down. The constant terror that they will stop outside your door; you wait for it, you know it's coming, but still sometimes you trick yourself into saying, "Not today. Maybe today, they're too busy for me. Maybe today, the Americans will come."

Today, they are not too busy for her. The familiar—dreaded—*clomp clomp* followed by silence. The torturous click of a key being inserted, a lock falling open. Then another *clomp,* hands under her armpits—if she had enough flesh still there to bruise, that tender area between upper arm and breast would be black and blue— and she's on her feet, feet that no longer work reliably on their own, and she's being dragged down the hall. There are grooves, she observes for the first time; grooves on the floor from so many people being dragged against their will.

And now she's in the office of yet another nameless Nazi—two of them, as a matter of fact—and this time, for the first time, there's a gun to her head.

"Give her up, Frau Auzello. Why do you play this game? You could be free. You could go home to the Ritz. You could have champagne and escargot tonight, a hot bath. What is this girl to you?"

"I don't know if Lily is a Jew," she begins wearily; how many times does she have to say it?

"All right, you win."

She raises her head, looks at him—denies the hope that begins to flower in her chest. "What do you mean?"

"You win, Frau. We will forget this Lily, leave her be."

"You will—I—" How does one thank a German? Blanche can't begin to form the words.

"Yes. We will go after your husband instead. If you won't give up your friend, we will arrest your husband. The esteemed Herr Auzello, director of the Ritz. We can find someone else to replace him. We'll find something to charge him with—he's been in prison once before. We'll say we discovered he was responsible for leaving that light on during the air raid."

"But no! You can't—*I* left that light on! I did it!"

"So you say. But you won't utter a word about your friend. How can we believe you? I think it's better that we arrest your husband." The man picks up the phone.

Something breaks inside Blanche as he does—the years of pretending, of hiding, falling away like a great iceberg breaking apart, shattering everything within its vicinity, sheets and sheets of ice filling the water, causing great waves, deafening noise. Her heart is pounding so loudly—it must be weak from malnutrition, so complicating this moment of truth is the terror that she'll drop dead before she can reveal it—before she can save Claude. She licks her parched, papery lips, she shouts—although it's really a hoarse whisper; she no longer has the strength to shout—"It's me! *I'm* the Jew! Not Lily. Forget about her—you want a Jew? Well, you have one—it's me! Blanche Rubenstein! So leave him—leave Claude alone!" She's weeping, wiping tears that aren't there because she's so dehydrated. "I'm the Jew—for God's sake, don't take Claude!" She drops to her knees, pleading.

The two Germans exchange glances, eyebrows raised. One cracks a smile, then the other—and to her horror, they are laughing.

"Why do you lie? You are Madame Auzello

of the Ritz. The French don't like Jews—the Ritz especially. Have you ever seen a Jew at the Ritz?" He guffaws.

"But it's true! I swear—my maiden name is Blanche Rubenstein, not Ross. My passport—it's false. I changed it—I'm not from Cleveland but from the Upper East Side of Manhattan!"

And she laughs, too; it's contagious. She laughs, because it really was so easy. For Claude, she erased her past.

For Claude, she reclaims it again.

"You've got it all wrong," she rasps. She looks up, searching the German, desperate to find something in his face she can recognize—humanity, pity. Even hatred will do at the moment. "I'm the Jew! I am—I'm Blanche Rubenstein!"

"You are Blanche Ross Auzello, Catholic." The other officer thumps her passport shut. "This is ridiculous. You're trying to cover up for your little Jewish friend. I'm weary of this." The officer drags her to her feet, pressing his gun against her temple, and the click of the safety being removed echoes in her brain, and she knows, with certainty, that she will die.

"Don't hurt Claude," she whispers, but she will not close her eyes. She doesn't want to see in their ugly faces their glee, their hunger. But she will not let them see her terror.

Her body is shaking violently, she swallows,

but there's no saliva. There's nothing left, nothing left of Blanche Rubenstein.

Blanche Auzello.

Then—the gun slides away from her flesh. Outside, there is commotion—boots running, the screech of brakes and rumble of motors, shouts. Her interrogators exchange looks, and for the first time since 1940, Blanche sees confusion, even fear, in Aryan eyes.

They leave her, and she shuffles to the window, looking out at chaos: Nazis are everywhere, those gray-green uniforms dashing about, almost comically. Papers are flying through the air like snow; she glances up and sees them being tossed out of windows, some on fire, the orange sparks like fireflies.

"Amerikaner! Amerikaner!"

Americans!

Blanche clings to the windowsill, peering out through the bars, and she's desperate to believe what she sees, what she hears, but she can't. Not yet.

"Amerikaner!"

The Americans—they must be here. Paris, thank God, is safe.

But wait—over there! A shadowy corner between two buildings—she sees it. She sees *her,* Lily, she's there, she's wearing the blue dress Blanche last saw her in, a faded blue, like a bleached summer sky. Blanche can't make out her body, only the blue of the dress, but it's Lily, it must be! Lily running, Lily flying; Lily fleeing, and Blanche wants to call to her, Blanche wants her to come back for her. But Lily must run away. She must have her chance.

Blanche must give her friend that chance. Because she's the reason Lily was arrested in the first place.

"You!"

One of the *Boche* is back in the room, and he's hauling Blanche out the door, dragging her up some stairs, through another corridor, and she's outside for the first time in months, but it's too bright, it's too big, there is no ceiling, no walls, she's so exposed, she can't even recognize fresh air, can't let it in her sick lungs. She's gasping, flailing, like a fish out of water.

"You," he repeats, shoving her against a brick wall stained with blood, and the gun is at her head once more.

"I'm the Jew," Blanche whispers again. "I'm the Jew."

"Leave her." Another voice, one of the other officers from before, is striding past, his arms full of files and papers. "Leave her, crazy bitch—she's blubbering nonsense. Let the Americans deal with her. Jews at the Ritz? Ha!"

They're gone. All of them. Vanished, a cloud of dust the only sign they were here at all.

No, no. That's not true. There are signs everywhere—the black spider of the Nazi flag hanging from windows, the papers that didn't burn. The crimson—almost black—bloodstains against walls where firing squads did their work. Stains on the ground, too. Stains everywhere.

People—or are they ghosts?—everywhere, too. A few yellow stars on striped prison shifts—once-pretty girls who were kept here for the officers instead of being shipped out to one of the camps. But mostly there are no stars here at Fresnes; all the yellow stars are no longer in France, perhaps no longer in this world at all. Unless they were yellow stars like her; hiding in plain sight, forced to watch the horrors in a silence that protected as well as shamed.

Prisoners are stumbling out of the buildings like sleepwalkers. They blink at the dazzling sun. Some crawl on their hands and knees, too weak to walk.

Blanche is one of these sleepwalkers. She shuffles a few steps toward where she glimpsed that blue dress. She searches the gaunt faces, the bruised and battered and skeletal faces, for Lily.

But then she looks for someone else. Even though he's fifteen kilometers away, at the Ritz.

"Claude! Claude!"

"Auzello?"

Blanche stops spinning, dizzy; there is someone at her feet. Someone who was once a man, but is now missing an arm, the stump not bandaged, just a shriveled black stick, and his eyes are bulging, his mouth is also swollen purple, and he can barely speak. His head has been shaved, but a few hairs have started to grow in—black, coarse. He is crumpled on the ground, his legs obviously broken; they are splayed like a marionette's. He is only just alive, and for not much longer. Blanche can tell that he's dying.

She stoops, cradles him in her arms. "What did you say?"

"Claude Auzello?" He has to pause, his breathing so labored Blanche can't hear anything else. "Are you . . . Blanche?" The man is burning with fever. "He is . . . very brave."

"Who?" she asks urgently. "Are you talking about Claude?"

But the man is unconscious, if not dead. And Blanche has to leave him there, leave him for someone else to bury. She has to get away from this place, before the Nazis return.

The prisoners who can still stand look at one another, confusion in their red-rimmed, watery eyes. For the first time in a long time, no one is here to tell them what to do.

Without a word, they shuffle toward the gates, which are flung open, fresh tire tracks scarring the gravel. A woman near Blanche falls, but she can't help her. Blanche steps over her.

Once, she stops to shake off her wooden clogs,

which are so big she can't even shuffle properly. Turning back, Blanche searches, one last time, for that blue dress. For Lily.

But Lily is gone. Blanche tells herself that she has run away, far away, where she'll be safe; that she is hiding somewhere, watching them all leave, making sure the Germans don't come back. And that she'll come find Blanche, later. Blanche has to tell herself that.

Because she has to keep walking. She has to go home, to the Ritz.

To Claude.

CHAPTER 32

CLAUDE,
August 24, 1944

"Monsieur Auzello, there is a call for you."

Claude nods, tamping down the flare of hope these words ignite. It's been months, and every call has disappointed him. There's no reason to think this one will be any different.

But it is different. The hotel is different, the streets are, the very air—you can see the tension vibrating, were you the kind of person who claimed to see such things. Were you the kind of person like his Blanchette.

"I'll take it." Claude follows the porter—François, that's his name, he's fairly new to the Ritz, just a youth, a schoolboy when the *Boche* first arrived—down the polished marble hall to his office, where there is a phone. A phone he knows very well is tapped by his guests.

His guests are, shall we say, otherwise occupied today? Something has happened. Several officers departed last night without settling their bills. "Charge it to the Vichy government," they barked, and Claude bowed politely and assured them he would, even though the

Vichy government hasn't got a franc—or more to the point, a Reichsmark—to its name.

It does seem as if a terrible reckoning is upon them all. If the Americans are truly on the outskirts of Paris, as is rumored, it's a reckoning for the *Boche*. But Claude can't help but think it's a reckoning for all who survived, as well.

He grips the phone, ready to lift it to his ear. Ready to be told something—perhaps it's nothing more than a fishmonger wanting to sell him his latest catch.

Perhaps it's something far worse.

"Hello? This is Claude Auzello."

The voice on the phone is not the one he longs to hear. He doesn't even recognize it; this is a stranger calling him. Which fills him with both terror, and hope.

And then Claude hears her name.

Claude cries out when he sees her. A ghastly notion of a woman slumped against a broken wooden fence by the side of the road.

As soon as Chanel confirmed this was where she had been taken, Claude had gone to Fresnes himself, countless times. Bringing food, wine, pastries, chocolate—"A little present from the Ritz," he always declared, removing the white linen towel with a flourish, revealing the delicacies. Every time, the basket was taken, greedily.

Every time, he was turned away without seeing her, without even confirmation that she was inside.

So despite the chaos everywhere—Claude heard gunfire, glimpsed an American tank down a side road, encountered citizens running to and fro, uncertain what to do; celebrate, hide, fight?—Claude leaped into one of the Ritz lorries and drove like a madman out of the city the moment he hung up the phone. She'd made it to a house about a kilometer from the prison, he was told. She could walk no farther.

But this isn't her, it can't be her. It cannot be his Blanchette.

This woman is forty pounds thinner than his Blanche. Her hair is patchy, gray. Her skin is drawn tight against her face. She is struggling for breath; he glimpses a broken tooth and nearly turns away. Her hands—once elegant, nails manicured and painted red—are shaking, the nails torn, and she makes no effort to stop the trembling. She is barefoot, her feet filthy and bleeding.

But her eyes—those eyes, they could be Blanche's.

"Blanche!" He rushes to her, terrified to gather her in his arms, she is so fragile. And when he does put an arm about her shoulder, to help her into the car, she gasps with pain. "What did they do to you, my love?" He can't help himself, even as he doesn't want to know.

Blanche shakes her head and closes her eyes as soon as he carries her to the passenger seat.

Claude grits his teeth at each jolt in the road, each honk of a horn, for there are still dangers about—Germans cut off from their regiments, left behind, cornered. Rumors of mines laid by the Resistance. Pockets of fighting still, even in the heart of the city.

He hears himself chatter as he has never chattered before, sharing gossip, anything to fill the silence, stifle the fear, drown out her ragged breathing—"Von Dincklage left, and now Chanel is back, bereft. And unprotected." Claude longs to hear Blanche's voice; he wishes it so desperately that he would do anything—break out into an aria, tell her he's shot Hitler himself—to have her speak, just once. Just to have her call him by his name. "And Arletty, too—her Nazi lover is gone. There are rumors that French citizens who—who collaborated, as they're calling it—are being locked in the very prisons that the Germans have just left. The Americans will take the city tomorrow, I think. The Germans are almost all gone from the Ritz; only a few equerries remain. But we must be careful, still. For a little while. And then, my love, we will celebrate! Paris will celebrate as it's never celebrated before!"

Still she does not open her eyes, does not utter a sound. Again, Claude's vocabulary is not equipped to deal with a situation, so he lapses into hopeless silence. Once, he thought French the most perfect language in the world; it had brought him his wife, hadn't it? She used to say that she'd fallen in love with him because of his accent. But the war has shattered that illusion, too. For war doesn't make sense in any language.

Finally, they turn down the Place Vendôme, to the square. The Nazi trucks and tanks are gone although the swastika still hangs over the doorway. But they are home. His heart swells with joy.

The Auzellos have returned to the Ritz.

As Claude carries Blanche up the few stairs, he spies the entire staff gathered inside the front entrance; Blanche raises her head and sees them, too. She struggles, tries to take a deep breath but cannot—her hand flies to her rib cage as she gasps with pain—and she rasps, "Let me down, please."

He obeys, though he is certain she will fall.

"Always the front door from now on," she whispers, her eyes, in her skeletal face, shining brightly. Bravely.

The staff cannot hide their horror at her appearance; Marie-Louise herself has tears in her eyes as she rushes to Blanche's side. Claude lifts his wife once again and carries her down the hall—the Hall of Dreams, they once called it, but the displays are empty; the Nazis took all the dreams with them when they left—to the rue Cambon side and gets her into the service lift. There is no way she can manage the stairs.

"Dear Claude," Marie-Louise murmurs, after he carries his wife—she weighs nothing—over the threshold of their suite, and lays her tenderly on their bed. "Dear Claude. Dear Blanche." Madame Ritz is sobbing, tears making tracks through her heavily powdered cheeks. "That this could happen here, in Paris. In my husband's home." She shakes her head and leaves, pressing Claude's hand in sympathy.

"My love," he says, looking at his wife, so slight, so fragile. "I—I only wanted to keep you safe," Claude whispers. "I only wanted to keep us all safe here."

"You did a lousy job of it." She laughs, and the sound is like glass being crushed beneath a Nazi boot.

"Don't." Claude can't bear it even as he can't help but admire her—that she can make a joke of this, this terror that she endured. "Don't. I am not worthy of you, Blanche. Of what you did for Paris—for me."

"No more lies, Claude." Now she is crying, not laughing, and Claude creeps gingerly upon the bed, cradling his body against hers, not caring about the filth, the lice, the smell. "No more lies between us. I told them—I told the damn Nazis I was a Jew."

"Is that why they—?" But Claude can't bring himself to say the word *torture*.

"No, they did that before. But they didn't believe me, Claude. They didn't believe there could be a Jew here—at the Ritz."

"We won't hide it anymore," Claude promises. "Only the truth from now on, my dearest."

She is so still, for such a long while, that he thinks she has fallen asleep; he has to listen carefully, but he can hear her breathing, ragged but steady. "I promise to keep you safe," he whispers. "For the rest of my life—I will sacrifice anything. To keep you safe."

And Claude doesn't know if these two promises—the promise to tell the truth and the promise to keep her safe—can both be kept, even in peacetime. The only thing he does know is, he has to at least try.

And one thing more:

No one will have to show Claude Auzello how brave his wife is, ever again. He will see it every morning, every night. In every conversation they have, every glimpse of her that he is allowed—every smile, every frown, every tear, every laugh.

And he will never be worthy of her.

THE RITZ,
August 25, 1944

"I have come to liberate the Ritz," he crows, hopping out of the Jeep, standing with his legs planted like thick trees, his arms upon his hips. His beard is longer and bushier—and whiter—than it had been when the Ritz saw him last.

But the Ritz still recognizes him. Hemingway himself—come to liberate the Ritz!

Claude Auzello, standing at the entrance, suppresses a sigh. The Ritz is already liberated; the last German left last night and as soon as he left on foot—snarling, spewing forth obscenities—the entire staff cheered and sobbed. They marched about like soldiers themselves, taking all the swastikas down; they celebrated in the Imperial Suite, bouncing upon the very bed that Göring had slept in, donning the marabou dressing gowns and dancing to that gramophone—odd, the German was very fond of the American Andrews Sisters, particularly "Bei Mir Bist du Schön." They sat, ten of them easily, in that enormous tub (after first, of course, scrubbing it) and drank the good champagne that Monsieur Claude managed to hide from the Germans in a storehouse across the Seine.

Hemingway takes a pistol—a German pistol, many of the staff can't help but recoil at the sight of it—from a holster strapped to his broad chest. He is in the uniform of an American soldier. There are four other Americans with him.

He bounds up the steps; Claude Auzello bows to him.

"I'm here to liberate the Ritz bar," Hemingway declares, throwing his head back. "Follow me, boys!" And he runs, his gun at the ready, down the wide entrance hallway, smiling his big white-teethed American smile; he looks healthy, well fed, and jubilant.

Emerging from the long hallway into the rue Cambon side, Hemingway bursts through the door of the bar, declaring, "I have done it! The Ritz is taken back by the Allies! Drinks for everyone!"

And soon the bar is flooded with familiar faces, Americans and Brits—all dusty, all wearing uniforms, but all noticeably well fed and giddy—are crowding into the bar. Robert Capa, Lee Miller, so many war correspondents. Picasso, too, has returned, after spending the Occupation holed up in his apartment (unlike Gertrude Stein and her friend Alice, who fled to the country). George Scheuer—Frank Meier's former lieutenant, the head bartender now that Frank is gone—is so busy popping champagne corks, for a while it sounds as if there is gunfire inside the hotel itself.

But no one flinches; everyone keeps drinking, laughing, slapping one another on the back.

And then—

"Hello, boys." It is Marlene Dietrich herself slinking her way toward Hemingway. "Papa," she purrs, and he drops to his knees and bows down to her. She is in an American Army uniform but it is tailored to hug her curves. Her blond hair is shining, in a page-boy cut. Her face is fully made up. She looks as if she's just walked off a movie set, but according to the whispers, she just got off an Army truck, having accompanied a regiment of U.S. soldiers into the city.

"The Kraut! Long live the Kraut!" For a moment, everyone flinches until they remember that this is Hemingway's nickname for her. And they cheer, along with the others, as the two embrace, and kiss passionately.

"You need a shave," she scolds him in the only German accent anyone wants to hear, ever again. "But first, a drink."

The party goes on. It will always go on, they think—they believe.

Now that the Germans have finally left the Hôtel Ritz.

On the Place Vendôme.

409

CHAPTER 33

BLANCHE,
September 1944

"Blanche, hey, Blanche!"

There are cheers as she ventures into the bar for the first time; cheers that lift her off her unsteady feet and ensconce her at her usual table. But there is shock, as well. Hemingway tries, but does not quite succeed, to hide his concern.

He pulls out her chair for her with a gentleness that's startling in a man as overwhelming as he can be, and buys her a drink. And then proceeds to tell her all about his adventures following the Army into France, his boredom in London waiting for the invasion. Blanche listens, nods, her usual role. But she can't help noticing that he doesn't ask about those who are no longer at the Ritz, like his "good pal" Frank Meier. Like Greep. Like his favorite shoeshine boy, Jacques. Like the man who used to shave him, Victor.

Dietrich—slim, blond, wearing trousers to Claude's disapproval—is singing her famous songs, encircled by a throng of admirers. Blanche is sniffing that single rose in a vase, put there by Claude, dear Claude, who is still afraid to let her out of his sight and so he's happy, for once, to have her spend all day at the bar, drinking martini after martini. Martinis she suspects won't obscure the thoughts, the memories, but damn, if she won't give them a chance to anyway.

Ernest downs his martini in one gulp. She notices, not for the first time, that his hands are as vast and creased as baseball gloves.

"Look at this, Blanche." He caresses a big black leather belt cinched tight around his protruding belly. "I took it off a Nazi. I call it my Kraut belt."

At the sight of it, she can't stop herself; she begins to shake, so she picks up the drink with two hands and brings it to her lips, manages to set it down without sloshing too much over the brim. He ignores this, friend to friend, drunk to drunk.

"Hey, what happened to that friend of yours? That little Russian, or whatever she was?"

Blanche eyes him. His fine-featured yet broad face shines with good health, good times. Privilege. Ignorance.

Blanche shrugs—that convenient Gallic shrug, invented for moments like this—and quickly changes the subject, asking him about his current, typically complicated, marital situation.

"Oh, Martha's coming soon, but Mary's here now, and so I need to make sure Martha stays at another hotel. We'll divorce. I'll marry Mary." He indicates a young woman with short brown hair seated near Marlene; she is plainly dressed to the point of dowdiness and seems to be eyeing Dietrich with jealousy. Everybody knows that Dietrich and Hemingway have always had a passion for each other, and the first night Dietrich came back to the Ritz, she spent it with Hemingway after giving him a very public shave; Capa captured it with his camera, and the photo has already run in the newspapers.

This is the kind of gossip that once filled Blanche's days. She rose every morning, eager to hear more of it. But now it just seems pointless. And unfair—these people who have had such a "marvelous" war can think about romance and deceit, can play these little games with deadly seriousness. They have room inside of them for that; their bellies are not full of hate and guilt.

"Mary's a reporter, too. We met in London. Martha's mad as hell with me, but I'm mad as hell with her. She got to land with the troops at Normandy." Finally his face does cloud over, but it is the petulance of a little boy who didn't get his way. "A goddamned woman landing with the first wave of troops, when my papers got all fouled up and I couldn't. It kills me, Blanche, it kills me. I've never known such tragedy."

She asks him to get her another martini, praying she won't throw it at his bragging face. But even if she does, what will happen to her? What could possibly happen to Blanche that she could ever care about, worry about, fear?

They are all like that, these Americans, these Brits, all those who spent the war on the other side of the Channel—too bright, too loud, too damn happy. And Blanche wishes she could be like them—Christ, she really does! She'd thought—she'd *known*—those long weeks at Fresnes, that if only she could get back to the Ritz, everything would be the way it used to be. So every morning, she dresses herself as before; she even bought a new frock from Chanel who took one look at her and said, "I like what you've done with your hair, Blanche."

Blanche handed her salesgirl an exorbitant amount of American money. An envelope with her name on it showed up one day, slid beneath the door of their suite, and she recognized the handwriting as Frank Meier's; inside was several hundred dollars and no note. She expected Claude would order her to turn the money over to Madame Ritz but surprisingly, he did not.

"I see you still *have* your hair, bitch," Blanche retorted. For how Coco wasn't rounded up with the other women who'd had Nazi lovers, and had her hair shaved like they had, no one knows. The fact that she's been handing out free bottles of Chanel No. 5 to all the American servicemen to take home to their girls must have been a factor. They're so besotted with her, they won't let any of the ravenous civilian tribunals touch a hair on her scheming little head.

But to Blanche's surprise, Coco refused the money and told the girl to wrap the dress anyway.

With her extra money, Blanche found nylons on the black market, thanks to a French baroness who seems overanxious to help some of those who have returned (apparently, her German lover did not take her back across the Rhine, and she is worried about her immediate future). Blanche went to a hairdresser—not that the shocked young woman could do much with her sparse hair but dye what was left of it, and suggest Blanche buy herself some new hats. Blanche puts on perfume, makeup, pearls; she had the seamstresses at the Ritz take in all her clothes, for they hang on her now. But it's only a costume; the person looking out from the mirror is someone else, not Blanche. Still, she marches forth from their suite clad in this familiar, expensive garb, remembering the filthy wool shift, the wooden clogs of Fresnes.

But always she sees herself from afar; she sees herself as she was *before,* knocking them back with the boys, laughing raucously, gossiping. Then Blanche drifts back down, like a balloon losing air, and she settles into the broken body she has now: the shoulder that refuses to heal, the headaches, the pain in her side whenever she moves too quickly, the shortness of breath, the tremors she can't control, the nervousness—

the least little sound makes her jump like a cat and break out into a sweat. Sometimes, she even soils herself and she thinks, Christ, is there no dignity left to her?

But still she tries; oh, she does try! She drinks, she sings along with Dietrich when she croons "Lili Marleen" and Dietrich calls Blanche a "Good Little Soldier." She roams the streets as she used to before, trying to recapture the magic, haunting old haunts—the Galeries Lafayette, Brasserie Lipp, the newly reopened shops on the avenue Montaigne (although they have precious little to sell).

Sometimes, she walks past Maxim's. She can't help herself. But she'll never go inside it again.

She's searching for the Paris she fell in love with, but it's difficult. There are bullet holes pock-marking walls and buildings, broken windows and streetlamps, barbed-wire barricades still visible, where members of the Resistance, along with civilians, decided to take on the panicked German troops themselves before the Allies arrived. The street signs are still in German and French, but somebody has made it their business to paint over the German words. The museums, like the Louvre, are vast, empty echoes of the past; there are still too many paintings and sculptures missing, looted by the Germans. Who knows if they'll ever be returned?

Just like the people who will never return.

Parisians are too thin, even for Parisians; they walk about in patched dresses and jackets that were fashionable five years ago—although who knows what's fashionable now?—and their shoes still have those wooden soles. Potatoes and leeks seem to be the only vegetables available in the meager little markets, although flowers, as always, are in profusion. Instead of those horrible German military bands with their tubas playing in the Luxembourg Gardens, the Americans, with their flashing trombones, play swing music— Glenn Miller, Benny Goodman—and the young people dance to it, slinging each other about, laughing, free—acting like young people should, and this in itself is a miracle.

The French performers who stayed and entertained the Germans during the Occupation, like Maurice Chevalier, have all conveniently taken a vacation elsewhere for the time being.

There are still soldiers, of course, but the sight of them no longer strikes terror and resentment in Parisians' hearts. These are their liberators— the Americans in their khaki uniforms, the smiles broad, flashing healthy white teeth; the British in their slightly darker versions, their smiles not so ready. And French soldiers, too—they came marching in in triumph, led by General Leclerc, along with the British and the Americans. And the citizens cheered them, wildly, even as they knew that were it not for the Brits and Yanks, the French Army would still be in North Africa. The French troops are browned by the sun; they look as if they've been on a holiday, not in a war. It isn't their fault, of course; it had been the government that told them to stop fighting, back in 1940. Still, there is a sense of shame mixed with relief, when Parisians see their own military uniforms.

Blanche wanders these strange yet familiar streets with her husband's permission; Claude thinks it's good for her to get away from the Ritz now and again. He's concerned for her, understands how fragile she remains, and she's grateful enough that one damned person in this world remembers what she's been through and allows her to talk about it. She meekly accepts his fussing and worrying: "Only go out during the day, Blanchette. I want you home at night." "Only a few blocks today, my love, you're looking tired." "How is your shoulder today, Blanche? Would you like me to schedule you a masseuse? Don't you think you ought to stay in bed today, my dear?"

Like a child, Blanche nods dutifully, she accepts his attentions, smothering though they may be. There is a surprising tenderness between these two; they both see it but they can't quite talk about it. Something young and fragile has sprung forth, like a new branch growing from a battered tree. They are both so damaged, in different ways, by these past years. They are a middle-aged married couple but they treat each other with such respect, such care. Sometimes Blanche feels shy in his presence; like a new bride.

Every day, he sends her flowers. But never violets. She looks for those, from another person. But she looks in vain.

Elise is still with them. She fusses over Blanche, concocting endless, delicious, nourishing things for her to eat. Although soup is the only thing she can reliably keep down.

"I did look, Blanche," Claude says to her one evening while they're sitting quietly in their apartment; they spend more nights there, as of late. Apparently, Blanche screams in her sleep. And she wouldn't want the Ritz guests to hear that now, would she? "There are no records left at Fresnes, of course—the Nazis burned everything, as you said. Martin appears to have vanished, as well—I told you about him. I asked everyone I knew who might have some contact with the Resistance. But no one has heard what became of her."

"I think she must be dead." This is the first time Blanche has said it aloud. "I think I got her killed." She hasn't been able to cry for Lily yet. Since she's returned, she's not been able to feel *anything*—not the sight of lovers huddled over a café table; not the newborn kittens and their contented mama discovered in a neighbor's attic; not even the sound of accordion music along the Seine has been able to stir in her any kind of romance or happiness or longing, as it once did.

Claude takes her hand in his. And even that can't make her feel content.

Blanche sits in an empty synagogue in the Marais, which is so heartbreakingly devoid of people. She shuts her eyes and tries to conjure up the music, the chanting, from the synagogue of her youth. Blanche's parents—German-born Jews—were not Orthodox; women sat with the men, English was mixed with Hebrew in the service. But Reform or Orthodox, certain things are the same everywhere—the Torah, the prayers. The swirling of a mystical antiquity and always, *always,* that palpable sense of suffering, waiting. With her eyes squeezed shut, Blanche tries, desperately, to reclaim her past. The past she'd so thoroughly expunged that not even the Nazis believed she was Jewish.

Blanche fervently waits for something to move her, something to flicker inside her—a connection, a chain to her ancestors that will link her even more tightly to those who were taken, who are still gone, who might never return.

But nothing does. She sits for nearly an hour, and all she feels is foolish. It's only after she leaves the building and is walking toward the

Seine, passing a carousel and seeing children on it, children so young they might not, please God, remember the horrors of these years, that she cries. Because on one of those children's jackets Blanche can make out the faint outline of the yellow star—obviously just removed so that the fabric, behind it, is a darker shade than the rest of the coat.

Blanche recognizes that outline, and she sits down on a bench, and she cries.

At dinner that evening, she finally cries for Lily.

"I did kill her, I know I did." Tears slowly slide down her cheeks, splashing into another of Elise's creamy soups that has gone untouched.

"No—I think—you can't know that. Lily killed Germans, Blanche. She made her choices and she knew she would probably die because of them."

"But if I'd not made such a scene at Maxim's— she might have gotten away with it."

"You must not live the rest of your life in pain because of this, my love. I think, perhaps, it's best that I leave the Ritz?" He looks uncertain for a moment, but then he nods decisively. "Yes, I— we will leave the Ritz. We will move to that farm we used to talk about, where I can take care of you all the time. And that way, perhaps, you can forget. Maybe we should go to America? To join your family there—I could surely find a job?"

"No!" Blanche drops her spoon in the soup,

splattering the tablecloth. "No! I'm not American anymore. Not after Fresnes. I belong here, in France—our scars are the same, France's and mine. Don't you see? I can't go back."

"But—"

"Claude." Blanche sighs, reluctant to voice this out loud for fear of what he will say. "What if she is looking for me?"

"Oh, Blanche . . ."

"Don't you see? The Ritz is the only place she'll know to look for me, if—when—she comes back."

Her husband's eyes are so anguished, and Lily is not the one he's mourning in this moment. Blanche sees herself reflected in those sympathetic eyes—a broken, delusional victim.

But that isn't how she wants to be seen; that's not how she—or Lily—deserves to be remembered. And so, drying her first—and last— tears for Lily, Blanche tells him about her plan.

When Blanche observed the child's jacket in the park, she walked over to take a closer look. Two nuns were in charge of this small group of children—Jewish children, pale from being hidden away these long years. Blanche recognized them right away; they looked like all the children in the photographs at her parents' house.

"Sister?" she asked one of the nuns.

"Yes?"

"Who are—who are they?" Blanche smiled at the tiny girl with the dark star outline on her jacket; the girl stuck her finger in her mouth and simply stared at Blanche until she blurted out, "Your dress is pretty!"

Blanche and the sister laughed, but then the nun took Blanche's arm and walked her away from the children.

"Orphans, I'm afraid. They were hidden in the country, taken there from the city when their parents were—rounded up. Kind people, Catholics, hid them, cared for them, as if they were their own children—they instructed them in the Church so they could be passed off as Catholics if the Nazis came looking for them."

"What will happen to them now? Will they be returned to their families?" But before the sister could answer, Blanche knew what she was going to say.

"There are no families to return them to. Their parents, older siblings—they're gone."

"But surely they have relatives in America, other countries—aunts or uncles who escaped, that they could go to?"

"Oh, we wouldn't want that, would we? These souls are Catholic now, bless them! Baptized, every one of them! We'll put them in Catholic homes, of course. They're so young, they'll never remember that they're—they'll never remember their past." The sister beamed at her charges,

sallow-skinned, dark-haired—expressions of utter sadness and patience in their eyes, when they weren't engaged in play.

How do you recognize a Semite?

Blanche Rubenstein knew all too well.

"Sister, you would be surprised about how much they'll remember. Trust me. It's not so easy to forget." Blanche reached into her purse and handed the sister the rest of her found money. "For Christ's sake—excuse me, Sister—buy them new coats, at least. Ones without stars."

"Claude," she says to him now—excited, perhaps even happy, for the first time in so long. "Claude, I have an idea. A way to, well—atone, maybe, for what I did. I'd like to help Jewish orphans find Jewish homes. Some of them are being raised as Catholic, so that they will never know where they came from or who they are. I'd like to do something about that."

She smiles across at her husband, whose face is full of admiration, not pity. She wants to keep that look in his face, now and forever. She lost it, once. She won't let that happen again.

"What you sacrificed for me, for all of Paris, and now that you want to do this—" he begins, but Blanche shakes her head.

"Oh, Popsy, don't make a big deal about it." She picks up her spoon, ravenous—another surprise. "At the time, it really didn't seem that important to me. That's not entirely true, it turns out. But this way—if I help these kids, if I get them back to their families, no matter how far away—I feel like I'm reclaiming my faith again. You don't mind, do you?" She peers at him, anxious; she never knows when his Catholicism will flare up like a persistent rash.

"Mind? I will help you, Blanchette. We can raise money, have fundraisers at the Ritz—we know lawyers, for I'm sure this is complicated, legally. I am only humbled that you would ask my help."

"Well, who the hell would I ask but my husband? You're a good man, Claude Auzello. Even if you do your best to hide it sometimes."

The Auzellos beam at each other across the table. They know, finally, the truth of each other; she's so proud of him, of what he did during the war, keeping the Ritz and all its employees together, and still finding a way to strike a blow against the Nazis, who were his guests. His captors. Blanche can't think of anyone else who had as difficult—as peculiar—a job as he did, during all this.

Blanche knows he's proud of her, too. Sometimes he can barely look her in the eye when he talks of what she did. He is humbled by her, but he shouldn't be. They're both brave as hell, these Auzellos and Rubensteins.

Finally, after twenty-one years, they have a marriage that even a Frenchman can't destroy.

CHAPTER 34
CLAUDE,
Autumn 1945

When the first contingent of Americans sails to France after VE Day, they experience something of a shock. As do Blanche and Claude.

"Blanche! You're alive!" Foxy Sondheim squeals, throws her fur muff in the air, and throws herself on Blanche.

"Last I looked, I was," Blanche replies, puzzled—she raises her eyebrows at Claude as Foxy begins to weep.

"But Winchell—Walter Winchell, in his column a year or so ago, said you'd been *shot* by the Nazis! We all thought you were dead—everyone in New York! We even threw *a wake* at the Ritz for you!"

"Really?" A huge grin lights up Blanche's face; she ushers Foxy into the bar and Claude brings them a bottle of champagne. Foxy is a tall New York fashion designer who was a loyal guest before the war; she's part of a group recently sent over by the U.S. Department of State. And Claude, of course, is anxious to remind these returning Americans and Brits that the Ritz is very much still open for business.

"I made Winchell's column? Did you hear that, Popsy?"

Blanche is truly tickled, making Foxy repeat the story for everyone who didn't hear it the first time. Then Blanche begins to tell Foxy about her work with the orphans—"I can put you down for, what? Five hundred dollars? It has to be American money—no francs, you cheapskate!"—and Foxy laughs, while Claude leaves them to reminisce and catch up.

But Foxy comes to him later and expresses her shock over Blanche's appearance.

"What happened to her, Claude? What really happened here, during the war?"

"We are so glad to have you back, Madame Sondheim," Claude replies. "How is your suite? The same as before, I sincerely hope? We are fine, do not worry about Blanche. She is a survivor."

"She sure is." Foxy hands him her dog's leash, which he takes with a resigned smile. "Like the Eiffel Tower itself!"

Yes, she is, Claude thinks proudly. Blanche is triumphant, precious, brave. She is everything Paris is, or should be—beauty untouched by these grim years, soul unbowed, unbroken. Yes, bad things have happened. But Paris—and Blanche— will survive; music will play once more, tourist boats filled with citizens, not soldiers, will meander up and down the Seine, broken windows will be replaced by newer, shinier ones, gardens that were trampled by boots will be replanted. But it will be—complicated.

Claude realizes this the moment the trains start arriving, disgorging their passengers that aren't people but skeletons. From Germany they come, starting this early autumn of 1945. From Poland. From Austria. From places called Bergen-Belsen, Auschwitz, Dachau. Skeletons who can barely walk, with tattoos of numbers on their forearms. Claude sees them, staggering about Paris, blinking, stunned at being alive. Stunned at seeing the Eiffel Tower again, the Tuileries, the Arc; tears in their eyes to find themselves back home. And Claude understands that they who had survived the Occupation in Paris aren't so noble, after all; what he has done wasn't really so brave, so wondrous. Not even what Blanche had endured can compare to what these survivors have seen, heard, experienced. He, like everyone else, has to look away when he encounters them—sitting in a café, wearing too many layers no matter the temperature; seated on benches in the gardens, faces turned toward the sun with eyes closed tightly, taking deep, shattering breaths of fresh air, of life itself, trying to fill out their bodies with this air, this life.

What was the Occupation, compared to the atrocities these souls have endured? Claude is ashamed to think of how he had chafed at what he had to do when the Nazis were at the Ritz—

the serving, the fetching, the bowing. He is so ashamed that he vows never to talk about it, or what he had done with Martin. And in this way he is like every other French citizen—collectively, almost as if they gathered in the Opéra and had a mass meeting about it, Parisians decide to draw a veil over those years. Unlike when the Great War ended, Claude realizes that there will be no getting together to swap war stories. This privilege is left to the Allies who had fought and liberated.

What is left to the French is too enormous and complicated, a great tangle of threads of all hues and heft that one cannot begin to unravel. There was bravery, but there was also collaboration. There was defiance, but there was also acquiescence. Some people suffered, but most did not.

So what can Paris do but—live on? Look forward? Take pride in the past that is distant, heroic—and plan for a future that is not predicated too much on national pride. In a way, this binds Parisians together, after the citizen tribunals run their course and the skeletons become, at least in appearance, people again: the unspoken consensus that it's best not to look too closely at the war years, and instead, concentrate on the future.

Like Blanche is doing, with her work with the orphans; she sells her clothing that she can no longer wear, her designer dresses, to raise funds. Several influential Jews form committees to look into these war orphanages, and there are tensions between the Catholic and the Jewish communities over it. But then again, if there weren't tensions between Parisians it wouldn't be Paris, would it? So Blanche raises money and argues with nuns and priests and it keeps her happy, keeps her busy.

Keeps her from thinking too much about Lily.

Many of these returning guests are on their way to cover the Nuremberg trials, and when those trials result in ten executions and one suicide (their old friend Hermann Göring), Claude shakes his head sorrowfully.

"We have just lost eleven steady customers," he says, and the roar of laughter that greets his little joke is very gratifying, indeed.

At the Ritz, commanding his staff, Claude does not feel old. At the Ritz, in its rosy, flattering light, Blanche does not look twice her age.

At the Ritz, everything will be as it was. Because that is what the Ritz does; it causes you to forget the very last thing you saw before you entered its opulence—even if that very last thing was the worst of humanity. The Ritz will provide relief, will provide distraction, will provide the best champagne to wash down bile, will provide the softest towels to absorb despair.

Balance—Claude had always believed himself

to be a man capable of apportioning the correct value to every part of his life. Work, religion, relaxation, friends, family, education, physical activity. Love. Devotion. In his mind, there was a scale, and on one side was the Ritz, and on the other side was Blanche, and the two scales were equal, symmetrical; the scales never moved, one never slid up while the other hung heavier.

But when Blanche was taken, he realized he had not apportioned her value correctly, after all. The scales were off; he'd been putting his thumb in the side that represented the Ritz.

He will never make that mistake again. He will do his duties, and do them well. He will continue to uphold the values of César Ritz, further his legacy, ensure its success. He will go to Mass, he will walk the streets at night, he will continue to have his favorite views of the Arc, his favorite gardens, his favorite cafés. He will sob unabashedly when he hears "La Marseillaise."

But his heart will be Blanche's, alone.

LILY

Blanche is dead.

It's been a very long time since that day in Fresnes prison. That day when Blanche called out my name, and I was so happy to hear it. So happy to have made a friend who could not deny me, even if it meant sealing my fate.

Heifer wouldn't have called my name. Lorenzo wouldn't have looked at me. None of them would mourn me. But Blanche, she did; Blanche rushed to me; Blanche called out "Lily!" And when they took me away, I didn't feel alone and forgotten. I never thought I would find hope in the midst of pain and despair; I never thought I would find graciousness in the midst of war.

But because of Blanche, I did.

I kept track of her at first, when she and the others left Fresnes that day. I kept track of her, and Claude, and the Ritz. I watched her courageously try to snatch at life again.

And for a long time, she succeeded.

Blanche and Claude Auzello grew old, suddenly. Blanche gained weight and no longer dyed her hair. Claude shriveled, his hair graying and thinning.

And these two who had battled, who had raged,

who began with a passion so fierce and heady that it blinded them for years—suddenly, they treated each other as old married couples do: with tenderness, with exasperation, but always with love, polished over time so that the rough edges were no longer visible and only the smooth patina showed.

Blanche worried about Claude's workload, his smoking, his incessant fussing over her. She fretted when she saw him being pushed aside, stuck in his old-fashioned ways as the Ritz moved into a new, more modern era. He worried about her drinking, her headaches, her sudden outbursts, more frequent as the years piled up and the memories, the pain took their toll—she screamed in German, said foul things, spat over the upstairs railing of the grand staircase. She would take to her bed for days unable to eat, unable to bear the light.

And Claude would despair. His inability to destroy her demons, to keep her safe, consumed him. "I must help her," he whispered so that only Robert and I—who were the only ones listening, it must be said—could hear. "I must keep her safe, I must protect her."

Oh, Claude.

It is devastating to see a loved one suffer; it is harder to bear than your own pain. Love is despair, love is delight. Love is fear, love is hope. Love is mercy.

Love is anger.

When Claude officially retired—unwillingly—the Auzellos were presented with a silver tray with the years of his service engraved on it, and they waved goodbye and Claude leaned on his wife as they walked out the door of the Ritz. They left with promises to return soon for a drink or tea or maybe lunch. But they will not keep those promises.

Because now, only a few days later, Blanche is dead.

And so is Claude.

An accident, it must have been—that's what everyone says. A tragic accident, because nobody who knows Claude Auzello can conceive of him hurting his wife—look at what she'd been through, in the war. He must have been cleaning his gun and it accidentally went off. Surely, it was only his despair at losing her that made him turn the gun on himself, that is what everyone says as they hear the news, weep, pray, toast to the memory of the Auzellos of the Ritz—and then go on about their business, the business of the living.

And soon, Claude and Blanche Auzello will be only memories. Nobody wants to remember the war years anymore, except for that one story about Hemingway, and how he told everyone he liberated the hotel even though he didn't. Nobody wants to tell the story of the French director and his American Jewish wife and how they really saved the Hôtel Ritz, on the Place Vendôme.

I do, though. I like that story, it's a fine story, even as I still wonder about the ending.

When Claude put his suffering wife to bed that night, what was he thinking?

When he watched her fall into a surprisingly peaceful sleep, not yet uttering the terrors she could no longer suppress, did he think of the first time he saw her?

When he reached for the pistol, the same one he'd carried since the war, did he only hope to relieve her of her misery? Was it weariness— his own as well as hers—that steadied his hand as he put the pillow over her head and pulled the trigger? Selfishness, so that he didn't have to care for her, didn't have to watch her continued descent into a place where he could not follow?

Or was it love?

Because I think Blanche suspected, before she climbed into their bed that evening. I think she knew what her husband was going to do—her despairing husband, robbed of his life, his Ritz, robbed of his dignity—and she gave him his release. Because Blanche, after all, was so very good at saving.

Whose love was strongest, that night— Claude's, or Blanche's? Or was it their love, combined, a steel conduit linking one to the other, forged by war and pain, that steadied his hand, that caused her to lie so still, so peacefully?

I've told you their story.

You decide.

In the early morning of May 29, 1969, a neighbor of the Auzellos on the avenue Montaigne heard a sound he thought was a tire popping. Three hours later, he heard the same sound. Soon after, the maid arrived to prepare breakfast.

When she went to awaken them, she found Blanche in bed, dead from a gunshot wound, and Claude, a gun in his hand, a mortal wound to his head, lying on the floor beside her.

It had been twenty-nine years since the Germans first arrived at the Ritz.

AUTHOR'S NOTE

When I'm searching for a new novel subject, there are many things I look for. A compelling protagonist, an intriguing but unknown slice of history, a setting that can be a character itself—all of these things have inspired me to write books. But sometimes, you come across what I call simply a "great big fat juicy story." And that's exactly what I found in *Mistress of the Ritz*.

I first encountered Blanche and Claude Auzello in the nonfiction book *The Hotel on Place Vendôme*, by Tilar J. Mazzeo, which introduced me to the role of the Hôtel Ritz during the German occupation: a part of history I knew nothing about. (See above.) It was also an inspiring setting that could be a character in a book. (Ditto.)

And in its pages, I found that great big fat juicy story, but one with many empty blanks.

Mazzeo's book first introduced me to the Auzellos, their background, and their wartime service. But the nature of the book made it impossible for the Auzellos to take center stage; theirs was only one of many sketched-out stories of life at the Ritz during the war years. I was left feeling that here was a novel begging to be written. And indeed, as I started researching

Blanche and Claude and the Ritz, that was the one question I kept seeing in articles and blogs and other books: Why hasn't someone written a novel about these two?

How could I resist?

Most of my previous novels have been about people with a very rich written history already. Certainly Anne Morrow Lindbergh, Truman Capote, Mary Pickford all have been written about, extensively, before. But there really isn't much out there about Blanche and Claude. We don't even know their exact dates of birth. There was the book I mentioned above, and then a very slight biography of Blanche called *Queen of the Ritz*, written by her nephew Samuel Marx. This book is frustrating, even though it consists of interviews that Marx conducted with Blanche long after the war. It never gets to the truth of Blanche's character, or her marriage beyond its arguments and Claude's mistresses. It's all surface, even when Blanche talks about her wartime exploits. She has a tendency, always, to default to humor, even when relating her imprisonment and torture. Her real character remains a mystery.

There is one other book, *The Ritz of Paris*, by Stephen Watts, that talks about the Ritz during the war and includes several interviews with Claude. (The book was written in 1963.) Again, when probed about what went on there during the war, and his own bravery, Claude draws a tight curtain over it. It is frustrating, to say the least.

So I would say that *Mistress of the Ritz*, more than any of my other novels, is "inspired" by a true story and real people, rather than based on them. With so few real details to go on—for example, Lily and J'Ali are name-checked in the few things written about Blanche, but I could not find any details about them elsewhere—and so few true glimpses into Blanche's and Claude's characters, my imagination was given free rein.

We know that Blanche first came to Paris in the early 1920s with her friend Pearl White, and that she was the lover of an Egyptian prince named J'Ali. We know that she, after a very short time, married Claude Auzello, the manager of the Hôtel Claridge, who soon became the manager of the Hôtel Ritz. We know that she forged her passport to erase her Jewish heritage. We know that Blanche worked with the Resistance and got several airmen out of the country, but the details are nonexistent. We know she was arrested—possibly more than once, although I keep it to only the one time in this novel. We know that *something* happened at Maxim's restaurant when she took Lily there to celebrate D-Day. We know the circumstances of her liberation from Fresnes, right down to the fact that she was about to be executed when the Allies literally arrived in the nick of time. We know that Lily disappeared.

We know that Claude worked with other hotel directors to convey messages through suppliers outside France, and that a man named Martin was his contact.

We know that in 1968, Claude killed Blanche in a murder-suicide.

And—that's it.

Why did Blanche risk her life, when she could have easily sat out the war in luxury? What was the aftermath like, when all her old pals—Hemingway, the Duke and Duchess of Windsor—returned to the Ritz after the war? How had Blanche changed? How had Claude? In the books I've mentioned, they don't seem to. Life just goes on as before, as if the war was only a minor interruption. But given their ending, that couldn't have been the truth of their lives. And as a novelist, that is my drive, always—imagining that truth, the *emotional* truth, of these real people's lives.

One more thing, for the World War II historians out there: There were actually two different von Stülpnagels occupying the Ritz; first there was Otto, then his cousin Carl-Heinrich, who replaced Otto when Otto was assigned to another post. Carl-Heinrich was the von Stülpnagel who was implicated in the plot to assassinate Hitler that took form in the bar of the Hôtel Ritz. For ease of reading, I combined these two von Stülpnagels into one composite.

From the beginning, I knew the Ritz was going to be the third major character of this book and that excited me; its very name invokes such intrigue and glamour! I was fortunate enough to spend three nights at the Ritz during my research period. While of course the Ritz has been—famously—redecorated and modernized since Blanche and Claude's reign, it was still important for me to get a good idea of the layout of the building, the luxury, the *feeling* that it inspires. Like Blanche says, it truly does make you sit up straighter, dress better, behave yourself in ways you might not outside its doors.

And then, there is Paris itself. My favorite city in the world. I've looked for years for a story set in Paris, just so I could finally declare my love for it in print.

I'm so glad that Blanche and Claude came along and provided me with that story. *Their* story—a great big fat juicy story.

ACKNOWLEDGMENTS

As always, it takes a village to write a book. I am indebted once more to my brilliant editor, Kate Miciak, who holds my feet to the fire with every book and makes me a better writer. And I wouldn't have a career if it wasn't for the passion and dedication of the best agent in the world, Laura Langlie.

It's a luxury to write when you know you have a fabulous team at your back, and I have just that at Penguin Random House. I'm thankful for each and every one of you: Kara Welsh, Kim Hovey, Gina Wachtel, Sharon Propson, Jennifer Garza, Susan Corcoran, Quinne Rogers, Leigh Marchant, Allyson Pearl, Robbin Schiff, Benjamin Dreyer, Loren Noveck, Allison Schuster, Jesse Shuman, Alyssa Matesic, and Gina Centrello. And my gratitude to all the fabulous Penguin Random House sales reps, who are the most passionate readers in the world.

Thank you to the Authors Unbound team.

I'm so grateful to François Grisor at the Ritz Paris for his help and the behind-the-scenes tour he gave me, and to Anne Michel, my editor at Albin Michel in France, for help in making contacts for me at the Ritz.

All my love to my family who support me even

when they don't think they do: Dennis Hauser, Alec Hauser, Ben Hauser, Emily Curtis, Norman Miller, Mark and Stephanie Miller.

And finally, always, thank you to the book-sellers and readers who keep asking me to write more books. Because of you, I will.

ABOUT THE AUTHOR

Melanie Benjamin has written the *New York Times* bestselling historical novels *The Aviator's Wife* and *The Swans of Fifth Avenue*, the nationally bestselling *Alice I Have Been*, and *The Girls in the Picture* and *The Autobiography of Mrs. Tom Thumb*. She lives in Chicago with her husband. When she isn't writing, she's reading.

Melaniebenjamin.com
Twitter: @MelanieBen
Look for Melanie Benjamin on Facebook

Books are produced in the United States using U.S.-based materials

Books are printed using a revolutionary new process called THINKtech™ that lowers energy usage by 70% and increases overall quality

Books are durable and flexible because of Smyth-sewing

Paper is sourced using environmentally responsible foresting methods and the paper is acid-free

Center Point Large Print
600 Brooks Road / PO Box 1
Thorndike, ME 04986-0001 USA

(207) 568-3717

US & Canada:
1 800 929-9108
www.centerpointlargeprint.com